IT WAS THE MOST EXQUISITE SENSATION SHE HAD EVER HAD....

At first she cantered the great stallion gently, and then, sensing the huge beast straining to go faster, she let him lope into a gallop as he made his way toward the rising sun.

She wanted to become part of the stallion's very body and soul. She felt like an ancient myth or Indian legend as she let him slow on the crest of a hill and she watched the sun begin in earnest its climb into the sky. It was only then that she heard the hooves behind her, then that she knew she'd been followed, and then that she turned in surprise. But when she saw him riding the ivory and onyx pinto toward her, she wasn't really surprised to see Tate Jordan. It was as though he were also part of the legend, as though he also belonged there, as though he, too, had fallen from the fiery golden morning sky.

DANIELLE STEEL

PALOMINO

A DELL TRADE PAPERBACK

A DELL TRADE PAPERBACK
Published by
Dell Publishing Co., Inc.
1 Dag Hammarskjold Plaza
New York, New York 10017

Dell ® TM 681510, Dell Publishing Co., Inc.

Printed in the United States of America

First printing—April 1981

Library of Congress Cataloging in Publication Data

Steel, Danielle.
Palomino.

I. Title.
PS3569.T33828P3   813'.54   80-28004
ISBN 0-440-56753-X (pbk.)

To Thaddeus
With all my love,
And all my heart,
And all my thanks,
For all that you
Have given me

d.s.

To ride over the hills,
on a fine horse,
with a dream,
looking for love,
before sunset,
is what life is about . . .
and to find it
is the culmination
of a lifetime.

PALOMINO

1

Hurrying up the steps of the brownstone on East Sixty-third Street, Samantha squinted her eyes against the fierce wind and driving rain, which was turning rapidly into sleet. It whipped her face and tingled as it pricked at her eyes. She made a soft purring noise, as though to urge herself on, and then stopped, gasping, as she fought with the lock, her key refusing to turn. Finally, finally, the door gave, and she fell into the warmth of the front hall. For a long moment she just stood there, shaking the dampness off her long silvery blond hair. It was a color one rarely saw, like spun silver meshed with fine gold; a towhead they had called her as a child, and she had hated it, and then in her teens and twenties her hair had won her lavish praise. Now at thirty she was used to it, and when John had told her that she looked like a fairy princess, she laughed at him, her blue eyes dancing, her beautiful, delicately angular face in sharp contrast to the full breasts and softly rounded hips. Her legs were long and thin and endless.

She was a woman of a thousand contrasts, huge dancing eyes with a sharp look that saw all, in sudden contrast to the sensual fullness of her mouth, the narrow shoulders, large breasts, the long graceful hands; the softness of her voice in contrast to the intelligent precision of her words. Somehow one expected Samantha Taylor to have a southern drawl, to languish on a velvet chaise longue, her form framed by a negligee trimmed in marabou. Instead she was given to jeans and bounded across rooms with a long stride. She was filled with energy and life, except tonight, except for the past hundred nights.

She stood now, as she had since late August, silent, still, waiting, the rain running off the tips of her hair, listening . . . but for what? There was no one here anymore. She was alone in the old brownstone. The couple who owned it had been in London for six months, their duplex apartment had been lent to a cousin who was almost never there. A reporter for *Paris-Match,* he spent more time in New Orleans, Los Angeles, and Chicago than he did in New York. And then there was the top floor. Samantha's domain . . . Samantha's . . . only hers now, although once upon a time it was Samantha and John's, an apartment they had put together with such devotion and such care. Every elegant inch of it, dammit. Samantha thought of it again with a small frown as she left her umbrella in the front hall and made her way slowly upstairs. She hated to come home now and managed to see to it that she came home later every night. It was almost nine o'clock this evening. But it had been later than that the night before. She wasn't even hungry. She hadn't been since she had first heard the news.

"You're what?" She had stared at him in horror on a broiling August evening. The air conditioner was broken, and the air was heavy and still. She had come to greet him at the front door, wearing only white lace underpants and a little lilac bra. "Are you crazy?"

"No." He had stared at her, looking wooden and strained. Only that morning they had made love. And now his Viking-like blond beauty seemed . . . beyond her reach. He looked like someone she didn't even know. "I can't lie to you anymore, Sam. I had to tell you. I've got to get out."

For what seemed like hours she had only stared at him. He couldn't mean it. He had to be kidding. But he wasn't. That was the insanity of it. He was deadly serious. She knew it from the look of agony on his face. She walked slowly toward him, but he shook his head and turned away. "Don't . . . please don't." His shoulders shook softly, and for the first time since he had spoken she felt pity slice through her like a shaft of pain. But why was she feeling sorry for him? Why? How could she feel sorry for *him* after what he had just said?

"Do you love her?" The shoulders she had loved so much only shook more, and he said nothing. But the pity began to fade now as Samantha moved toward him. Anger began to boil within her soul. "Answer me, dammit." She yanked hard on his shoulder, and he turned to look into her eyes.

"Yes. I think so. But, Sam, I don't know. I just know I have to get out of here for a while so I can figure it out."

She stalked across the room, stopping only when she reached the far side of the delicate French rug that looked like a carpet of flowers beneath her bare feet. There were tiny violets and small dusty-colored roses, and a myriad of still smaller flowers one had to stoop to see. The overall impression was one of pastel pinks and reds and mauves; it was a warm link to the soft pinks and mauves and deep dusty green on the couches and chairs that filled the large wood-paneled room. The house was an old brownstone, and the top floor was theirs. And Samantha had taken two years to decorate it, lovingly, with beautiful pieces of Louis XV furniture that she and John bought together at antique shops and auctions at Sotheby Parke Bernet. The fabrics were all French, the vases constantly filled with freshly cut flowers, the paintings all Impressionistic, and the overall feeling of the apartment was decidedly European and very elegant. Yet there was a cozy side to it too, as there was to Sam. It wasn't the beauty of the apartment she was seeing now as she stood with her back to her husband, wondering if they would ever be the same again. It was as though one of them had just died, as though everything had been instantly and irretrievably shattered and would never be repaired. And all with a few well-chosen words.

"Why didn't you tell me?" She turned and her face was filled with accusation.

"I . . ." He began but couldn't finish. There was nothing he could say now to make it better, to take back the pain he had just inflicted on the woman he had once so greatly loved. But seven years was a long time. It should have been long enough to solder them to each other forever, and yet it hadn't, and somehow, somehow, during the election coverage the year before, he had slipped. He had meant to end it when they all got back from Washington. He had really meant to. But Liz hadn't let him, and it had gone on. And on, and on . . . until now she had forced his hand. And the bitch of it was that she was pregnant and refused to get rid of the kid. "I didn't know what to tell you, Sam. I didn't . . . and I thought—"

"I don't give a damn what you thought!" Suddenly her eyes blazed at the man she had known and loved for eleven years. They had become lovers at nineteen. He had been the first man she had ever slept with, when they were both at Yale. He had been so big and blond and beautiful, a football hero, the big man on campus, the golden boy everybody loved, including Sam, who worshiped him from the first moment they met. "You know what I thought, you son of a bitch? I thought you were faithful to me. That's what I thought. I thought you gave a damn. I thought"—her voice quavered for the first time since he'd said the awful words—"I thought you loved me."

"I do." There were tears running slowly down his cheeks as he said the words.

"Oh, yeah?" She was crying openly now and she felt as though he had just torn out her heart and thrown it on the floor. "Then how come you're moving out? How come you walked in here like a crazy person, dammit, and when I said, 'Hi, babe, how was your day?' you said, 'I'm having an affair with Liz Jones and I'm moving out.' " Her voice was growing hysterical as she advanced on him. "Can you explain that to me? And just how long have you been involved with her anyway? God damn you, John Taylor . . . God damn you. . . ." As though she couldn't stop herself, she rushed at him, fists flailing, and then pulling at his hair, trying to maul his face; he resisted her with ease and pulled her arms behind her as he forced her down to the floor, where he cradled her in his arms.

"Oh, babe, I'm so sorry. . . ."

"Sorry?" It was a shriek between laughter and tears as she struggled free. "You come in here and tell me that you're leaving me for someone else and you're 'sorry'? Jesus Christ . . ." She took a deep breath then and pushed away from him. "Let me go, dammit." She looked at him with raw pain, and when he saw that she was calmer, he let go of her arms. She was still breathless from her attack on him, but now she walked slowly to the dark green velvet couch and sat down. She looked smaller suddenly, and very young, the thick sheet of pale blond hair hanging down as she buried her face in her hands, and then slowly she raised her face again, her eyes awash with tears. "Do you really love her?" Somehow it was impossible to believe.

"I think so." He nodded slowly. "The worst part is that I love you both."

"Why?" Samantha looked past him into an empty space, seeing nothing and understanding still less. "What was missing between us?"

Slowly he sat down. It had to be told. She had to know. He had been wrong to keep it from her for so long. "It happened during the election coverage last year."

"And it's been going on since then?" Her eyes widened as she wiped away fresh tears with the back of one hand. "Ten months, and I didn't know it?" He nodded and said nothing. "My God." And then she looked at him strangely. "Then why now? Why did you walk in here today like this and tell me? Why don't you stop seeing her? Why aren't you trying to save a marriage we've had for more than seven years? What the hell do you mean 'I'm having an affair and I'm moving out'? Is that all this means to you?"

She was beginning to shriek again and John Taylor almost cringed. He hated this, hated what he was doing to her, but he knew he had to, he had to go. Liz had something he desperately wanted, she had a quality that he needed, a kind of low profile that pleased him. He and Samantha were too much alike in some ways, too visible, too spectacular, too quick, too beautiful. He liked Liz's sensible plainness, her less-dazzling intelligence, her quiet style, her willingness to take a backseat, to be obscure, while helping him to be more of what he was. She was the perfect foil for him, it was why they worked so well as a team. On camera, doing the news, John was undeniably the star, and Liz helped make him look that way. He liked that. She was so much quieter than Samantha, so much less flamboyant, so much less exciting, and he had finally discovered that that was what he wanted. He didn't feel anxious when he was with her, he didn't have to compete. He was automatically the star.

And there was more to it now. She was pregnant and it was his child, he knew it. It was the one thing he wanted more than all else. A son, to play with and love and teach to play football. It was what he had always wanted, and what Samantha couldn't give him. It had taken the doctors three years to discover what the problem was, and when they did, they were sure. Samantha was sterile. She would never have a child. "Why now, John?" Samantha's voice dragged him back to the present, and he slowly shook his head.

"It doesn't matter. It's not important. It just had to be done. I had to tell you. There is no good day for something like this."

"Are you willing to end it?" She was pushing and she knew it, but she had to ask, had to push him; she still couldn't understand what had happened, and why. Why on this blistering hot day had her husband come home from the television station where he reported the news every night and told her that he was leaving her for someone else? "Will you stop seeing her, John?"

Slowly he had shaken his head. "No, Sam, I won't."

"Why?" Her voice had dwindled, childlike, and there

had been a fresh wave of tears. "What does she have that I don't have? She's plain, and she's boring . . . and you—you always said you didn't like her . . . and you hated working with her, and—" She couldn't go on, and he watched her, almost feeling her pain as his own.

"I have to go, Sam."

"Why?" She grew frantic as he moved into the bedroom to pack his clothes.

"Because I do, that's all. Look, it's not fair of me to stay here and let you go on like this."

"Please stay. . . ." Panic crept into her voice like a dangerous beast. "It's okay, we'll work it out . . . honest . . . please . . . John. . . ." The tears were streaming down her face, and he suddenly turned hard and distant as he packed. He became almost frantic, as though he had to leave in a hurry before he fell apart too.

And then suddenly he turned on her. "Stop it, dammit! Stop it . . . Sam, please. . . ."

"Please what? Please don't cry because my husband is leaving me after seven years, eleven if you count the time at Yale before we were married? Or please don't make you feel guilty while you leave me for some goddamn whore? Is that what you want, John? For me to wish you luck and help you pack? Christ, you walk in here and blow my whole life apart and what do you want from me? Understanding? Well, I can't give it to you. I can't do anything except cry, and if I have to, I'll beg . . . I'll beg, do you hear me . . . ?" And with that, she collapsed in a chair and began to sob again. With a firm hand he clasped the suitcase into which he had thrown half a dozen shirts, a pair of sneakers, two pairs of dress shoes, and a summer suit. Half of it was hanging out of the suitcase, and he was carrying a fistful of ties in one hand. It was impossible. He couldn't think straight, let alone pack.

"I'll come back Monday when you're at work."

"I'm not going to work."

"Why not?" He looked disheveled and distracted, and Samantha-looked up at him and laughed softly through her tears.

"Because my husband just left me, you jackass, and I don't think I'm going to feel like going to work on Monday. Do you mind?"

He hadn't smiled, hadn't softened in any way. He just looked at her awkwardly, nodded, and walked quickly out the door. He dropped two ties as he went, and after he was gone, Samantha picked them up and held them for a long time as she lay on the couch and cried.

She had done a lot of crying on the couch since August, but John hadn't come back. In October he had gone to the Dominican Republic for a long weekend, gotten a divorce, and five days later married Liz. Samantha knew now that Liz was pregnant, and when she had first heard, the news had cut through her like a knife. Liz had announced it one night on the broadcast, and Sam had watched her, her mouth open, shocked. So that was why he had left her. For a kid . . . a baby . . . a son that she couldn't give him. But in time she came to understand that it wasn't only that.

There had been a lot about their marriage that she hadn't seen, hadn't wanted to see, because she loved John so much. His sense of competition with her, his sense of insecurity over Sam's success in her own field. No matter that he was one of the top newscasters in the nation, no matter that people flocked for his autograph everywhere they went, John always seemed to feel that his success was an ephemeral thing, that any day it could be over, that they might replace him, that the ratings could change his life. For Sam, it was different. As assistant creative director of the second largest advertising agency in the country, her position was tenuous, but less so than his. Hers was a fickle profession as well, but she had too many award-winning campaigns behind her to make her feel vulnerable to the winds of change. As she sat alone in her apartment all through the autumn, she remembered bits and pieces, snatches of conversations, things he had said. . . .

"For chrissake, Sam, you've made it to the top at thirty. Shit, with bonuses you make more money than I do." And now she knew that that had bugged him too. But what should she have done? Quit? Why? In her case why not work? They couldn't have a baby and John had never wanted to adopt one. "It's not the same if it's not your own." "But it becomes your own. Look, we could adopt a newborn, we're young enough to qualify for the best. A baby would mean so much, sweetheart, think about it. . . ." Her eyes had glowed when they discussed it, his had always glazed, and then he would shake his head. The answer to the question of adoption was always no. And now he didn't have to worry about it anymore. In three more months he would have his first child. His own. The thought of it always hit Samantha like a physical blow.

Samantha tried not to think about it as she reached the top landing and opened her front door. The apartment had a musty smell these days. The windows were always closed, the heat was too high, her plants were all dying and she had neither thrown them out nor taken care of them. The entire apartment had an aura of unlove, of disuse, as though someone were only changing clothes there, but nothing more than that. And it was true. Samantha hadn't cooked anything more than coffee there since September. She skipped breakfast, ate lunch with clients as a rule, or with other executives of Crane, Harper, and Laub, and dinner she usually forgot. Or if she was absolutely starving, she grabbed a sandwich on the way home and ate it in the waxed paper, juggling it on one knee as she glanced at the news on TV. She hadn't seen her plates since the summer and she didn't really care. She hadn't really lived since the summer, and sometimes she wondered if she ever would again. All she could think of was what had happened, how he had told her, why he had left her, and that he was no longer hers. Pain had given way to fury, which led to sorrow, which grew to grief, which reverted once again to anger, until at last by Thanksgiving her emotions were so frayed at the edges that she was numb. She almost blew the biggest campaign of her career, and two weeks before that she had had to go into her office, lock the door, and lie down. For a moment she had felt as though she were going to have hysterics, faint maybe, or perhaps just put her arms around someone—anyone—and burst into tears. It was as though there were no one now, no one to whom she belonged, no one who cared. Her father had died when she was in college, her mother lived in Atlanta with a man she found charming but whom Sam did not. He was a doctor, and pompous and self-satisfied as hell. But at least her mother was happy. Anyway, Sam wasn't close to her mother, and it wasn't to her that she could turn. In fact she hadn't told her of the divorce until November, when her mother had called one night and found Sam in tears. She had been kind, but it did little to strengthen the bond between them. For Sam and her mother it was too late. And it wasn't a mother that she longed for, it was her husband, the man she had lain next to, and loved, and laughed with for the last eleven years, the man she knew better than her own skin, who made her happy in the morning and secure at night. And now he was gone. The realization of it never failed to bring tears to her eyes and a sense of desolation to her soul.

But tonight, cold as well as weary, for once Samantha didn't even care. She took off her coat and hung it in the bathroom to dry, pulled off her boots, and ran a brush through her silvery gold hair. She looked in the mirror without really seeing her face. She saw nothing when she looked at herself now, nothing except a blob of skin, two dull eyes, a mass of long blond hair. One by one she peeled off her clothes as she stood there, dropping the black cashmere skirt, the black and white silk blouse she'd worn to work. The boots she'd pulled off and thrown on the floor beside her were from Celine in Paris, and the scarf she unknotted at her neck was a black and white geometrical pattern from Hermès. She had worn large pearl and onyx earrings and her hair had been severely knotted at her neck. The coat, which hung damply beside her, was bright red. Even in her dazed state of loss and sorrow, Samantha Taylor was a beautiful woman, or as the creative director of the agency called her, "a hell of a striking girl." She turned the tap and a rush of hot water ran into the deep green tub. Once the bathroom had been filled with plants and bright flowers. In summer she liked to keep pansies and violets and geraniums there. There were tiny violets on the wallpaper, and all of the fixtures were French porcelain, in a brilliant emerald green. But like the rest of the apartment, it lacked luster now. The cleaning woman came to keep everything from getting dusty, but it was impossible to hire someone to come three times a week to make the place look loved. It was that that had left it, as it had left Samantha herself, that polish, that luster that comes only with a warm touch and a kind hand, the rich patina of good loving that shows on women in a myriad tiny ways.

When the tub was full of steaming water, Samantha slipped slowly into it, let herself just lie there, and closed her eyes. For a brief moment she felt as though she were floating, as though she had no past, no future, no fears, no worries, and then little by little the present forced itself into her mind. The account she was currently working on was a disaster. It was a line of cars the agency had coveted for a decade, and now she had to come up with the whole concept herself. She had come up with a series of suggestions relating to horses, with commercials to be shot in open country or on ranches, with an outdoorsy-looking man or woman who could make a big splash in the ads. But her heart wasn't really in it, and she knew it, and she wondered briefly for how long this would go on. For how long would she feel somehow impaired, damaged, as though the motor ran but the car would never again get out of first gear? It was a feeling of dragging, of pulling down, like having lead hair and hands and feet. When she stepped out of the tub, with her long silky hair piled in a loose knot atop her head, she wrapped herself carefully in a huge lilac towel and then padded barefoot into her room. Here again there was the feeling of a garden, a huge four-poster was covered with white eyelet embroideries and the bedspread was scattered with bright yellow flowers. Everything in the room was yellow and bright and frilly. It was a room she had loved when she did the apartment, and a place she hated now as she lay in it night after night alone.

It wasn't that there had not been offers. There had been, but she was immobilized by the interminable sensation of being numb. There was no one whom she wanted, no one about whom she cared. It was as though someone had turned off the faucet to her very soul. And now as she sat on the edge of the bed and yawned softly, remembering that she had eaten only an egg-salad sandwich for lunch and skipped both breakfast and dinner, she jumped as she heard the buzzer from downstairs. For a moment she thought about not answering, and then, dropping the towel and reaching hastily for a quilted pale blue satin robe, she ran toward the intercom as she heard the bell again.

"Yes?"

"Jack the Ripper here. May I come up?"

For a fraction of an instant the voice was unfamiliar in the garbled static of the intercom, and then suddenly she laughed, and as she did she looked like herself again. Her eyes lit up, and her cheeks still wore their healthy glow from the warm tub. She looked younger than she had in months. "What are you doing here, Charlie?" she shouted into the speaker in the wall.

"Freezing my ass off, thanks. You gonna let me in?" She laughed again and rapidly pressed the buzzer, and a moment later she could hear him bounding up the stairs. When he arrived in her doorway, Charles Peterson looked more like a lumberjack than the art director of Crane, Harper, and Laub, and he looked more like twenty-two than thirty-seven. He had a full, boyish face and laughing brown eyes, dark shaggy hair and a full beard, which was now dusted with sleet. "Got a towel?" he said, catching his breath, more from the cold and the rain than from the stairs.

She rapidly got him a thick lilac towel from her bathroom and handed it to him; he took off his coat and dried his face and beard. He had been wearing a large leather cowboy hat that now funneled a little river of ice water onto the French rug. "Peeing on my carpet again, Charlie?"

"Now that you mention it . . . got any coffee?"

"Sure." Sam looked at him strangely, wondering if anything was wrong. He had come to visit her once or twice before at the apartment, but usually only when something major was on his mind. "Something happen with the new account that I should know?" She glanced out at him from the kitchen with a worried look, and he grinned and shook his head as he followed her to where she stood.

"Nope. And nothing's going to go wrong. You've been

16

on the right track with that all week. It's going to be fabulous, Sam."

She smiled softly as she started the coffee. "I think so too." The two exchanged a long, warm smile. They had been friends for almost five years, through countless campaigns, winning awards and teasing and joking and working till four A.M. to coordinate a presentation before showing it to the client and the account men the next day. They were both the wunderkinder of Harvey Maxwell, titular creative director of the firm. But Harvey had sat back for years now. He had found Charlie at one agency and hired Samantha from another. He knew good people when he found them. He had given them their heads and sat back with glee as he watched what they created. In another year he would retire, and it was everyone's bet, including Samantha's, that she would inherit his job. Creative director at thirty-one was not bad at all. "So what's new, kiddo? I haven't seen you since this morning. How's the Wurtzheimer stuff going?"

"Well . . ." Charlie threw up his hands with an expression of acceptance. "How much can you do for one of the largest department stores in St. Louis that has big bucks and no taste?"

"What about the swan theme we talked about last week?"

"They hated it. They want flash. Swans ain't flash."

Sam rolled her eyes and sat down at the large butcher-block table as Charlie sprawled his lanky form into one of the chairs across from her. It was strange, she had never been drawn to Charlie Peterson, not in all the years they had worked together, traveled together, slept on planes together, talked into the wee hours together. He was her brother, her soul mate, her friend. And he had a wife she loved almost as much as he did. Melinda was perfect for him. She had decorated their big friendly apartment on East Eighty-first with brightly colored tapestries and beautifully woven baskets. The furniture was all covered in a deep mahogany-colored leather and everywhere one looked were wonderful little art objects, tiny treasures Melinda had discovered and brought home, everything from exotic seashells they had collected together in Tahiti, to one perfect marble she had borrowed from their sons. They had three boys, all of whom looked like Charlie, a large unmannerly dog named Rags, and an enormous yellow Jeep Charlie had driven for the past ten years. Melinda was also an artist, but she had never been "corrupted" by the workaday world. She worked in a studio and had had two successful shows of her work in the past few years. In many ways she was very different from Samantha, yet the two women had a gentleness in common, a softness beneath the bravado that Charlie treasured in both. And in his own way he loved Samantha, and he had been rocked to the core by what John had done. He had never liked him anyway and had always pegged him for an egocentric ass. John's rapid desertion of Samantha and subsequent marriage to Liz Jones had proved to Charlie that he was right, as far as he was concerned at least. Melinda had tried to understand both sides, but Charlie hadn't wanted to hear it. He was too worried about Sam. She'd been in lousy shape for the

past four months, and it showed. Her work had suffered.
Her eyes were dead. Her face was gaunt.

"So what's doing, madame? I hope you don't mind my
coming over so late."

"No." Samantha smiled as she poured him a cup of
coffee. "I just wonder how come you're here. Checking up
on me?"

"Maybe." His eyes were gentle above the dark beard.
"Do you mind that, Sam?"

She looked up at him sadly and he wanted to take her in
his arms. "How could I mind that? It's nice to know
someone gives a damn."

"You know I do. And so does Mellie."

"How is she? Okay?" He nodded. They never had time
to talk about things like that in the office.

"She's fine." He was beginning to wonder how he was
going to lead into what he wanted to tell her. It wasn't
going to be easy, and he knew that she might not take it
well.

"So? What's up?" Samantha was suddenly looking at
him with amusement. He feigned an innocent expression
and Samantha tweaked his beard. "You've got something
up your sleeve, Charlie. What is it?"

"What makes you say that?"

"It's pouring rain outside, it's freezing cold, it's Friday
night, and you could be at home with your warm, cozy
wife and your three charming children. It's difficult to
imagine that you came all the way over here just for a cup
of coffee with me."

"Why not? You're a lot more charming than my

children. But"—he hesitated briefly—"you're right. I didn't just happen to drop by. I came up here to talk to you." God, it was awful. How could he tell her? He suddenly knew that she'd never understand.

"And? Come on, out with it." There was a spark of mischief in her eye that he hadn't seen for a long time.

"Well, Sam . . ." He took a deep breath and watched her closely. "Harvey and I were talking—"

"About me?" She looked instantly uptight, but he nodded and went on. She hated people talking about her now. Because they always talked about how she was and what John had done.

"Yeah, about you."

"Why? The Detroit account? I'm not sure he understands my concept, but—"

"No, not about the Detroit account, Sam. About *you*."

"What about me?" She thought that was over, that they weren't talking about her anymore. There was nothing left to talk about. The separation was over, the divorce had come and gone, and John was married to someone else. She had survived it. So? "I'm fine."

"Are you? I think that's amazing." He looked at her with feeling and a trace of the anger he had felt all along for John. "I'm not sure I'd be so fine in your shoes, Sam."

"I don't have any choice. Besides, I'm tougher than you are."

"You probably are." He smiled gently. "But maybe not as tough as you think. Why not give yourself a break, Sam?"

"What's that supposed to mean? Go to Miami and lie on the beach?"

"Why not?" He forced a smile and she looked at him, shocked.

"What are you telling me?" Panic crept rapidly into her face. "Is Harvey firing me? Is that it? Did he send you here to play hatchet man, Charlie? They don't want me anymore because I'm not as cheerful as I used to be?" Just asking the questions, she felt her eyes fill with tears. "Christ, what do you expect? I had a rough time . . . it was . . ." The tears began to choke her and she hurriedly stood up. "I'm okay, dammit. I'm fine. Why the hell—" But Charlie grabbed her arm and pulled her back down to her seat with a gentle look in his eyes.

"Take it easy, babe. Everything's okay."

"Is he firing me, Charlie?" A lone, sad tear crept down her cheek. But Charlie Peterson shook his head.

"No, Sam, of course not."

"But?" She knew. She already knew.

"He wants you to go away for a while, to take it easy. You've given us enough to run with for a while on the Detroit account. And it won't kill the old man to think about business for a change. We can get along without you, as long as we have to."

"But you don't have to. This is silly, Charlie."

"Is it?" He looked at her long and hard. "Is it silly, Sam? Can you really take that kind of pressure and not buckle? Watching your husband leave you for someone else, seeing him on national television every night chatting with his new wife as you watch her pregnant belly growing? Can you really take that in stride without missing a step? Without missing a goddamn day at work, for chrissake, insisting on taking on every new account in the house. I expect you to crack yourself wide open sooner or later. Can you really put yourself on the line like that,

Sam? I can't. I can't do that to you, just as your friend. What that son of a bitch did to you almost brought you to your knees, for God's sake. Give in to it, go cry somewhere, let go of it all and then come back. We need you. We need you desperately. Harvey knows that, I know it, the account guys know it, and you damn well better know it, but we don't need you sick or crazy or broken, and that's how you're going to wind up if you don't take the pressure off now."

"So you think I'm having a nervous breakdown, is that it?" She looked hurt as well as shocked, but Charlie shook his head.

"Of course not. But hell, a year from now, you could. The time to take care of the pain is now, Sam, not later, when it's buried so deep that you can't find it anymore."

"I've already lived with it for this long. It's been four months."

"And it's killing you." It was a flat statement on his part and she didn't deny it.

"So what did Harvey say?" She looked sad as her eyes met those of her friend. She felt somehow as though she had failed, as though she should have been able to handle it better.

"He wants you to go away."

"Where?" She wiped a tear from her cheek with the back of her hand.

"Anywhere you want."

"For how long?"

He hesitated for only an instant before answering. "Three or four months." What they had decided was that she would be better off away until John and Liz had had their much publicized child. Charlie knew what a blow it was to Samantha, and he and Harvey had talked it out over many a lunch, but neither could have been prepared for the look Charlie saw now on her face. It was a look of total disbelief, of shock, almost of horror.

"*Four months?* Are you crazy? What the hell is going to happen to our clients? What the hell will happen to my job? Jesus, you really took care of it, didn't you? What is it? You want my job all of a sudden, is that it?" She jumped up from the table again and stalked away, but he followed her and stood facing her, looking down at her with sorrow in his eyes.

"Your job is a sure thing, Sam. But you've got to do this. You can't push yourself like this anymore. You have to get out of here. Out of this apartment, out of your office, maybe even out of New York. You know what I think? I think you should call that woman you like so much in California and go stay with her. Then come back when it's out of your system, when you're back among the living. It'll do you a hell of a lot of good."

"What woman?" Samantha looked blank.

"The one you told me about years ago, the one with the horse ranch, Carol or Karen something, the old woman who was the aunt of your college roommate. You used to talk about her as though she were your dearest friend." She had been. Barbie had been her closest confidante besides John, and they had been college roommates. She had died two weeks after graduation in a plane crash over Detroit.

There was suddenly a gentle smile in Samantha's eyes. "Barbie's aunt . . . Caroline Lord. She's a wonderful woman. But why on earth would I go there?"

"You like to ride, don't you?" She nodded. "Well, it's a beautiful place and it's about as different and as far from Madison Avenue as you can get. Maybe what you need is to park your fancy business wardrobe and pour that sexy body of yours into some jeans and chase cowboys for a while."

"Very funny, that's all I need." But the idea had struck some kind of chord. She hadn't seen Caroline in years. She and John had stopped to visit her once, it had been a three-hour drive north and east from L.A. and John had hated it. He didn't like the horses, thought the ranch was uncomfortable, and Caroline and her foreman had looked askance at him for his prissy city ways. A horseman he wasn't, but Samantha was an elegant horsewoman. She had been since she was a child. There had been a wild pinto pony on the ranch when they visited and she had ridden it, to Caroline's dismay. But she hadn't gotten hurt in spite of the horse throwing her half a dozen times as she tried to help break him to the saddle, and John had been instantly impressed by her skill. It had been a happy time in Sam's life and seemed a long time in the past as she looked up at Charlie now. "I'm not even sure she'd have me. I don't know, Charlie. It's a crazy idea. Why don't you guys just leave me alone to finish my work?"

"Because we love you, and you're going to destroy yourself like this."

"No, I'm not." She smiled valiantly at him, and slowly he shook his head.

"It doesn't matter what you say to me now, Sam. It was Harvey's decision."

"What was?"

"Your leave of absence."

"It's definite, then?" Once again she looked shocked and again he nodded his head.

"As of today. Three and a half months leave, and you can extend it to six if you want." They had called the station to ascertain Liz's due date, and tacked two more weeks on from there.

"And I won't lose my job?"

"No." He slowly pulled a letter out of his pocket and gave it to Samantha to read. It was from Harvey and guaranteed her job even if she stayed away for six months. It was unheard of in their business, but as Harvey had put it, Samantha Taylor was "a fairly extraordinary girl."

Sam looked up sadly at Charlie. "Does this mean I'm off as of today?" Her lower lip trembled.

"That's what it means, lady. You're on vacation as of right now. Hell, I wish I were."

"Oh, my God." She sank into a chair and covered her face with one hand. "Now what am I going to do, Charlie?"

He gently touched her shoulder. "Do what I told you, baby. Call your old friend on that ranch."

It was a mad suggestion, but after he left, she began to think about what she was going to do. She went to bed still in a state of shock. For the next three and a half months, she was out of a job. She had nowhere to go, nothing to do, nothing she wanted to see, and no one to see it with. For the first time in her adult life she was totally without plans. All she had to do was have one meeting with Harvey the next morning to explain everything on her desk and after that she was free. As she lay there in the dark, feeling frightened, suddenly she began to giggle. It was crazy really, what the hell was she going to do with herself until April 1? April fool . . . the joke's on you . . . Europe? Australia? A visit to her mother in Atlanta? For an instant she felt freer than she ever had before. When she had left Yale, she had had John to think of, and now she had no one at all. And then, on an impulse, she reached for her address book in the darkness and decided to follow Charlie's advice. She flicked on the light and found the number easily under *L*. It would be nine thirty in California, and she hoped that it wasn't too late to call.

The phone was answered on the second ring by the familiar smoky voice of Caroline Lord. There followed a lengthy explanation on Sam's part, friendly silences from Caroline as she spoke, and then a strange, anguished sob as Sam let herself go at last. Then it was like coming home to an old friend. The older woman listened, really listened. She gave Sam a kind of comfort she had forgotten over the years. And when Sam hung up the phone half an hour later, she lay staring at the canopy above her, wondering if maybe she really was going crazy after all. She had just promised to fly to California the following afternoon.

2

It was a frenzied morning for Samantha, she packed two suitcases, called the airlines, left a note and a check for the cleaning woman, and attempted to close up the apartment as best she could. Then, with her two suitcases, she took a cab to the office, where she gave Charlie the key to the apartment and promised to send Christmas presents for the boys from the coast. Then she met with Harvey for more than two hours, explaining everything he wanted to know.

"You know, you don't have to do this for me, Harvey. It isn't what I want." Her eyes reached out toward him as they concluded the meeting that would send her on her way.

He eyed her quietly from across his vast marble and chrome desk. "It isn't what you want, Sam, but it's what you need, whether you know it or not. Are you getting out of town?" He was a tall, spare man with iron-gray hair that he wore as closely cropped as any Marine. He wore white Brooks Brothers shirts, striped suits, looked like a banker, and smoked a pipe, but behind the steely gray eyes was a brilliant mind, a creative spirit, and a rare and beautiful soul. He had been, in a sense, like a father to Samantha, and now that she thought it over, it didn't really surprise her that he was sending her away. But they hadn't spoken of her plans all morning. All they had talked about were the accounts.

"Yes, I'm going away." She smiled at him from across the forbidding desk. It was easy to remember how frightened she had been of him at first, and how much she had come to respect him over the years. But the respect was mutual, as she knew. "In fact"—she looked at her watch—"my plane leaves in two hours."

"Then get the hell out of my office." He put his pipe down and grinned, but Sam hesitated for a moment in her chair.

"You're sure I'll get my job back, Harvey?"

"I swear it. You have the letter?" She nodded. "Good. Then if you don't get your job back, you can sue me."

"That's not what I want. I want the job."

"You'll get it, and probably mine eventually too."

"I could come back in a few weeks, you know." She said

it tentatively, but he shook his head and the smile faded quickly from his eyes.

"No, Sam, you can't. April first, and that's it."

"For any special reason?" He didn't want to tell her, so again he shook his head.

"No, that was the date we picked. I'll send you plenty of memos to keep you abreast of what's happening here, and you can call me anytime you want. Does my secretary know where to find you?"

"Not yet, but she will."

"Good." He came around the desk then and pulled her toward him without saying another word. He held her close for a long moment and then kissed the top of her head. "Take it easy, Sam. We'll miss you." His voice was gruff and there were tears in her eyes as she held him close for one more moment and then strode rapidly toward the door. For just one tiny instant she felt as though she were being banished from her home, and she felt panic wash over her as she considered begging him not to make her leave.

But when she left his office, Charlie was waiting for her outside in the hallway, and he smiled gently at her, slung an arm over her shoulders, and gave her a squeeze. "Ready to go, kiddo?"

"No." She smiled damply at him and then sniffed, burrowing closely into his side.

"You will be."

"Yeah? What makes you so sure?" They were walking slowly back to her office, and more than ever she wanted to stay. "This is crazy. You know that, don't you, Charlie?

I mean, I have work to do, campaigns to coordinate, I have no right to—"

"You can keep talking if you want to, Sam, but it won't make any difference." He looked at his watch. "Two hours from now I'm putting you on that plane."

Samantha suddenly stopped walking and turned to look at him belligerently, and he couldn't resist smiling at her. She looked like a very beautiful and totally impossible child. "What if I won't get on it? What if I just won't go?"

"Then I'll drug you and take you out there myself."

"Mellie wouldn't like that."

"She'd love it. She's been begging me to get out of her hair all week." He stopped, eyeing Samantha.

Slowly she smiled. "I'm not going to talk you out of it, am I?"

"Nope. Nor Harvey. It really doesn't matter where you go, Sam, but you've got to get the hell out of here, for your own sake. Don't you want to? Don't you want to get away from all the questions, from the memories, from the chance of running into . . . them?" The word had a painful ring to it, and she shrugged.

"What difference does it make? When I turn on the news in California, they'll still be there. The two of them. Looking . . ." Her eyes filled with tears just thinking of those two faces that she was magnetically drawn to every night. She always watched them, and then hated herself for it, wanting to turn the knob to another channel but unable to move her hand. "I don't know, dammit, they just look like they belong together, don't they?" Suddenly her face pulled into a mask of sadness and the tears began to roll down her face. "We never looked like that, did we? I mean—"

But Charlie said nothing, he only pulled her into his arms. "It's okay, Sam. It's okay." And then as she cried softly into his shoulder, oblivious of the glances of secretaries hurrying past her, he swept a long strand of the blond hair off her forehead and smiled down at her again. "This is why you need a vacation. I think it's called emotional exhaustion, or hadn't you noticed?"

She grunted disapproval and then chuckled softly through her tears. "Is that what they call it? Yeah . . ." She pulled away from him, sighed, and wiped the tears from her cheeks. "Maybe I do need a vacation." And then, valiantly swinging her hair back over her shoulders, she attempted to glare at her friend. "But not for the reasons you think. You bastards have just worn me out."

"You're damn right we have. And we have every intention of doing so again when you return. So enjoy yourself while you're out there. Horse freak." A hand on both their shoulders suddenly made them both turn.

"Haven't you left yet, Samantha?" It was Harvey, pipe clenched in his teeth and a bright light in his eyes. "I thought you had a plane to catch."

"She does." Charlie grinned at her.

"Then put her on it, for chrissake. Get her out of here. We have work to do." He smiled gruffly, waved the pipe, and disappeared down another hallway as Charlie looked at her again and saw the sheepish smile.

"You don't really have to put me on the plane, you know."

"Don't I?" She shook her head in answer, but she

wasn't paying attention to the art director, she was looking at her office as though for the last time. Charlie caught her expression and he grabbed her coat and bags. "Come on, before you get maudlin on me. Let's catch that plane."

"Yes, sir."

He crossed the threshold and waited, and with two hesitant steps she followed him. With a deep breath and one last glance behind her she softly closed the door.

3

The plane ride across the country was uneventful. The country drifted below her like bits and pieces of a patchwork quilt. The rough brown nubby textures of winter fields drifted into snowy white velvets, and as they reached the West Coast there were signs of deep satiny greens and rich shiny blues, as lakes and forests and fields ran beneath them. At last, with a fiery sunset to welcome them, the plane touched down in L.A.

Samantha stretched her long legs out in front of her, and then her arms as she looked out the window once again. She had dozed most of the way across the country, and now she looked out and wondered why she had come. What point was there in running all the way to California? What would she possibly find there? She knew as she stood up, tossing her long blond mane behind her, that she had been wrong to come all this way. She wasn't nineteen years old anymore. It didn't make any sense to come and hang out on a ranch and play cowgirl. She was a woman with responsibilities and a life to lead, all of which centered around New York. But what did she have there really? Nothing—nothing at all.

With a sigh she watched the rest of the passengers begin to deplane, and she buttoned her coat, picked up her tote bag, and fell in line. She had worn a dark brown suede coat with a sheepskin lining, jeans, and her chocolate leather boots from Celine. The tote bag she had brought was in the same color and tied around the handle was a red silk scarf, which she took off and knotted loosely around her neck. Even with the worried frown between her eyebrows, and the casual clothes she had worn on the trip, she was still a strikingly beautiful woman, and heads turned as men noticed her making her way slowly out of the giant plane. None of them had seen her during the five-hour trip because she had only left her seat once and that to wash her face and hands before the late lunch that was served. But the rest of the time she had just sat there, numb, tired, dozing, trying to reason out once again why she had let them do this, why she had allowed herself to be talked into coming west.

"Enjoy your stay. Thank you for flying . . ." The phalanx of stewardesses spoke the familiar words like a chorus of Rockettes, and Samantha smiled at them in return.

PALOMINO

A moment later Samantha was standing in the Los Angeles airport, looking around with a sense of disorientation, wondering where to go, who would find her, not sure suddenly if they would even meet her at all. Caroline had said that the foreman, Bill King, would probably meet her, and if he wasn't available, one of the other ranch hands would be there. "Just look for them, you can't miss 'em, not in that airport." And then the old woman had laughed softly, and so had Sam. In an airport filled with Vuitton and Gucci and gold lamé sandals and mink and chinchilla and little bikini tops and shirts left open to the navel, it would be easy to spot a ranch hand, in Stetson and cowboy boots and jeans. More than the costume, it would be easy to spot the way they moved and walked, the deep tan of their skin, their wholesome aura as they moved uneasily in the showily decked-out, decadent crowd. Sam already knew from her other visits to the ranch that there would be nothing decadent about the ranch hands. They were tough, kind, hardworking people who loved what they did and had an almost mystical tie to the land that they worked on, the people they worked with, and the livestock they tended with such care. They were a breed Samantha had always respected, but certainly a very different breed than she was accustomed to in New York. For a moment, as she stood there, watching the typical airport chaos, she suddenly realized that once she got to the ranch she would be glad she had come. Maybe this was what she needed after all.

As she looked around for the sign that said BAGGAGE CLAIM, she felt a hand on her arm. She turned, looking startled, and then she saw him, the tall, broad-shouldered, leathery old cowboy that she remembered instantly from ten years before. He stood towering over her, his blue eyes like bits of summer sky, his face marked like a landscape, his smile as wide as she remembered it; a feeling of great warmth exuded from him as he touched his hat and then enfolded her into a great big bear hug. It was Bill King, the man who had been the foreman on the Lord Ranch since Caroline had bought it some thirty years before. He was a man in his early sixties, a man of slight education, but with vast knowledge, great wisdom, and even greater warmth. She had been drawn to him the first time she'd seen him, and she and Barbara had looked up to him like a wise uncle, and he had championed their every cause. He had come with Caroline to Barbara's funeral and had stood discreetly behind the family with a floodtide of tears coursing down his face. But there were no tears now, there were only smiles for Samantha as the huge hand on her shoulder squeezed her still harder and he gave a small shout of glee.

"Damn, I'm happy to see you, Sam! How long has it been? Five, six years?"

"More like eight or nine." She grinned up at him, equally happy to see him and suddenly delighted that she had come. Maybe Charlie hadn't been so wrong after all. The tall, weathered man looked down at her with a look that told her she had come home.

"Ready?" He crooked an arm and with a nod and a smile she took it, and they went in search of her baggage, which was already spinning lazily on the turntable when they got downstairs. "This it?" He looked at her questioningly, holding the large black leather suitcase with the red and green Gucci stripe. He held the heavy case easily in one hand, her tote slung over his shoulder.

"That's it, Bill."

He frowned at her briefly. "Then you can't be meaning to stay long. I remember the last time you came out here with your husband. You must have had seven bags between the two of you."

She chuckled at the memory. John had brought enough clothes with him for a month at Saint-Moritz. "Most of that was my husband's. We had just been to Palm Springs."

He nodded, saying nothing, and then led the way to the garage. He was a man of few words but rich emotions. She had seen that often during her early visits to the ranch. Five minutes later they had reached the large red pickup, stowed her suitcase in the back, and were driving slowly out of the parking lot of the Los Angeles International Airport, and Sam suddenly felt as though she were about to be set free. After the confinement of her life in New York, her job, her marriage, and now the confusion of bodies pressing around her on the plane and then in the airport terminal after the trip, finally she was about to go out to open places, to be alone, to think, to see mountains and trees and cattle, and to rediscover a life she had almost forgotten. As she thought of it, a long, slow smile lit up her face.

"You look good, Sam." He cast an eye at her as they left

the airport, and he shifted into fourth gear as they reached the freeway beyond.

But she only smiled and shook her head at him. "Not as good as all that. It's been a long time." Her voice softened on the words, remembering the last time she had seen him and Caroline Lord. It had been a strange trip, an awkward mingling of past and present. The ranch hadn't been much fun for John. And as they drove along the highway, Sam's mind filled with memories of the last trip. It seemed a thousand years later when she felt the old foreman's hand on her arm, and when she looked around, she realized that the countryside around them had altered radically. There was no evidence of the plastic ugliness of the L.A. suburbs, in fact there were no houses in sight at all, only acres and acres of rolling farmland, the far reaches of large ranches, and uninhabited government preserves. It was beautiful country all around her, and Sam rolled down the window and sniffed the air. "God, it even smells different, doesn't it?"

"Sure does." He smiled the familiar warm smile and drove on for a while without speaking. "Caroline sure is looking forward to seeing you, Sam. It's been kind of lonely for her ever since Barb died. You know, she talks about you a heck of a lot. I always wondered if you'd come back. I didn't really think so after the last time." They had left the ranch early, and John had made no secret of the fact that he'd been bored stiff.

"I would have come back, sooner or later. I was always hoping to stop here when I went to L.A. on business, but I never had enough time."

"And now? You quit your job, Sam?" He had only a

vague idea that she had something to do with commercials, but he had no clear picture of what, and he didn't really care. Caroline had told him that it was a good job, it made her happy, and that was all that counted. He knew what her husband did, of course. Everyone in the country knew John Taylor, by face as well as by name. Bill King had never liked him, but he sure as hell knew who he was.

"No, Bill, I didn't quit. I'm on leave."

"Sick leave?" He looked worried as they drove through the hills.

Sam hesitated for only a moment. "Not really. Kind of a rest cure, I guess." For a minute she was going to leave it at that and then she decided to tell him. "John and I split up." He raised a questioning eyebrow but said nothing, and she went on. "Quite a while ago actually. At least it seems like it. It's been three or four months." A hundred and two days, to be exact. She had counted every one of them. "And I guess they just thought I needed the break at the office." It sounded lousy to her as she said it, and suddenly she felt panic rise in her as it had that morning when she spoke to Harvey. Were they really firing her and just didn't want to tell her yet? Did they think she couldn't take the pressure? Did they think she'd already cracked up? But when she looked at Bill King, she saw that he was nodding, as though it all made perfect sense to him.

"Sounds right to me, babe." His voice was reassuring. "It's damn hard to keep on going when you hurt." He stopped for a moment and then went on. "I found that out years ago when my wife died. I thought I could still handle my job on the ranch I was working on then. But after a week my boss said, 'Bill, my boy, I'm givin' you a month's money, you go on home to your folks and come back when the money's gone.' You know, Sam, I was mad as fire when he did it, thought he was telling me that I couldn't handle the job, but he was right. I went to my sister's outside Phoenix, stayed for about six weeks, and when I came back, I was myself again. You can't expect a man nor a woman to keep going all the time. Sometimes you have to give him room for grief."

He didn't tell her that he had taken three months off twenty-five years later, time off from the Lord ranch, when his son was killed during the early days of Vietnam. For three months he had been so stricken that he had barely been able to talk. It was Caroline who had nursed him out of it, who had listened, who had cared, who had finally come to find him in a bar in Tucson and dragged him home. He had a job to do on the ranch, she had told him, and enough was enough. She barked at him like a drill sergeant and heaped work on him until he thought he would die. She had shouted, yelled, argued, bullied, until finally one day they had almost come to blows out in the south pasture. They had gotten off their horses, and she had swung at him, and he had knocked her right on her ass, and then suddenly she had been laughing at him, and she laughed until the tears ran from her eyes in streams, and he laughed just as hard and knelt beside her to help her up, and it was then that he had kissed her for the first time.

It had been eighteen years ago that August, and he had never loved another woman as he loved her. She was the only woman he had actually ached for, longed for, lusted after, laughed with, worked with, dreamed with, and respected more than he respected any man. But she was a very special kind of woman. Caroline Lord was no ordinary woman. She was a superwoman. She was brilliant and amusing, attractive, kind, compassionate, intelligent. And he had never been able to understand what she wanted with a ranch hand. But she had known her mind from the beginning and never regretted the decision. For almost twenty years now she had secretly been his woman. And she would have made the affair public long before, had he let her. But he felt that her position as mistress of the Lord Ranch was sacred, and although here and there it was suspected, no one had ever known for certain that they were lovers, the only thing anyone knew for certain was that they were friends. Even Samantha had never been sure that there was more between them, though she and Barbara had suspected and often giggled, but they had never really known.

"How's Caroline, Bill?" She looked over at him with a warm smile and saw a special glow come to his eyes.

"Tough as ever. She's tougher than anyone on that ranch." And older. She was three years older than he. She had been one of the most glamorous and elegant women in Hollywood in her twenties, married to one of the most important directors of her day. The parties they had given were still among the early legends, and the home they had built in the hills above Hollywood was still on some of the tours. It had changed hands often but was still a remarkable edifice, a monument to a bygone era rarely equaled in later years. But at thirty-two Caroline Lord had been widowed, and after that, for her, life in Hollywood had never been the same again. She had stayed on for two more years, but they had been painful and lonely, and then suddenly without explanation she had disappeared. She had spent a year in Europe, and then another six months in New York. It took her another year after that to decide what she really wanted, but as she drove for hours, alone in her white Lincoln Continental, she suddenly knew where it was she longed to be. Out in the country, in nature, away from the champagne and the parties and the pretense. None of it had had any meaning for her after her husband was gone. All of that was over for her now. She was ready for something very different, a whole new life, a new adventure, and that spring, after looking at every available piece of property in a two-hundred-mile radius of Los Angeles, she bought the ranch.

She paid a fortune for it, hired an adviser and the best ranch hands around. She paid everyone a handsome wage, built them pleasant, cozy quarters, and offered them a kind of warmth and comfort that few men could deny. And in return, she wanted sound advice and good teaching, she wanted to learn how to run the ranch herself one day, and she expected them all to work as hard as she did herself. It was in her first year at the ranch that Bill King found her, took the place in hand, and taught her all he knew himself. He was a foreman of the kind most ranchers would die for, and it was purely by accident that he landed on the Lord Ranch. And even more so that he and Caroline Lord wound up as lovers. All that

Samantha knew of Bill's history on the ranch was that he had been there almost since the beginning and had helped make the place a financial success.

Theirs was one of the few California cattle ranches that showed a profit. They bred Angus cattle and sold a few Morgan horses as well. Most of the big ranches were in the Midwest or the Southwest; only a precious few in California had good luck, and many were kept in operation as tax losses by their owners—city dwellers, stockbrokers, lawyers, and movie stars who bought them as a kind of game. But the Lord Ranch was no game, not to Bill King or Caroline Lord, or to the men who worked there, and Samantha also knew that while she stayed there she would be expected to perform certain chores as well. No one came to the ranch just to be lazy. It seemed indecent, considering how hard everyone else worked.

When Sam had called Caroline this time, she had told Sam that at the moment they were short two men and Samantha was welcome to help out. It was going to be a busy vacation for Samantha, of that she was sure. She figured that most likely she would do small jobs in the stables, take care of some of the horses, and maybe help clean out some of the stalls. She knew just how unlikely it was that she would get a chance to do much more. Not that she wasn't able to. Samantha had long since proven her skill on a horse. A rider at five, in horse shows at seven, Madison Square Garden at twelve, and three blue ribbons and a red, jumping competitions thereafter, and a couple of years when she had dreamed of the Olympics and when she had spent every living moment she had with her own horse. But once she'd gone to college there hadn't been much time for horses, the dream of the Olympics faded, and in the years afterward she almost never had time to ride. It was only when she had visited the ranch with Barbara, or when she met someone with horses once in a great while, that she still got a chance to ride. But she knew that as a "city gal," she would not likely be trusted by hands to work with them, unless Caroline interfered on her behalf.

"Been riding much lately?" As though reading her thoughts, Bill leaned toward her with a smile.

She shook her head. "You know, I don't think I've been on a horse in two years."

"You'll be mighty sore by this time tomorrow."

"Probably." They exchanged a quiet smile as they drove on in the early evening. "But it'll probably feel good. That's a nice kind of sore." Tired knees and aching calves—it wasn't like the aching spirit she had borne these last months.

"We've got some new palominos, a new pinto, and a whole mess of Morgans, all of which Caroline bought this year. And then"—he almost grunted as he said it—"she's got this crazy damn horse. Don't ask me why she bought it, except some damn fool nonsense about he looks like a horse in some movie her husband made." He looked at Sam disapprovingly. "She bought herself a Thorough-bred. Hell of a fine horse. But we don't need a horse like that on a ranch. Looks like a damn racehorse . . . runs like one too. She's going to kill herself on it. No doubt about it. Told her so myself."

He glared at Sam and she smiled. She could just

imagine elegant Caroline on her Thoroughbred, racing across the fields as though she were still a young girl. It would be wonderful to see her again, wonderful to be back there, and suddenly Samantha felt a wave of gratitude wash over her. She was so glad she had come after all. She cast a sideways glance at Bill as he drove the last few miles toward the ranch that had been his home for more than two decades, and Samantha found herself wondering again just exactly how far his involvement with Caroline went. At sixty-three, he was still virile and handsome, the broad frame, the long legs, the strong arms, the powerful hands, and the brilliant blue eyes all combined to give him an aura of power and style. On him the Stetson looked marvelous, on him the blue jeans seemed to be molded to his legs. None of it looked trite or silly. He was the best of his breed, the proudest of his kind. The rugged lines of his face only helped to enhance the well-chiseled features, and the deep husky baritone voice was precisely what it had been. He was easily six feet four without the Stetson, and with it, he was literally a towering man.

As they drove through the front gates of the ranch, Samantha breathed a sigh of relief—of pain—of lots of feelings. The road stretched on for another mile after the sign that said LORD RANCH with a handsomely carved L, which they also used in their brand. Samantha felt like an anxious child as she caught her breath, expecting to see the house suddenly loom toward them, but it was another ten minutes before they rounded the last turn in the private road, and then suddenly there it was. It looked almost like an old plantation, a beautiful big white house

with dark blue shutters, a brick chimney, a wide front
porch, broad front steps, surrounding flower beds, which
became a riot of color in the summer, and, behind it all, a
veritable wall of gigantic, handsome trees. Just down the
slope from the house was a single willow tree and a little
pond, which was covered with lillies and filled with frogs.
Near at hand were the stables, beyond them the barns, and
all around were cottages for the men. In Sam's mind it
always stood out as the way a ranch should look, but
whenever she had seen others, she had rapidly discovered
that few did. Few other ranches were as impeccably kept, as
handsome, as well run . . . and none of them boasted either
Caroline Lord or Bill King.

"Well, little lady, how does it look to you?" The pickup
had stopped, and as he always did, Bill looked around with
obvious pride. He had helped to make the Lord Ranch
something special, and that was just what it was, most of all
to him. "Does it look different?"

"No." She smiled as she looked around her in the
darkness. But the moon was high, the house was well lit,
there were lights on in the men's cottages and the main
hall where they ate and played cards, there was a strong
light near the stables, and it was easy to see that not much
had changed.

"There are a few technical improvements, but you can't
see them."

"I'm glad. I was afraid it might all have changed."

"Nope." He sounded the horn twice, and as he did so the
door to the main house opened and a tall slim white-haired
woman stood in the doorway, smiling first at Bill,

and then instantly at Sam. There was only a moment's hesitation as she stood gazing at the young woman, and then with a light step she ran down the stairs, held out her arms, and took Samantha in a tight hug.

"Welcome home, Samantha. Welcome home." And then suddenly, as she smelled the dusty rose of Caroline Lord's perfume, felt her thick white hair brush her cheek, she felt tears in her eyes and a sense of having come home. After a moment the two women parted, and Caroline stood back and looked at her with a smile. "My God, you're pretty, Sam. Prettier even than last time."

"You're crazy. And good Lord, look at you!" The older woman was as tall and as thin and as ramrod straight as she ever had been, her eyes were bright, and her whole being suggested sparkle and life. She was as pretty as she had been the last time Sam saw her in her fifties, and now at sixty-six, she was still beautiful, and even in jeans and a man's cotton shirt she had her own undeniable style. There was a bright blue scarf knotted at her neck, she wore an old Indian belt, and her cowboy boots were a deep jade-green. Samantha happened to look down as she followed Caroline up the steps to the ranch house and gasped with a little exclamation of delight. "Oh, God, they're wonderful, Caroline!"

"Aren't they?" Caroline had understood instantly and looked down at them with a girlish smile. "I had them made specially. It's a final extravagance at my age, but what the hell. It may be my last chance." Sam was suddenly struck by that kind of reference, and it jolted her just to realize that Caroline thought like that now. Sam was silent as she walked into the familiar house, and Bill followed her with her bags. The entrance hall that they stood in boasted a handsome Early American table, a brass chandelier, and a big bright-colored hooked rug. In the living room beyond there was a huge fire blazing in the fireplace, surrounded by a cluster of comfortable well-upholstered chairs covered in a deep blue. It was a color picked up again in an antique rug, this one littered with bright flowers woven into the hooked design. The room was entirely done in blues and reds and greens, there was a brightness to it that seemed to perfectly reflect Caroline herself, and all of it was set off by the many antique pieces in rich woods. There were leather-bound books, brass fixtures everywhere, andirons in front of the fireplace, candelabra, buckets and planters, and sconces on the walls with lights like delicate candles. It was a wonderful old-fashioned room with elegance and warmth, much like Caroline herself, and it was perfectly in keeping with the fact that it was on the ranch. It was a room that would have been perfect in *Town & Country* or *House and Garden,* but which, of course, Caroline had never shown. It was her home and not a showplace, and after the very visible years she had spent in Hollywood she felt very strongly about her privacy now. In effect, for all but a few, she had virtually disappeared some twenty-five years before.

"Do you need some more firewood, Caroline?" Bill was looking down at her from his great height, his snow-white hair revealed now that he had his big-brimmed Stetson in his hand.

She smiled and shook her head, looking ever more youthful, the light in his eyes reflected in her own. "No, thanks, Bill. I've got enough for the rest of the night."

"Fine. Then I'll see you ladies in the morning." He smiled warmly at Sam, nodded respectfully to Caroline, and with his long stride rapidly left the living room and went out. They heard the door close gently behind him, and as Samantha and Barbara had decided a hundred times during the visits while they were in college, Sam decided once again that the two couldn't be involved with each other after all. Not if they said good night to each other like that. And their greetings were never more personal than they had just been, friendly nods, casual smiles, warm greetings, serious conversations about the ranch. Nothing else was ever evident between them, and yet as one watched them one had a feeling, as though they had some secret understanding, or as Sam had once put it to Barbara, "as though they were really husband and wife."

But before Samantha could ponder the matter further, Caroline put a tray on a low table near the fire, poured a cup of hot chocolate, uncovered a plate of sandwiches, and waved to Sam to sit down.

"Come on, Sam, sit down and make yourself comfortable." And then, as she did, the older woman smiled at her again. "Welcome home."

For the second time that evening Sam's eyes filled with tears and she reached a long graceful hand toward Caroline. They held hands for a moment, as Sam held the bony fingers tight.

"Thank you for letting me come here."

"Don't say that." Caroline let go and handed her the hot chocolate. "I'm glad that you called me. I've always loved you. . . ." She hesitated for a moment, glancing into the fire and then back at Sam, "Just as much as I loved Barb." And then she sighed softly. "Losing her was like losing a daughter. It's hard to believe it's been almost ten years." Sam nodded silently, and then Caroline smiled at her. "I'm glad to know that I didn't lose you too. I've loved your letters, but for the last few years I've been wondering if you'd ever come back."

"I wanted to, but . . . I've been busy."

"Do you want to tell me about all that, or are you too tired?" It had been a five-hour flight, and then a three-hour drive. By California time it was only eight thirty, but by Sam's time, in New York, it was eleven thirty at night. But she wasn't even tired, she was just exhilarated to see her old friend.

"I'm not too tired . . . I just don't know where to start."

"Then start with the hot chocolate. Then the sandwiches. Then talk." The two women exchanged another smile, and then Sam couldn't resist reaching out to her again, and Caroline gave her a warm hug. "Do you know how good it is to have you back here?"

"Only half as good as it is to be back." She took a big bite out of a sandwich and then sat back against the couch with a broad grin. "Bill says you have a new Thoroughbred. Is he a beauty?"

"Oh, God, Sam, he sure is!" And then she laughed again. "Better even than my green boots." She looked down with amusement and then back at Sam with a sparkle in her eye. "He's a stallion and so full of fire that even I can hardly ride him. Bill is terrified I'll kill myself riding him, but when I saw him, I really couldn't resist.

The son of one of the other ranchers near here bought him in Kentucky, and then needed some quick money so he sold him to me. It's almost a sin to ride him just for pleasure, but I can't help it. I just have to. I don't give a damn if I'm an arthritic old woman, or what kind of fool anyone thinks me, he is the one horse in my lifetime I want to ride till I die." Sam flinched again at the mention of death and old age. In that sense both she and Bill had changed since the last time. But after all, they were both in their sixties now, maybe it was indeed a preoccupation that was normal for their age. Nonetheless it was impossible to think of either of them as "old people," they were too handsome, too active, too powerful, too busy. And yet, it was obviously an image of themselves that they both now had. "What's his name?"

Caroline laughed out loud and then stood up and walked toward the fire, holding out her hands for warmth. "Black Beauty, of course." She turned toward Samantha, her exquisite features delicately lit by the fire until she looked almost like a carefully etched cameo, or a porcelain figure.

"Has anyone told you lately how beautiful you are, Aunt Caro?" It was the name Barbara had used for her, and this time there were tears in Caroline's eyes.

"Bless you, Sam. You're as blind as ever."

"The hell I am." She grinned and nibbled at the rest of her sandwich before taking a sip of the hot chocolate that Caroline had poured from a Thermos jug. She was the same gracious hostess she always had been in the days when Samantha had first visited the ranch and all the way back to her legendary parties in Hollywood in 1935. "So."

Sam's face sobered slowly. "I guess you want to know about John. I don't suppose there's much more than what I told you the other night on the phone. He had an affair, he got her pregnant, he left me, they got married, and now they await the birth of their first child."

"You say it so succinctly." Then after a moment, "Do you hate him?"

"Sometimes." Sam's voice fell to a whisper. "Most of the time I just miss him and wonder if he's all right. I wonder if she knows that he's allergic to wool socks. I wonder if anyone buys him the kind of coffee he loves, if he's sick or healthy or happy or freaked out, if he remembers to take his asthma medicine on a trip . . . if —if he's sorry—" She stopped and then looked back at Caroline still standing by the fire. "That sounds crazy, doesn't it? I mean, the man walked out on me, cheated on me, dumped me, and now he doesn't even call to find out how I am, and I worry that his feet itch because his wife might make a mistake and buy him wool socks. Is that crazy?" She laughed but it was suddenly a half sob. "Isn't it?" And then she squeezed her eyes shut again. Slowly she shook her head, keeping her eyes tightly closed, as though by closing them she wouldn't see the images that had danced in her head for so long. "God, Caro, it was so awful and so public." She opened her eyes. "Didn't you read about it?"

"I did. Once. But it was just some vague gossip that you two were separated. I hoped that it was a lie, just some stupid publicity to make him seem more appealing. I know how those things are, how they get planted and don't mean a thing."

"This one did. You haven't watched them together on the broadcast?"

"I never did."

"Neither did I." Samantha looked rueful. "But I do now."

"You ought to stop that."

Samantha nodded silently. "Yeah, I will. There's a lot I have to stop. I guess that's why I came out here."

"And your job?"

"I don't know. I've somehow managed to keep it through all this. At least I think so if they meant what they said when I left. But to tell you the truth, I don't know how I did it. I was a zombie every waking minute I was in the office." She dropped her face into her hands with a soft sigh. "Maybe it's just as well that I left." She felt Caroline's hand on her shoulder a moment later.

"I think so too, Sam. Maybe the ranch will give you time to heal, and time to collect your thoughts. You've been through a tremendous trauma. I know, I went through the same thing when Arthur died. I didn't think I'd live through it. I thought it would kill me too. That's not quite the same thing as what happened to you, but in its own way death is a rejection." There was a vague frown in her eyes as she said the last words, but it rapidly flitted away as she smiled again at Sam. "But your life isn't over, you know, Samantha. In some ways perhaps it's just begun. How old are you now?"

Samantha groaned. "Thirty." She made it sound like eighty and Caroline laughed, a delicate, silvery sound in the pretty room.

"You expect me to be impressed?"

"Sympathetic." Samantha spoke with a grin.

"At my age, darling, that's too much to ask. Envious, perhaps, that would be more like it. Thirty." She looked dreamily into the fire. "What I wouldn't give for that!"

"What I wouldn't give to look like you do now, age be damned!"

"Flattery, flattery . . ." But it was obvious that it pleased her, and then she turned to Sam again with a question in her eyes. "Have you been out with anyone else since it happened?" Sam rapidly shook her head. "Why not?"

"Two very good reasons. No one decent has asked me, and I don't want to. In my heart I'm still married to John Taylor. If I went out with another man, it would feel like cheating. I'm just not ready. And you know?" She looked somberly at the older woman. "I don't think I ever will be. I just don't want to. It's as though part of me died when he walked out that door. I don't care anymore. I don't give a damn if nobody ever loves me again. I don't feel lovable. I don't want to be loved . . . except by him."

"Well, you'd better do something about that, Samantha." Caroline eyed her with gentle disapproval. "You've got to be realistic, and you can't wander around like a mobile dead body. You have to live. That's what they told me, you know. But it does take time. I know that. You've had how many months now?"

"Three and a half."

"Give it another six." She smiled softly. "And if you're not madly in love by then, we'll do something radical."

"Like what? A lobotomy?" Samantha looked serious as she took another sip of hot chocolate.

"We'll think of something, but I don't really think we'll have to."

"Hopefully by then I'll be back on Madison Avenue, killing myself with a fifteen-hour workday."

"Is that what you want?" Caroline looked at her sadly.

"I don't know. I used to think so. But now that I look back at it, maybe I was in competition with John. Still, I have a good shot at becoming creative director of the agency, and there's a lot of ego involved in that."

"Do you enjoy it?"

Samantha nodded and smiled. "I love it." And then she cocked her head to one side with a shy smile. "But there have been times when I've liked this kind of life more. Caro—" She hesitated, but only for an instant. "Can I ride Black Beauty tomorrow?" She suddenly looked like a very young girl.

But Caroline slowly shook her head. "Not yet, Sam. You ought to warm up on one of the others. How long has it been since you've been on a horse?"

"About two years."

"Then you don't want to start with Black Beauty."

"Why not?"

"Because you'll land on your fanny halfway out the gate. He's not easy to ride, Sam." And then more gently, "Not even for you, I suspect." Caroline had seen years before that Samantha was a splendid rider, but she knew only too well that Black Beauty was an unusual horse. He even gave her a hard time, and he terrified the foreman and most of the ranch hands. "Give it time. I promise I'll let you ride him when you feel sure of yourself again." They both knew that that wouldn't take Sam long. She had spent too much time with horses to feel rusty for long. "You know, I was hoping you wanted to do some serious riding. Bill and I have spent the last three weeks tearing our hair out over the ranch papers. We have a lot of things to tie up at year end. As I told you, we're two men short on top of it. We could use an extra hand. If you want to, you could ride with the men."

"Are you serious?" Samantha looked stunned. "You'd let me do that?" Her big blue eyes lit up by the light of the fire, her golden hair was alight with its glow.

"Of course I would let you. In fact I'd be grateful to you." And then, with a gentle smile, "You're as competent as they are. Or you will be again after a day or two. Think you'd survive starting out with a full day in the saddle?"

"Hell yes!" Samantha grinned, and Caroline walked toward her with a look of affection in her eyes.

"Then get to bed, young lady. You have to be up at four o'clock. In fact I was so sure you'd say yes, I told Tate Jordan to expect you. Bill and I have to go into town." She looked at her watch then. It was a simple watch that Bill King had given her that Christmas. Once, thirty years earlier, the only watches that had graced her wrist had been Swiss and encrusted with diamonds. There had been one in particular that her husband had bought her in Paris, at Cartier's. But she had long since put it away. Sometimes she found it hard to believe that she had ever had another life. She stood looking at Samantha now with a warm smile and gave the younger woman another firm hug. "Welcome home, darling."

"Thank you, Aunt Caro."

With that, the two women walked slowly down the hall. Caroline knew that the fire was safely contained in the fireplace, and she left the tray for the Mexican woman who arrived every morning to work on the ranch and clean her house.

She walked Samantha to her bedroom doorway and watched as Sam eyed the room with delight. It was a different room than she had shared with Barbara during the summers. Caroline had long since turned that room into a study. It had pained her too much to remember the young girl who had visited and lived there, growing into young womanhood in the pink frills of that room. This room was entirely different. It was equally feminine, but stark white. Everything was white eyelet and wonderfully frilly, from the canopied bed to the handmade cushions to the wicker chaise longue. Only the wonderful patchwork bedspread folded back on the bed introduced some colors, and here were a riot of bright colors, reds and blues and yellows, all carefully worked in a log-cabin design. There were matching cushions on two comfortable wicker chairs near the fireplace. And on the large wicker desk rested a huge vase of multicolored flowers. And through her windows Samantha would have a perfect view of the hills. It was a room in which one would want to spend hours, if not years. The touches of Hollywood hadn't entirely left Caro. She still decorated every room with the special touches and infinite good taste that had characterized her Hollywood years.

"It sure doesn't look like the bedroom of a ranch hand."

Sam chuckled as she sat down on the edge of the bed and looked around.

"Not exactly. But if you'd prefer, I'm sure one of the men would be happy to share a bunk in one of the cottages." They grinned at each other, kissed again, and then Caroline softly closed the door. Samantha could hear the heels of the cowboy boots echo on the hardwood floors all the way down the hallway to the other side of the house where Caro had her own apartment: a large bedroom, a small den, a dressing room, a bathroom, all done in bright colors not unlike the quilted bedspread, and here she still kept a few pieces of long-ago-collected art. There was one very fine Impressionist painting. The others were all pieces she had bought in Europe, some with her husband, some after she lost him, but they were the only treasures she still kept from her old life.

In her own room Sam slowly unpacked her suitcase, feeling as though in the space of a few hours she had entered an entirely different world. Could she really have been in New York that morning, sleeping in her own apartment, talking to Harvey Maxwell in his office? Could one come this far in so short a time? It seemed more than unlikely as she listened to the horses neighing softly in the distance and felt the winter wind brush her face as she opened the window and looked out. Outside there was a landscape lit by the moon beneath a sky brilliant with every star in the heavens. It was a miraculous scene and she was more than glad to be there, glad to be visiting Caroline, and glad to be away from New York. Here she would find herself again. She knew as she stood there that she had done the right thing. And as she turned away from the window, somewhere in the distance she heard a door close near Caroline's bedroom, and for a moment she wondered, as she and Barbie had so long ago, if it was Bill King.

4

The alarm went off next to Sam's bedside at four the next morning. She groaned as she heard it and then reached out a hand to turn it off. But as she did she felt the breeze on her fingers and suddenly realized that something was different. She opened one eye, looked around, and realized that she wasn't at home. Not in her own at least. She looked around once more, in total confusion, and then up at the frilly white canopy above her, and suddenly she knew. She was at Caroline Lord's ranch, in California, and that morning she was going to ride with the other hands. The idea sounded a little less appealing than it had the previous evening. The prospect of leaping out of bed, taking a shower, and actually leaving the building before she even had breakfast, and then, after being faced with a plate heaped high with sausages and eggs, getting on a horse, all probably before six A.M., sounded exceedingly grim. But this was what she had come west for, and as she considered sleeping in for the first morning, she knew she couldn't do it. Not if she was going to make friends with the men. Besides, letting her ride with the men was a privilege Caroline had given her. And if she was to be respected by the ranch hands, she would have to show herself as tough, as willing, as knowing, as good with a horse, as ready to ride, as any of them.

She wasn't greatly encouraged when she peered into the darkness after her shower and saw that the countryside was shrouded in a thin veil of rain. She climbed into an old pair of blue jeans, a white button-down shirt, a thick black turtleneck sweater, wool socks, and her own riding boots that she had worn religiously when she rode in the East. They were beautiful custom-made boots from Miller's and not at all the kind of thing to wear on a ranch, but she figured that she could buy a pair of cowboy boots in town that weekend, and in the meantime she'd have to make do. She pulled her long blond hair into a tight knot at the nape of her neck, splashed some more cold water on her face, grabbed an old blue down parka that she had worn skiing and a pair of brown leather gloves. Gone were the days of Halston, Bill Blass, and Norell. But what she was going to be doing was no longer that kind of work. Elegance didn't matter, only warmth and comfort. And she knew that when she returned to her room that evening she would do so with every muscle shrieking, every joint aching, her seat numb, her knees raw, her eyes blurred from the wind, her face tingling, her hands clenched in the position she would use all day with the reins. Knowing that was certainly no incentive to get up. She slipped out of her room into the hall and noticed the narrow sliver of light under Caroline's door. She thought of saying good morning, but it seemed an ungodly hour to disturb anyone, and on tiptoe Sam continued toward the front door. She closed it softly behind her, pulling the hood of her parka over her head and pulling the string tight in the soft rain, her boots making little squishing noises in the puddles that had already formed on the ground.

It seemed to take forever to reach the main hall where the men ate and where some of them gathered at night to play pool or cards. It was a large, freshly painted, rambling building, with beamed ceilings, a brick fireplace tall enough to stand in, a record player, a TV, several game tables, and a handsome antique pool table. As Sam had always known her to, Caroline Lord treated her men well.

For just an instant as Sam reached the doorway, her hand froze on the knob and she suddenly wondered what she had done. She was about to invade the all-male sanctum, share their meals with them in the morning and at lunchtime, work beside them, and pretend to be one of them. What would they think of the intrusion? Suddenly Samantha's knees trembled as she wondered if Caroline or Bill had warned them, and she stood there almost too terrified to go inside. As she stood there in the rain, hesitating, with her hand on the doorknob, a voice just behind her muttered, "Come on, dammit, man, it's cold." She wheeled around, startled at the voice she hadn't expected, and found herself face to face with a stocky man with dark brown hair and dark eyes, of approximately her own height and age. He looked as surprised as she did, and then with a rapid hand to his mouth at the error, his face broke into a broad grin. "You're Miss Caroline's friend, aren't you?" She nodded speechlessly, attempting to smile. "Sorry . . . but could you open the door anyway? It is cold!"

"Oh . . ." She heaved the door wide. "I'm sorry. I just. . . did she . . . did she say anything about me?" Her porcelain cheeks were flushed from embarrassment and the chill rain.

"Sure did. Welcome to the ranch, miss." He smiled and moved past her, welcoming but not particularly anxious to say more. He instantly greeted two or three of the other ranch hands and then moved toward the huge open kitchen, greeted the cook, and grabbed a cup of coffee and a bowl of Cream of Wheat.

Samantha saw then that the room was filled with men like the one who had just entered, all wearing blue jeans, sturdy jackets, heavy sweaters, their hats left on pegs on the wall, their cowboy boots clattering loudly as they made their way across the wood floor. There were more than twenty of them in the large hall that morning, talking in small groups or drinking coffee alone. Half a dozen were already seated at the long table, eating eggs and bacon or hot cereal, or finishing a second or third cup of coffee. But wherever one looked, there was a man engaged in his own morning ritual, in a man's world, about to engage in man's work, and for the first time in her life Samantha felt totally out of place. She felt her face flush hotly again as she walked hesitantly toward the kitchen, smiled nervously at two of the men as she helped herself to a cup of black coffee, and then attempted to disappear into the woodwork at the far end of the room.

At first glance there was not a single face she remembered. Most of them were young and probably relatively new there, and only two or three of them looked as though they could have worked anywhere for a long time. One was a broad, heavyset man in his early or mid-fifties who looked a lot like Bill King. He had the same kind of build, but his eyes weren't as warm and his face wasn't as kind. He glanced only once at Samantha and then turned his back to her to say something to a young freckled redhead. They both laughed and then walked across the room to a table where they joined two other men. For an instant of paranoia Samantha wondered if she would be the source of amusement, if it had been totally crazy of her to come here, and even crazier for her to want to ride with the men. This was a far cry from her days here with Barbara, when they had come to play around on the ranch. For one thing they had both been very young and very pretty and it had delighted all the men just to watch them hang around and ride. But this was different. Samantha was trying to masquerade as their equal, something they would surely not tolerate, if they even noticed her presence at all.

"Aren't you going to have some breakfast?" The voice next to her was husky but gentle, and Sam found herself looking into the face of another man of the old foreman's vintage, but this one did not look as unpleasant as the first one. In fact, after another glance at him, she gave a soft gasp.

"Josh! Josh! It's me, Sam!" He had been there every summer when she had come with Barbara, and he had always taken care of them. Barbara had told Sam how gently he had taught her to ride when she was a little girl. He had a wife and six kids somewhere, Sam remembered. But Sam had never seen them anywhere on the ranch. Like most of the men he worked with, he was used to living his life in an exclusively male world. It was a strange, solitary life, a lonely existence carried out among others who were equally apart. A society of loners who banded together, as though for warmth. And now he looked at Samantha, blankly for a moment and then with rapid recognition and a warm smile. Without hesitation he reached out and hugged her, and she could feel the rough stubble of his beard against her cheek.

"I'll be damned! It's Sam!" He gave a soft whoop and she laughed with him. "Now why the hell didn't I figure it out when Miss Caroline told us about her 'friend'?" He slapped his leg and grinned at her some more. "How've you been, dammit? Boy, you look good!" She found it hard to believe with her face still half asleep and her body encased in her worst and oldest clothes.

"So do you! How are your wife and kids?"

"Grown and gone, thank God. Except for one and the wife." And then he lowered his voice, as though telling some terrible secret. "They live here on the ranch now, you know. Miss Caroline made me. Said it wasn't right for them to live in town with me living here."

"I'm glad."

He rolled his eyes in answer and they both laughed.

"Aren't you going to eat some breakfast? Miss Caroline told us that a friend of hers was coming from New York to help us out." He grinned evilly for a moment. "You should have seen their faces when she told them her friend was a woman."

"They must have been thrilled." Samantha said sarcastically as they made their way toward the kitchen. She was dying for some coffee and the food was beginning to smell good now that she had found Josh.

And then as she helped herself to a large bowl of oatmeal, Josh leaned toward her conspiratorially. "What are you doing here, Sam? Aren't you married?"

"Not anymore." He nodded sagely and she volunteered no other information as they went and sat down at one of the tables. For a long time as Sam ate her oatmeal and nibbled at some toast, no one joined them, and then eventually curiosity got the better of two or three of the men. One by one Josh introduced them, and for the most part they were younger than Sam and had the rugged look of hardworking men who all but lived in the outdoors. It was by no means an easy profession, particularly at this time of year. And it was obvious how Bill King had come by the rugged lines in his face that made him look like a heavily carved statue, they had been worn by time and the elements as he rode for some fifty years on the different ranches where he worked. Josh's face was no different as

Sam watched him, and she could easily see that some of the others would look very much like them in a short time.

"Lotta new faces, huh, Sam?" She nodded, and he left her for a second for more coffee. She noticed on the big clock over the fireplace that it was five forty-five. In fifteen minutes they would all head for the barn to claim their horses and officially their workday would begin. She wondered who was going to assign her a horse for the day. Caroline hadn't mentioned it the previous evening, and she was suddenly anxious as she looked around for Josh. But he had disappeared somewhere with one of his cronies, and Sam found herself looking around her like a lost child. Despite the few curious glances cast her way, on the whole there was no visible interest and she suspected that what was happening was that they didn't want to pay attention to her, so most of them pretended to look away. It made her want to shout or stand on a table, just to catch their attention once and for all, tell them that she was sorry she was invading their world and that if they wanted her to she'd go home now, but the precise way in which they were ignoring her was beginning to drive her nuts. It was as though they were determined that she shouldn't be there, so they pretended to themselves and each other that she was not.

"Miss Taylor?" She spun around at the sound of her name and found herself staring into a broad chest wearing a thick wool plaid shirt in blue and red.

"Yes?" Her eyes traveled upward until she found herself looking into a pair of eyes of a color she had seldom seen. They were almost emerald with gold flecks.

The hair was black and the temples were touched with gray. The face was leathered, the features sharp, and he was taller than any other man on the ranch, including Bill King.

"I'm the assistant foreman here." He offered only his title, no name. And there was something cold and forbidding in his voice as he said it. Had she met him in a dark alley, a chill would have rippled up her spine.

"How do you do?" She wasn't quite sure what to say to him, and he was looking down at her with a tight frown.

"Are you ready to come out to the barn?" She nodded in answer, awed by his commanding style, as well as his great height. She noticed, too, now that the others were watching, wondering what he was saying to her and obviously noticing that there was no trace of warmth in the way he spoke, no welcoming words, and no smile.

Actually she had wanted another cup of coffee but she wasn't about to tell him that as he led the way to the door. She grabbed her jacket off the peg where she had finally left it, struggled into it, pulled up the hood, and closed the door behind her, feeling somehow like a child who has done something wrong. The idea of Samantha riding with them clearly irked him as he walked rapidly into the barn. Samantha shook the rain off her hood as she slipped it off her hair and watched him. He picked up a clipboard with a list of men's names and those of horses, and then with a pensive frown he walked to a nearby stall. The name outside the stall was LADY, and for some reason she wasn't sure she could have explained she found herself instantly irritated by his choice. Just because she was a woman she had to ride Lady? She instinctively felt that she was going to be stuck with that horse during the entire duration of her stay and found herself fervently hoping that Lady would at least prove to be a decent mount.

"You ride fairly well?" Again she only nodded, afraid to toot her own horn, afraid to offend him, when the truth would have been that she probably rode better than most of the men on the ranch, but he would have to see that for himself, if he even bothered to look. Samantha watched him again as he went back to his list, and found herself watching the sweep of his neck as his dark hair brushed his collar. He was a powerful, sensuous-looking man, somewhere in his early forties. There was something almost frightening about him, something fierce and stubborn and determined. She could sense it without knowing him, and she felt almost a ripple of fear go through her as he turned to her again and shook his head. "No good. She might just be too much for you. I want you to ride Rusty. He's on the far side of the barn. Grab one of the free saddles in the tack room and mount up. We ride out in ten minutes." And then with a look of annoyance, "Can you be ready by then?" What did he think, she wondered, that it took her two hours to saddle a horse?

Suddenly as she watched him her temper flared. "I can be ready in five. Or less." He said nothing in answer and merely walked away, put the clipboard back on the wall from which he'd taken it, and strode quickly across the barn to the stalls, where he saddled his own horse and led it slowly outside. Within five minutes all the men had returned from breakfast and the barn was a madhouse of

70

catcalls and laughter and noises mixed with the sounds of horses shifting their feet, greeting their habitual riders, and whinnying at each other as the men who rode them took them from their stalls, creating a veritable traffic jam at the entrance as the entire group emerged into the damp yard beyond and congregated happily in the light rain.

Most of the men had donned slickers over their jackets, and Josh had handed Sam one as she walked her horse slowly outside. He was a large unexciting-looking chestnut, with no particular verve and no spark to his step. Samantha already suspected that what she could anticipate was a horse that would want to stop by the stream, walk when he could, nibble at bushes, graze on whatever grass he could find, and beg to go home whenever Sam happened to turn even slightly in the direction of the barn. It promised to be a day filled with aggravation, and she found herself suddenly remorseful over her anger about Lady only moments before. But more than that, what she felt as she waited was that she wanted to prove to the assistant foreman that she was worthy of a much better mount. Like Black Beauty, she smiled to herself as she thought of Caroline's Thoroughbred stallion. She was looking forward to riding him, and wouldn't that just show this rigid chauvinist ranchman what kind of a rider she was. She wondered if Bill King had ever been like him, and had to admit to herself that he had probably been worse. Bill King had been, and was still, a tough foreman, and this one hadn't really done much to Sam except offer her a pretty tame horse, which, she had to admit in spite of herself, was a reasonable thing to do with an unknown rider out from a place like New York. How did he know she could ride, after all? And if Caroline hadn't tried to prejudice them in her favor, it was just as well.

The men sat on horseback in the rain in their slickers, chatting in little clusters, waiting for the assistant foreman to give them their instructions for the day. The twenty-eight ranch hands never rode together, but usually broke into four or five groups to perform whatever needed doing at various ends of the ranch. Every morning Bill King, or his assistant, moved among them, verbally giving out assignments, telling which men to work with which others and where. Now, as he did every morning when Bill King wasn't around, the tall, dark-haired assistant foreman quietly moved among them, giving them their assignments for the day. He assigned Josh four men to work the south end of the ranch, looking for strays and cattle in trouble. Two other groups went to check some fences he thought were down. Another foursome had two sick cows to bring in down by the river. And he and another four men and Samantha were checking the north boundaries for three cows he knew were loose and about to calve. Samantha followed the group quietly out of the main compound, riding sedately on Rusty and wishing that the rain would stop. It seemed forever before they got into a good canter, and she had had to remind herself again that in a Western saddle you didn't post to trot. It was odd to sit in the big comfortable saddle, she was far more accustomed to the smaller, flatter English saddles she had always used for jumping and competition in Madison Square Garden, but this was a whole other life.

Only once did she smile to herself and wonder what was happening that morning in her office. It was insane to think that only two days before she had been wearing a blue Dior suit and conducting a creative meeting with a new client, and now she was out looking for stray cows on a ranch. The very thought of it almost made her laugh aloud as they crested a small hill, and she had to concentrate to keep from openly smiling, the whole contrast of what she had done and what she was doing was so totally absurd. Several times she noticed the assistant foreman's eyes on her, as though checking to see if she could manage her mount. Once she almost said something unpleasant to him as he reminded her to rein in as he rode past her, while Rusty was desperately trying to nibble at some grass. For just a moment Samantha had let the animal have his way, hoping to pacify the dull-spirited beast before they moved on. The dark-haired tyrant seemed to think that Samantha couldn't control him, and the very thought of that almost made her scream. "I did it on purpose," she wanted to shout after him, but he seemed totally uninterested in her doings as he moved on to talk quietly to two of his men. She noticed also that all of them seemed to regard him as something of an authority. The men had the same way of dealing with him as they did with Bill King, with quiet awe, curt respectful answers, and quick nods. No one questioned what he suggested, no one argued with what he said. There was very little humor exchanged between him and the others, and he smiled very rarely as the men talked or he talked to them. Somehow Sam found that he annoyed her. The very sureness with which he spoke was an open challenge to her.

"Enjoying your ride?" he asked her a little while later as he rode along beside her for a moment.

"Very much," she said through clenched teeth as the pouring rain grew worse. "Lovely weather." She smiled at him, but he didn't answer. He only nodded and moved on, and she mentally accused him of being a humorless pain in the ass. As the day wore on, her legs grew tired, her seat ached, the insides of her knees screamed from the no-longer-unfamiliar friction of saddle against jeans. Her feet were cold, her hands were stiff, and just as she wondered if it would ever end they broke for lunch. They stopped at a small cabin on the far reaches of Caroline's ranch, set aside for just such occasions. It boasted a table, some chairs, and the equipment they needed to assist them with making lunch: hot plates and running water. Sam discovered that the assistant foreman himself had brought the necessary provisions in his saddlebag, and everyone was handed a fat sandwich filled with turkey and ham, and two huge Thermoses were brought out and rapidly emptied. One had been filled with soup, the other with coffee, and it wasn't until she was cherishing the last of her coffee that he spoke to her again.

"Holding up all right, Miss Taylor?" There was the faintest trace of mockery in his voice, but this time there was a kinder light in his eyes.

"Fine, thanks. What about you, Mr. . . . er . . . you know, I don't know your name." She smiled sweetly at him and this time he grinned. There was definitely some pepper to the girl. He had sensed that right at the first, when he had suggested Lady. He had seen the look of annoyance flare up in her eyes, but he hadn't given a damn what kind of horse she wanted. He was going to give her the quietest mount on the place. He didn't need some dizzy broad from New York breaking her ass on the north boundary that morning. That was all he needed, but so far she seemed to have managed all right. And he had to admit that it was hard to figure out what kind of rider she was on that lazy horse.

"My name's Tate Jordan." He held out a hand, and once again she wasn't sure if he was mocking her or being sincere. "How are you enjoying your stay?"

"Terrific." She smiled angelically at him. "Great weather. Superb horse. Wonderful people. . . ." She faltered a moment and he raised an eyebrow.

"What? Nothing to say about the food?"

"I'll think of something."

"I'm sure you will. I must say, I'm surprised you decided to ride today. You could have waited for a better day to start out."

"Why should I? You didn't, did you?"

"No." He looked at her almost derisively. "But that's hardly the same thing."

"Volunteers always try harder, or didn't you know that, Mr. Jordan?"

"I guess I didn't. We haven't had too many around here. Have you been out here before?" He looked her over with interest for the first time, but it was curiosity, rather than any friendship he was intending to form.

"Yes, I have, but not in a long time."

"Did Caroline let you ride with the men before too?"

"Not really . . . oh, once in a while . . . but it was more for fun."

"And this time?" The questioning eyebrow raised again.

"I guess this is for fun too." She smiled at him more genuinely this time. She could have told him it was therapy, but she wasn't about to disclose her secrets to him. On the spur of the moment she decided to thank him instead. "I do appreciate your letting me ride with you. I know it must be difficult having someone new around." She wasn't going to apologize for being a woman. That would have been too much to bear. "I hope that eventually I might be of some use."

"Maybe so." He nodded at her then and moved on. He didn't speak to her again for the rest of the afternoon. They never found the strays they had been concerned about, and by two o'clock in the afternoon they met up with one of the parties mending fences and joined them. Samantha was of only minimal use in what they were doing, and the truth of it was that by three o'clock she was so tired, she was ready to fall asleep, in the pouring rain, on the horse, and despite whatever conditions prevailed. By four she was looking truly miserable, and by five thirty when they went back, she was sure that once she got off the horse she would never move again. She had been on horseback and in the rain for eleven out of eleven and a half hours, and she thought that there was a distinct possibility that she might die that night. She could barely crawl off the horse when they got back to the barn, and only Josh's firm hands assisting her kept her from falling bowlegged and exhausted onto the ground. She met his concerned look with an exhausted chuckle and gratefully took a firm hold of his supporting arm.

"I think maybe you overdid it today, Sam. Why didn't you go home early?"

"Are you kidding? I'd have died first. If Aunt Caro can do it, so can I. . . ." And then she looked ruefully at her old buddy. "Or can I?"

"I hate to tell you this, babe, but she's been doing it for a lot longer than you have, and every day. You're going to hurt like the devil by tomorrow."

"Never mind tomorrow! You should know what it feels like right now." All of this was being conducted in whispers from just inside Rusty's stall. Rusty was already impervious to them, gorging himself on hay.

"Can you walk?"

"I'd better. I'm sure as hell not going to crawl out of here."

"Want me to carry you?"

"I'd love it." She grinned at him. "But what would they all say?" They both laughed at the thought of it, and then as Sam glanced up, suddenly her eyes took on a new sparkle. She had just noticed a name on a pretty little bronze plaque outside another stall. "Josh." Suddenly her eyes didn't look as though she were in any kind of agony. "Is that Black Beauty?"

"Yes, ma'am." He said it with an admiring grin, for her as much as for the Thoroughbred. "Want to see him?"

"I would take my last dying steps across a bed of nails to see him, Joshua. Take me to him." He put an arm under hers to support her and helped her hobble across the barn to the other stall. All of the others had gone by then, and there were suddenly no other voices in the barn except theirs.

From the distance the stall appeared to be empty, but as Samantha approached it she saw him in the far corner and whistled softly as he walked slowly toward them and nuzzled her hand. He was the most beautiful horse she had ever seen in her entire lifetime, a masterpiece of black velvet with a white star on his forehead and two perfectly matched white socks on his front legs. His mane and his tail were the same perfect shiny raven-black as the rest of his body, and his eyes were large and gentle. His legs were incredibly graceful, and he was also the biggest horse Sam thought she had ever seen. "My God, Josh, he's incredible."

"He's a beauty, ain't he?"

"Better than that, he's the best-looking horse I've ever seen." Sam sounded awed. "How big is he?"

"Seventeen and a half hands, almost eighteen." Josh said it with pride and pleasure and Samantha whistled softly in the big barn.

"What I'd give to ride that."

"Think she'll let you? Mr. King doesn't even like her to ride him, you know. He's got a hell of a lot of spirit. Almost threw her a couple of times, and that ain't easy to do. I ain't seen a horse yet could throw Miss Caro."

Samantha never took her eyes off the horse. "She said I could ride him, and I'll bet he doesn't try to throw me."

"I wouldn't chance it, Miss Taylor." The voice from directly behind her wasn't Josh's voice, it was another voice, a deep, smoky one that spoke softly, but without

78

warmth. She turned slowly to see Tate Jordan and suddenly her eyes blazed.

"And why don't you think I should chance it? Do you think Rusty is more my style?" She was suddenly very angry as exhaustion, pain, and annoyance mingled almost beyond control.

"I don't know about that. But there's a world between these two horses, and Miss Caroline is probably the best woman rider I've ever seen. If she has trouble with Black Beauty, you can bet that you'd fare a lot worse." He looked too sure of himself, and Josh looked suddenly uncomfortable at the exchange.

"Oh, really? How interesting, Mr. Jordan. I notice that you qualify Caroline as the 'best *woman* rider' you've ever seen. I take it you don't feel she compares with men?"

"It's a different kind of riding."

"Not always. I'll bet you that I could handle this beast a lot better than you could."

"What makes you think so?" His eyes flashed, but only for an instant.

"I've been riding Thoroughbreds for years." She said it with the venom of sheer exhaustion, but Tate Jordan looked neither pleased nor amused.

"Some of us haven't had those advantages. We just do the best we can, with whatever we've got." As he said it she felt her face flush; he touched his hat, nodded at her without looking at the ranch hand beside her, and then strode out of the barn.

For a moment there was silence, and then Josh watched her to see what was happening in her face. She tried to look nonchalant as she patted Black Beauty's muzzle, and then glanced over again at Josh. "Irritating son of a bitch, isn't he? Is he always like that?"

"Probably. Around women. His wife ran off and left him years ago. She ran off with the ranch owner's son, married him too. And he even adopted Tate's boy. Till they was killed. His wife and the ranch owner's boy got themselves killed in a car wreck. Tate got his boy back, though the boy still don't use his name. I don't think Tate cares much what name the boy uses. He's crazy as hell about his son. But he don't never mention his wife. I think she left him with kind of a sour taste in his mouth about women. Except for—" Josh blushed furiously for a moment. "Except for . . . you know, easy women. I don't think he's never been involved with no one else. And hell, he says his boy's twenty-two, so you know how long that's been."

Sam nodded slowly. "Do you know the boy?"

Josh shrugged and shook his head. "Nope. I know Tate got him a job around here last year, but he don't usually say much about himself, or the boy. He keeps pretty private. Most of the men do. But he goes to see him about once a week. He's over at the Bar Three."

Another loner, Sam found herself thinking, wondering if cowboys were anything but. She was intrigued about something else about him. He showed a quick intelligence, and she found herself wondering briefly just who and what Tate Jordan was, as Josh shook his head with his familiar grin. "Don't let it worry you none, Sam. He don't mean no harm. It's just his way. Underneath all them porcupine quills he's gentle. You should see him with the kids on the ranch. He must have been a good father to his boy. And Tate's got an education too. Not that that makes much difference here. His dad was a rancher and sent him to some fine schools. Even went to college and got some kind of degree in something, but his old man died and they lost the ranch. I think that's when he went to work on the other ranch and his wife ran off then with his boss's son. I think it must have all done something to him. I don't think he wants much more than he got. For himself or his boy. He's just a ranch hand like the rest of us. But he's smart and he'll be a foreman someday. If not here, then he'll do it somewhere else. You can't deny what a man is. And ornery or not, he's a hell of a good man on a ranch." Sam thought of what she'd just heard. She knew more than she really wanted to, thanks to Josh's loose tongue. "Ready to head back to the big house?" He looked warmly at the pretty young woman with the tired face and the damp clothing. "Can you make it?"

"If you ask me that again, Josh, I'll kick you." She glared at him ferociously and he laughed.

"Hell no, you won't." He laughed more. "You couldn't lift your leg high enough to kick a short dog, Samantha." And then he laughed over his joke all the way to the big house. It was a few minutes after six when Caroline opened the door to them, and Josh left her at the front door in Caroline's care. She couldn't help smiling at her young friend as Sam struggled into the cozy living room and collapsed, groaning, onto the couch. She had shed the damp jacket on the way, and as her pants had stayed dry beneath the slicker, she knew that she wasn't damaging the furniture and she needed to sit down.

"Good God, girl, did you ride all day?" Sam nodded,

barely able to speak, she was so tired and stiff. "Why in heaven's name didn't you come home when you'd had enough?"

"I didn't want to look like a sissy. . . ." She groaned horribly but managed to grin at Caroline, who collapsed on the couch with a chuckle and a smile.

"Oh, Samantha, you foolish girl! You'll be in agony tomorrow!"

"No, I won't. I'll be back on that damn horse." And then she groaned again, but more at the memory of the horse than at the pain.

"Which one did they give you?"

"A miserable old beast called Rusty." Sam looked at Caroline with open disgust and Caroline laughed harder.

"Oh, God, they didn't. Did they really?" Samantha nodded. "Who on earth did that? I told them you could ride as well as any of the men."

"Well, they didn't believe you. At least Tate Jordan didn't. He almost gave me Lady, and then decided Rusty was more my speed."

"Tomorrow tell him you want Navajo. He's a beautiful Appaloosa, no one rides him except Bill and myself."

"Will that make the other men resent me?"

"Did they today?"

"I'm not sure. They didn't say much."

"They don't say much to each other either. And if you rode with them since this morning, how could they possibly resent you? My God, and all those hours on the first day!" She looked truly horrified at what Samantha had done.

"Wouldn't you have done the same thing?"

She thought about it for a minute, and then, with a sheepish grin, nodded yes.

"By the way, I saw Black Beauty."

"What do you think of him?" Caroline's eyes glowed.

"I think I'd like to steal him, or at least ride him. But"—her eyes suddenly flashed again—"Mr. Jordan doesn't think I ought to. According to him, Black Beauty isn't a horse for a woman."

"What about me?" Caroline looked vastly amused.

"He thinks you're the 'best *woman* rider' he's ever seen. I challenged him about that, why not the 'best rider' without qualifying it?" But Caroline only laughed at her. "What's so funny, Aunt Caro? You *are* the best damn rider I've ever seen."

"For a woman," she countered.

"You think that's funny?"

"I'm used to it. Bill King thinks the same thing."

"Liberated in these parts, aren't they?" Samantha groaned as she got off the couch and pointed herself in the direction of her room. "In any case if I can squeeze a better horse out of Tate Jordan tomorrow, I'll feel as though I've won a major battle for womankind. What was the name of that Appaloosa?"

"Navajo. Just tell him I said so."

Samantha rolled her eyes as she disappeared down the hall. "Good luck," Caroline called after her. But as she washed her face and brushed her hair in the pretty bedroom, she realized that it was the first time in three months that she hadn't moved heaven and earth to watch John and Liz's evening broadcast, and she hadn't even missed it. She was in another world now. A world of horses named Rusty, and Appaloosas, and assistant foremen who thought they ruled the world; but it was all very simple and very wholesome, and the most pressing problem she had was what horse she was going to ride the next day.

She thought once more to herself as she lay in bed shortly after dinner that it was the most blissfully simple existence she had known since she was a child. And then, as the thoughts faded from her mind, just before she drifted into sleep, she heard the familiar door close again and she was sure this time that she heard muffled footsteps and soft laughter in the hall.

5

The next morning Samantha climbed out of bed with a horrific groan, she staggered to the shower and stood there for a full fifteen minutes with the hot water raining down on her sore limbs. The insides of her knees were almost scarlet from her eleven-hour day in the saddle, and she padded her long johns with wads of cotton as she gingerly stepped back into her jeans. The only encouraging sign for the day ahead was that it was no longer raining, and she glanced around her in the early morning darkness, noticing that there were still stars in the sky, as she made her way to the main dining hall for breakfast.

This morning she felt less timid as she walked in, hung her jacket on a hook, and went straight to the coffee machine, where she filled a tall steaming mug. She saw her old friend Josh at a far table and went over to him with a smile as he beckoned to her to sit down.

"How you feelin' today, Samantha?"

She grinned ruefully at him and lowered her voice conspiratorially as she took over the empty chair. "It's a good thing we're riding today, Josh, that's all I can tell you."

"How's that?"

" 'Cause I sure as hell couldn't walk. I just about crawled here from the big house." Josh and the other two men chuckled and one of them praised her for her hard ride the day before.

"You sure are a damn fine rider, Samantha." Not that she had had the opportunity to show them her stuff in the driving rain.

"I used to be. It's been a long time."

"Don't make no difference," Josh told her firmly. "You got a good seat, good hands, you got 'em for the rest of your life. You gonna ride Rusty again today, Sam?" He raised one eyebrow and she shrugged as she sipped her coffee.

"We'll see. I don't think so." Josh only smiled. He knew that Sam wouldn't put up with an old nag like that for long. Sure as hell not after she saw Black Beauty. It would be a miracle if she wasn't riding him before long. "What did you think of the big boy?" He grinned with pleasure.

"Black Beauty?" Her eyes filled with a special light as she said his name. There was something about horsepeople and a Thoroughbred stallion. It was a kind of passion other people would never understand. Josh nodded and grinned. "He's the best piece of horseflesh I've ever seen."

"Miss Caro going to let you ride him?" He couldn't resist asking.

"If I can talk her into it—and don't think I won't try!" Sam smiled back over her shoulder as she headed for the line waiting for breakfast. She returned five minutes later with a plate of sausages and fried eggs. Two of the men had moved to another table, and Josh was already squaring the hat on his head. "Going out early, Josh?"

"I told Tate I'd give him a hand in the barn before we ride out this morning." He smiled at her, turned to call out to one of his friends, and then disappeared.

Twenty minutes later when Samantha went out to the barn to saddle up, she looked around hesitantly for Tate, not entirely sure how to broach the change of mounts with him. But on a day like this there was no way she was going to ride a nag like the one he'd assigned her. She was sure that if Navajo was Caroline's suggestion, he would be much more her style.

A couple of the men nodded to her as they walked past her. They seemed less annoyed by her presence than they had been the previous morning. She suspected that even though they had been expecting her they hadn't imagined her quite as she was. But she also knew that if nothing else would win them over, riding as hard and as long as they did in the driving rain would eventually win their hearts. And if she was going to spend the next three months on Caroline's ranch, acting like any other ranch hand, then it was important to her that the men come to accept her as one of them. Still she knew that one or two of the younger ones had been stunned by her looks and her youth, and she had caught one of them staring at her in fascination the evening before when she had pulled the rubber band out of her hair at the end of the long day and shook out her wet mane of silvery blond hair. She had smiled at him briefly and he had blushed furiously and turned away.

"Morning, Miss Taylor." The firm voice broke into Sam's reverie, and when she looked up at Tate Jordan, she suddenly knew that however uncomfortable he may have made her, or wanted to, she was not willing to ride a bad horse all day in order to prove that he was in charge. There was something stubborn and determined just in the way he looked at her, and it set her back up just watching the way he moved his head. "Tired after yesterday?"

"Not really." Not to him would she admit the aches and the pains. Tired? Of course not. Just to look at him one knew how powerful and important he thought he was. Assistant foreman on the Lord Ranch. Not bad, Mr. Assistant Foreman. And Sam knew it was possible that at sixty-three, Bill King might retire at any moment and leave Tate Jordan his oversize shoes to fill. Not that Jordan would fill them as impressively as Bill King had, or as intelligently or as kindly or as wisely. . . . She didn't know why, but Tate Jordan annoyed the hell out of her, and there was an unspoken friction between them one could sense instantly as he brushed past. "Ahh . . . Mr.

88

Jordan." She suddenly felt an odd pleasure in putting a spoke in his wheels.

"Yes?" He turned to face her, holding a saddle perched on one shoulder.

"I thought I'd try a different ride." Her eyes were cool as glass as his slowly began to blaze.

"What did you have in mind?" There was an undertone of challenge.

She was dying to say Black Beauty, but decided not to waste the irony of the suggestion on him. "Caroline thought that Navajo might do."

He looked momentarily annoyed, but then nodded and turned away, muttering distractedly over his shoulder, "Go ahead." The very words irritated Samantha. Why did she need his permission for what horse she rode? Reason provided a simple answer, but she still bristled at his style as she found Navajo's stall and his saddle and bridle in a little tack room just beyond it and went back to saddle up. He was a beautiful Appaloosa, mottled whipped-cream-and-chocolate face, rich brown flanks, and the characteristic white hindquarters with big brown spots. He was gentle as Samantha put the saddle on him and then strapped the girth beneath him, but it was also evident as she led him out of his stall that he had a great deal more spirit than Rusty. In fact she had to work to control him once she was astride, and he pranced for a full five minutes as she attempted to join the others beginning to move out. She had been assigned the same group as the previous day, and she saw Tate Jordan watching her with open disapproval as they rode toward the hills.

"Think you can manage him, Miss Taylor?" His voice was clear as a bell and Samantha suddenly felt a strong urge to hit him as he rode alongside her and observed the frisky maneuvers of her horse.

"I'll certainly try, Mr. Jordan."

"I think we probably should have given you Lady." Samantha said nothing at all in answer and moved on. Half an hour later they were all engrossed in what they were doing: looking for strays and once again checking fences. They found a sick heifer, which two of the men roped in order to lead back to one of the main cattle barns. And by the time they stopped for lunch, they had already put in six hours of work. They stopped in a clearing and tied the horses to the surrounding trees. The usual sandwiches and soup and coffee were handed around, and conversation was sparse but relaxed. No one said much to Samantha, but she was comfortable with them nonetheless and let her thoughts drift as she sat for a few moments with her eyes closed in the winter sun.

"You must be tired, Miss Taylor." It was that voice again. She opened one eye.

"Not really. I was enjoying the sunshine. Does that bother you very much?"

"Not at all." He smiled pleasantly. "How are you enjoying Navajo?"

"Very much." She opened both eyes and smiled at him. And then she suddenly couldn't resist teasing him a little. "Not as much as I'd enjoy Black Beauty of course." She smiled mischievously at him and it was hard to tell if she meant it or not.

"That, Miss Taylor"—he returned the smile to her like

a rapid volley in tennis—"is a mistake I hope you never make." He nodded wisely. "You'd get hurt. And that"— he smiled gently at her again—"would be a great shame. A stallion like that, there are damn few people who should ride him. Even Miss Lord herself has to be careful when she takes him out. He's a dangerous beast, and not . . ." He looked for the right words. ". . . not the kind of horse a 'sometime rider' ought to play with." The green eyes looked infinitely patronizing as he gazed down at her with his steaming cup of coffee in his hand.

"Have you ridden him?" The question was blunt and her eyes didn't smile.

"Once."

"How did you find him?"

"He's a beautiful animal. No doubt about that." The green eyes smiled again. "He's quite a different ride than Navajo." But there was an implication in his words that suggested that Navajo was all she could handle. "Looks like he gave you a little bit of a hard time when we started out."

"And you thought I couldn't handle it?" She was almost amused.

"I was concerned. After all, if you get hurt, it's my responsibility, Miss Taylor."

"Spoken like a true foreman, Mr. Jordan. But I don't really think Miss Lord would hold you responsible for what happens to me with a horse. She knows me too well."

"What does that mean?"

"That I'm not used to riding horses like Rusty."

"But you think you're up to a stallion like Black Beauty?" He knew that neither Caroline Lord nor Bill King would let her ride him. Hell, they'd only let him ride the exquisite Thoroughbred once.

Samantha nodded quietly. "Yes, I think I could ride him."

He looked amused. "Do you? You're that sure of yourself, are you?"

"I just know how I ride. I ride hard. I take chances. I know what I'm doing, and I've been riding since I was five. That's been a while."

"Every day?" There was a challenge again. "Ride much in New York, do you?"

"No, Mr. Jordan." She smiled sweetly. "I don't." But as she said it she vowed to ride Black Beauty as soon as Caroline would let her, because she wanted to, and because she wanted to show this arrogant cowboy that she could.

A moment later he strode back toward his men and gave them the signal. They mounted up and spent the rest of the afternoon checking the boundaries of the ranch. They found some more loose heifers at the outermost reaches and drove them home at sunset, when once again Samantha wondered if she would even be able to get off her horse. But Josh was waiting for her outside the barn when they got there, and he gave her a hand as she swung her leg over Navajo with a groan.

"You gonna make it, Sam?"

"I doubt it." He grinned at her in answer as she untacked her horse and almost staggered to the tack room to put her saddle and bridle away.

"How'd it go today?" He followed her and stood in the doorway.

"All right, I guess." She realized with a tired smile that she was beginning to speak like the rest of the cowboys, in the same sparse fashion. Only Jordan spoke differently than they did, and only when he was speaking to her. Then the education he'd had was obvious; the rest of the time he sounded just like them. Not unlike Bill King, who was subtly different when he was with Caroline, but not as much. Bill King and Tate Jordan were very different men. Jordan was much less of a rough diamond than most.

"Long way from New York, ain't it, Samantha?" The wizened little old cowboy grinned, and she rolled her eyes.

"It sure is. But that's why I came out here."

He nodded. He didn't really know why she had come. But he understood. A ranch was a good place to be when one had problems. Lots of hard work, fresh air, good food, and good horses would cure almost anything. Your belly got full, your rump got tired, the sun came up and went down, and another day went by with nothing more complicated to worry about than if your horse needed new shoes or the fence on the south forty needed fixing. It was the only life Josh had ever known but he had seen plenty of other people try other things and come back to it. It was a good life. And he knew it would do Sam good too. Whatever she was running away from, it would help her. He had noticed the dark circles under her eyes the previous morning. They already looked clearer today.

Together, they wandered past Black Beauty, and

almost instinctively Sam reached out and patted his neck.
"Hello, boy." She spoke softly to him and he whinnied as
though he knew her. She gazed at him thoughtfully, as
though once again seeing him for the first time. And then
an odd light came into her eyes as she left the big barn
with Josh at her side, bid him good night, and walked
slowly back to the big house, where Bill King was talking
to Caroline. They stopped when she came in.

"Hello, Bill . . . Caro." She smiled at them both. "Am I
interrupting something?" She looked embarrassed for a
moment, but they were both quick to shake their heads.

"Of course not, dear." Caroline kissed her and Bill King
picked up his hat and got up.

"I'll be seein' you tomorrow, ladies." He was quick to
leave them and Samantha sprawled out on the couch with
a sigh.

"Hard day?" Caroline looked at her gently as she lay
there. She herself hadn't ridden all week. She and Bill still
had a lot of paperwork to do before year's end, and there
were only two weeks left in which to do it. She'd at least
have to get out and ride Black Beauty one of these days
before he became totally wild, but she didn't really even
have time for that. "Are you very tired, Sam?" Caroline
looked sympathetic.

"Tired? Are you kidding? After sitting at a desk for all
these years? I'm not tired. I'm broken. If Josh didn't drag
me off that horse every night, I'd probably have to sleep
out there."

"That bad, huh?"

"Worse." The two women laughed and the Mexican
woman who helped Caroline with the cleaning and

cooking signaled from the kitchen. Dinner was ready. "Mmm, what is it?" Samantha wrinkled her nose happily on the way into the big handsomely done country kitchen.

"Enchiladas, chiles rellenos, tamales. . . . All my favorites, I hope some of them are yours."

Samantha smiled at her happily. "After a day like that you could feed me cardboard, as long as there was lots of it, with a bath and a bed at the end of the meal."

"I'll remember that, Samantha. Otherwise how's it going? Everyone being civil to you, I hope?" She furrowed her brows as she asked the question, and Samantha nodded and smiled.

"Everyone's perfectly pleasant." But there was a tiny catch in her voice and Caroline was quick to hear it.

"Except?"

"No except's. I don't think Tate Jordan and I will ever be best friends, but he's perfectly civilized. I just don't think he approves of what he calls 'sometime riders.' "

Caroline looked amused. "Probably not. He is an odd sort. In some ways he thinks like a rancher, but he's perfectly happy to break his back working on the ranch. He is the last of the real thing. Real cowboys, the hard-riding, hardworking, down-to-the-core ranchman who would die for the ranchers he works for and do anything he could to save the ranch. He's a good man to have here, and one day," she sighed softly, "he'll be the right man to step into Bill's shoes. If he stays."

"Why wouldn't he? He has a hell of a nice life here. You've always provided your men with more comforts than anyone else."

"Yes." She nodded slowly. "And I've never been

convinced that that mattered to them as much as I thought it should. They're a funny breed. Almost everything they do is a matter of pride and honor. They'll work for one man for nothing because they feel they owe him or because he's done right by them, and then leave someone else because they feel they should. It's impossible to predict what any of them will do. Even Bill. I never even fully know with him what he's going to do."

"It must be quite something to try and run a ranch like that."

"It's interesting." Caroline smiled. "Very interesting." And then suddenly she noticed Samantha glancing at her watch. "Something wrong, Sam?"

"No." Sam looked suddenly strangely quiet. "It's six o'clock."

"Yes?" For a moment Caroline didn't understand and then she did. "The news broadcast?" Samantha nodded. "Do you watch it every night?"

"I try not to." The look of pain was back in Sam's eyes as she said it. "But in the end I always do."

"Do you think you ought to?"

"No." Slowly Samantha shook her head.

"Do you want me to have Lucia-Maria bring the television in? She can, you know." But Sam shook her head again.

"I have to stop watching sometime." A tiny sigh escaped her. "I might as well stop watching right now." It was like fighting an addiction. The addiction of staring into John Taylor's face every night.

"Can I offer anything to help distract you? A drink? A

rival newscast? Hard candy? Some tissues to shred?" She was teasing and Samantha laughed then. What a wonderful woman she was and she seemed to understand it all.

"I'll be all right, but come to think of it . . ." She looked across the table at Caroline, looking like a very young girl with an enormous request, like Mom's mink stole for the senior prom. And the long blond hair loose on her shoulders only helped to make her look younger in the soft light. "I do have a favor to ask."

"What's that? I can't imagine anything here you can't have."

"I can." Samantha grinned like a little kid.

"And what might that be?"

Samantha whispered the two magic words. "Black Beauty."

For a moment Caroline looked pensive, and then suddenly she looked amused. "So that's it, is it! I see. . . ."

"Aunt Caro . . . may I?"

"May you what?" Caroline Lord sat back in her chair with a regal air and a twinkle in her eye.

But Samantha would not be easily put off. "May I ride him?"

There was no answer for a long moment as Caroline grew anxious. "Do you think you're up to it yet?"

Samantha nodded slowly, knowing the truth of what Josh had said: If you had it, you never lost it. "I do."

Caroline nodded slowly. She had watched Sam riding into the main compound as she and Bill had stood at her large picture windows. Sam just had horses in her bones.

It was a part of her, instinctively, even after not riding for over a year. "Why do you want to ride him?" She cocked her head to one side, her dinner forgotten.

When Samantha answered, her voice was gentle and her eyes had a faraway look, her ex-husband's broadcast forgotten, along with the woman to whom he had fled. All she could think of now was the ravishingly beautiful black stallion in the stables and how badly she wanted to feel him beneath her as together they raced into the wind. "I don't know why." She looked up at Caroline honestly. And then she smiled. "I just feel as though, as though"— she faltered for a moment, her eyes distant again—"as though I have to. I can't explain it, Caro. There's something about that horse." She smiled a distant smile, which was instantly reflected in Caroline's eyes.

"I know. I felt it too. That was why I had to have him. Even if it makes no sense for a woman my age to have a horse like him. I had to, just this one last time." Samantha nodded her complete understanding and as the two women looked into each other's eyes they felt the same bond that had always held them together, across the years, across the miles. In some ways they were as one, as though in their souls they were mother and daughter.

"Well?" Samantha looked at her hopefully.

"Go ahead." Caroline smiled slowly. "Ride him."

"When?" Sam almost held her breath.

"Tomorrow. Why not?"

6

In the morning as Samantha poured her aching body out of bed, she only felt its pain for the first few instants. After that she remembered her conversation with Caroline, and nothing hurt anymore as she ran to the shower and stood there, with the hot water pounding down on her shoulders and her head. This morning she wasn't even going to take the time for breakfast. She didn't care about breakfast. Not today. All she needed was a cup of coffee from Caroline's kitchen, and after that she would sail out to the barn. Just thinking about it made her smile. It was all she could think of this morning. And the smile was still dancing in her eyes as she ran the last steps to the barn. Two of the men were talking quietly in one corner, but other than that there was no one there. It was still much too early for most of them to be there. They were eating breakfast and trying to wake up as they gossiped about the local news and the usual ranch talk in the main dining hall.

Quietly, almost stealthily, Samantha picked up Black Beauty's saddle and walked toward his stall. But as soon as she had done so she saw the two men eyeing her, one with raised eyebrows. They had both stopped talking and were watching her with a silent question. Just as silently she nodded and slipped into the stall. She made soft murmuring noises to soothe him, running a hand down the long graceful neck and patting the powerful flanks as he eyed her nervously at first, backing and sidling, and then stopping as though to sniff the air near where she stood. She rested the saddle on the stall door, and then slipping the bridle over his head, she led him from the stall.

"Ma'am?" The voice surprised her as she looped the reins around a convenient post so she could saddle Black Beauty. She turned around to see who it was. It was one of the two men who had been watching her, and she realized then that he was a good friend of Josh. "Miss Taylor?"

"Yes?"

"Uh . . . do you . . . I don't mean . . ." He was mortified, but clearly worried, and Sam smiled her golden smile. This morning her hair was loose down her back, her eyes brilliant, her face pink from the chill December air. She looked incredibly beautiful as she stood beside the coal-black Thoroughbred stallion, like a tiny palomino at his side.

"It's all right." She was quick to reassure him. "I have Miss Lord's permission."

"Uh . . . ma'am . . . does Tate Jordan know?"

"No." She shook her head firmly. "He doesn't. And I don't see why he should. Black Beauty belongs to Miss Caroline, doesn't he?" The man nodded, and Sam smiled the dazzling smile again. "Then there shouldn't be any problem."

He hesitated and then backed off. "I guess not." And then with a worried frown, "You ain't scared to ride him? He's got one hell of a lot of power in those long limbs."

"I'll bet he does." She looked at his legs with pleasure and anticipation and then swung the saddle onto his back. For Black Beauty, Caroline had also acquired an English saddle, and it was this that Samantha was strapping to him now. It was as though he knew the feel of the smooth brown leather, unlike the cumbersome Western saddle Samantha had been riding for two days. This was a saddle she knew better, and a breed of horse she had often ridden, but a horse as fine as this one was a rare gift in any horseman's life.

A few minutes after she had saddled him, she tightened the girth again, and then hesitantly one of the two ranch hands moved closer and gave her a leg up onto the gigantic black horse. At the feel of a rider on his back, Black Beauty pranced nervously for a moment, and then with the reins well in hand, Samantha nodded at the two ranch hands and walked Black Beauty quickly away. He pranced and sidestepped quite a lot on the way to the first gate, and then as she let him through it, she allowed him to break into a trot, which rapidly became a swift canter as they made their way across the fields. The sky was by then streaked with the first signs of daybreak, and the light around her was pale gray becoming almost gold. It was a magnificent winter morning and she had beneath her the most magnificent horse she had ever ridden. Unconsciously a broad smile broke out on her face and she let Black Beauty gallop as she moved with him across the fields. It was the most extravagant feeling of freedom she had ever known and it was almost like flying, as together, like one body, they sailed along. It seemed hours later when she forced herself to make him change direction, and slowing him only a little, she began to head home. She still had to ride with the men that morning, and what she had done was forfeit breakfast to ride this magnificent horse across the fields. It was only a quarter of a mile from the main complex that she finally succumbed to temptation and jumped the huge horse across a narrow stream, which he cleared with ease, and only after they had passed it did she notice that not far from them Tate Jordan was riding his own handsome black and white pinto and glaring at her as she raced along. She reined in a little, veered and rode toward him, wanting, just for one moment, to rush him and show him how well she rode. But instead she resisted the temptation and just allowed herself to gallop gaily in his direction on the back of the handsome beast. She slowed him down to a canter, and Black Beauty was prancing happily as they reached Tate.

"Good morning! Want to run with us?" In her eyes was

victory beyond measure, and the answering look in Tate
Jordan's eyes was fierce.

"What the hell are you doing on that horse?"

"Caroline said I could ride him." She sounded like a
petulant child as she slowed him further, and Tate fell
into step beside her as they rode back. She was
remembering everything he had said to her the day
before and she was enjoying her moment of triumph as
he fumed. "Remarkable, isn't he?"

"Yeah. And if he'd stumbled at the stream back there,
he'd have a remarkably broken leg, or didn't you think of
that when you raced him toward it to jump it? Didn't you
see the rocks back there, dammit? Don't you know how
easily he could slip?" His voice carried across the early
morning silence, and Samantha looked at him with
annoyance as they rode on.

"I know what I'm doing, Jordan."

"Do you?" He eyed her with unbridled fury. "I doubt
that. Your idea of knowing what you're doing is showing
off and going as fast as you can. You could ruin a lot of
horses that way. Not to mention what you could do to
yourself."

As she rode along beside him she wanted to scream.
"Do you really think you could do better?"

"Maybe I know enough not to try. A horse like that
should be a racehorse or a show horse. He doesn't belong
on a ranch. He shouldn't be ridden by people like you, or
me, or Miss Caro. He should be ridden by highly trained
people, Thoroughbred people, or he shouldn't be ridden
at all."

"I told you, I know what I'm doing." Her voice rose in

the stillness, and without warning, he reached out and grabbed her reins. Almost instantly both horses and their riders came to a full stop.

"I told you yesterday, you don't belong on that horse. You'll hurt him or kill yourself."

"Well." She looked at him angrily. "Did I?"

"Maybe next time you will."

"You can't admit it, can you? That a woman can ride as well as you. That's what galls you, isn't it?"

"The hell it is. Damn city playgirl, you come out here to have a good time and play at 'ranch girl' for a few weeks, ride a horse like that, jump him on terrain you don't know—dammit, why don't people like you stay where they belong? You don't belong here! Don't you understand that?"

"I understand it perfectly, now let go of my horse."

"Damn right I will."

He threw the reins at her and drove off. And feeling somehow as though she had lost rather than won, she rode back to the barn, but more sedately. She didn't know why, but his words had hurt. And there was one grain of truth in his tirade. She had been wrong to jump Black Beauty headlong over the stream. She didn't know the country she was riding, at least not well enough to take chances like that. But on the other hand, it had felt wonderful, flying over the countryside on a horse with the speed of the wind.

She could see the men gathering in the yard of the complex and hurried back into the barn to put Black Beauty in his stall. She was going to rub him down just for a moment, cover him with his blanket, and then leave.

She could give him a good rubdown that night, but when she reached his stall, Tate Jordan was already waiting, his green eyes like smoldering emerald fire, his face harder than she had seen it before, but he was looking taller and more handsome than any cowboy on a poster and for an insane moment she thought of her agency's new car ads. He would have been perfect as the male model, but this was not a commercial, and this wasn't New York.

"Just what exactly are you planning to do with that horse?" His voice was low and taut.

"Rub him down for a minute and then cover him up."

"And that's it?"

"Look." She knew what he was saying and now her delicate skin flushed to the roots of her golden hair. "I'll come back later and take care of him properly."

"When? In twelve hours? Like hell you will, *Miss* Taylor. If you want to ride a horse like Black Beauty, you'd damn well better live up to the responsibility. Walk him, cool him off, rub him down. I don't want to see you out with the others for another hour, if then. Is that clear? I know you're not much on taking advice or suggestions, but how are you on orders, do you understand them? Or is that a sometime thing with you too?" As she looked at him she almost wanted to slap him. What a hateful man he could be, but he was also a man who loved horses, and he was right about what he had just said.

"Fine. I understand." Her eyes dropped, and she took Black Beauty's bridle in her hands and prepared to walk away.

"Are you sure?"

"Yes, dammit! Yes!" She turned back to shout at him,

and there was an odd light in his eyes. He nodded and walked back toward his own horse, the reins looped easily over one of the hitching posts outside. "By the way, where will you all be working today?"

"I don't know." He strode past her. "Find us."

"How?"

"Just gallop the hell all over the ranch. You'll love it." He grinned sarcastically at her as he got back on his horse and rode off, and Samantha wished for only a moment that she were a man. At that precise moment she would have loved to hit him, but he was already gone.

As it turned out, it took her two hours to find them. Two hours of riding through brush, of following a few familiar trails and getting lost on others. At one point she almost wondered if Tate hadn't purposely chosen some activity that would keep them out in the more remote areas so she wouldn't find them. But at last she did. And despite the chill December air, she was warm in the bright winter sunshine after riding everywhere she could think of looking for them. She had found two other small work groups, and one larger one, but of Tate's there had been no sign.

"Have a nice ride?" He looked at her with amusement as she stopped and Navajo pawed the ground.

"Charming, thank you." But there was a feeling of victory nonetheless to have found them at all, and she watched the emerald eyes glinting in the sun. And then, without saying anything further, she wheeled her horse and joined the men, dismounting a few moments later to help carry a newborn calf in a sling made of a blanket. The mother had died only hours before, and the calf looked as if she might not make it either. One of the men hoisted the small, scarcely breathing animal in front of his saddle and rode steadily toward the livestock barn, where he would bring her to another cow in the hopes of giving her a foster mother. It was only half an hour later when Sam spotted the next one on her own, this one even smaller than the first, and the mother had obviously been gone for several more hours. This time with no assistance she fashioned the sling on her own, hoisted the calf onto her saddle with the help of a young ranch hand who was far too intrigued by Samantha to be of much use with the calf. Then, without waiting for instructions, she began to canter at a steady pace after the other ranch hand, toward the main barn.

"Can you manage it on your own?" She looked up, startled, to see Tate Jordan riding along smoothly beside her, his sleek black and white pinto making an interesting pair with her brown and white Appaloosa.

"Yeah, I think I can manage." And then with a look of concern at the animal in front of her saddle, "Do you think this one will live?"

"I doubt it." He spoke matter-of-factly as he watched her. "But it's always worth a try." She nodded in answer and rode harder, and this time he veered away and turned back. A few minutes later she was at the main barn, and the orphaned calf was taken into expert hands that worked on him for over an hour, but the little calf didn't live. As she walked back to Navajo waiting patiently outside the livestock buildings, she felt tears sting her eyes, and then as she swung her leg over the saddle she suddenly felt anger. Anger that they hadn't been able to save him, that the poor little beast hadn't survived. And she knew there were others like him out there, whose mothers had, for one reason or another, died as they delivered in the cold night. The men always had an eye out for livestock in trouble on the hills, but it was inevitable that there were some who escaped their notice and died on the hills every year. It was common for those who delivered in winter. The others had come to accept it, but Samantha had not. Somehow the orphaned calves seemed almost symbolic of the children she could not bear, and now she rode back out to the others with a vengeance and a determination that the next one she brought back would live.

She brought in three more that afternoon, riding hell for leather as she had that morning on Black Beauty, the calves wrapped in the blankets, the men watching her with combined intrigue and awe. She was a strange and beautiful young woman, bent low over her horse's neck, riding as no woman had on the Lord Ranch before, not even Caroline Lord. The extraordinary thing was that as they watched her fly across the hills, Navajo moving like a brown streak until they saw him no more, they knew just how good Samantha was. She was a horsewoman like few others, and as they rode back to the barn that night the men joked with her as they hadn't before.

"Do you always ride like that?" It was Tate Jordan again, his dark hair ruffled beneath the big black Stetson, his eyes bright, his beard beginning to cast a shadow across his face by the end of the day. There was a kind of rugged masculinity about him that had always made women pause when they saw him, as though for just a

moment they couldn't catch their breath. But Samantha
did not suffer from that affliction. There was something
about the self-assured way he moved that annoyed her.
He was a man who was sure of his world and his job, his
men and his horses, and probably his women as well. For
a moment she didn't answer his question, and then she
nodded with a vague smile.

"For a good cause."

"And this morning?" Why did he want to push her?
she wondered. Why did he care?

"That was a good cause too."

"Was it?" The green eyes pursued her as they rode
home after the long day.

But this time Samantha faced him frankly, her blue
eyes locking into his green. "Yes, it was. It made me feel
alive again, Mr. Jordan. It made me feel free. I haven't felt
like that in a long time." He nodded slowly and said
nothing. She wasn't sure if he understood, or if he even
cared, but with a last look at her he moved on.

7

"Aren't you going to ride Black Beauty this morning?"

For a moment she almost snapped at him as she swung a leg over Navajo and settled herself in the saddle, and then for no particular reason, she grinned at him. "No, I thought I'd give him a rest, Mr. Jordan. How about you?"

"I don't ride Thoroughbreds, Miss Taylor." The green eyes laughed at her as his lively pinto danced.

"Maybe you should." But he said nothing and rode off to lead his men into a distant part of the ranch. Their group was larger than usual, and today Bill King and

111

Caroline were riding with them too. But Samantha scarcely saw them. She was too busy doing the job she had been assigned to do, and by now she knew that the men were beginning to accept her. They hadn't planned to, they hadn't really wanted to. But she had worked so hard and ridden so well, and hung in for such endless hours, and worked so diligently to save the orphaned calves, that suddenly this morning it was "Heyyyyyo! Over here . . . Sam! . . . Hey, Sam, dammit . . . right now!" No more Miss Taylor, not a single ma'am. She totally lost track of time and everything except her work and her surroundings, and it wasn't until dinner that night that she stopped to talk to Caroline again.

"You know, Sam, you're a marvel." She poured a second cup of coffee for Samantha and sat back in the comfortable kitchen chair. "You could be in New York, sitting behind a desk, creating exotic commercials, and living in an apartment that's the envy of everyone you know, and instead you're out here, chasing cows, carrying sick calves, knee deep in manure, mending fences with my men, taking orders from men who have a fifth-grade education, getting up before dawn, and riding all day long. You know, there aren't many people who would understand that." Not to mention the fact that she had once been the wife of one of the most desirable young men on TV, Caroline thought. "What do you think about what you're doing?" Caroline's blue eyes danced at her and Samantha smiled.

"I think I'm doing the first sensible thing I've done in a very long time, and I love it. Besides"—she grinned girlishly—"I figure if I stick around here long enough, I'll get to ride Black Beauty again."

"I hear Tate Jordan didn't take too kindly to it."

"I don't think he takes too kindly to me on the whole."

"You been scaring him half to death, Samantha?"

"Hardly. As arrogant as he is, it would take a lot more than me to scare him."

"I don't think that's the case. But I hear he thinks you can ride. From him that's high praise."

"I suspected that this morning, but he'd rather die than say so."

"He's no different than the rest. This is their world, Samantha, not ours. On a ranch a woman is still a second-class citizen, most of the time anyway. They're all kings here."

"Does that bother you?" Samantha watched her, intrigued, but the older woman visibly softened as she grew pensive, and something very gentle veiled her eyes.

"No, I like it like that." Her voice was strangely gentle, and then she smiled up at Samantha and looked almost like a girl. In that flash of a moment it explained everything about Bill King. In his own way he ruled her, and she loved it. She had for many years. She respected his power and his strength and his masculinity, his judgment about the ranch and his way of handling the men. Caroline owned and ran the ranch, but it was Bill King behind her who had always helped run it, who silently held the reins along with her. The ranch hands respected her, but as a woman, a figurehead. It was Bill King who had always made them jump. And Tate Jordan who was making them jump now. There was something terribly macho and animal and appealing about all of it. It was a pull one wanted to resist as a modern woman, yet one couldn't. The lure of that kind of masculinity was almost too strong.

"Do you like Tate Jordan?" It was an odd, direct question, yet Caroline said it in such a naive way that Samantha laughed.

"Like him? I don't think I could." But that wasn't what Caroline had meant, and she knew it, and now she laughed a little silvery laugh as she sat back in her chair. "He's good at what he does. I suppose I respect him, though he's certainly not an easy man to get along with, and I don't think he much likes me. He's attractive, if that's what you mean, but unapproachable too. He's an odd man, Aunt Caro." Caroline nodded silently. She had once said almost the same things about Bill King. "What made you ask?" There was certainly nothing between them, nothing Caroline could have sensed or seen as she had watched them all work all day long.

"I don't know. Just a feeling. I get the impression he likes you." She said it simply, as young girls do.

"I doubt that." Samantha looked both amused and skeptical. And then she spoke more firmly. "But in any case that's not why I'm here. I'm here to get over being involved with one man. I don't need to cure it by getting involved with another. And certainly no one here."

"What makes you say that?" Caroline looked at her strangely.

"Because we're all foreigners to each other. I'm a stranger to them, and I suppose in their own way, they're strangers to me. I don't understand their ways any more than they understand mine. No," she sighed softly, "I'm here to work, Aunt Caro, not play with the cowboys." Caroline laughed at the words she used and shook her head.

"That's how those things start though. No one ever intends . . ." For a moment Sam wondered if Caroline was trying to tell her something, if after all this time she was going to admit to an affair with Bill King, but the moment passed quickly, and now Caroline stood up, put the dishes in the sink, and a few minutes later began to turn off the kitchen lights. Lucia-Maria had long since gone home. Samantha was suddenly sorry that she hadn't encouraged Caroline to say more, but she had the impression that Caroline was anxious not to say anything further. Silently a door had already closed.

"You know, the truth of it is, Aunt Caro, that I'm already in love with someone else."

"Are you?" The older woman instantly stopped what she was doing and looked stunned. She had had no inkling before that Samantha was already involved.

"Yes."

"Would it be rude to ask who?"

"Not at all." Samantha smiled at her gently. "I'm very much in love with your Thoroughbred horse." They both laughed and bid each other good night a few minutes later. And tonight Sam found herself listening for the now familiar opening and closing of the front door. She was certain now that it was Bill King coming to spend the night with Caroline, and she wondered why they hadn't married if this had gone on for as long as she now suspected it had. Maybe they had their reasons. Maybe he already had a wife. She found herself pondering, too, the questions Caroline had asked about Tate Jordan and wondered why Caroline should suspect Samantha of being attracted to him. She wasn't really. If anything, he annoyed her. Or did he? She suddenly found that she was questioning herself. He was brutally handsome, like someone out of a commercial . . . like someone out of a dream. But he wasn't her kind of dream; tall, dark, and handsome. She smiled to herself, her mind instantly darting back to John Taylor . . . John with his glorious golden beauty, his long legs, his huge, almost sapphire-colored eyes. They had been so perfect together, so alive, so happy, they had done everything together . . . everything . . . except fall in love with Liz Jones. That John had done alone.

At least, she consoled herself as she pulled her mind willfully away from him again, she hadn't been watching the newscast. At least she didn't know how the pregnancy was going or have to listen to Liz thank another thousand viewers for little hand-knit booties and crocheted blankets or "darling little pink hats." It had been almost unbearable, but she hadn't been able to stop watching the broadcasts while she was still in New York. Even when she worked late, she watched them. It was as though there were an alarm clock buried somewhere in her body that let her know when it was six o'clock and then forced her inexorably toward a television set so she could watch the program. At least here she hadn't thought of it in almost a week. And in another week it would be Christmas, and after she survived that—her first

Christmas without John, the first time in eleven years that she wouldn't be with him—then she knew that she'd live. And in the meantime all she had to do was work from morning till night, follow the cowboys, spend twelve hours a day riding Navajo, find those little orphaned babies, and bring them back alive. And day by day, month by month, she'd make it. She was finally beginning to know that she would live. She congratulated herself again on the wise decision to come west as her eyes closed and she drifted off to sleep, and this time along with Liz and John and Harvey Maxwell there were suddenly other people in her dreams too: Caroline trying desperately to tell her something that she could never quite hear; and Josh, laughing, always laughing; and a tall dark-haired man on a beautiful black horse with a white star on its forehead and two white socks. She was riding behind him, bareback, holding tightly to him as they raced along through the night. She was never quite sure where they were going or from where they had come, but she knew that she felt perfectly safe there as they rode along in perfect unison. And as she woke up with her alarm at four thirty, she felt oddly rested, but she couldn't quite remember her dream.

8

Just before they would normally have had their lunchbreak, Tate Jordan gave the signal and the large group of men working together gave a whoop and headed home. Sam was among them, joking with Josh about his wife and children, and being teased by two of the other men. One of them was accusing her of probably having run away from a boyfriend who beat her "and rightly so after listening to you run that big mouth of yours," but the other one claimed that she was probably the mother of eleven children and too lousy a cook so they threw her out.

"You're all right." Samantha laughed with the men she was riding with. It had been an easy morning's work and they were all anxious to knock off work early for lunch. It was the twenty-fourth of December, and that night there would be a huge Christmas feast in the main hall, wives and children and even girl friends were invited. It was an annual event, beloved by all. It made them all feel more than ever like a family, linked together and bonded by their love for the ranch. "The truth is that I had fifteen illegitimate children and they all beat me, so I ran away. How's that?"

"What, no boyfriend?" One of the old timers guffawed. "A pretty little palomino like you and no boyfriend, awww come on!" They were all beginning to liken her to a palomino, but she was fond enough of horses and she took it as a compliment. The truth was that she was daily beginning to look more like one. Her long shining hair was whitening in the sun, and her face was getting tanned a rich honey-brown. It was a beautiful combination, and one which all of the men had noticed, whether they mentioned it or not. "Don't tell me you ain't got no man, Sam!" The old timer persisted in the question a number of them had pondered when she wasn't around.

"Nope. Of course there were fifteen fathers for the fifteen illegitimate children, but now"—she laughed along with them and then shrugged, calling over her shoulder as she rode ahead back to the barn—"I'm too mean for any man."

Josh watched her go with a gentle look in his eyes, and the man riding closest to him leaned closer to ask him, "What's really her story, Josh? Got any kids?"

"Not that I know of."

"Married?"

"Not anymore." But he said nothing further. Partly because he figured if Sam wanted them to know something she'd tell them, and besides that, he didn't know any more about her life himself.

"I think she's out here running away from something," a very young cowboy volunteered, blushing.

"Mebbe so," Josh agreed and moved on. No one really wanted to discuss it. It was Christmas, they had their own women and children to think of and it was her business after all. Despite the superficial gossipy tendencies that exist in any situation of communal living, the ranch on the whole bred considerable respect. These were, for the most part, men who believed in keeping their own counsel, and they thought too highly of each other and their own privacy to pry. Most of them were not overt talkers, and most of their conversation usually centered around the livestock and the ranch. Sam was safe in their midst and she knew it. It was part of why being there was so right for her. No one was going to ask about John or about Liz or about why she had never had babies, and how did she feel now that she was divorced. . . . "Tell me, Mrs. Taylor, now that your husband has ditched you for another woman, how do you feel about . . . " She had been all through that in New York. And now she was free.

"See you later!" She called the words gaily to Josh as she made her way hurriedly to the big house. She was going to shower and change into fresh jeans, and then she had promised to come back over to the main hall to help decorate the tree. There were groups and committees devoted to everything from singing Christmas carols to baking. Christmas was an event second to none on the Lord Ranch.

When she walked into the house, Caroline was poring over an enormous ledger with a deep frown, and Samantha snuck behind her and gave her a big hug.

"Oh! You startled me!"

"Why don't you relax for a change? It's Christmas!"

"Do I look like Scrooge yet?" Caroline's face relaxed into a warm smile. "Should I say 'Bah humbug'?"

"Not yet. Wait till tomorrow. And then we can all haunt you with the ghost of Christmas Past!"

"Oh, there have been a few of those." For a moment Caroline became pensive as she put the big ranch ledger away. Suddenly she had thought back to Hollywood and her extravagant Christmases there. And as she watched her Samantha knew exactly what was on her mind.

"Do you miss all that still?" What she meant was "Do you still miss your husband?" and Samantha's eyes were suddenly sad as she asked. It was as though she needed to know for herself how long it would go on.

"No." Caroline answered the question gently. "I'm not sure I ever really did, not after the beginning. Oddly enough, this was always more my style. For a long time I didn't know that, but I discovered that once I came here. I've always been happy here, Samantha. It's the right place for me to be."

"I know. I've always sensed that about you." She envied her. Sam had not yet found her own place. All she had was the apartment she had shared with John Taylor. There was nothing that was exclusively Sam's.

"Do you miss New York terribly, Sam?"

Sam shook her head slowly. "No, not New York. Some of my friends. My friend Charlie and his wife, Melinda, and their three little boys. One of them is my godson." She felt suddenly lonely and bereft as she said it, homesick for the people she had left behind. "And my boss maybe, Harvey Maxwell. He's the creative director at CHL. He's been like a father to me. I suppose I miss him too." And then, as she said the words, she felt a wave of loneliness overtake her as she thought of John again—and this first Christmas without him. Involuntarily her eyes suddenly filled with tears and she looked away, but Caroline saw them and gently reached out and took her hand.

"It's all right. I understand. . . . " She reached out and pulled Samantha to her. "I remember what it was like when I first lost my husband. That was a very difficult year for me too." And then after a moment, "But it gets better. Just give it time." Sam only nodded, and her shoulders shook gently as she bowed her head on Aunt Caro's delicate shoulder, and then a moment later she sniffed and pulled away.

"I'm sorry." She smiled in embarrassment through her tears. "How maudlin. I don't know why that happened."

"Because it's Christmas and you were married to him for all those years. It's perfectly normal, you know, Sam. For God's sake, what do you expect?" But again, as she sat there, as she had been a thousand times since she'd heard that John had left Sam, Caroline was outraged at what he had done. How could he leave this perfectly exquisite young woman for that cold little bitch that she had stealthily watched on TV the other night, trying to understand what had happened, trying to see some reason why he had chosen her instead of Sam. The only reason she could see was the baby, but that hardly seemed a reason to go totally crazy and leave a woman like Sam. Nonetheless he had done it, however little she understood what he had done. "Are you going over to help decorate the tree?"

Sam nodded and smiled valiantly again. "I also promised to bake cookies, but you may be sorry about that. The men I've been working with all tease me that any woman who can ride the way I do probably can't cook. And the worst of it is that they're right." They both laughed and Sam gently kissed Aunt Caro and then held her close one more time. "Thank you." It was a fierce whisper.

"For what? Don't be silly."

"For being my friend." She let go of the older woman then, and when she did, there were tears in Caroline's eyes as well.

"Foolish woman. Don't ever thank me for being your friend! Or I won't be!" She tried to look angry but couldn't, and then shooed Sam out the door to go decorate the tree. A half an hour later Sam was in the main dining hall, perched on a tall ladder, hanging silver and green and red and blue and yellow baubles on the tree. There were small children working on the lower branches, and tiny ones hanging up little paper ornaments they'd made.

124

There was an older group stringing popcorn and cranberries together, and a circle of men and women choosing ornaments and making as much noise, or more, as their kids. It was a large and happy congregation, with women circulating large bowls of popcorn, platters of brownies, boxes of cookies, all made on the ranch or sent from "back home." There were people working everywhere in the best of the Christmas spirit, even Tate Jordan had come in, and as the official ranch giant, he had just agreed to put the star on the top of the tree. He was carrying a child on each shoulder and the black Stetson hung on a hook near the door. It was only when he reached the tree that he saw Samantha, and then, setting the children down, he smiled. From her perch on the ladder for once she was actually taller than he.

"Put you to work, did they, Sam?"

"Of course." She smiled, but ever since her earlier moment of nostalgia there had been something sparkling missing from her smile. For a moment he commandeered the ladder and clambered up it quickly to hang the huge gold star. He added a few angels and some bright Christmas balls near the top, adjusted the lights, and then stepped down and handed Samantha up again. "Very nice."

"There have to be some advantages to being as tall as I am. Do you want a cup of coffee?" He said it casually, as though they had always been friends, and this time when she answered there was more life in her smile.

"Sure."

He came back with two cups and some cookies and proceeded to hand her an assortment of ornaments, which she hung from her perch as occasionally she sipped her coffee and munched a cookie and he commented on where she should hang the next ball. At last she grinned at him after he had just told her where to hang a little silver angel.

"Tell me, Mr. Jordan, do you always give orders?"

He stopped to think for a moment and then nodded. "Yeah, I guess I do."

She sipped her coffee and watched him. "Don't you find it tiresome?"

"No." And then he looked at her pointedly. "Do you . . . find it tiresome to give orders, I mean?" He sensed that she was used to running things too. There was something about her that suggested an aura of command.

She answered without hesitation. "Yes. Very."

"And that's why you're here?" It was a very direct question and she looked at him for a minute before answering.

"Partially." As she answered he found himself wondering if she had had a nervous breakdown. He was sure that there was a serious reason why she had come to the ranch, and he was also sure that this was not just an ordinary housewife running away from home. But there was nothing to indicate that she was even slightly crazy. He really had no clue.

"Samantha, what do you do when you're not in California working on ranches?"

She didn't really want to answer but she liked his openness as he stood there talking to her. She didn't want to spoil their working relationship by being cute with glib answers and scaring him away. This was a man she liked and respected, sometimes detested, but thought was good at his job. What was the point of playing games with him now?

"I write commercials." It was an oversimplification of her job, but it was a start. In an odd way she was not unlike the assistant foreman at Crane, Harper, and Laub. Realizing that suddenly made her smile.

"What's so funny?" He looked puzzled as he watched her.

"Nothing. I just realized that in some ways our jobs are alike. At the advertising agency where I work there's a man named Harvey Maxwell. He's kind of like Bill King. And he's also old and one of these days he's going to retire, and—" Suddenly she was sorry she had said it. All he would do is resent her if he thought she was going to step into the man's job, but Tate Jordan was smiling as she abruptly ended her recital.

"Go ahead, say it."

"Say what?" She tried hard to look blank.

"That you'll probably get his job."

"What makes you think that?" Despite the fresh suntan she was blushing. "I didn't say that."

"You didn't have to. You said our jobs were alike. So you're an assistant foreman, are you?" For some reason she couldn't fathom, he looked pleased, as though that amused him. "Very nice. Do you like what you do?"

"Sometimes. Sometimes it's hectic and crazy and I hate it."

"At least you don't have to ride twelve hours in the rain."

"There is that." She returned the smile, suddenly intrigued by this big gentle man who had been so harsh and so demanding during her first days on the ranch, and so livid with her for riding Black Beauty, and now he seemed like a totally different person as they drank coffee and ate cookies next to the Christmas tree. She looked at him closely for a moment and then decided to ask him something. She suddenly felt that she had nothing to lose. As he stood there he looked impossible to anger, impossible to annoy. "Tell me something. Why did you get so furious with me for riding Black Beauty?"

He stood very still for a moment and then set down his coffee cup and looked deep into her eyes. "Because I thought it was dangerous for you."

"Because you didn't think I was good enough to ride him?" This time it wasn't a challenge, it was a straight question, and he gave her a straight answer.

"No, I knew you were good enough that first day. The way you sat on Rusty in the pouring rain and even got a little work out of the old nag, I knew damn well you were good. But it takes more than that to ride Black Beauty. It takes caution and strength, and I'm not sure you're long on either. In fact I'm sure you're not. One day that horse is going to kill somebody. I didn't want it to be you." He paused for a moment, his voice husky. "Miss Caroline should never have bought him. He's a bad horse, Sam." He looked at her strangely. "I feel it in my gut. He frightens me." And then he startled her again by speaking ever so softly. "I don't want you to ride him again." She said nothing in answer, and after a long moment she looked away. "But that's not like you, is it?

To turn down a challenge, to pass up a risk? Maybe especially now."

"What do you mean by that?" She was puzzled by what he had just said.

He looked her straight in the eye again as he answered. "I have the feeling you've lost something very precious to you . . . someone, most likely—that's the only thing most of us give a damn about. Maybe right now you don't care about yourself as much as you should. That's a bad time to ride a demon horse like that stallion. I'd rather see you on any horse on the ranch except that one. But I don't suppose you'd give up riding a Thoroughbred stallion just for me." She wasn't sure what to say to him when he stopped talking, and her voice was husky when she answered at last.

"You're right about a lot of things, Tate." His name was new and strange on her lips, and when she lifted her eyes to his, her voice grew softer. "I was wrong to ride him—the way I did. I took a lot of chances that morning." And then after a brief pause, "I won't promise you that I won't ride him again, but when I do, I'll be careful. I will promise you that. Broad daylight, terrain I know, no jumping over a rock bed and a stream I can barely see. . . ."

"My God, how reasonable!" He looked down at her and grinned. "I'm impressed!" He was teasing her and she grinned.

"You should be! You can't imagine the crazy things I've done on horses over the years."

"You ought to quit doing stuff like that, Sam. It's not worth the price you may have to pay." They both fell silent for a moment. They both knew of the accidents that befell others, the paraplegics who spent the rest of their lives in wheelchairs because they risked a mad jump and fell. "I never did see the point of that crazy Eastern jumping. Christ, you can kill yourself like that, Sam. Is it worth it?"

She let her eyes drift into his. "Does it matter?"

He looked at her long and hard. "It may not matter to you right now, Sam. But one of these days it will again. Don't do something foolish. You can't change that back." She nodded slowly and smiled. He was a strange and perceptive man, and she could see that he had qualities she hadn't originally noticed. At first she had seen him only as a tyrannical but effective assistant foreman. Now she saw that he was a man of much greater depth. The years he had spent around people and ranchers and ranch hands, living and losing and working till he almost dropped, hadn't been wasted. He had learned what he did well, and along with it he had learned to read people—no simple art. "More coffee?" He looked down at her again with a small smile and she shook her head.

"No, thanks, Tate." This time his name seemed easier on her lips. "I should be moving on. I'm on the cookie-making detail. What about you?" He grinned at her and stretched to whisper in her ear.

"I'm Santa." He said it with mixed embarrassment and glee.

"What?" She looked at him with confused amusement, not sure if he was kidding.

"I'm Santa." He said it again, barely doing more than mouth the words, and then, leaning closer to her, he explained. "Every year I get all dressed up in a costume and Miss Caroline's got this huge bag of toys for the kids. I play Santa."

"Oh, Tate, you?"

"Hell, I'm the tallest guy here. It makes sense." He tried to pass it off as ordinary but it was obvious that he enjoyed it. "The kids really make it all worthwhile." And then he looked down at her questioningly again. "You got kids?"

She shook her head slowly, her eyes giving away nothing of the emptiness she felt. "You?" She had momentarily forgotten the ranch gossip she'd heard from Josh.

"I've got one. Works on a ranch near here now. He's a good kid."

"Does he look like you?"

"Nope. Not at all. He's kind of slight and redheaded like his mother." He smiled slowly as he said it, thinking of the boy with obvious pride.

Her voice was husky again when she spoke to him. "You're a very lucky man."

"I think so too." He smiled at her. And then his voice lowered again as it almost caressed her. "But don't worry, little palomino, one of these days you're gonna be lucky too." He touched her gently on the shoulder then and moved on.

131

9

"S anta . . . Santa! . . . Over here. . . ."

"Now just a minute, Sally. You've got to wait for me to come over to that side of the room." Tate Jordan in the heavy white beard and red velvet costume was slowly making his way around the room, endowing each child with a much awaited present, bestowing candy canes and other candies, pats on the cheek, hugs, and even kisses. It was a side of Tate Jordan that no one knew except the people who saw him do this every year on the ranch. It made one actually believe in Santa, just to watch him chuckle and cavort and pull yet another surprise from his enormous sack. Had he not told her earlier that evening that he was playing Santa, Samantha would never have suspected that it was he. Even his voice sounded different as he chatted and chuckled gently, exhorting children to be good to their mommies and their daddies this year, to stop teasing their little sisters, to do their homework, and to stop being mean to the cat or the dog. He seemed to know everything about everyone, which of course wasn't difficult on a ranch. But as they touched him and were touched by him, the children were ecstatic, and even Samantha was caught up in the magic of his "ho ho ho." The entire performance seemed to take him hours, and when he was through, after eating a whole plate of cookies and six glasses of milk, he vanished with a last "Ho ho ho" toward the barn, not to be seen again for another year.

Forty-five minutes later, bereft of makeup, padded belly, white wig, and red suit, he reappeared in the main hall, unnoticed as he wandered through the crowd admiring the toys and the dolls and tickling and teasing the children. Soon he made his way to where Samantha stood, with Bill and Caroline, in a simple black velvet skirt with a very pretty white lace blouse. Her hair was knotted loosely at her neck and tied with a black velvet ribbon, and she was wearing makeup for the first time since she had come to the ranch.

"Is that you, Sam?" he teased after accepting a glass of punch and a fervent thank-you to his employer.

"I could say the same to you, you know." And then in a

soft voice, "That was just terrific. Are you that good every year?"

"I get better and better." He grinned happily. The Santa Claus role always made Christmas for him.

"Is your son here?"

"No." He shook his head quickly. "Jeff's boss isn't as generous as mine." He smiled at Samantha. "He's working tonight."

"That's too bad." She looked genuinely sorry.

"I'll see him tomorrow. And it's all right. He's a big guy now. He doesn't have time for his old man." But there was no resentment as he said it. He had enjoyed watching his son become a man. For a moment he wanted to ask Samantha why she had had no children, he had been watching her all evening as she hungrily eyed all the little boys and girls, but he finally decided that it was far too personal a question and he settled instead for a question about New York.

"It's a lot colder there, but I don't think I've ever been anywhere where there's as much Christmas spirit as this."

"That has nothing to do with California. That's Caroline Lord, and nothing else." Samantha nodded, and this time when they exchanged a smile their eyes met and held.

Shortly thereafter Samantha met Josh's wife and two of his married children, and a number of the men she'd been riding with for the last two weeks sheepishly brought her their wives or their girl friends, their sons and their daughters and their nieces, and for the first time since she'd come there, she knew that she belonged.

"Well, Sam? Very different from your usual Christmas?" Caroline was looking at her with a warm smile and Bill was standing nearby.

"Very different. And I love it."

"I'm glad." It was only a few minutes after Caroline had warmly hugged her and wished her a merry Christmas that Samantha noticed that she seemed to have disappeared. And shortly thereafter she realized that the old foreman had too. She wondered how many others had noticed. But Samantha was equally aware of the fact that she never heard any gossip about them on the ranch. She wondered if perhaps she was jumping to inappropriate conclusions. It didn't seem likely that she was, but one never knew.

"Tired?" It was Tate Jordan's voice just above her again, and she turned toward him with a little nod.

"I was just about to go back to the house. I was looking for Aunt Caro, but I guess she's already gone."

"She always leaves quietly so as not to spoil anyone's fun." He spoke with nothing but the greatest admiration. It was a bond that he shared with Sam. "Are you ready to go too?" Sam nodded and tried unsuccessfully to squelch a yawn. "Come on, sleepyhead, I'll walk you home."

"Can I help it if the guy I work for is a slave driver? It's a wonder I don't fall out of my saddle half dead by the end of the day."

"Once or twice"—he grinned at her—"I thought you might." And then he laughed out loud. "That first day, Sam, I thought you'd stick it out if you died in the saddle."

"I almost did. Josh almost had to carry me home."

"And you still got up on Black Beauty after that! You're crazy!"

"About that horse . . . yes!" He looked unhappy after she said it, and she changed the subject as they stepped into the frosty night. "Feels like snow."

"It does, but it's not very likely. At least I hope not." He looked up at the sky but didn't seem overly concerned. And by then they had already reached the door of the big house, where Sam lived.

Samantha hesitated for a moment and then as she opened the door she stepped aside and looked up at the dark-haired giant with the deep green eyes. "Would you like to come in, Tate, for a glass of wine or a cup of coffee?" But he was quick to shake his head, almost as though she had suggested something outrageous that he could never accept.

"I promise," she said, grinning at him, "I won't attack you. I'll sit on another couch." He let out a roar of laughter as she said it, and it was difficult to recognize the man she had been at odds with for more than two weeks.

"It's not that, but ranch etiquette, I guess. This is Miss Caroline's house. It wouldn't be appropriate for me to . . . it's difficult to explain. . . . "

Samantha smiled at him pleasantly from the doorway. "Would you like me to wake her so she can ask you in herself?"

He rolled his eyes. "Hardly, but thanks for the thought. Another time."

"Chicken." She looked like a kid as she stood there, and he laughed.

10

Because she had done so for the past ten days, Samantha woke up at four thirty the next morning. She forced herself to lie in bed, pretending even to herself to be asleep, and finally, after an hour of lying with her eyes closed and her mind racing, she got out of bed. It was still dark outside and the stars were shining brightly, but she knew that in little over an hour, life on the ranch would begin. Christmas morning or no, the animals would begin stirring, there would be men in the corral tending to the horses, even though no one would be riding the hills.

On bare feet Samantha silently padded to the kitchen, plugged in the electric coffee maker Caroline used, and then sat waiting in the dark kitchen, letting her mind drift back to the night before. It had been a lovely Christmas party she had shared with the others. Like one gigantic family, all of them linked to each other, each one caring about the other, the children familiar with everyone who lived there, happy and shouting and running around the big beautifully decorated Christmas tree. Thinking about the children at the Christmas party the night before suddenly made her think of Charlie and Melinda's children. This was the first Christmas that she hadn't sent them gifts. She remembered her promise to Charlie with a pang, but she had been nowhere near a store. As Samantha sat in the empty kitchen she felt suddenly very lonely, and without warning, her thoughts shifted instantly and very painfully to John. What was his Christmas like this year? How did it feel to be married to a woman who was pregnant? Had they already done the nursery? The pain Samantha felt knife through her was almost beyond bearing, and as though by reflex action she felt herself reach for the phone. Without thinking, yet desperately wanting to reach out and hear a friendly voice, she dialed a familiar number and only a moment later she heard Charlie Peterson answer the phone. His mellifluous voice boomed into the receiver with a resounding rendition of "Jingle Bells." He was halfway into the second verse before Sam could squeeze in her name.

"Who? . . . 'O'er the fields we go . . . ' "

"Shut up, Charlie! It's me, Sam!"

"Oh . . . hi, Sam. . . . 'Dashing all the wayyyy . . . ' "

"Charlie!" She was laughing as she listened, between rounds of trying to outshout him, but despite the amusement of listening to him, there was another pang of loneliness and she felt terribly far away. She suddenly wished she were with them, and not three thousand miles away on a ranch. There was no choice but to wait for him to finish singing.

"Merry Christmas!"

"You mean you're through? You're not going to sing 'Silent Night'?"

"I wasn't planning to, but if you're making a special request, Sam, I'm sure I could. . . . "

"Charlie, please! I want to talk to Mellie and the boys. But first"—she almost gulped as she said it—"tell me how things are at the office." She had forced herself not to call. Harvey had practically ordered her not to and she had obeyed. They had her number if they needed her, and her boss had thought it would do her good to forget about them as completely as she could. And actually she had done better than she had expected to. Until now. "How are my accounts doing? Have you lost them all yet?"

"Every one of them." Charlie beamed into the phone with pride and lit a cigar, and then suddenly he frowned and looked at his watch. "What in hell are you doing up at this hour? It must be . . . what? Not even six o'clock in the morning out there! Where are you?" He suddenly wondered if she had abandoned the ranch and returned.

"I'm still here. I just couldn't sleep. I've been getting up at four thirty every morning, now I don't know what to do with myself. This feels like the middle of the afternoon."

Not quite, but she was certainly wide awake. "How are the kids?"

"Wonderful." There was a moment's hesitation in his voice, and he hurried on to ask her how she was. "They riding you ragged out there, I hope?"

"Absolutely. Come on, Charlie, tell me what's happening back there." Suddenly she wanted to know everything, from the office gossip to who was threatening to steal which account from another house.

"Nothing much, kiddo. New York hasn't changed much in the last two weeks. What about you?" He sounded serious for a moment and Sam smiled. "You happy out there, Sam? You all right?"

"I'm fine." And then with a small sigh, "It was the right thing to do, much as I hate to admit it. I guess I needed something as radical as this. I haven't watched the six o'clock news all week."

"That's something at least. If you're up at four thirty, you're probably asleep by six o'clock at night."

"Not quite, but close."

"And your friend . . . Caroline, and all the horses? They're okay?" He sounded so much like a New Yorker that it made her laugh as she pictured him puffing on his cigar and staring into space wearing his pajamas and his bathrobe and maybe something the children had given him for Christmas, like a baseball cap or a mitt or a pair of red-and-yellow-striped socks.

"Everyone here is fine. Let me talk to Mellie." She did, and Melinda didn't catch Charlie's signal. She almost instantly told Sam the news. She was pregnant. The baby was due in July, and she had just found out that week. For just a fraction of a second there was a strange silence and then suddenly Sam was full of effusive congratulations as in the distance Charlie closed his eyes and groaned.

"Why did you tell her?" He was whispering hoarsely at his wife as she attempted to continue to talk to Sam.

"Why not? She'll find out when she comes back anyway." Melinda had put her hand over the phone, whispered back to him, then took her hand away and went on. "The kids? They all say they want another brother, but if it isn't a girl this time, I quit." Charlie made impatient gestures, let her say a rapid good-bye, and recovered the phone.

"How come you didn't tell me, kiddo?" Sam tried to sound nonchalant, but as always when she heard that kind of news, especially lately, it touched something very old and sad and still sensitive near her very core. "Afraid I couldn't take it? I'm not mentally ill, you know, Charlie, I'm just divorced. That is *not* the same thing."

"Who cares about that stuff anyway." There was something sad and worried in his voice.

"You do." Sam's voice was very soft. "And Mellie does. And I do. And you're my friends. She was right to tell me. Don't yell at her when you get off the phone."

"Why not?" He grinned guiltily. "She needs to be kept in line."

"Some way you have of keeping her in line, Peterson. It's a good thing you're the most overpaid art director in the business. You're going to need it for all those kids."

"Yeah," he growled contentedly, "ain't I just." And then after a long moment, "Well, kid, be good to your horses, and call if you need us. And Sam"—there was a heavy pause—"we all think about you a lot, and we miss you. You know that, don't you, babe?" She nodded, unable to speak, her voice and her eyes instantly filled with tears.

"Yeah, I know." It was all she could finally choke out. "And I miss you too. Merry Christmas!" And then, as she smiled through her tears and blew him a kiss, she hung up. She sat in the kitchen afterward for almost half an hour, her coffee cold in the cup, her eyes riveted to the table, her heart and her mind three thousand miles away in New York. And when she looked up again, she saw that outside the day was slowly breaking, the night had faded from deep blue to pale gray, and she stood up and slowly walked with her cup over to the sink. She stood very still and knew exactly what she wanted to do. With a determined step she walked down the hall, slipped quietly into her clothes, and bundled herself up in two warm sweaters and a jacket, put on the cowboy hat Caroline had lent her a few days before, and with a last look over her shoulder to make sure that no one was stirring, she walked quietly out of her room, down the hall, and out the front door, closing it softly behind her.

It took her only a few moments to reach the stables, and when she did, she stopped a few feet away from his stall. There was no sound stirring within, and she wondered if he was still sleeping, the giant shining ebony animal she suddenly knew that she wanted to ride. She gently opened the half door and stepped inside, running a hand smoothly down his neck and his flanks and speaking so gently that she almost cooed. He was awake, but he wasn't restless. Black Beauty looked as though he had been waiting for her to come; he gazed meaningfully at her from behind the bristling black lashes, and Samantha smiled at him as she quietly let herself out of the stall, went to get his saddle and bridle, and returned to prepare him for their ride. There had been no one in the stable to see her when she got there, and there was still no one there now.

When she led him slowly out the main door a few minutes later into the early morning, there was no one in the vast yard outside. She walked Black Beauty to a nearby block and quickly climbed it. After hoisting herself into the saddle with ease and pulling the reins taut, she moved away toward the now familiar hills. She knew exactly where she wanted to ride him, she had seen a trail through some woods a few days before and now she knew that this was where she wanted to go. At first she cantered gently toward her destination, and then after a while, sensing the huge beast straining to go faster, she let him lope from a canter into a gallop as he made his way toward the rising sun. It was one of the most exquisite feelings she could remember, and she held her knees to his flanks and pressed harder as effortlessly they cleared a series of low bushes and then a narrow stream. She remembered the first time she had jumped him but knew that this was different. She was taking no chances with Black Beauty this morning, but she wasn't angry either. She only wanted to become a part of Black Beauty's very body and soul. She felt like an ancient myth, or Indian legend, as she let him slow on the crest of a hill, and she watched the sun begin in earnest its climb into the sky. It was only then that she heard the hooves behind her, then that she knew she'd been followed, and then that she turned in surprise. But when she saw him riding the ivory and onyx pinto toward her, she wasn't really surprised to see Tate Jordan. It was as though he were also a part of the legend, as though he also belonged there, as though he too had fallen from the fiery golden morning sky.

He rode toward her in a straight line, with the pinto at a full gallop, making his way toward her with almost fierce determination, and then at the last moment he swerved to fall in right at her side. She eyed him carefully for an instant, not sure of what she'd see there, afraid that once again he'd be angry, that he'd spoil the moment, and that the friendship that had been conceived only the night before would already die. But what she saw instead in those deep green eyes that looked at her so fiercely was not anger this time, but something much gentler. He said nothing to her, he only watched her, and then nodded and led the pinto on. It was clear that he wanted her to follow him, and she did, with Black Beauty moving effortlessly down the trails that he sought out, over hills, and into little valleys, until at last they were on a part of the property she had never seen. There was a small lake there, and a little cabin, and as they came over the last hill and saw it Tate and the steaming pinto slowed. He turned then to smile at her in the early morning, and Samantha returned the smile as she watched him rein in his horse and dismount.

"Are we still on the ranch?"

"Yes." He looked up at her. "Over past that clearing is where it ends." The clearing was just behind the cabin.

Samantha nodded. "Whose is that?" She indicated the cabin, wondering if there was anyone there.

Tate didn't give her a direct answer. "I found it a long time ago. I come here now and then, not often, but when I want to be alone. It's all locked up, and no one knows I come out here." It was a bid for secrecy and Samantha understood.

"Do you have the keys?"

"More or less." The handsome leathered face broke into a grin. "There's a key on Bill King's ring that fits it. I helped myself to it once."

"And made a copy?" Samantha looked shocked, but he nodded his head. Above all else Tate Jordan was an honest man. If Bill King had asked him, he would have told him. But Bill never had, and Tate figured he wouldn't care. Above all he didn't want to draw attention to the forgotten cabin. It meant a lot to him.

"I keep some coffee in there, if it hasn't gone stale. Want to get down for a bit and step inside?" He didn't tell her that he kept a bottle of whiskey there too. Nothing with which to commit excesses, but something to keep him warm and soothe his mind. He came here sometimes when he was worried, or if something was bothering him and he needed to be alone for a day. Many was the Sunday he had spent at this cabin, and he had his own ideas as to what kind of purpose it had once served. "Well, Miss Taylor?" Tate Jordan watched her for a long moment and she nodded.

"I'd like that." The lure of coffee appealed to her, this morning it was unusually cold. He gave her a hand down and helped her tie up the handsome horse, and then he led the way toward the door of the cabin, extracted his copy of the key, opened the door, and stepped aside to let her in. Like the rest of the cowboys on the ranch, he was always gallant. It was like a last touch of the Old West, and she looked up and smiled at him as she walked slowly in.

There was a dry, musty smell in the cabin, but as she looked around her her eyes widened instantly in surprise. The large airy single room was decorated in pretty flowered chintzes, they were somewhat old-fashioned, but still very handsome and very appealing. There was a little couch, two thickly cushioned wicker chairs, and in a corner by the fire was a huge handsome leather chair that Samantha knew instantly was an antique. There was a small writing desk in a corner, there was a radio, a small record player, there were several shelves of books, a large friendly fireplace, and a number of funny objects that must have meant something to the person who owned the cabin: two large handsome trophies, a boar's head, a collection of old bottles, some funny old photographs in ornate old-fashioned frames. There was a thick bear rug spread out in front of the hearth and a delicate antique rocking chair with a needlepoint footstool standing nearby. It was like a haven in a fairy tale, hidden deep in the forest, the kind of place one would want to come to hide from the rest of the world. And then through an open doorway Sam saw a small pretty little blue room with a large handsome brass bed and a beautiful quilt, soft-blue walls, another impressive bear rug, and a little brass lamp with a small shade. The curtains were blue and white and very frilly, and there was a large handsome landscape of another part of the ranch hanging over the

148

bed. It was a room where one would want to spend the rest of one's life.

"Tate, whose is this?" Samantha looked vaguely puzzled, and Tate only pointed to one of the trophies perched on a little shelf on the near wall.

"Take a look."

She moved closer and her eyes widened as she looked at the trophy and then Tate and then back again. It bore the legend WILLIAM B. KING 1934. The second one was Bill King's too, but dated 1939. And then Sam looked over her shoulder again at Tate, this time with fresh concern.

"Is this his cabin, Tate? Should we be here?"

"I don't know the answer to the first question, Sam. And to the second, probably not. But once I found this place, I could never stay away." His voice was deep and smoky as his eyes reached out for Sam's.

She looked around silently and nodded again. "I can see why."

As Tate moved quietly toward the kitchen she began to look at the old photographs, and although she thought there was something familiar about them, she was never really sure. And then, feeling almost embarrassed, she drifted into the bedroom, her eye caught by the large landscape over the bed. As she reached it and could easily read the signature, suddenly she stopped. The artist had signed her name in red in the lower right-hand corner. C. Lord. Sam turned around then and was about to flee the tiny bedroom, but the room was blocked by Tate's vast frame in the doorway. He was holding out a cup of steaming instant coffee and watching her face.

"It's theirs, isn't it?" Here was the answer to her question, the question she and Barbara had mused over so often, and laughed about, and giggled over. Finally, in this tiny cozy blue room with the patchwork quilt and the huge brass bed that almost filled the room, she knew. "Isn't it, Tate?" Suddenly Sam wanted confirmation, from him if no one else. He nodded slowly and handed her the bright yellow cup.

"I think so. It's a nice place, isn't it? Somehow, all put together it's just like them."

"Does anyone else know?" She felt as though she had uncovered a holy secret and had a responsibility to both of them to know if it was secure.

"About them?" He shook his head. "At least no one's ever been sure. But they've been awfully careful. Neither of them ever gives it away. When he's with the men he talks about 'Miss Caroline' just like the rest of us, even calls her that most of the time to her face. He treats her with respect, but no particularly marked interest, and she does the same with him."

"Why?" Samantha looked puzzled as she sipped her coffee and then set down the cup and sat on the edge of the bed. "Why didn't they just let people know years ago and get married if that was what they wanted?"

"Maybe they didn't want that." Tate looked as though he understood it, and as she looked up at his weathered face, it was clear that Sam did not. "Bill King's a proud man. He wouldn't want it said that he married Miss Caro for her money, or for her ranch or her cattle."

"So they have this?" Sam looked around her in fresh amazement. "A little cottage in the woods, and he tiptoes in and out of her house for the next twenty-five years."

"Maybe it kept the romance fresh for them." Tate Jordan was smiling as he sat down next to Samantha on the bed. "You know, there's something very special about what you see here." He looked around himself with warmth and respect that were almost akin to awe. "You know what you see, Samantha?" He didn't wait for the answer but went on. "You see two people who love each other, whose lives blend perfectly, her paintings and his trophies, their old photographs and records and books, his comfortable old leather chair and her little rocking chair and her footstool by the fire. Just look at it, Sam." Together they glanced out of the bedroom doorway. "Just look. You know what you see out there? You see love. That's what love is, those copper pots, and that old needlepoint cushion, and that funny old pig's head. That's two people you see out there, two people who've loved each other for a long time, and still do."

"You think they still come here?" Sam was almost whispering and Tate laughed.

"I doubt it. Or if they do, not much anyway. I probably come here more than they do. Bill's arthritis has been bothering him a lot the last few years. I suspect"—he lowered his voice—"that they stay pretty close to the big house." As he said it Samantha remembered the nightly opening and closing of doors. Yet even after all these years they met in hidden ways at midnight hours.

"I still don't understand why they keep it a secret."

Tate looked at her for a long time and then shrugged. "Sometimes that's just the way it is." And then he smiled at her. "This isn't New York, Samantha. A lot of old-fashioned values still apply." It didn't make sense to her anyway. In that case they should have gotten married. Good Lord, it had gone on for twenty years after all.

"How did you find this place, Tate?" She stood up again and wandered back out to the living room and a few minutes later sat down in Caroline's comfortable old rocking chair.

"I just happened on it one day. They must have spent a lot of time here years back. It's got the same kind of feeling as a real home."

"It is a real home." Sam stared into the empty fireplace dreamily as she said it, thinking back to the elegant apartment she had left behind her in New York. It had none of the qualities she felt here, not anymore, none of the love, none of the warmth, none of the tender comfort, the solace that she felt just sitting in the old rocking chair.

"Feel like you could stay forever, don't you?" He smiled at her and let his huge frame down into the leather chair. "Want me to light a fire?"

She quickly shook her head. "I'd worry too much about it after we left."

"I wouldn't leave it burning, silly."

"I know that." They exchanged another smile. "But I'd worry anyway. You know, maybe a stray spark or something . . . this is too special to mess with. I wouldn't want to do anything to jeopardize what they have here." And then, looking at him more seriously, "I don't even feel like we should be here."

"Why not?" The sharp chin jutted out just a little.

"It's not ours. It's theirs, and it's private and secret.

They wouldn't want us to be here, or to know about them. . . ."

"But we knew about them anyway, didn't we?" He asked the question gently and she nodded slowly.

"I always suspected. Barb—Aunt Caro's niece and I— we used to talk about it for hours, trying to guess, assuming and then not assuming. We were never really sure."

"And once you grew up?"

She smiled in answer. "Then I sensed it. But still I always wondered."

He nodded slowly. "So did I. I always thought I knew for certain. But I didn't really. Until I came here. This tells its own story." He looked around again. "And what a nice story it tells."

"Yeah." Sam nodded agreement and began to rock slowly in the old chair. "It would be nice to love someone like that, wouldn't it? Enough to build something together, and to keep it together for twenty years."

"How long did your marriage last, Sam?" It was the first personal question he had asked her, and she looked at him squarely and answered him quickly, seemingly without emotion. But she couldn't help wondering how he knew she'd ever been married.

"Seven years. Yours?"

"Five. My boy was just a little guy when his mom took off."

"I'll bet you were glad when you got him back." And then suddenly she blushed furiously, remembering the story and what an insensitive thing she had inadvertently said. "I'm sorry, I didn't mean—"

"Hush." He waved a hand gently. "I know what you meant. And hell, I was glad. But I was damn sorry his mom died."

"Did you love her even after she left you?" It was an outrageous question but suddenly it didn't matter. It was as though here, in this shrine of Bill and Caro's, they could say anything and ask anything they wanted, as long as it mattered, as long as it wasn't designed to hurt.

Tate Jordan nodded his head slowly. "Yes, I loved her. In some ways I still do, and she's been dead near fifteen years. It's a funny thing. You don't always remember the way things got in the end. What about you, Sam, you too? You remember your husband when you first loved him, or remember what a son of a bitch he was at the end?"

Sam laughed softly at his honesty and nodded her head as she rocked. "God, isn't that the truth. Why? I keep asking myself. Why do I remember him when we went to college, when we got engaged, on our honeymoon, on our first Christmas? How come my first thought of him isn't with his socks and my guts hanging out of his suitcase when he walked out the door?" They both smiled at the image she'd created, and Tate shook his head and then turned to her again, his eyes filled with questions.

"Was that how it was, then? He walked out on you, Sam?"

"Yes," she answered bluntly.

"For someone else?" She nodded, but she didn't look pained this time. She was just admitting to a simple truth. "That's how it was with my old lady too." Sam noticed as she listened that now Tate sounded more like the other cowboys. Maybe here he could relax. He no longer had to

154

impress her, and there was no one else around. "Tears
your heart out, doesn't it? I was twenty-five years old, and
I thought I'd die."

"So did I." Sam looked at him intently. "So did I. In
fact," she sighed softly, "I guess everyone in my office did
too. That's why I'm here. To get over it. To get away."

"How long has it been?"

"Since last August."

"That's long enough." He looked matter-of-fact and
she bridled.

"Is it? For what? To forget him? To not give a damn
anymore? Well, you're wrong on that one, buddy, try
again."

"Do you think about him all the time?"

"No." She answered him honestly. "But too much."

"You divorced yet?"

She nodded. "Yes, and he's already remarried, and
they're having a baby in March." Might as well tell him
everything at one sitting. And in an odd way it felt good
to get it all out of the way, all the painful truths, the true
confessions. It was wonderful to get it over with. But she
found now that he was watching her intently.

"I'll bet that hurts a lot."

"What?" For a moment she didn't follow what he was
saying.

"About the baby. Did you want children?"

She hesitated for only an instant, and then nodded as
she suddenly left the rocking chair. "As a matter of fact,
yes, Mr. Jordan. But I'm sterile. So my husband got what
he wanted—somewhere else. . . ." As she stood at the
window, looking out at the lake, she didn't hear him

coming, and then suddenly he was standing behind her, with his arms around her waist.

"It doesn't matter, Sam . . . and you're not sterile. Sterile is someone who can't love, who can't give anything, who is locked up and closed up and sold out. That's all that matters and that's not you, Sam. That's just not you." He turned her around slowly to face him and there were tears in her eyes. She didn't want him to see them, but she couldn't resist the magnetic pull of his hands as he had turned her slowly by the waist. He gently kissed both her eyes, and then pressed his mouth down on hers for so hard and so long that at last she had to fight for breath.

"Tate . . . don't . . . no . . ." She was fighting, but weakly, and he only pulled her closer to him again. She could smell the scent of saddle soap and tobacco on him and feel the rough wool of his shirt beneath her cheek as she turned away and rested her face against his chest.

"Why not?" He put a finger under her chin and made her look up at him again. "Sam?" She said nothing, and he kissed her again. His voice was gentle in her ear when he spoke to her, and she could feel her heart pounding against her chest. "Sam, I want you, more than I've ever wanted any woman before."

She spoke softly, but with feeling, as her eyes gazed into his. "That isn't enough."

He nodded slowly. "I understand." And then after a long moment, "But I don't offer anything more than that anymore."

Now it was her turn. She smiled gently and asked the same question. "Why not?"

"Because—" He hesitated and then chuckled softly in the pretty little cabin. "Because I really am sterile. I don't have all of that left to give."

"How do you know? Have you tried lately?"

"Not in eighteen years." His answer was quick and honest.

"And you think it's too late to love anyone again?" He didn't answer and Sam looked around, her eyes pausing at the trophies and then coming back to him. "Don't you think he loves her, Tate?" He nodded. "So do I. He can't be any braver than you are, and he's one hell of a man." And then as she looked at Tate, "So are you."

"Does that mean . . ." He spoke softly, his lips playing with hers and her heart wreaking havoc between her ribs, wondering what she was doing kissing this stranger, this cowboy, and trying to justify to him why he should fall in love. She wanted to ask herself what in hell she thought she was doing, but there wasn't time. "Does that mean," he went on, "that if I told you I loved you, that we'd be making love right now?" He looked amused, and with a small smile she shook her head. "I didn't think it did. So what are you trying to convince me of, and why?"

"I'm trying to convince you that it's not too late to fall in love again. Look at them, when they started out, they were older than we are now. They had to be."

"Yeah . . ." But he didn't sound convinced. And then he turned his eyes back to her with a pensive expression. "What difference does it make to you if I ever fall in love again?"

"I'd like to know that it's possible."

"Why? Are you doing research for science?"

"No," she whispered. "For myself."

"So that's it." He ran a hand gently down her pale blond mane, fighting with the pins that held it firmly in the knot at the nape of her neck, and then suddenly he unleashed it and it all came tumbling down her back. "My God, your hair is lovely, Sam . . . palomino. . . ." He said it ever so softly. "Little palomino . . . how beautiful you are. . . ." The sun glinted in the window and danced among the gold threads in her hair.

"We should go back now." She said it gently but firmly.

"Should we?"

"We should."

"Why?" His lips were kissing her chin and her jawbone and her neck. She wasn't objecting, but she was also not going to let him go any farther than that. "Why should we go back now, Sam? Oh, God, you're so lovely. . . ." She could feel a shiver run through him, and she pulled away slowly with a small shake of her head.

"No, Tate."

"Why not?" For a moment there was fire in his eyes, and she was almost afraid.

"Because it's not right."

"For chrissake, I'm a man, you're a woman . . . we're not children here. What do you want?" He raised his voice in lustful irritation. "The perfect romance, a wedding ring on your finger before you go to bed?"

"What do you want, cowboy? Just a quick roll in the hay?" The force of her words hit him like a bullet, and he looked stunned as slowly he shook his head.

"I'm sorry." He spoke coldly and then moved to the

sink to wash their cups. But when he had finished, she was still standing there, watching him, and she spoke up.

"I'm not sorry. I like you. In fact"—she reached out and put a hand on his arm—"I like you a hell of a lot. But I don't want to get hurt next time."

"You can't have the kind of guarantees you want, Sam. Not from anyone. And not from me. The only guarantees you'll ever get are lies." There was some truth in that and she knew it, but it wasn't just the promises she wanted but something real.

"You know what I want?" She looked around at the cabin as she asked the question. "I want this. I want this kind of meshing and blending and loving after more than twenty years."

"You think they were so sure of that in the beginning? You think they knew then what they do now? Hell no. She owned the ranch and he was a ranch hand. That was all they knew."

"You think so?" Samantha's eyes exploded sparks at him. "You know what else I'll bet they knew then?"

"What?"

"I'll bet they knew they were in love. And until I find that, until a man loves me and I love him, then I'm not coming out to play again."

He opened the door and locked it behind them. "Come on." But she had seen as she walked past him that he wasn't angry. He had understood all that she had told him, and she found herself wondering what he would do now, and what she would do herself. For a moment, just a moment, she had wanted to abandon all restraint and caution, but she had decided not to. Not because she didn't want him, but because she wanted him so much. Tate Jordan was one hell of a man.

"Can we come back here?" She eyed him squarely as he cupped his hands and offered her a leg up to the huge Thoroughbred horse.

"Do you really want to?"

She nodded slowly, and he smiled at her and said nothing. She took the leg up and flew into her saddle. A moment later she had the reins in her hands, her heels in the horse's flanks, and she was flying beside Tate Jordan into the wind.

11

"Have a nice ride, dear?" Caroline looked at her benevolently as Samantha strode into the living room, her hair loose, her face flushed, her eyes bright. She looked like a vision of youth and health and beauty, and Caroline couldn't help envying her a little as she watched the young limbs coil into a comfortable chair.

"Very, thanks, Aunt Caro." She was dying to tell her that she had seen their cabin, but she knew she couldn't. But still the excitement lingered. From that and the kiss she and Tate had shared in Black Beauty's stall. It had been a kiss that seared her very edges and reached into the nether regions of her soul. He was a man different from any other, more powerful and more independent and more alluring than any she had ever known or ever would.

"See anyone this morning?" It was a casual question, born of thirty years of almost communal living on a large ranch. Not a single hour went by that one didn't hang out with someone, talk about something, and hear something about someone else.

Sam had been about to say "No one," and then decided to tell Caroline the truth. "I saw Tate Jordan."

"Oh." It was a very small word without any great emphasis or interest. "How is Santa Claus after last night? The kids sure enjoy him every year."

Sam was tempted to say "So do I," but didn't dare say it. "They should. He's a very nice man."

"You mean you've relented? You don't hate him anymore?"

"I never did." She tried to look casual as she poured herself a cup of coffee. "We just didn't see eye to eye over my ability to ride your horse."

"And he's changed his mind?" Samantha nodded with a grin of satisfaction. "No wonder you like him. How heartily we approve of those who approve of us. He's a good man though, no matter what he may have said about your riding Black Beauty. He knows this ranch every bit as well as Bill and I." Every bit . . . even the cabin, Samantha found herself thinking and had to take a sip of coffee so as not to smile.

"What are you doing today, Aunt Caro?"

"The books, as usual."

"On Christmas?" Samantha looked shocked.

Caroline nodded dutifully. "On Christmas."

"Why don't we have Christmas dinner instead?"

"As I recall," Caroline said, looking at her with amusement, "we already did that last night."

"That was different. That was everyone. Why don't you and I cook dinner today for Bill King and Tate?" Caroline eyed her very hard for a moment and then shook her head.

"I don't really think that would work."

"Why not?"

Caroline sighed softly. "Because they're ranch hands, Samantha, and we're not. There really is a very definite hierarchy on a ranch."

"Don't you ever have dinner with Bill?" Sam looked shocked.

"Very rarely. Only on state occasions, when someone gets married or dies. Only on nights like last night, at Christmas, do all the fences come down. The rest of the time, you are who you are, and they—they're careful to keep the fences up, Sam."

"But why?"

"Out of respect. That's just the way it is." She seemed to accept it, but it continued to annoy Sam.

"But it's all so stupid. What difference does the hierarchy make, for heaven's sake! Who cares?"

"They do." Caroline's voice was like a splash of cold water. "They care very much, about form, about position, about who you are and the respect they feel they owe you. As a ranch owner, you're put on a pedestal by them, and they never let you come down. It's tiring sometimes, but that's the way it is. You have to accept it. If we invited Bill and Tate here today, they would be genuinely shocked." But Sam found it hard to believe as she remembered Tate's earlier entreaties to sleep with him at the cabin. It hadn't occurred to her yet that that was different; it was private. It wasn't like having dinner together at the big house.

"Well, it still doesn't make any sense to me."

Caroline smiled warmly at her. "It never did to me either, but I accept it now, Sam. It's simpler that way. That's just the way they are." Was that the reason for the cabin, then? Because he was a ranch hand and she was something very different, the ranch owner? Could all the secrecy have been for something as simple as that? She was suddenly dying to ask her but knew that she could not. "There will be cold turkey dinners all day at the main hall, Samantha. You could go over there and chat with whoever's around. But I really have to work with Bill for a few hours in my office. I feel terrible about neglecting you on Christmas, Sam, but we have to get this done." Caroline and Bill's single-minded purpose together, over all the years, had always been the ranch. But now Sam found herself wondering if they ever missed the cabin. They would have to. It was such a perfect place to hide out. She wondered, too, how long it had been since they had last been there, how often they had gone in the beginning, if they'd had it then . . . and she wondered, too, how soon she would go there again with Tate.

"I'll be fine, Aunt Caro. I have some letters to write. I'll go get something to eat at the main hall when I get hungry." And suddenly she realized that she wanted to catch a glimpse of Tate again. It was as though he had got under her skin that morning and now she couldn't get him out. All she could think of was him, and his hands and his lips and his eyes. . . .

But when she went to the main hall for lunch half an hour later, she found that there was no sight of him, and Josh mentioned to her casually when she saw him near the barn a few hours later that Tate had gone to the Bar Three Ranch, twenty-five miles away, to visit his son.

12

In the silvery early morning darkness Tate Jordan gave
the signal, and the two dozen ranch hands who followed
his orders kicked their horses and followed him toward
the main gate. Today most of them were rounding up
young bulls for castration, and Tate himself and another
small group were riding to a narrow canyon to see if the
bridge there was down. When they reached it an hour
later, they saw that all was pretty much in order, but on
the way back they found that two trees had been hit by
lightning and had gone through the roof of a shed,
damaging a tractor and some small tools. For two hours

the men worked pulling branches away from the building, checking over the tools, trying to start the tractor, and finally activating a huge saw so that they could remove the broken trees. It was grueling work for all of them, and most of all Samantha, and when they stopped at long last for lunch, Samantha's long blond hair was damp from her efforts and her thick flannel shirt clung to her chest.

"Coffee, Sam?" Tate handed it to her as he did to the others, and only for a fraction of an instant did she think that she saw something special lingering in his eyes. But a moment later when he gave her some more instructions on what he wanted done with the broken tools, she felt certain that she'd imagined the earlier attention. It was obvious that their relationship was once again strictly business. And by the end of the day she was sure. He treated her well now, as he did the others, joked with her once or twice, and told her to rest when he saw that she could do no more. But he offered her no special words, no particular encouragement, as she sweated and labored. At the end of the day, when she left Navajo in his stall, Tate said nothing to her as he left the barn and headed back to his own cabin not far from the main hall.

"Hard work today, eh, Sam?" Josh called to her over his shoulder as he put up his saddle, and she nodded, glancing briefly at Tate's back and suddenly wondering if the moments at the hidden cabin had been a kind of aberration, a brief flash when they both had lost control and then regained it. And she was suddenly glad that she hadn't succumbed to the powerful attraction she had felt. By now he would have been laughing at her, she thought briefly, trying to remember what Josh had said. "You look beat."

"Don't we all! It's always hard work out here." But she didn't look unhappy about it as she said it, and she was glad, as she had been that morning, that she had been spared the all-day session of castrating the young bulls. From what she had seen of it years before it was a bloody and unpleasant experience, and she would rather have spent the day as she had with Tate and the others, fighting with the branches of the stricken trees and wrestling with the awkward farm tools in the crushed shed. "See you tomorrow!" She waved at him with a tired smile and headed toward the big house, suddenly eager for a hot bath and some dinner, and shortly thereafter her warm bed. Her life on the ranch seemed to grow simpler daily. She slept, she got up, she ate, and she worked her tail off. But it was just what she had wanted. She barely had any time to think. Though lately there were thoughts that seemed to crowd her: visions of Tate's face as they had stood side by side in the cabin, talking about Bill and Caro . . . and themselves.

When she walked into the friendly ranch house, she called out to Caroline but was met with only silence. And a few minutes later, in the kitchen, she found a note that explained that Caroline had driven a hundred miles with Bill King. There were problems with some of the tax material that couldn't be explained on the phone, so they had gone to see the accountant. They would either be back late that night or in the morning, but in either case obviously, Sam was not to wait up. There was a chicken already roasted in the oven, a big baked potato alongside it, and a salad in the fridge. But despite the hard day's work Sam found that she wasn't as hungry as she'd thought a few moments earlier. The prospect of eating alone didn't have much appeal. Instead she wandered slowly into the living room, thinking that later she'd make herself a sandwich, but almost without thinking, she stooped, flicked a switch, and turned on the TV. And then she could almost feel something akin to an electric shock run through her as she heard John's voice boom into the cozy living room, and then moments later saw Liz's swelling belly and her smiling face. It brought home again just what had happened, and as Sam watched them her eyes held the same sadness that she had brought with her from New York. She was staring at them and listening to them go through their usual patter, when she suddenly realized that for the past few minutes someone had been knocking on the door. For what had seemed like hours she had been mesmerized by the two smiling people on the evening newscast, and she had been almost unable to tear herself away. With a quick flick of the switch they disappeared from the screen, and with a small unhappy frown around her eyes, Sam walked to the door and pulled it open. Gone was the New York caution of "Who is it?" Here it could only be ranch hands or friends, there were simply no foes. As she pulled open the door she found herself staring at a navy-blue plaid shirt and a familiar denim jacket, and she let her eyes move rapidly upward until they reached Tate Jordan's face.

"Hi, Tate." She looked tired and distracted as she stood there, her mind still crammed with the images of her ex-husband and his new wife.

"Something wrong?" He looked instantly worried as he watched her, but she shook her head. "You look like you've had bad news."

"No." She looked vague as she said it. Even if she felt lousy, she could hardly call it "news" anymore. "Not really. I guess I'm just tired." She smiled at him but it wasn't the easy, relaxed smile he was growing used to, and he wondered what had made her unhappy enough to look like that. He thought maybe she'd had a phone call from back home, or a nasty letter from her ex-husband. He knew that kind of look himself from his own hassles with his ex-wife years before.

"You worked your ass off out there today, little Palomino." His smile was like a reward at the end of a hard day, and this time when Sam grinned it was real.

"I'm glad you noticed." But she knew by now that Tate Jordan saw everything. It was part of why he was such a valuable man to have on the ranch. He knew all of his men, the quality of their work, their loyalty, their devotion, what they took from and gave to the Lord Ranch in every possible way. And then, eyeing him with a question, she stood aside. "Would you like to come in?"

"I didn't mean to bother you, Sam." He looked momentarily embarrassed as he stepped inside. "I just heard that Bill and Caroline drove in to see the accountant. I thought I'd make sure you were okay. Want to come over to the hall for dinner?" She was touched by his thoughtfulness and suddenly wondered if she saw something more in his smile. But it was difficult to tell with Tate Jordan. There were times when one could read nothing at all in the deep green eyes and even less on the

171

heavily lined face. "Have you already eaten?" He could smell the chicken still in the oven, and she shook her head.

"No, Caroline left me a chicken, but I wasn't . . . I didn't have time to . . ." She flushed suddenly, remembering the evening broadcast she had sat and stared at instead of eating. And then, as she looked at him, she waved at the kitchen and cocked her head to one side, brushing her thick blond mane off her shoulders and down her back.

"Do you want to have dinner with me here, Tate? There's plenty to eat out there." They could divide the potato, there was the whole chicken, and the salad was big enough to feed half the men on the ranch. Caroline always cooked as though she were expecting an army. It came from years of being surrounded by ranch hands and friends.

"Wouldn't that be a lot of trouble for you?" He looked hesitant, his big bulk suddenly seeming too large for the low ceilings, but Samantha quickly shook her head.

"Don't be silly. Caroline left enough food here for ten." He laughed and followed her into the kitchen, and as they chatted about the ranch and the day's work, she set the table, and a few minutes later they were devouring the chicken and the salad as though they ate dinner together every day.

"What's New York like?" He looked at her, grinning, after he had finished his meal.

"Oh . . . crazy, I guess, is the best way to describe it. Too crowded, too noisy, too dirty, but exciting too.

Everyone in New York seems to be doing something: going to the theater, starting a business, rehearsing for a ballet, going broke, getting rich, getting famous. It really isn't a place for mere mortals."

"And you?" He eyed her carefully as she got up to pour them both coffee.

"I used to think I loved it." She shrugged as she set down the cups of steaming coffee and sat down again. "Now sometimes I'm not so sure. It all seems terribly far away right now, and not very important. It's funny, three weeks ago I couldn't have left my office to get a haircut without calling three times in an hour just to make sure everything was okay. And now I've been gone for almost three weeks and who knows the difference? They don't. I don't. It's as if I never lived back there." But she also knew that if she had flown back that night, by the next morning it would seem as though she had never left, and she would feel once again that she never could. "I think the thing about New York is that it's addictive. Once you break the habit, you're all right, but while you're hooked"—she smiled warmly at him—"watch out!"

"I've known women like that in my lifetime!" His eyes danced mischievously as he sipped the steaming coffee in the delicate white cup.

"Have you now, Mr. Jordan? Would you care to tell me about that?"

"Nope." He smiled again. "What about you? Did you leave anyone waiting for you in New York, or did you run away from all of that too?"

Her eyes grew serious for a moment after he asked her

173

and then she shook her head. "I didn't run away, Tate. I left. For a vacation..." She hesitated again. "A sabbatical, I think they called it at the office. And no, I didn't leave anyone waiting back there. I thought you understood all of that the other day."

"It never hurts to ask."

"I haven't been out with anyone since my husband."

"Since August?" She was surprised that he had remembered but she nodded. "Don't you think it's about time?"

She didn't want to tell him that she was beginning to think so right now. "Maybe. It'll all happen at the right time."

"Will it?" He spoke softly as he leaned toward her and kissed her as he had before. Once again she felt her heart pounding against the table as her body moved toward him, and with one hand he gently cupped her face as the other smoothed her silken hair. "My God, you're beautiful, Sam. You take my breath away, do you know that?" He kissed her again, and then pushed the plates across the table and pulled her toward him, until suddenly they were both breathless as they kissed in the silent house. It was then that Sam gently pulled away from him, with a small embarrassed smile on her lips.

"Aunt Caro would be shocked, Tate."

"Would she?" He looked unconvinced. "Somehow I doubt that." And at the same moment they both found themselves thinking of Caroline and Bill King on their little trip. They would probably spend the night together somewhere on the road. It made Sam think again of the little hidden cabin, and Tate smiled as his mind drifted back to it too. "If it weren't so dark we could ride out there. I liked being there with you, Sam."

"At the cabin?" She had understood immediately what he had been thinking, and he nodded.

"I felt the other day"—his voice caressed her and he stood up—"as though it had been made just for us." She smiled at him and slowly he pulled her to her feet until she stood before him, dwarfed by his size, her own tall frame tiny beside his, her breasts suddenly pressed against him as he pulled her to him, and her mouth hungry for his once again as gently he stroked her back and her hair. He pulled away then and his voice was only a whisper. "I know this sounds crazy, Sam, but I love you. I knew it the first time I saw you. I wanted to touch you and to hold you and to run my hands through that palomino hair." He smiled gently down at her but Samantha looked pensive. "Do you believe me, Sam?"

Her big blue eyes found his green ones and she looked troubled. "I don't know what I believe, Tate. I was thinking of what I said to you the other day, that just making love with someone wouldn't be enough. Is that why you said all this?"

"No." His voice was still a whisper, his mouth near her ear as he kissed her neck. "I said it because I mean it. I've been thinking about you a lot since the other day. What you want isn't different from what I feel, Sam." His voice grew stronger as he reached out and took her hands. "You just want me to put words to my feelings. I'm not used to doing that. It's easier to say 'I want to make love to you' than it is to say 'I love you.' But I've never met a woman I've wanted as much as I want you."

"Why?" She spoke in a hoarse whisper with all the hurt John had left her sharply etched in her eyes. "Why do you want me?"

"Because you're so lovely. . . ." He reached out gently and touched her breasts with his powerful yet careful hands. "Because I like the way you laugh and the way you talk . . . and the way you ride that damn horse of Caro's . . . the way you work like an ox with the men even though you don't have to . . . because I like"—he grinned and let his hands slip around her—"the way your ass sits on top of your legs." She laughed in answer and gently pushed his hands away. "Isn't that good enough reason?"

"Good enough reason for what, Mr. Jordan?" She was teasing him now as she turned away from him and began to clear the table, but before she could get their plates to the sink, he had taken them from her, set them down, and picked her up easily in his arms and carried her out of the room, making his way across the living room until he reached the long hall that led to her room. "Is this the way, Samantha?" His voice was ever so gentle and his eyes burned into hers. She wanted to tell him to stop, to turn back, but she found that she couldn't. She only nodded and pointed vaguely down the hall, and then, giggling suddenly, she pushed away from him.

"Come on . . . stop, Tate. Put me down!" His laughter joined hers but he didn't do as she told him. Instead he stopped at a halfway-opened door at the end of the hall.

"Is this yours?"

"Yes." She crossed her arms as he held her in his as though she were a very small child. "But I didn't invite you in, did I?"

"Didn't you?" One eyebrow rose and he crossed the threshold and looked around with interest. And then with no further words he set her down on the bed, took her in his arms, and kissed her hard on the mouth. The games between them were suddenly over, and the passion he unleashed in her took her very much by surprise. She was stunned at the force with which he held her to him, at the hunger of his mouth and his hands and his whole body as it reached out for hers. It seemed only moments later that he lay beside her and that her clothes seemed to melt away from her body, as did his. All she was aware of was the soft doeskin of his flesh against hers, the gentleness of his hands—ever searching, ever thrilling—the endless legs wound around hers, and his mouth drinking her own. He held her closer to him until she could bear it no longer and she pressed against him, moaning softly, longing to be his. It was then that he pulled away from her, that he looked hard into her eyes, asking her a question without words. Tate Jordan had never taken a woman, and would not take this one, not ever, and not now, unless this was what she wanted, unless he was certain, and as he searched her eyes she nodded slowly, and then seconds later he took her, pressing deep and hard into her flesh with his own. She gave a sharp gasp of pleasure as he thrust deeper, and then with another moan she let herself go to the ecstasy he brought her to again and again and again.

It seemed hours later when he lay still beside her, the room was dark, the house quiet, and she felt his long powerful body stretched out next to her, content, sated, and she felt with pleasure his lips gentle on her neck. "I

love you, Palomino. I love you." The words sounded so
real, but suddenly she wanted to ask him "Do you?" Was
it real? Would anyone ever really love her again? Love
her and mean it, love her and not hurt her, love her and
not go away? A small trickle of tears suddenly fell from
the corner of her eye to the pillow, and he looked at her
sadly and nodded his head. He pulled her into his arms
then and cradled her gently, crooning to her softly
meaningless words as one would have to a wounded
animal or a very small child. "It's all right, babe. It's all
right now, I'm here with you. . . ."

"I'm sorry. . . ." Her words were muffled as suddenly
the sobs of a lifetime broke from her, and the grief that
had lived pent up inside her broke from her like a flock of
wild birds. They lay like that, locked together, for almost
an hour, and when her tears were spent, she felt a
familiar stirring beside her and she smiled slowly and
reached down to touch him, and then guide him to the
same spot again.

"You all right now?" His voice was husky in the
darkness, and she nodded. "Answer me."

"I'm all right." He would go no farther and his eyes
were riveted to hers.

"You sure?"

"Yes, I'm sure." With her body she showed him the
gratitude that she didn't know the words for, arching
toward him and giving him as much pleasure as he had
given her. It was a meshing of two people beyond any she
had ever known in the years before him, and as she lay
beside Tate Jordan and slept, Samantha wore a small
happy smile.

PALOMINO

When the alarm went off at her bedside the next morning, she awoke slowly, with a smile, expecting to see him, and what she saw instead was a note beneath the small clock. He had set it for her when he had left her bed quietly at two o'clock that morning. He had turned on the alarm and written her a note on a little scrap of paper. It said only I LOVE YOU, PALOMINO. And as she read it she lay back on her pillows again, closed her eyes, and smiled. This time there were no tears.

13

At the end of the day's work Samantha looked as fresh and alive as she had at the beginning, and Josh commented on it with disgust as she hung up her saddle with a grin.

"Christ, woman! Look at you, Sam, tough as nails. Three weeks ago you could hardly walk after a day's ride, you were so out of shape. Now you fly off that damn horse and look as bright-eyed at six o'clock at night as you do in the morning when you get up. Makes me sick. You ought to be carrying *me* back to *my* cabin. My ass is sore as hell, and my arms are killing me from roping those damn steers. Maybe what you need is to shake your butt and work a little harder."

"Bullshit. I worked harder than you did today!"

"Oh, yeah?" He snarled playfully at her and swatted her behind with his hat as she walked past.

"Yeah!" She ran past him with a grin on her face and a long blond ponytail tied with a bright red ribbon. She had almost flown in her saddle all day long. All she had been able to think of was Tate Jordan, but neither of them had given anything away as they worked. If anything, he had been indifferent and almost surly, and she had done her best to ignore him the few times they might have had occasion to speak. He spoke to her casually only once over coffee at lunchtime and then strolled away to chat with some of the other men while Sam hung back with the ranch hands she knew best. It was only now that the day was over that she allowed her thoughts to soar toward Tate again. All day she had remembered moments of their night together, an instant, a glimmer, the shape of his leg as he had lain naked and uncovered amidst the tousled sheets, a look in his eye as he leaned toward her to kiss her again, the way the back of his neck looked as he lay down for a moment with a happy sigh and let her run long, tantalizing fingers slowly down his tingling spine. She loved the way he looked and the way he felt and what he did to her, and now it was all she could think of as she ran back to Aunt Caro's house. She had no idea when she might see him alone again. His cabin was highly visible, so near to the main hall where the men ate, and Aunt Caro was back from her brief trip with Bill. It was obvious that a meeting between them would take some arranging, but she felt certain that he would find a way. The thought that now he and Bill King would both tiptoe into the house and then creep out again at midnight brought a gurgle of laughter to her lips as she opened the front door.

"My, aren't you happy this evening, Miss Samantha." Caroline eyed her with pleasure from where she sat. And for the first time in four months she saw John's familiar face and felt not a twinge. She checked for a moment, narrowed her eyes pensively as she watched him, and then shrugged with a small quiet smile as she went to her room to wash up.

"I'll be back in a minute, Aunt Caro."

When she returned, they shared dinner, only tonight Samantha found herself wondering where Tate was. Was he in the main dining hall with the others? Had he opted to stay in his cabin and cook for himself, as a few of the men did? But most of them preferred to eat dinner with the others. Even the men with wives on the ranch often came to the main hall after dinner for coffee and a smoke and the companionship of the men they rode with all day long. Suddenly Samantha ached to be with them, but she also sensed that if she joined them all of a sudden in the evening they would begin to wonder why she was there. They accepted her in their midst in the daytime, but in the evening they expected her to stay at the big house with Caroline, where she belonged. It would have shocked them to see her there in the evening, and it would have been impossible to seek out Tate without causing comment. Someone would have easily figured it out. Gossip on any ranch was rampant, and there was a kind of sensitive radar that all of them seemed to have. Romances and marriages and divorces were almost instantly discovered, along with illicit affairs and illegitimate babies, which made it all the more remarkable that Bill King and Caroline had kept their secret for so long. Even if some of the old timers, or those who knew them well, suspected, no one on the ranch had ever been sure. Samantha found now that she respected that and understood all the more how difficult the clandestine life-style must have been. Now she felt herself fairly throbbing with excitement, aching to be with the man, to talk to him, to laugh, to tease him, to touch him, to go for a walk in the night air, to look up at him with interest and pride and hold his hand, and after that to come back to her bedroom and discover each other's bodies once again, as they had the night before.

"Do you want some more salad, Samantha?" They were halfway through dinner before Samantha seemed to remember where she was. For half an hour she had been silent and dreamy and drifting as Caroline watched her and wondered what was the cause. Sam didn't look unhappy, so she didn't think she was upset that Caroline had been watching the newscast. She didn't look homesick. In fact she looked fine, so it had to be something else. "Something wrong, Sam?"

"Hmm?"

"Something right?"

"What? . . . Oh . . . I'm sorry." Samantha blushed like a schoolgirl and then shook her head with a brief girlish laugh. "No, I was just distracted. It was a long day today, but I enjoyed it." It was the only way she could explain the outrageous glow she knew she wore and the look on her face.

"What on earth did you do?"

"Nothing special. Roped some horses, checked the fences, the men roped some steers this afternoon. . . ." She tried to remember. Mostly she had dreamed about Tate. "It was just a nice day really."

The wise old woman watched her closely. "I'm glad that you're happy here on the ranch."

Samantha's face grew oddly serious as she remembered. "I am, Aunt Caro. I'm happier here than I've been anywhere else in a long time."

Caroline nodded and addressed herself to her salad as Samantha went back to dreaming of Tate. But it wasn't until the next morning that she saw him. The night before she had heard Bill King come and go, with envy this time. But there had been no way that Tate could come to her, and as she lay in her bed, longing for him, she smiled to herself, it was like being eighteen and having an illicit affair. She felt suddenly young and girlish, terribly clandestine, and impatient to be with him again.

It was seven o'clock the next morning, Sunday, when she gulped her coffee, zipped up her jeans, donned her jacket, brushed her hair one last time, and then ran out to the barn, hoping that she might find him there. As it turned out, when she got there, there was no one. The men who had come to feed the horses had already gone back to the main hall to eat, and she was alone in the huge barn with the familiar horses, each one in its stall, quietly eating or resting or softly greeting each other, as Samantha slowly made her way to Black Beauty's stall.

She ran a hand slowly down his muzzle and then felt the soft whiskered lips brush her hand, looking for something to eat.

"I didn't bring you anything this morning, Beauty. I'm sorry, boy."

"Never mind him." The low voice came from behind her. "What did you bring me?"

"Oh!" She wheeled around to face him, startled, and before she could catch her breath, he had taken her swiftly in his arms, almost crushing the air out of her lungs as he held her and kissed her quickly, and then let her go.

"Good morning, Palomino." He spoke in a whisper and she blushed.

"Hello . . . I missed you."

"I missed you too. Do you want to go to the cabin this morning?" Anyone even a few feet from them couldn't have heard him speaking, and Samantha nodded quickly with a bright light of anticipation in her eyes.

"I'd like that."

"I'll meet you at the south fence, in the clearing. Do you know where that is?" He looked suddenly worried as he watched her as though he were afraid she might get lost, but she only laughed.

"Are you kidding? Where do you think I've been all week long while you've been working?"

"I don't know, babe." He grinned at her. "Same place I've been, I suspect. Halfway out of your head."

"You're not far wrong." And then, as he made to go, she grabbed at his sleeve and whispered, "I love you."

He nodded, brushed her lips with his own, and

whispered in answer, "I love you too. See you at ten." And then he was gone, his heels clicking loudly on the barn floor, and a moment later as he turned a bend there was a shouted greeting to two of the men coming to tend their horses. A moment earlier and they would have seen him kissing Samantha. Instead all they saw now was Sam diligently feeding Caroline's best horse.

14

They met at five minutes before ten in the south clearing, their horses fresh, the sky blue, their eyes bright with desire. It was a little crazy, this brand-new passion, she couldn't explain it but deep in her gut, she knew that she had to be with him, and she was ready to make a commitment to him for the rest of her life. She tried to explain it to him later that morning, as they lay in the big comfortable brass bed in the pale blue bedroom, their bodies tired, their hearts light, and his arm encircling her as she nestled at his side.

"I don't know, Tate, it's as if . . . as if I've always been waiting for you. As if suddenly I know what I was born for. . . ."

"You mean screwing?" He grinned at her and rumpled the exquisite hair.

"Don't call it that." She looked hurt.

"I'm sorry." He kissed her softly and touched her face. "Making love. That's what it is, you know, no matter what I call it."

"I know it is." She moved closer to him with a happy smile and closed her eyes. "It must be wrong to be this happy. It's certainly indecent." Her eyelids fluttered and he kissed the tip of her nose.

"Is it? Why?" He looked just as happy as she as he lay there. "Why don't we have a right to feel like this?"

"I'm not sure. But I hope we do and for a very long time." Their thoughts went in unison to Bill and Caroline, who had lain in the same bed before them and were still together after such a long time.

"It's crazy, Tate, it's all so new between us and it just doesn't feel like it, does it?"

"No, but if you don't stop talking about it, I'm going to start treating you like you've been around for the last twenty years."

"And then what?"

"I'll ignore you."

"Just try it." She ran a slender finger up the inside of his thigh and stopped interestingly where his legs joined.

"And just what is that all about, Miss Samantha?"

"Hang around and I'll show you." She teased in a sultry voice and he put a hand between her thighs. They were the oddest combination of teasing and serious, and through the entire morning there was always the feeling that they had been there before and been part of each other's lives for a very long time. It was almost impossible to realize that the relationship was a brand-new one, and Tate seemed to feel as comfortable as she did as they wandered naked through the tiny house.

"Did you see the photo albums, babe?" he called out to her as she made sandwiches in the cheerful little kitchen from the provisions he'd brought. He sat on the couch, with a blanket over his naked shoulders, his feet extended toward the bright fire. The fireplace hadn't been cleaned since the last person had used it, so they felt certain that no one would discover that they'd been there from whatever ashes they eventually left in the grate.

"Yeah, they're great, aren't they?" There were photographs of Bill and Caroline, and other people on the ranch, dating all the way back to the early fifties, and the two new lovers chuckled fondly as they glanced through the pages, watching people cavort years ago in front of outdated cars, in funny bathing suits and odd hats. There were a few pictures of rodeos, and there were even some photographs of the ranch before some of the newer buildings had been built. "Gee, it used to be a lot smaller."

He smiled in answer. "One day it should be a lot bigger than this. This could be the finest ranch in the state, maybe one of the best in the country, but Bill King is getting old, he isn't as anxious to see it grow. Leastways not anymore."

"What about you? Is that what you want, Tate? To run

this ranch someday?" He nodded slowly, being honest with her. He had a great deal of ambition, all of it centered around this ranch.

"Yeah. I'd like to make it something very special one day, if Miss Caro will let me. I'm not sure she will, while old Bill is around."

Samantha spoke softly, almost reverently. "I hope he always will be, Tate, for her sake."

He nodded slowly. "So do I. But one day, one day . . . there are some things I'd like to change on this ranch." Closing the album carefully, he began to tell her. An hour later he glanced at the electric clock in the kitchen and stopped. "Listen to me, Sam, I could go on like this for hours." He smiled sheepishly but it was obvious that she had enjoyed it.

"I like hearing about it." And then after a minute, "Why don't you start your own ranch?"

But he laughed and shook his head. "With what, little Palomino? Good wishes and old beer cans? Do you have any idea what it would cost to start a decent ranch? A fortune. Not on my pay, babe. No, all I want is to be one hell of a foreman, not an assistant foreman, but the real thing. The man in power. Hell, most of the ranchers don't know their ass from a hole in the ground. The foreman is the one who keeps the place running."

"You do that here." She eyed him proudly and he gently touched her hair and then cupped a hand under her chin.

"I try, little Palomino. I try when I'm not playing hookie with you. You could make me almost sorry I'm working. All I wanted to do yesterday was come here with you, and make love to you and sit by the fire and feel good."

Samantha stared into the fire with dreams in her eyes. "So did I." And then after a moment she turned her eyes back to him. "What are we going to do, Tate?"

"About what?" He was teasing her. He knew what she meant.

"Don't be cute. You know what I mean." And then she giggled. "The other night I had this vision of you and Bill King tiptoeing into the house and bumping into each other in the dark." They both laughed at the image and he pulled her close, with a pensive look in his eyes. He had already mulled over the possibilities, and all of them were complicated, none of them was ideal.

"I don't know, Sam, it would be a lot easier if it were summer. We could come here every night after work and ride back in the moonlight under the stars. But it's dark as hell now when we finish, and I'd be afraid one of the horses might stumble and get hurt."

"We could carry lanterns."

"Sure." He grinned at her. "Or hire a helicopter, why not?"

"Oh, shut up. Well . . . what are we going to do? Do you want to try sneaking into Aunt Caro's?"

He shook his head slowly. "No. They'd hear us; just like you told me you hear him coming in every night. And my place is so damn wide open. All it would take would be for one of the men to see you, just once, and it would be all over for us."

"Would it?" Samantha looked strained as she said it.

193

"Would it really be so awful if they knew?" He nodded slowly. "Why?"

"It's not right, Sam. You are who you are and I am who I am. You don't want them talking and neither do I." But the truth was that she didn't give a damn. She thought she loved him, and she didn't give two pins what anyone said. What could they do to hurt them? But she saw in his face that it was a sacred rule. Ranchers didn't fall in love with ranch hands.

Samantha looked at Tate squarely. "I'm not going to play the same game they've played, Tate, not forever. If we stay together, I want people to know it. I want to be able to be proud of what we have, not afraid of who might find out."

"We'll cross that bridge later." But she had the feeling that he wasn't prepared to move an inch in her direction, and suddenly she bridled and the light in her eyes was as stubborn as his.

"Why? Why not start dealing with it right now? Okay, I understand that we don't have to advertise to everybody right this minute that we're having an affair. But hell, Tate, I'm not going to sneak around forever."

"No." He said it very quietly. "Eventually you're going back to New York." The words hit her like a wave of cold water, and when she spoke again, there was ice and pain in her voice.

"What makes you so sure?"

"Because that's where you belong, just like I belong here."

"Is that right? How do you know that? How do you know that I'm not like Caroline, that I haven't decided I don't want that kind of life anymore, not that my life is like hers was?"

"You know how I know?" He looked at her with the full wisdom of his forty-plus years. "Because when Caroline came here, she was a widow, she wanted to give up the life she had shared with her husband, because he was gone. And she was forty years old, Sam, that's not the same as thirty or thirty-one. You're young, you still have a lot of living to do, a lot of your crazy commercials to put together, a lot of deals to make, a lot of buses to catch, phone calls to make, planes to miss, parties to go to. . . ."

"And I couldn't do some of that here?" She looked hurt and he eyed her gently, with wisdom and tenderness and love.

"No, little one, you couldn't. This isn't the place for that. You came here to heal, Sam, and that's what you're doing, and maybe I'm just part of that. I love you. I never laid eyes on you before three weeks ago, and I haven't really given a damn about a woman in years, but I know I love you. I knew it the first day we met. And I hope you love me. But what happened to Bill and Caro is a miracle, Sam, they don't belong together, and they never will. She's educated, he isn't. She's led one hell of a fancy life, and his idea of class is a solid-gold toothpick and a fifty-cent cigar. She owns the ranch and he ain't got a hill of beans. But she loves him, and he loves her, and this was all she wanted. For my own reasons I think she was a little crazy, but she'd had another life, and maybe after that this was enough for her. You're different, Sam, you're so much younger, and you've got a right to so much more than I could give you here." It was totally crazy, they had known each other for less than a month, and only been lovers for two days, and yet they were talking about the future as though it really mattered, as though there were even a question of their staying together for the rest of time. Samantha eyed him with amazement and then looked at him with a small smile.

"You're crazy, Tate Jordan. But I love you." And then she took his face in her hands and kissed him, hard, on the lips and then sat back and crossed her arms. "And if I want to stay here, if this is the life I want, whether I'm thirty or ninety or eighteen, then that's my decision. I am not Caroline Lord, and you are not Bill King, and you can save your damn self-sacrificing speeches, mister, because when the time comes, I'm going to do exactly what I want to do. If I don't want to go back to New York, you can't make me, and if it's you I want for the rest of my life, then I'll follow you to the ends of the earth and bug you to death until you announce it to every last goddamn ranch hand, and Caroline and Bill. You're not going to get rid of me as easily as you'd like to. You got that?" She was grinning at him, but she saw that there was still a broad streak of resistance in his eyes. It didn't matter though, he didn't know her, and the truth of it was that with only one recent exception, what Sam Taylor wanted, she got. "Got that, mister?"

"Yeah, I got it." But without saying more, this time it was Tate who kissed her and silenced her almost completely as he threw off the warm blanket and cast it over both of them. Only moments later they were once more blended together, their legs and their arms and their bodies one shimmering tangle as their lips held and the fire crackled nearby. And when it was over, he pulled his lips from hers breathlessly and carried her back to the little blue bedroom where they began again. It was after six o'clock when they noticed that it was nighttime. They had slept and made love and slept and made love all afternoon, and now regretfully Tate swatted her bottom, and then went into the bathroom to run a hot tub. They took a bath together, his endless limbs wrapped around her, as she giggled and told him stories of her early summers on the ranch.

"You know, we still haven't solved our problem."

"I didn't know we had one." He lay his head back on the edge of the tub and closed his eyes in the hot bath.

"I mean about where and how to meet."

He fell silent for a long moment as he thought it over and then shook his head. "Damn, I wish I knew. What do you think, Sam?"

"I don't know. My room at Aunt Caro's? I could let you in the window." She laughed nervously. It really had overtones of being fifteen years old and very "fast." "Your place?"

He nodded slowly. "I guess so. But I don't like it." And then suddenly he brightened. "I've got it. Hennessey's been bitching for two months about his house. Says the cabin's too small for him, it sits in the wind, and it's too far from the chow hall. He's been driving us all nuts."

"So?"

"I'll trade him. His place is on the edge of the camp, almost behind Caro's. At least if you go there, no one should see you. It's a hell of a lot better than where I am right now."

"You don't think they'll suspect?"

"Why should they?" He grinned at her in the steam from the bathtub. "I don't plan to pinch your ass every day at breakfast or kiss you on the mouth before we ride."

"Why not, don't you love me?"

He said nothing, but only leaned forward, kissed her tenderly, and then fondled her breasts. "Matter of fact, little Palomino, I do."

She raised herself on her knees in the old bathtub and then knelt facing him with everything she felt in her eyes. "So do I, Tate Jordan. So do I."

They rode back that night after seven, and Sam was intensely grateful that she knew Caroline had gone to dinner at another ranch. Otherwise Caroline would have been frantic. But the day had slipped past them, with their chatter and their laughter and their loving, and now as Sam came back to the main ranch house she felt a sudden loss at not being with him. It was as though someone had severed her right arm. It was an odd feeling to have about a man she had known for so little time, but isolated as they were from the rest of the world, there was something special and intense about their feelings, and she found herself longing for him again as she sat alone in the empty house. Caroline had left her a note that expressed concern at her long absence but not panic, and she had also left a warm dinner on the stove, which Sam only picked at before going to bed at eight thirty and lying there in the dark, thinking of Tate.

When Caroline came home that night with Bill King beside her, they tiptoed stealthily into the darkened house, and Bill went immediately to her room. Sam's presence in the house had made things a little awkward, and Caroline had to remind him every night not to close the front door so hard, but he didn't hear. Now Caroline walked softly down the hall to Sam's room, opened the door, peered into the moonlit darkness, and saw the beautiful young woman asleep in her bed. She stood watching her for a moment, feeling that her own youth had come back to haunt her, and then silently she walked into the room. She thought that she knew what was happening, yet as she had known it for herself, it was something that couldn't be changed or stopped. One had to live one's life. She stood there for a long time, gazing down at Samantha, her hair fanned out on her pillow, her face so unlined and so happy, and with tears in her eyes, Caroline reached out and touched the sleeping girl's hand. It did nothing to wake Sam as she lay there, and on still-silent feet Caroline left the room again.

When she returned to her own room, Bill was waiting in his pajamas and taking a last puff on his cigar. "Where were you? Still hungry after all that dinner?"

"No." Caroline shook her head, oddly quiet. "I wanted to make sure that Sam was all right."

"Is she?"

"Yes. She's sleeping." They had thought so when they saw the darkened house.

"She's a nice girl. That guy she was married to must've been a damn fool to run off with that other woman." He hadn't been impressed with what he'd seen of Liz on TV.

Caroline nodded silent agreement and then wondered how many of them were damn fools. She to have let Bill force silence on her for two decades, keeping their love for each other a secret; Bill for living like a criminal, as he tiptoed in and out of her house for more than twenty years; Samantha for falling for a man and a way of life that were both as foreign to her and possibly as dangerous as jumping off the top of the Empire State Building; and Tate Jordan for falling in love with a girl he couldn't have. Because Caroline knew exactly what was happening. She sensed it in her bones, in her gut, in her soul. She had seen it in Sam's eyes before Sam even knew it, sensed it on Christmas when she saw Tate look at Sam while she was busy doing something else. Caroline saw it all, and yet she had to pretend that she saw nothing, knew nothing and no one, and suddenly she didn't want that anymore.

"Bill." She looked at him strangely, took his cigar away, and set it down in the ashtray. "I want to get married."

"Sure, Caro." He grinned and fondled her left breast.

"Don't." She brushed him away. "I mean it." And something suddenly told him that she did.

"You're senile! Why would we get married now?"

"Because at our age you shouldn't be sneaking in and out of our house in the middle of the night, it's bad for my nerves and your arthritis."

"You're crazy." He lay back against the headboard with a look of shock.

"Maybe. But I'll tell you something. By now I don't think we'll surprise anyone. And what's more, I don't think anyone would care. No one would remember what or where I come from, so all your old arguments are nonsense. All they know after all this time is that I'm

Caroline Lord and you're Bill King of the Lord Ranch. Period."

"Not period." He looked suddenly ferocious. "They know you're the rancher and I'm the foreman."

"Who gives a damn?"

"I do. And you should. And the men do. There's a difference, Caro. You know that after all these years. And I'll be damned"—he almost roared it at her—"if I'll make you a laughingstock. Running off and marrying the foreman—the hell I will."

"Fine." She glared at him. "Then I'll fire you, and you can come back as my husband."

"Woman, you're crazy." He wouldn't even discuss it. "Now turn the light out. I'm tired."

"So am I...." She looked at him unhappily. "Of hiding, that's what I'm tired of after all these years. I want to be married, dammit, Bill."

"Then marry another rancher."

"Go to hell." She glared at him and he turned off the light, and the conversation was ended. It was the same conversation they had had a hundred times over the last twenty years, and there was no winning. As far as he knew, she was the rancher, and he was the foreman. And as she lay on her side of the bed, her eyes filled with tears, her back to him, she fervently prayed that Samantha would not fall hopelessly in love with Tate Jordan, because she knew that it would end no differently than this. There was a code that these men followed, a code that made sense to no one but them, but they lived by it, and Caroline knew that they always would.

15

The exchange of cabins between Tate Jordan and Harry Hennessey was completed within four days. Hennessey was enchanted with Tate's offer, and with the appropriate amount of grumbling, Tate eventually moved his things. He claimed that he didn't particularly like his cabin, was sick and tired of hearing Hennessey bitch, and had no vested interest in any of the cabins. To him, it was one and the same. No one took any particular notice of the transaction, and by Thursday night Tate had unpacked all his things. In her room at Aunt Caro's, Samantha waited patiently in the dark until nine thirty, when Caroline was safely in her room. Samantha left via her window and padded through the garden at the rear of the house, until only a few moments later she reached Tate's front door. His new cabin was almost directly behind the house and could be seen by no other. It was even protected from the view of the big house by the fruit trees at the back end of the garden, so there was no one who could see Samantha slip quietly through the door. Tate was waiting for her, barefoot, bare-chested, and in blue jeans, his hair almost blue-black, with salt at the temples and liquid green fire in his eyes. His skin was as smooth as satin, and he folded her rapidly into his arms. Moments later they were between clean sheets on his narrow bed. It was only after they had made love that they indulged in conversation, that she giggled about sneaking out her window and told him that she was sure that at that very moment Bill King was tiptoeing through the front door.

"Doesn't this all seem ridiculous at our age?" She was amused but he wasn't.

"Just think of it as romantic." Like Bill King with his concern for Caro, Tate Jordan had no intention of turning Sam into a laughingstock on the ranch. She was no quick piece of ass, no easy lay from New York. She was one hell of a special lady, and now she was his woman, and he would protect her if he had to, even from herself. And she understood nothing of the code of behavior between ranchers and ranch hands. What they did was their business and no one else's, and always would be, no matter what Samantha said. It was a point that she no longer chose to argue, there were always too many other things to say. She knew his position now, and he was well aware of hers, there was nothing left to be said for the moment about their clandestine arrangements. And it was comfortable enough for a while. For some reason, in her own mind, she had decided to make it an "open secret" by summer. She figured by then they would have been lovers for six or seven months, and he would be less uptight about the others knowing the score. And she realized as she thought of the summer that suddenly she was thinking of staying on at the ranch. It was the first time that she had admitted to herself that she might stay there, and it brought up the question of what she would do with her job in New York. But she figured that there was time to work that out too. It was still only December, although it already felt as though she had been on the Lord Ranch, and was Tate Jordan's woman, for a number of years.

"Happy?" he asked her just before they drifted off to sleep, linked together, her legs entwined in his, and his arm around her shoulders.

"Mmmm. . . ." She smiled at him with her eyes closed, and he kissed her eyelids once just before she drifted off to sleep. She awoke when he did at four o'clock the next morning and made her way back through the orchards behind the garden, slipped in through her half-open window, and turned on the lights. She showered as she always did, dressed, went to the main hall to breakfast, and thus, for Samantha Taylor, began a new life.

16

On Valentine's Day she got a card from Charlie
Peterson from her office that made reference to her
empty office. For the first time she thought of the job
waiting for her in New York. She told Tate about it that
night as she lay in his arms. It was a nightly ritual now.
She was there each night no later than nine o'clock, after
eating dinner with Aunt Caro and then taking a bath.

"What's he like?" Tate watched her with interest as
she flung herself on the couch with a happy grin.

"Charlie?" She narrowed her eyes at the man who now
felt like her husband. "Are you jealous?"

"Should I be?" His voice was even.

"Hell no!" The words were blended with a shout of laughter. "He and I have never been involved, besides he has a wife and three sons and she's pregnant again. I just love him like a brother, you know, kind of like my best buddy. We've worked together for years."

He nodded. And then, "Sam, don't you miss your job?"

She was silent and pensive for a moment before answering and then shook her head. "You know, the amazing thing is that I don't. Caroline says it was that way for her too. When she left her old life, she just left it. And she never had any desire to go back. I feel that way too, I miss it less and less every day."

"But you miss it some?" He had trapped her, and she rolled over on her stomach now and looked into his eyes as she lay on the couch and he sat near her with his back to the fire.

"Sure, I miss some of it. Like sometimes I miss my apartment, or some of my books, or my things. But I don't miss my life there. Or my job. Most of the things that I do miss are all the things that I could bring here if I wanted to. But the job . . . it's so strange, I spent all that time working so hard, and trying so damn hard to become important, and now . . ." She shrugged at him and looked like a very young, very blond sprite. "I just don't give a damn about that anymore. All I care about is if the steers are rounded up, if there's work to be done, if Navajo needs new shoes, if the fence in the north pasture is down. I don't know, Tate, it's as though something happened. As though I became a different person when I left New York."

"But somewhere in you, Sam, is still that old person. That person who wanted to write prize-winning commercials and be important in your line of work. You're going to miss that one day."

"How do you know that?" She looked suddenly angry. "Why do you keep pushing me to be what I don't want to be anymore? Why? Do you want me to go back? Are you scared of the commitment, Tate, of what it might mean?"

"Maybe. I have a right to be scared, Sam, you're a hell of a woman." He knew that she wasn't willing to keep their life together a secret forever, that she wanted their love out in the open. That was something that worried him a great deal.

"Well, don't push me. Right now I don't want to go back. And if I do, I'll tell you."

"I hope so." But they both knew that her leave of absence had only six more weeks to run. She had promised herself that she would make a decision by mid-March. She still had a month. But only two weeks later, as they rode slowly back from the secret cabin where they still spent idyllic Sundays, he looked mischievous and told her that he had a surprise.

"What kind of surprise?"

"You'll see when we get home." He leaned over toward her from where he sat on his pinto and kissed her full on the lips.

"Let's see . . . what could it be . . . ?" She managed to look both naughty and pensive, and also very young, at the same time. She had her long blond hair in two pigtails tied with red ribbons, and she was wearing a brand-new pair of red snakeskin cowboy boots. Tate had teased her horribly about them, telling her that they were even worse than Caro's green ones, but with the Blass and Ralph Lauren and Halston wardrobe cast off since she'd arrived at the ranch, they had been her only whimsical purchase in three months. "You bought me another pair of boots? Violet ones this time?"

"Oh, no . . ." he groaned as they rode slowly home.

"Pink?"

"I think I'm going to throw up."

"All right, something else. Let's see . . . a waffle iron?" He shook his head. "A new toaster?" She grinned, she had set fire to theirs only last week. "A puppy?" She looked hopeful and he smiled but once again shook his head. "A turtle? A snake? A giraffe? A hippopotamus?" She laughed and so did he. "Hell, I don't know. What is it?"

"You'll see."

As it turned out, it was a brand-new color television, which he had just bought through Josh's brother-in-law in the nearest town. Josh had promised to drop it off at Tate's place on Sunday. And Tate had told him to leave it inside while he was out. And when he and Samantha came through the door, he pointed with an expression of pride mixed with glee.

"Tate! Babe, this is great!" But she was a lot less excited than she knew he was. She had been perfectly happy without one. And then she pouted coyly. "Does this mean the honeymoon is over?"

"Hell no!" He was quick to prove it, but afterward he turned on the TV. The Sunday news report was on. It was a special weekly wrap-up usually done by someone else, but tonight for some reason John Taylor was handling it, and as Sam saw him she suddenly stopped and stared at him, as though she was seeing him for the first time. It had been almost three months since she'd seen his face on TV, five since she'd seen him in person, and she realized now that she didn't care anymore. All that terrible hurt and pain had faded and all that was left now was a vague feeling of disbelief. Was this truly the man she had once lived with? Had she really loved that man for eleven years? Now as she watched him she thought he looked plastic and pompous, and suddenly the clear realization of how totally self-centered he was came to her for the first time and she wondered why she had never seen it before. "You like him, Sam?" Tate was watching her with interest, his angular rugged countenance in complete contrast to the baby-smooth golden boy looks of the younger man on the TV screen. And with an odd little smile Sam slowly shook her head, and then turned to face Tate.

"No, I don't."

"You're sure watching him pretty close." And then Tate grinned. "Go on, you can tell the truth. Does he turn you on?"

This time it was Samantha who grinned. She smiled with a look of freedom and relief and suddenly, finally, she knew it was over. She no longer had any tie whatsoever to John Taylor. She was her own woman now, and it was Tate Jordan whom she loved. In fact she didn't even give a damn if they'd had their baby, and she didn't care if she never saw either John or Liz again. But Tate was persistent as he watched her, sprawled out in

211

the bed he had bought to accommodate their loving, with the soft blue blanket held to her chest.

"Come on, Sam, does he?"

"Nope," she finally answered with a note of triumph. She kissed Tate playfully on the neck then. "But you do."

"I don't believe you."

"Are you kidding?" She whooped with laughter. "After what we just did all day you can doubt that you turn me on? Tate Jordan, you are craaaaaazzyyyy!"

"I don't mean that, silly. I mean about him. Look . . . look at that pretty blond newsman." He was teasing her and Sam was laughing. "Look how pretty he is. Don't you want him?"

"Why? Can you get me a special deal? He probably sleeps in a hair net, and he's sixty years old and has had two face-lifts." For the first time in her life she was enjoying making fun of John. He had always taken himself so damn seriously, and she had let him. The face and body and image and life and happiness of John Robert Taylor had been of prime importance to both of them. But what about her? When had Sam really mattered, if ever? Certainly not at the end when he ran off with Liz. Her face grew serious again as she remembered.

"I think you like him and you're too chicken to admit it."

"Nope. You're wrong, Tate. I don't like him at all." But she said it with such an air of conviction that he turned his head to look at her again, this time with a look of serious inquiry that hadn't been there before.

"Do you know him?" She nodded, but she looked

neither moved nor amused. Mostly she looked indifferent, as though they were talking about a plant or a used
car. "Do you know him well?"

"I used to." She could see Tate bridle, and she wanted to
tease him just a little. She placed a hand on his powerful
naked chest and then smiled. "Don't get yourself excited,
sweetheart. It was nothing. We were married for seven
years." For a moment everything seemed to stop in the
little room. She could feel Tate's whole body tense beside
her, and he sat up in the bed next to her and stared down
at her with a look of dismay.

"Are you putting me on, Sam?"

"No." She looked at him matter-of-factly, unnerved by
his reaction, but not sure what it meant. It was probably
just shock.

"He was your husband?"

She nodded again. "Yes." And then she decided that the
occasion needed further explanation. It wasn't every day
that one saw the ex-husband of one's current lover on the
television screen as one went to bed at night. She told him
everything.

"But the funny thing is that I was just thinking as I
watched him that I really don't give a damn anymore.
When I was in New York, every night I used to watch that
damn broadcast. I'd watch both of them, John and Liz,
doing their cutesy little routine and talking about their
precious baby as though the whole world cared that she
was pregnant, and it used to turn me inside out. Once
when I came in, Caro was watching it, and I almost felt
sick. And you know what happened tonight when that
plastic face came on the screen?" She looked at Tate

expectantly but got no answer. "Absolutely nothing happened. Nothing. I didn't feel a damn thing. Not sick, not nervous, not pissed off, not left out. Nothing." She smiled broadly. "I just don't care."

With that, Tate got up, stalked across the room, and turned off the set. "I think that's wonderful. You used to be married to one of America's best-looking young heroes, clean-cut preppie John Taylor of television fame, and he leaves you and you find yourself a tired old cowboy, some ten or twelve years older than our hero, without a goddamn dime to his name, shoveling shit on a ranch, and you're trying to tell me that this is bliss? Not only is this bliss, but it's permanent bliss. Is that it, Samantha?" He was steaming, and Samantha felt helpless as she watched. "Why didn't you tell me?"

"Why? What difference does it make? Besides, he is not nearly as well known or successful as you seem to think he is." But that wasn't quite true.

"Bullshit. You want to see my bank account, baby, and compare it to his? What does he make every year? A hundred grand? Two? Three? You know what I make, Samantha? You want to know? Eighteen thousand before taxes, and that was a big raise for me because I'm the assistant foreman. I'm forty-three years old, for chrissake, and compared to him, I don't make shit."

"So what? Who gives a damn?" She was suddenly shouting as loud as he was, but she realized that it was because she was scared. Something had just happened to Tate when he learned that she and John had been married, and it frightened her. She didn't expect him to take it this hard. "The point is . . ." She made a conscious effort to lower her voice as she smoothed the blanket over her legs. By now Tate was pacing the room. "The point is what happened between us, what kind of people we were, what we were like to each other, what happened at the end, why he left me, how I felt about him and Liz and their baby. That's what matters, not how much money he makes or the fact that they're on TV. Besides, *they're* on television, Tate, I'm not. What difference does it make? Even if you're jealous of him, just look at him, dammit, he's a fool. He's a plastic little preppie that made good. He got lucky, that's all, he's got blond hair and a pretty face and the ladies around America like that. So what? What does that have to do with you and me? If you want to know what I think, I think it has absolutely nothing to do with us. And I don't give a shit about John Taylor. I love *you*."

"So how come you didn't tell me who you were married to?" He sounded suspicious of her now, and she lay back in the bed and tugged at her hair, trying not to scream before she sat up to face him again, which she did with a look in her eye almost as ferocious as the look in his.

"Because I didn't think it was important."

"Bullshit. You thought I'd feel like two cents, and you know something, sister?" He walked across the room and started to pull on his pants. "You were right. I do."

"Then you're crazy." She was shouting at him openly now, trying to fight his illusions with the truth. "Because you're worth fifty, a hundred, John Taylors. He's a selfish little son of a bitch who hurt me, for chrissake. You're a grown man, and a smart one, and a good one, and you've done nothing but be good to me since we met." She looked around the room where they had spent all their evening hours for three months, and saw the paintings he had bought her to cheer the place up, the comfortable bed he had bought, even the color TV now to amuse her, the pretty sheets they made love on, the books he thought she'd like. She saw the flowers that he picked her whenever he thought no one was looking, the fruit he had brought just for her from the orchards, the sketch of her he had done one Sunday at the lake. She thought of the moments and the hours and the gestures, the rolls of film they had taken and the secrets they had shared and she knew once again, for the hundredth time, that John Taylor wasn't fit to lick Tate Jordan's boots. There were tears in her eyes when she spoke again and her voice was suddenly husky and deep. "I don't compare you to him, Tate. I love you. I don't love him anymore. That's all that means anything. Please try to understand that. That's all that matters to me." She reached out to him but he kept his distance, and after a few minutes she let her hand drop to her side as she knelt naked on the bed with tears rolling slowly down her face.

"And you think all of that will mean something to you in five years? Oh, lady, don't be so naive. Five years from now I'll be just another cowboy, and he'll still be one of the most important people on television in this country. You think you won't stare at the set every night while you wash dishes and ask yourself how you wound up with me? This isn't playacting, you know. This is real life. Ranch life. Hard work. No money. This isn't a commercial you're making, lady, this is real." She began to cry harder now at the fierceness of his words.

"Don't you think it's real to me?"

"How could it be, for chrissake? How could it be, Sam? Look at what you come from and how I live. What's your apartment in New York like? A penthouse on Fifth Avenue? Some fancy-schmancy number with a doorman and a French poodle and marble floors?"

"No, it's a top floor in a town house, a walk-up, if that makes you feel any better."

"And it's filled with antiques."

"I have some."

"They ought to look real cute here." He said it with feeling and turned away from her to put on his shoes.

"Why the hell are you so angry?" She was shouting again and crying at the same time. "I'm sorry if I didn't tell you I was married to John Taylor. As it so happens, you're much more impressed with him than I am. I just didn't think it mattered as much as you seem to think."

"Anything else you didn't tell me? Your father is the president of General Motors, you grew up in the White House, you're an heiress?" He looked at her with hostility, and stark naked, she sprang from his bed like a long, lithe cat.

"No, I'm an epileptic and you're about to give me a fit." But he didn't even smile at her attempt to tease him out of his mood. He simply went into the bathroom and closed the door, while Sam waited, and when he came out, he glanced at her impatiently.

"Come on, put on your clothes."

"Why? I don't want to." She felt terror creep into her heart. "I'm not leaving."

"Yes, you are."

"No, I'm not." She sat down on the edge of the bed. "Not until we hash this thing out. I want you to know once and for all that that man doesn't mean anything to me and that I love you. Do you think you can get that through your fat head?"

"What difference does it make?"

"It makes a big difference to me. Because I love you, you big dummy." She lowered her voice and smiled gently at him, but he didn't return the smile. Instead he looked at her pointedly and picked up a cigar, but he only played with it, he didn't light it.

"You should go back to New York."

"Why? To chase after a husband I don't want? We're divorced. Remember that? I like it that way now. I'm in love with you."

"What about your job? You're going to give that up for ranch life too?"

"As a matter of fact . . ." She took a deep breath and almost trembled. What she was about to say now was the biggest step of all, and she knew that she hadn't yet completely thought it through, but it was the time to say it, tonight. She didn't have more time to think it out. ". . . that's exactly what I've been thinking of doing. Quitting my job and staying here for good."

"That's ridiculous."

"Why?"

"You don't belong here." He sounded exhausted as he said the words. "You belong there, in your apartment, working at your high-powered job, getting involved with some man in that world. You don't belong with a cowboy, living in a one-room cabin, shoveling horse shit, and roping steer. Besides, for chrissake, you're a lady."

"You make it sound very romantic." She tried to sound sarcastic again but tears stung her eyes.

"It isn't romantic, Sam. Not a bit. That's the whole point. You think it's a fantasy and it's not. Neither am I. I happen to be real."

"So am I. And that's the issue. You refuse to believe that I'm real too, that I have real needs and am a real person and can exist away from New York and my apartment and my job. You refuse to believe that I might want to change my life-style, that maybe New York doesn't suit me anymore, that this is better and it's what I want."

"So buy yourself a ranch, like Caroline."

"And then what? You'll believe I'm for real?"

"Maybe you can give me a job."

"Go to hell."

"Why not? And then I could sneak in and out of your bedroom for the next twenty years. Is that what you want, Sam? To end up like them, with a secret cabin you're too old and tired to go to, and all you've got left are secret dreams? You deserve a lot better, and if you're not smart enough to know that, then I am."

"What's that supposed to mean?" She eyed him with terror, but he would not meet her eyes.

"Nothing. It just means put your clothes on. I'm taking you home."

"To New York?" She tried to sound flip and failed.

"Never mind the smart shit, just put on your clothes."

"Why? What if I don't want to?" She looked like a

frightened belligerent child, and he walked over to where she had dropped her clothes in a pile when they made love earlier that evening; he scooped them all up and dumped them in her lap.

"I don't care what you want. This is what I want. Get dressed. I seem to be the only grown-up here."

"Like hell you are!" She jumped to her feet and dropped the pile of clothes to the floor. "You're just locked into your old-fashioned ideas about ranchers and ranch hands, and I won't listen to that bullshit anymore! It's a cop-out and you're wrong and it's stupid." She was sobbing as she stooped to the floor, picked up her clothes piece by piece, and began to dress. If he was going to be like this, she would go back to the big house. Let him stew in his own juice overnight.

Five minutes later she was dressed and he stood looking at her, with despair and disbelief, as though tonight he had discovered a side of her he had never known, as though she were suddenly a different person. She stood staring at him unhappily and then walked slowly toward the door.

"Do you want me to walk you home?"

For a moment she almost relented, but then she decided not to. "No, thanks, I can manage." She tried to calm herself as she stood in the doorway. "You're wrong, you know, Tate." And then she couldn't help whispering softly, "I love you." As tears filled her eyes she closed the door and ran home, grateful that once again Caroline was away at a nearby ranch. She did that often on Sundays, and tonight Samantha didn't want to see her as she came through the front door, her face streaked with tears.

17

The next morning Sam lingered in Caroline's kitchen over coffee, staring bleakly into the cup and thinking her own thoughts. She wasn't sure if she should try to talk to him again that evening, or let it sit for a few days and let him come to his senses on his own. She replayed in her mind the previous night's conversation, and her eyes filled with tears again as she stared into her cup. She was grateful that this morning there was no one around her. She had decided not to go to breakfast in the main hall. She wasn't hungry anyway, and she didn't want to see Tate until they went to work. She was careful not to go to the barn until five minutes before six, and when she saw him, he was in a far corner, with his familiar clipboard, quietly issuing orders, waving toward the far boundaries, pointing toward some of the animals they could see on the hills, and then turning to point to something else. Quietly Sam saddled Navajo as she did every morning, and a few minutes later she was mounted and waiting out in the yard. But for some reason he had put Josh in charge of Sam's group today, and it was obvious that he wouldn't be riding, or at least not with them. All of which annoyed Sam further, it was as though he was going out of his way to avoid her. And with a nasty edge to her voice she leaned toward him and said loudly as her horse walked past him, "Playing hookie today, Mr. Jordan?"

"No." He turned to look at her squarely. "I've got some business to discuss with Bill King." She nodded, not sure what to answer, but as she turned Navajo at the gate to lock it behind the others, she saw him standing in the yard, watching her with a look of sorrow, and then quietly he turned and walked away. Maybe he was sorry about the fuss he had made about her ex-husband. Maybe he had understood that the differences that existed between them were differences that may have mattered to him, but not to Sam. For an instant she wanted to call out to him, but she didn't dare, the others might hear her, so she spurred Navajo on and joined them for the usual hard day's work.

Twelve hours later, riding more slowly and slumping with fatigue in the heavy Western saddles, they all rode back into the main yard and dismounted, led their horses into the barn, and removed the bridles and the saddles and put them away. Samantha was particularly exhausted that evening, she had spent the whole day thinking about Tate and everything he had said the night before. She was vague and distracted when she said good night to the others, and she looked strained when she walked in Caroline's front door.

"You look beat, Sam. Are you feeling all right, dear?" Caroline looked at her worriedly and hoped that it was only hard work that had made her look so worn. But she had a sudden uneasy suspicion that it was more serious than that. But she was not going to add still further to Samantha's worries. She said nothing, only urged Sam to take a hot bath before dinner, while she put on some steaks and made some soup and a salad. But when Sam came back, it was in clean jeans and a plaid flannel shirt, and she looked more than ever like a tidy cowgirl, as Caroline commented with a smile.

Nonetheless dinner that evening was less than joyful and it seemed hours before Sam could flee through her window and make her way through the garden and past the orchard to the little cabin where she went to see Tate. But when she got there, she knew with a terrible certainty that he was even more upset than she had imagined. The lights were off and it was too early for him to be asleep. Either he was pretending or he was hanging out at the main hall with the others, which was unlike him, but certainly effective if he was trying to avoid her. Tentatively she knocked on the door and there was no answer. She turned the knob as she always did and walked in. But what greeted her was not the usual disarray of Tate's belongings. What met her eyes instead was a dusty, barren emptiness that engulfed her, and the sound of astonishment that she made reverberated against the empty walls. What had he done? Had he actually switched cabins again to avoid her? She felt a wave of panic engulf her as she realized that she had no idea where he was. With her heart pounding, as she steadied herself in the doorway, she reassured herself that wherever he was he couldn't have gone very far. She knew that somewhere in the complex there were still two or three empty cabins, and he had obviously spent the day moving lock, stock, and baggage to avoid her. If it hadn't been so unnerving, and such a sign of how ferociously he felt about what they had discussed the previous evening, she would have been amused. But as she walked back to Caroline's house in the darkness, she was anything but amused.

She scarcely slept that night as she tossed and turned, wondering why he had done something as radical as switch cabins, and at three thirty she got up, unable to bear it anymore. She puttered around her room for another half an hour, showered, and was still ready too early. She had another half hour to kill, with a cup of coffee in Caroline's kitchen, before she could go to the main hall to eat. And this morning she definitely wanted to be there. If she could catch him even for a moment, she wanted to ask him why he had changed cabins and tell him that he was acting like an impetuous child.

But as she stood on line, waiting for bacon and eggs and her third cup of coffee, she heard two of the men talking and turned to Josh with an expression of horror and a blank stare.

"What did they just say?"

"They were talking about Tate."

"I know. What did they say?" Her face looked ghostly pale. She couldn't have heard right.

"They said it's too bad."

"What's too bad?" She was trying desperately not to scream.

"That he left yesterday." Josh smiled pleasantly and moved forward in the line.

"For where?" Her heart began to pound in her ears so loudly, she could barely hear his answers, but he only shrugged before answering this time.

"No one seems to know. His boy over at the Bar Three ought to know though."

"What the hell do you mean?" She was almost shouting.

"Christ, Sam, take it easy. Tate Jordan. He quit."

"When?" She thought for a moment that she might faint.

"Yesterday. That was why he stuck around to talk to Bill King. To tell you the truth, yesterday morning he told me he was going to when he asked me to ride for him. He told me he'd been wanting to do it for a long time. He said it was time to move on." Josh shrugged. "Damn shame. He would have been good in Bill King's shoes."

"So he just left? No two-week notice, no breaking in someone new to do his job for him? That's it?" There were already tears stinging her eyes.

"Yeah, Sam, this ain't Wall Street. When a man wants to move on, he does. He bought himself a truck yesterday morning, put all his stuff in it, and took off."

225

"For good?" She could barely choke out the words.

"Sure. Ain't no sense coming back. Never the same if you do. I did it once. It was a mistake. If he was unhappy here, then he done the right thing." Oh? Did he? How lovely to hear it. And then Josh looked at her more closely. "You okay, Sam?"

"Yeah. Sure." But she was terrifying-looking, she was so gray. "I haven't been sleeping too well lately." She had to fight back the tears . . . had to . . . had to . . . besides, there was no reason to panic. Bill King would know where he was, and if he didn't, the boy would. She'd go and see him herself. But she wasn't going to let this man slip through her fingers. Never. And after she found him, he'd never do something like this to her again.

"You know"—Josh was still staring at her—"you looked lousy yesterday too. Think maybe you're getting the flu?"

"Yeah." She tried to look unaffected by what he had just told her about Tate Jordan. "Maybe."

"Then why the hell don't you go back to the big house and climb back into bed?"

She started to resist him and then knew that there was no way she could ride for the next twelve hours, driving herself mad, wondering where Tate had gone. So she nodded vaguely, thanked Josh for the suggestion, and left the main hall. She hurried back to the big house, let herself in through the front door, and then just stood there, as uncontrollable sobs racked her and she dropped to her knees beside a couch and bowed her head in despair. She felt as though she wouldn't survive this second loss in her life, not now, not Tate. As she agonized

226

over what had happened, sobbing uncontrollably into the couch, she suddenly realized that Caroline was next to her, gently touching her shoulder and then smoothing the tangled blond hair. Samantha looked up after a few moments, her face red and swollen, her eyes wild, and looked into her friend's eyes to learn what she could there, but Caroline only nodded and cooed gently and took her into her arms and slowly brought her to sit on the couch.

It was fully half an hour before she could speak. Caroline said nothing. She only sat there and rubbed her back gently and waited. There was nothing one could say. It cut her to the core to realize that Sam had come to her to recover from one major loss and had now sustained another. She knew in her gut about Sam and Tate. She had agonized over it the day before when Bill had told her that Tate Jordan had left. But it was too late to stop him, or to discuss it. He had already left when Bill told Caroline in the late afternoon, and all she could think of was how Samantha would take the news. But Caroline hadn't dared to tell her the night before. She had hoped it would wait.

Samantha looked at her then, her face blotched, her eyes hideously bloodshot and swollen, and there was no dissimulation in the look she gave her friend. "He's gone. Oh, God, Caro, he's gone. And I love him. . . ." She couldn't go on then, and Caroline nodded slowly. She understood only too well. She had tried to tell her that here things were different, that there were things that would matter to him that didn't seem important to her.

"What happened, Sam?"

"Oh, God, I don't know. We fell in love at Christmas. . . ." She looked around nervously suddenly, wondering if any of the Mexican women were cleaning, but there was no one in sight. "We went to—" She looked at Caroline in embarrassment. "We found your cabin and we met there at first, but not often. We weren't snooping—"

"It's all right, Sam." Caroline's voice was very quiet.

"We just wanted someplace to go and be alone."

"So did we." Caroline said it almost sadly.

"And then he switched cabins with someone else and I used to go to him every night . . . through the orchard. . . ." Her speech was disjointed and her face awash with tears. "And then the other night, he . . . we were watching television and John came on doing a special broadcast, and we were just kidding around at first, and he wanted to know . . . if I thought John was handsome or something . . . and I happened to mention that we'd been married . . . and Tate went nuts. I don't understand it." She gulped horribly and went on. "He just went crazy, telling me that I couldn't be married to a movie star one minute and a cowboy the next, that I'd never be happy, that I deserved better, that—" She couldn't go on then, she was overwhelmed by tears. "Oh, God, and now he's left. What will I do? How will I find him?" Panic ran through her again as it had all morning. "Do you know where he's gone?" Caroline shook her head sadly. "Does Bill?"

"I don't know. I'll call him up right now at his office and ask him." She walked away from Sam then and stepped to the phone on her desk. Sam listened in agony to the entire conversation, and it was clear at the end of it that Bill knew nothing at all, and he was sorry that Tate had gone too. He had been counting on him to take over for him one day when he was too old to run the ranch. But now that would never happen. He knew that Tate was gone for good.

"What did he say?" Samantha looked at her dismally as she came back and sat down.

"Not much. He said that Tate said he'd be in touch one of these days, but Bill says he wouldn't count on it. He knows the way these men are. He left no forwarding address."

"Then I'll have to find his son at the Bar Three." She said it almost with desperation, but Caroline shook her head.

"No, Sam. The boy quit and went with him. That much Bill knew. They packed the truck up together and then left."

"Oh, my God." Samantha dropped her head into her hands and began to sob again, softly this time, as though her heart were already shattered and there were nothing left.

"What can I do for you, Sam?" There were tears now in Caroline's eyes too. She realized how easily it could have happened to her years earlier, and the conversation Sam had related sounded exactly like an argument that she and Bill had had for years. Eventually they had resolved it differently, but Bill was a good deal less stubborn than Tate. He was also just a shade less noble, a fact for which Caroline was deeply grateful as she sat helplessly and watched the agony of her young friend.

Sam looked at her now, in answer to her question. "Help me find him. Please, oh, if you could do that . . ."

"How?"

Sam sat back against the couch and sniffed as she thought. "He'll go to a ranch somewhere. He won't want any other kind of work. How would I get a list of ranches?"

"I can tell you all the ones I know in this area, the men can tell you others. No, let me ask them, we'll cook up some excuse, some reason. Sam"—Caroline's eyes lit up—"you'll find him."

"I hope so." She smiled for the first time in hours. "I won't stop until I do."

18

By mid-April Sam had contacted sixty-three ranches. At first she had called the ones in the area, looking for Tate, then those farther north, some farther south, then she had begun to call other states. Arizona, New Mexico, Nevada, Texas, Arkansas, she had even called one in Nebraska that one of the men had suggested. He had talked to Tate about the place and said the food and the pay were real good. But no one had seen Tate Jordan. Sam left her name and address and Caroline's number and asked them to call her if Tate should appear. She used Caroline Lord's name everywhere and it helped her, and the two pored hourly over directories, want ads, listings, advertisements, and the names they got from the men. She had long since asked her office for an extension and had promised them some kind of definitive answer by May 1. If she wasn't coming back to New York, they wanted to know by then. Until then the job would be hers. But she didn't give a damn about her job, all she wanted was Tate Jordan, and he was nowhere to be found. It was as though a month before he had dropped off the face of the earth never to be seen again. He had to be somewhere, Sam knew, but the question was where? It was becoming an obsession with her. She no longer rode with the men, no matter that that began rumors or confirmed their suspicions. From the day that he left she rode with them no more.

She went to the cabin once alone, but couldn't bear it, and had ridden home on Black Beauty, her face covered with tears. Now she seldom even rode the big black Thoroughbred, even when Caroline encouraged her to do so. All she wanted to do was stay at the house, make phone calls, go over lists, look at maps, write letters, and try to figure out where he was. So far it had all been fruitless, and secretly Caroline was beginning to think that it might stay that way. The truth was that it was a big country, and there were countless ranches. There was always the possibility that he had gone to a different line of work entirely, or that he wasn't using his real name. She was much too familiar with the scores of drifters who had worked on the ranch in the years she had owned it to be able to hold out great hope to Sam. It was entirely possible that he would turn up somewhere, someday, but it was equally possible that he would never be seen or heard from again. It was even possible that he had left the country, gone to Canada or Mexico, or even one of the big ranches in Argentina. Often the ranch owners let men like Tate work without papers, or with falsified ones, just so they could have them on their ranches. As ranch foremen went, Tate had a long list of good credentials, he was a reliable, hardworking man, and he had a great deal of expertise to offer any ranch. Any ranch owner with half a brain would recognize that, the question was— which ranch owner and which ranch.

By the end of April there was still nothing, and Sam had three days to call her office and tell them where things stood. She had told them a month before that Caroline was ill and it was suddenly difficult for her to leave when she had said she would. They had been understanding at first, but now Charlie was calling. The fun was over. Harvey wanted her back. They were suddenly having big trouble with her automobile client, and if she was coming back at all, then Harvey wanted it to be right now. She couldn't really blame him, but she couldn't tell them either that she was in worse shape now than she had been when she left New York. More than ever, now that he was gone, she knew how much she loved Tate, how much she respected him and his way of life. It was particularly painful to her now when she saw Bill and Caro, and it was agonizing for Caroline to share in Samantha's loss.

"Sam." As she looked at her young friend over coffee on the last day of April, she sighed deeply and decided to tell her what she thought. "I think you should go back."

"Where?" She was glancing again at one of her lists of ranches and wondered if Caroline had thought of one they should try again. But Caroline was quick to shake her head.

"I meant New York."

"Now?" Sam looked shocked. "But I haven't found him."

Caroline gritted her teeth for what she wanted to say next, much as she hated to hurt Sam. "You don't know that you ever will."

"That's a rotten thing to say." Sam looked at her angrily and pushed away her coffee. She had been testy and nervous since the whole nightmare had begun. She never slept, she never ate, she never got fresh air anymore. She only did one thing. She looked for Tate. She had even driven to some of the ranches, and flown briefly to one.

"But it's true, Sam. You have to face the truth now. You may never find him again. I hope like hell that you do, but you can't spend the rest of your life looking for a man who wants to be left alone. Because if you find him, you don't know that you'll be able to convince him that what you think is right and that he's wrong. He thinks that the two of you are too different. It could just be that he's right. And even if he isn't, if this is what he wants, you can't force him to change his mind."

"What brought this on? Have you been talking about it to Bill?"

"No more than I have to." Sam knew that he disapproved of her relentless search for Tate. He called it a "fool manhunt" and thought Sam was wrong to push. "The man said what he wanted to tell her when he left here, Caro. There's nothing more to say." But then once he had admitted that if he had done the same thing he hoped that she would have tried as hard to find him. "I just think you ought to face the possibilities, Sam. It's been a month and a half."

"So maybe it'll just take a little longer."

"And a little longer . . . and a little longer . . . and a little longer than that. And then what? You spend twenty years looking for a man you barely knew."

"Don't say that." Sam looked exhausted as she closed her eyes. She had never worked as hard on any job as she had on the search for Tate. "I knew him. I know him. Maybe in some ways I knew him too damn well, and that scared him off."

"It could have," Caroline agreed. "But the point is that you can't go on living like this. It'll destroy you."

"Why should it?" The bitterness in her voice was easy to read. "Nothing else has." John and Liz had had their baby the month before, a little girl, and they had even shown her and victorious Liz in the delivery room on the evening news. But Sam didn't care about that anymore either. All she wanted was to find Tate.

"You have to go back, Sam." Caroline sounded as stubborn as Sam herself.

"Why? Because I don't belong here?" She looked at Caroline angrily, but this time Caroline nodded at what she said.

"That's right. You don't. You belong back in your own world, at your desk, in your office, in your own apartment, with your own things, meeting new people and seeing old friends, being who you really are and not who you

235

pretended to be for a while. Sam"—she reached out and touched her hand—"I'm not tired of having you here. If it were up to me, you could stay forever. But it's not good for you, don't you see that?"

"I don't care. I just want to find him."

"But he doesn't want you to find him. If he did, he would let you know where he is. He must be taking care that you don't find him, Sam, and if that's true, then you've lost the battle. He could hide from you for years."

"So you think I should quit. Is that it?"

There was a long silence between them, and then Caroline nodded almost imperceptibly. "Yes."

"But it's only been six weeks." Tears flooded her eyes as she tried to combat the logic of what Caroline had said. "Maybe if I wait another month—"

"If you do, you won't have a job, and that won't do you any good either. Sam, you need to go back to a normal life."

"What's normal anymore?" She had almost forgotten. It had been a year since she had been "happily" married to John Taylor, since she had led a perfectly ordinary life as an advertising executive in Manhattan, married to a man she loved and whom she thought loved her.

"Normal?" She looked at Caroline in horror. "You must be kidding. I wouldn't know normal anymore if it introduced itself and bit me on the ass!" Caroline laughed at her bleak humor but the look in her eyes didn't waver, and at last Sam sat back in her chair with a long pensive sigh. "But what the hell am I going to do in New York?"

"Forget all this for a while. It'll do you good. You can always come back."

"I'd just be running away again if I left here."

"No, you'd be doing something healthy. This isn't a life for you here, not like this." It hadn't been since he left.

Sam nodded silently, left the table, and walked slowly back to her room. She placed the call to Harvey Maxwell two hours later and then she went out to the barn and saddled Black Beauty. She rode him for the first time in three weeks that afternoon, riding him headlong into the wind, at full gallop, taking every chance, every jump, every hedge, every stream. Had Caroline seen her, she would have feared for the horse's life, as well as that of her young friend. Had Tate seen her, he would have killed her.

But she was alone now, riding as fast and as hard as she could until she knew that the horse could go no more. She cantered him back to the main compound then and walked him slowly around the corral for half an hour. She knew that she owed that much to the animal, no matter how unhappy she was. And then, when she felt that she had sufficiently walked him and he was cooler, she led him back to his stall and took off the English saddle, stood looking at him for a long time, and then patted his flanks one last time with a whispered, "Good-bye, old friend."

19

The plane landed at Kennedy Airport on a glowing spring evening, and Samantha looked down at the city with a blank stare. All she could think of as she unfastened her seat belt was the last she had seen of Caroline at the airport, standing tall and proud next to the old foreman, with tears running down her cheeks as she waved good-bye. Bill had said almost nothing to her as she stood on tiptoe to kiss his cheek in the crowded terminal, and then suddenly he had squeezed her arm and growled fondly, "Go on back to New York, Sam, and take care now." It was his way of saying that he thought she

239

was doing the right thing. But was she? she wondered as she picked up her tote bag and moved into the aisle. Had she been right to come home so soon? Should she have stayed longer? Would Tate have turned up if she'd just waited another month or two? Of course he still might appear, or call from somewhere. Caroline had promised to continue to ask around, and of course if anyone heard from him, she had promised to call Sam. Other than that there was nothing anyone could do. Sam knew that much herself as she sighed deeply and stepped into the airport.

The crowd around her was almost overwhelming, the noise level, the bodies, the confusion. After five months on the ranch she had forgotten what it was like to deal with that many people, to move as quickly as they were moving. She felt totally devoured by the press of people around her as she made her way to the baggage-claim area, feeling like a tourist in her own town and looking appropriately bewildered. There was of course not a single available porter, there were hundreds of people waiting for taxis, and when she finally got one, she had to share it with two Japanese tourists and a plastics salesman from Detroit. When he asked her where she had come from, she was almost too tired to answer, but finally murmured something about California.

"You an actress?" He seemed intrigued as he looked her over, taking in the shining blond hair and the deep tan. But Sam was quick to shake her head as she looked absentmindedly out the window.

"No, a ranch hand."

"A ranch hand?" He stared at her in open disbelief and

240

she turned to look at him with a tired smile. "This your first time in the big city?" He looked hopeful but she shook her head and did whatever she could to discourage the conversation after that. The two Japanese tourists were chatting animatedly in their own language, and the driver spoke only in curses, darting between lanes of traffic. It was an appropriate reentry into her city, and as they crossed the bridge from Queens into Manhattan, she looked at the skyline and suddenly wanted to cry. She didn't want to see the Empire State Building and the U.N. and all the other buildings. She wanted to see the big house, the barn, the beautiful redwood trees, and that vast expanse of blue sky. "Pretty, isn't it?" The perspiring plastics salesman from Detroit moved closer, and Sam only shook her head and edged closer to the door next to where she sat.

"No, not really. Not after what I've seen lately." She eyed him angrily, as though her return to New York were all his fault. He eyed one of the Japanese girls after that, but she only giggled and went on chattering in Japanese with her friend.

Mercifully the driver dropped Sam off first, and she stood for a long moment on the sidewalk, staring at her house, suddenly afraid to go in, sorry she'd come home, and longing more painfully for Tate than she ever had. What in hell was she doing here in this strange town, all alone, surrounded by all these people, going back to the apartment she had lived in with John? All she wanted was to go back to California, to find Tate, to live and work on the ranch. Why couldn't she have that? Was it so much to ask? she wondered as she unlocked the front door and struggled up the stairs with her bags. No twelve-hour day in the saddle had exhausted her as this one had, with a five-hour plane trip, two meals, a movie, and the emotional shock of coming back to New York. Groaning under the weight of her bags, she dropped them next to her front door on the landing, hunted for her key, fitted it in the lock, and shoved open the front door. The place smelled like the inside of a vacuum cleaner as she stepped inside. It was all there, where she had left it, looking vacant and unloved, and different somehow, as though while she'd been gone all the furniture had subtly altered, shrunken or grown or only slightly changed color. Nothing looked exactly the same as it had. Yet it was, every bit of it, just as it had been when she and John had lived there. She felt like an intruder now, or a ghost returning to a scene from her past.

"Hello?" She wasn't even sure why she said it, but when no one answered, she closed the front door and sat down on a chair with a sigh, and then as she looked around, the sobs overtook her, her shoulders shook, and she dropped her face into her hands.

The phone rang insistently twenty minutes later, and she sniffed and blew her nose in a handkerchief and answered the phone, not even sure why she did. After all this time it was obviously going to be a wrong number, unless it was Harvey or Charlie. They were the only two people in New York who knew that she was coming back.

"Yes?"

"Sam?"

"No." She gave a half-smile through her tears. "It's a burglar."

"Burglars don't cry, silly." It was Charlie.

"Sure they do. There's no color TV here to rip off."

"Come on over to our place, I'll give you mine."

"I don't want it." And then slowly the tears began flowing again, she sniffed loudly and closed her eyes as she tried to catch her breath. "Sorry, Charlie. I guess I'm not exactly thrilled to be home."

"Sounds like it. So? Why'd you come back?" He sounded matter-of-fact as he said it.

"Are you crazy? You and Harvey have been threatening murder and mayhem for the last six weeks, and you want to know why I'm here?"

"Okay, so come help us out with your crazy client and then go back. For good, if that's what you want." Charlie's approach to life was always so damn practical.

"It's not that simple."

"Why not? Look, Sam, life is very short and can be very sweet if you let it. You're a big girl, you're free now, you should be able to live wherever you want to. If what you want is to run around with a bunch of horses for the rest of your life, then go do it."

"That simple, huh?"

"Sure. Why not? Tell you what, why don't you just try it out here for a while, kind of like a tourist, see how it feels to you after a couple of months, and if you're not happy . . . hell, Sam, you can always split."

"You make it all sound so easy."

"That's how it should be. In any case, pretty lady, welcome back. Even if you don't want to be here, we're happy as hell to have you around."

"Thanks, love. How's Mellie?"

"Fat, but pretty. The baby's due in another two months, and this one's a girl, I just know it."

"Sure, Charlie, sure. Haven't I heard that at least two other times?" She smiled at the phone and wiped the tears off her face. It was at least nice to be back in the same town with him again. "The truth of it is, Mr. Peterson, you only know how to make boy babies. It's all the basketball games you go to, something in the air there gets into your genes."

"All right, so maybe what I need to do more of in future is go to strip joints. That makes sense...." They chuckled together as Sam looked around her at the depressing apartment.

"I thought you were going to water my plants, Charlie." There was more laughter than reproach in her voice as she gazed at the long-gone wisps of brownish green.

"For five months? You must be kidding. I'll buy you new ones."

"Don't bother. I love you anyway. Tell me, by the way, how bad things really are in the office, now that you've got me home."

"Bad."

"Terrible-bad or just medium-bad?"

"Excruciatingly bad. Another two days and I'd have had an ulcer or killed Harvey. That son of a bitch has been driving me nuts for weeks. The client hasn't liked a single storyboard we've shown them, they think it all looks too prissy, too sissy, too clean."

"Didn't you use my horse theme?"

"Hell yes, we've seen every horsey model there is this

side of the Mississippi, auditioned every female jockey, every trainer, every—"

"No, no, for chrissake, Charlie. They're right if that's what you're doing. I meant *horses*. Cowboys. You know, macho, sunsets, as in riding into the sunset on a big beautiful stallion. . . ." As she said it her mind went instantly to Black Beauty and, of course, Tate. "That's what you need for those cars. You're not selling a little woman's car, you're selling a low-cost sports car, and they want to give an impression of power and speed."

"And you don't think a racehorse can do that?"

"Hell no." She sounded adamant, and at his end he grinned.

"I guess that's why this one's your baby."

"I'll take a look at what you've got tomorrow."

"See you then, kid."

"Give my love to Mellie, Charlie, and thanks for calling." She hung up and looked around again and sighed, whispering to herself, "Oh, Tate—why?"

Bit by bit she unpacked her suitcase, dusted things off, tidied up, looked around, and tried to convince herself that this was her home. At ten o'clock she was grateful to climb into bed with a notepad and some memos from Harvey. She wanted to get a head start on what she had to do the next day. It was after twelve o'clock when she set down the notepad, turned off the light, and tried to go to sleep. In the end it took her another two hours, as she lay thinking of the ranch and waiting to hear the familiar sounds that never came.

20

Samantha's return to the office the next morning felt, to her, like a strange trip backward in time toward a point that seemed totally foreign, her desk and her office and her colleagues suddenly seemed like part of another life. She could barely imagine a time when she had spent ten hours a day there, when the workings of Crane, Harper, and Laub had preoccupied her every waking hour. Now the problems they dealt with seemed so childish, the clients they talked about so foolish and tyrannical, the concepts and the presentations and the ideas all seemed like child's play to her. She couldn't somehow bring herself to be truly frightened that they might lose a client, to care if someone were going to be angry, or the meeting might go awry. She listened with a serious expression all morning and when it was over, she felt as though she had wasted her time. Only Harvey Maxwell, the creative director, seemed vaguely to sense her feelings and he looked at her sharply after everyone else had left the conference room on the twenty-fourth floor.

"Well, Sam, how does it feel?" He eyed her closely, his brows knit, his pipe in his hand.

"Strange." She had always tried to be honest with him.

"That's to be expected. You've been gone for a long time."

She nodded slowly. "Longer than I should have been maybe." She looked up at him, her eyes hooked into his. "It's hard to come back after such a long time. I feel—" She hesitated and then decided to say it. "As though I've left a big part of me there."

He sighed, nodded, and attempted to relight his pipe. "I feel that too. Any special reason?" His eyes sought hers. "Anything I ought to know about? You fall in love with a cowboy, Sam, and plan to go back?" But he was asking her more than she wanted to tell him, so she only shook her head.

"Not really."

"I'm not sure I like your answer, Sam." He put down his pipe. "It's a little vague."

But Sam spoke to him quietly. "I came back. You asked me to and I did, maybe that's all we both need to know for now. You let me go away at a time when I needed to do that desperately, much more than I realized at the time. And now you need me, so here I am. I'm here for as long as you need me. I won't run out on you, Harvey. I promise." She smiled but Harvey Maxwell did not.

"But you think you might go back, Sam?"

"Maybe. I don't know what will happen." And then with a small sigh she gathered up her things. "Why don't we just worry about our client right now? What do you think about my ranch themes for the commercials, a cowboy riding along in the twilight or at sunrise, with a herd of cattle behind him . . . a man mounted on a splendid horse, emerging from the landscape, yet at one with his surroundings—"

"Stop!" He held up a hand and grinned. "You'll make me buy the car. I like it. Work up some storyboards with Charlie and let's see if we can get this show on the road."

The storyboards she worked up over the next three weeks with Charlie were the best that any of them had ever seen. What they had on their hands was not only a series of powerful commercials, they had another award-winning campaign. As Sam sat back in her chair after the first client meeting, she looked happy and proud.

"Well, kiddo, you did it." Charlie threw his arms around her as they waited for Harvey to join them. He had walked the client out to the elevator while Sam and Charlie talked. "They loved it!"

"They should. Your artwork was stupendous, Charlie."

"My pleasure." He grinned and stroked his beard, and a moment later Harvey joined them, beaming for once and waving toward the boards set up around the room. There were four commercials they had presented, in the hopes of talking the client into one or two. The client had accepted all four.

"Well, children, did we make a successful presentation or did we make a successful presentation?" Harvey couldn't get the grin off his face and Samantha smiled back happily at him. It was one of the first times she had looked happy since she'd come back, but it felt good to be doing something constructive, and to have done it so well.

"When do we start?"

"They want to go into production on it immediately. How soon can you start, Sam? Do we have any locations lined up? Christ, you must know enough ranches to get things rolling. What about the one you've been living on for the last six months?"

"I'll call. But we're going to need three more. And I think"—she mused about it while gnawing her pencil— "I think we're going to want some entirely different locations. Each ranch should be different, special, set apart from the others. We don't just want repeats of the one we shot before."

"What are you suggesting?"

"The Northwest, the Southwest, the Midwest, California . . . maybe even Hawaii . . . Argentina?"

"Oh, Jesus. I knew it. Well, figure it all out and work it into the budget. We still have to get that past them, but I don't really think we'll have a problem with it. Just do me a favor, start finding locations. It sounds like this may take a little time. And call your friend out at your ranch. At least that will give us one. If we have to, we can start there." Sam nodded. She knew that this shoot, like countless others, was going to be entirely hers. Now that she was back, Harvey was already talking about retiring again, and she knew that he would leave all the location work to her.

"I may have to fly out and look at some places next week, Harvey. Sound okay to you?"

"That sounds fine." He left them then, still with a broad smile on his face, and Samantha and Charlie went back to their offices, Samantha to her white-on-white office with chrome and glass desk, beige leather couch and chairs, and lithographs all coordinated in the same white and beige. Charlie's office looked more like an artsy-crafty attic, cluttered and colorful and amusing, with odd-shaped boxes, huge plants, and funny signs. It looked exactly like an art director's office, one wall was white, one yellow, two were a deep heather blue, and the rug on the floor was dark brown. He had, of course, chosen his own decor. Sam's was part of the general scheme of the whole CHL office, all of it done in soft sand colors and cool textures with modern lines, and not a great deal of soul. But it was restful to work there. She never even saw the decor when she was working, and when she saw clients, she usually met them in one of the conference rooms, or at The Four Seasons for lunch.

She knew when she looked at her watch that it was the wrong time to call Caroline to ask if they could film there. At noon in California Caroline would be out in the hills with Bill and the other men. But she got out the list she had already glanced at that morning in anticipation and began to make phone calls to see what she could do. She knew damn well that she couldn't just pick up the phone and call ranches where she knew no one. She would have to fly out to the areas, then drive around and make her pitch to them in person, asking them if they would allow a commercial to be filmed on the ranch. It usually took weeks to find locations, but she was going to do it right, because she was going to produce the best damn commercials that anyone had ever seen. She was doing it as much for the client now as for herself. It meant a great deal to her to make everything perfect, to make it special and important and striking and effective—and maybe even to find Tate. That was a possibility that hadn't escaped her. It wasn't why she had pushed for the concept. The cowboy-on-horseback theme was perfect for the product, but it also could be that while she was traveling and looking for locations, and maybe even while she was out there again for the shooting, maybe then someone on one of the ranches might have heard of Tate. The prospect of finding him was a goal she never lost sight of, and now it loomed larger than ever as she called the travel department and asked them to book her on flights to Phoenix, Albuquerque, Omaha, and Denver, and all during the following week.

"Looking for a location?" the voice asked.

"Yeah." Sam was already deeply engrossed in the notes on her desk. She had a list of places she wanted to see, most of them concentrated in those four areas, and then of course there was Aunt Caro's ranch.

"Sounds like fun."

"It should be." And Sam's eyes began to dance.

21

The phone rang at the Lord ranch at six o'clock that evening as Sam sat in her apartment in a bathrobe, once again looking around at the lifeless decor. She decided as she waited for the phone to be answered that she was going to have to do something about the way the place looked, if she stayed there.

"Hello?" It was Caroline, and Sam immediately broke into a smile.

"Boy, it's good to hear your voice."

"Sam?" Caroline smiled in answer. "Are you all right?"

"I'm fine. I'm just working on a crazy project. And

aside from wanting to know how you all are, I wanted to ask you a favor, but you have to say no if that's what you want."

"First tell me how you are, and how it feels to be back." Samantha noticed that Caroline sounded tired, but she put it down to a long day's work and reported in full on her return, how grim the apartment looked, what it felt like to go back to the office, and then her voice came alive with excitement as she explained about the commercials and her search the following week for other ranches.

"And you know what that means, don't you?" Her voice fairly flew. "It means that maybe, just maybe, if I get lucky"—she barely dared to do more than whisper—"I could just find Tate. Hell, I'm going to be all over this country." For a moment, Caroline said nothing.

"Is that why you're doing it, Sam?" Caroline sounded sad for her. She wanted Sam just to forget him. It would be better for her in the end.

"No, it isn't." She withdrew a little. She had heard the dismay in the older woman's voice. "But it's why I'm so excited about it. This is a great opportunity for me."

"I'd say so professionally, in any case. This could be very important for you, if the commercials come out as well as you seem to think they will."

"I'm hoping they do, which is part of why I called. Aunt Caro, how would you feel about our shooting at the ranch?" It was a candid, open question but there was a moment of silence at the other end.

"Normally, Sam, I'd have loved it. If nothing else, it would give us an excuse to see you. But I'm afraid that

254

right now it's out of the question." There was a catch in her voice as she said it, and Sam frowned. "Is something wrong, Aunt Caro?"

"Yes." A little sob shook her, but she pulled herself together quickly. "No, really, I'm all right. Bill had a little heart attack last week. Nothing major. He's already back from the hospital, and the doctor says that it's nothing to be unduly alarmed about, but . . ." Suddenly fresh sobs shook her. "Oh, Sam, I thought if something happened . . . I don't know what I'd do. I couldn't live without him." It was the first time that they had faced that, and she was terrified now that she'd lose him. "I just couldn't go on if something happened to Bill." She sobbed softly into the phone.

"My God, why didn't you call me?" Samantha looked stunned.

"I don't know, it all happened so quickly. And I stayed at the hospital with him, and I've been awfully busy since he got home. He was only there for a week, and the doctor says it's nothing. . . ." She was repeating herself in her anxiety and Sam could feel tears sting her eyes too.

"Do you want me to come out there?"

"Don't be silly."

"I'm serious. I don't have to be here. They lived without me all winter, they can manage fine. Especially now that I've done all the groundwork for them, all they have to do is find the locations and then have a production house do the film. I could be out there tomorrow, Aunt Caro. Do you want me?"

"I always want you, darling." The older woman smiled

through her tears. "And I love you very much. But we're fine really. You take care of your commercials and I'll take care of Bill and he'll be fine. I just didn't think that right now the disruption—"

"Of course not. I'm sorry I asked you, but I'm not really. If I hadn't asked, I would never have known about Bill. You're a rat not to have called me! You're sure you can manage?"

"Positive. And if I need you, I'll call you."

"Promise?"

"Solemnly." Caroline smiled again.

And then Sam asked the next question gently. "Is he staying at the house?" She hoped so, it would be a lot easier for Aunt Caro, and a lot more agreeable for him.

But Caroline sighed and shook her head. "No, of course not. He's so stubborn, Sam. He's staying at his old cabin. Now I'm the one sneaking in and out all night long."

"That's ridiculous. Can't you pretend to put him up in the guest room? Hell, he's been the foreman there for almost thirty years, would that be so shocking?"

"He thinks so, and I'm not supposed to upset him so I let him have his way."

"Men!" Sam snorted as she said it and Caroline laughed.

"I completely agree."

"Well, give him my love and tell him to take it easy, and I'll call you in a few days to see how he is." And then just before she hung up, she called out to her old friend, "I love you, Aunt Caro."

"I love you too, Sam dear." And now they were bound in a common secret, the lives of women who loved ranch

256

hands, who had to live shackled by the insane rules of courtship peculiar to ranch hands and ranchers. And now that Caroline had almost lost her beloved foreman, she suddenly knew how great was Sam's pain.

22

For ten days Sam flew from the Midwest to the Southwest, and then up north again, and only Caroline's insistence that Bill was so much better kept her away from California as well. In each place she stopped she rented cars, stayed at small motels, drove hundreds of miles, and spoke to every conceivable rancher she could lay her hands on, and for her own purposes she spoke to the ranch hands as well. For the purposes of Crane, Harper, and Laub, at the end of ten days she had just what she needed, four splendid ranches, each one totally different, surrounded by varied but always majestic countryside. They were all settings that would make extravagantly beautiful commercials. But for her own purposes, again and again Sam struck out. And as she flew back to New York her sense of victory at having found what she had wanted was vastly outweighed by her depression over not finding Tate. She had called Caroline from her hotel room every evening, inquired about Bill, and then told her who she had talked to, what they had said, and pondered for another hundred times what might have happened to Tate, where he might have gone, which direction he might have taken. By now she had spoken to so many ranchers since he had vanished three months before that she felt certain that if someone found him, saw him, met him, or hired him they would surely drop her a note. She had left her card at all the ranches she had visited, and surely some of that effort would pay off. Maybe he was just taking time to visit relatives along the way and was headed for a specific destination. But again Caroline reminded her that he could be anywhere, on any ranch, and there was always the possibility that he would never surface in Sam's life again. She felt that, for Sam's sake, it had to be faced.

"I'll never give up completely," Sam had said stubbornly only the night before.

"No, but you can't spend the rest of your life waiting either." She didn't say it, but Sam had thought quickly "Why not?" Instead they had turned the conversation back to Bill and his health. Caroline thought he was much improved, but still weak.

And now, as the plane landed in New York, Sam thought of him again, and inevitably of Tate. She knew also that for the next month she would think of him every day, every moment, as she interviewed actor after actor after actor to play the role in the commercials. They had already agreed with the client that what they wanted was not four cowboys, but one man. One man who would embody all that was powerful and masculine and good and true and sexy in this country. And all Sam could think of was someone who looked like Tate.

In the ensuing weeks, as she spent hours meeting the actors sent over by the city's biggest modeling agencies, she compared them all to him. She wanted someone tall, broad shouldered, in his early forties, with a deep mellifluous voice, kind, with interesting eyes and strong hands, a good seat in the saddle . . . what she really wanted was Tate. It was as though each time her secretary announced another group of actors to audition, Sam went to meet them expecting to see him. What she saw instead were dazzling blondes with broad shoulders; tall, dark, handsome men; ex-football-players, and even an ex-hockey-goalie; men with rugged faces, deep-set eyes, and strong chins; but most of them seemed too plastic, some had bad voices, faces that were too pretty, one looked more like a ballet dancer than a cowboy. In the end, after four weeks of looking, she found her man, and it was a good thing. The shoot was only two weeks away, scheduled for July fifteenth.

The man they chose was actually English, but his Western accent was so perfect that no one would have known. For years he had been a Shakespearean actor at Stratford-on-Avon, and two years before he had decided to come to New York and start doing commercials, because he was tired of demanding roles with too little pay. Now he was advertising soft drinks, men's underwear, and a line of tools in national commercials that were paying him a handsome wage. He had shoulders from one side of the room to the other, a handsome angular face that was good-looking but not too pretty, deep blue eyes, and dark reddish-brown hair. He looked totally the part, and every man in America would want to identify with him and their wives would dream of the car being advertised, in the hopes that the cowboy in the commercial might somehow appear at the wheel. He was exactly what they needed for the commercial, and the only thing that amused Samantha, as she told Charlie, was that their new Western hero was decidedly gay.

"Does he look it?" Charlie looked worried.

"Hell no, he's an actor. And he is gorgeous!"

"Well, do yourself a favor, don't fall in love with him."

"I'll try not to." But the best part was that she liked him. His name was Henry Johns-Adams, and if nothing else he would be good company on the trip. He was extremely well-read, terribly polite, very cultured, and he seemed to have a good sense of humor as well. It would be a real relief from some of the self-centered, undisciplined egomaniacs she had had along on other shoots. "You coming west with us, Charlie?"

"I don't know, Sam. I hate to leave Mellie. If she has the baby by then, it'll be okay. If not, I may have to send two of my assistants. Can you manage?"

"If I have to." And then with a gentle smile, "How's she feeling?"

"Fat, exhausted, fed up, bitchy. But I love her anyway.

And it's almost over. The baby's due at the end of next week."

"What are you going to name him?" She hadn't gotten off his back about it being a boy again.

"Her. And you'll see. We're not telling what we're going to name her. It's a surprise this time."

"Come on, tell me, Charlie. Charlotte, if it's a girl?" She loved to tease him and he pinched her behind as he shook his head and disappeared.

As it turned out, Mellie had the baby that weekend, a week early for a change and a girl this time, finally. The surprise was that they named her Samantha. When Charlie told her in the office on Tuesday after the Fourth of July weekend, there were tears in Sam's eyes.

"Do you mean it?"

"Sure I do. Want to come see her?"

"Are you kidding? I'd love to. Mellie's not too tired?"

"Hell no. The fourth one's easy. It sounds disgusting but she walked out of the delivery room. Freaked me out, but the doctor said it was okay."

"It makes me nervous just hearing about it." Like all women who have never had children, Samantha was amazed by the entire process and the whole mystique.

They went to the hospital together at lunchtime, and Mellie looked happy and healthy and glowing in a lace-trimmed pink bathrobe, with pink satin slippers, a huge grin on her face, and the tiny pink and white baby nestled in her arms. For a long moment Sam said absolutely nothing. She just stood and stared at the delicate bundle, her eyes riveted to the baby's face.

"She's so beautiful, Mellie." Sam said it in a whisper, in

tones of awe, and Charlie chuckled from where he stood just behind her.

"Yeah. But we would have named her Samantha even if she'd been ugly." Sam turned around and made a face at him. It dispelled the enormity of the moment, and Sam's sudden longing for what she could never have, the miracle of childbirth and her own child. Lately she had seldom let her thoughts wander in that direction, but for the first time in a long time, as she stood there gazing down at the new baby, she felt her heart ache for the lost dream.

"Want to hold her?" Melinda looked lovelier than Sam had ever seen her. There was a kind of quiet glow that seemed to emanate from the very depths of her soul and at the same time envelop the baby as it lay precious and protected in its mother's arms.

"I don't think so." Sam shook her head and sat down on a corner of the bed, her eyes still riveted to the small child. "I'd be afraid to break her."

"They're tougher than they look." It was the claim of every mother. "Here . . . try it." Without warning, Melinda dropped the baby into Sam's arms and settled her there as they all watched the baby stretch, curl herself up again, and then smile. She was sound asleep as she lay there, and Sam could feel the baby's warmth in her arms.

"She's so tiny!"

"No, she's not!" Mellie laughed. "She weighs eight and a half pounds!"

But a moment later the brand-new Samantha discovered that she was hungry and awoke, looking for her mother, with a yowl. The elder Samantha returned her to the safety of Melinda, and a few minutes later she and Charlie went back to the office, as Samantha felt again how much was missing in her life. It was one of those times when the fact that she was sterile weighed on her like a boulder on her guts.

And then, as she stopped in the doorway of her office, she remembered and called out to Charlie. "Does this mean you're coming west with me?"

He nodded, smiling, "I would have had to anyway."

"How come?" She looked surprised.

"Just to be sure you don't rape our cowboy!"

"Not likely." She grinned at him and disappeared into her office. The agony of seeing the baby subsided slightly, though it didn't leave her completely for the rest of the day.

23

"Everybody ready?" Charlie looked at them with a broad grin, and then bowed at the entourage and waved them onto the airplane. They were traveling on a commercial airline to Arizona, but there were so many of them, it seemed as though they had bought out most of first class. There were seven people from the production company, and in addition Sam, Charlie, their two assistants, Henry Johns-Adams—the English actor—and his friend. To add to the mountain of luggage and equipment and miscellaneous crates and boxes. Henry and his roommate had brought along their dog, a tiny white poodle named Georgie, which Samantha prayed would not manage to dart underneath the feet of any horses. If it did, it was so little that it would probably be all over, and most likely so would the shoot.

In addition they were being met in Arizona by a makeup person and a hairdresser, both of whom had been workin in L.A. and would continue on with the group from Crane, Harper, and Laub for the rest of the trip.

"Think they got all our luggage?" Henry's friend whispered to Samantha nervously, and she convinced him that it was assuredly all on the plane. "But there's so much."

"They're used to it. Besides"—she smiled reassuringly—"this is first class." As though that made a difference, as though they wouldn't just as easily lose one of his matched Vuitton suitcases as they would one of the crew's pieces of Samsonite luggage or one of the zillion-dollar pieces of equipment. And once again she realized what a great deal of work she'd have on this journey. Having thought up the concept, almost completely written the ads herself, found the locations, cast the leading man, organized the troupes, selected the production house and approved their bid, what she was going to do now, for the next two weeks, in four different locations, was reassure everyone that they would be fed soon, it would only take a few more takes, the weather would be cooler tomorrow, the air conditioning in the hotel would be repaired by noon, and the food couldn't possibly be this bad in the next town. And having a nervous gay boyfriend and a French poodle along wouldn't help anything. On the other hand Henry Johns-Adams had already proven to be even tempered, amusing, and a good sport, and Sam was hopeful that he would keep both his lover and his pet in line. She didn't mind his being gay, but she was a little uptight about having him bring his little entourage. Nonetheless, he had insisted, and they wanted him badly enough to have brought his mother and fourteen of his dearest friends.

The drinks on the plane helped everyone's nerves and their spirits. Charlie was in grand form and entertained them all, and finally, half an hour out of Tucson, they all relaxed. They had no work to do that day. They were going to drive a hundred and fifty miles to their location, in three rented station wagons, with all the equipment, and then they'd all have a good dinner and a good night's sleep and get to work bright and early the next day. Sam's ranch hours were about to stand her in good stead, because she figured that she'd be up every morning by four thirty. And every night, for an hour or two after work, she had a plan. She had already made up the list of additional people she wanted to talk to, and after working on whichever ranch all day, she'd hang out with the ranch hands for a while and just chat. Maybe one of them had worked with Tate somewhere, maybe one of them would know a link—a relative, an old employer, someone who might know where he was by now. It was worth a try. Anything was. As the plane lowered its landing gear Samantha smiled to herself, feeling hopeful. You never knew, maybe one of these days she would walk onto a ranch, look up at a tall handsome cowboy leaning against a fence post, and it wouldn't be a stranger this time. It would be Tate, with those green eyes, and the gentle smile, and the mouth that she so loved. . . . Tate. . . .

"You okay, Sam?" Charlie had tapped her arm, and when she turned in surprise, he was looking at her strangely.

"Huh?" She still looked startled.

"I've been talking to you for about ten minutes."

"That's nice."

"I wanted to know who you want to drive the other two cars." She quickly brought her mind back to business and gave instructions, but it wasn't what she was thinking about as they landed and her eyes lingered on the horizon, wondering if by the next day, or the day after, she would have found him. . . . Tate, are you there? She wanted to whisper the words, but she knew that there would be no answer. There was no way of knowing. She just had to keep looking. But that was why she was here.

They were among the first off the plane, and she organized the group quickly, picking up the station wagons, assigning drivers, handing out maps, buying boxes of sandwiches for the trip, giving out vouchers for their motel in case they arrived separately from each other in the three cars. She had thought of everything, as she always did.

In the car she drove she had Charlie, the hairdresser, the makeup artist, the star, his boyfriend, the poodle, and all the Vuitton luggage. The equipment, the crew, and the assistants went in the two other cars.

"All set?" Charlie looked around behind him and then handed out cans of cold fruit juice. It was hotter than hell in Arizona, and they were all relieved to be in an air-conditioned car. Henry was in the process of telling funny stories about being on tour in England, the boyfriend had kept them all in stitches with tales of what it had been like to discover he was gay in Dubuque, the hairdresser and makeup girl had plenty of stories to tell about their recent trip to L.A. to coif and paint a noted rock star, and the trip went along pleasantly until they reached the hotel. Here, predictably, unfolded the first drama. The hotel owner didn't allow dogs, didn't think much of Henry's friend, looked with horror at the hairdresser's flaming-red hair with the little blue punk fringe across the front, and scowled horribly at "them ugly brown bags." Henry's friend almost caressed his beloved Vuitton and threatened to sleep in the car if he had to, but he was not leaving the dog. A hundred dollar bill, which would appear on the expense account as tips and miscellaneous, helped grease the way for Georgie to stay in the hideous turquoise vinyl splendor of the hotel too.

"You look beat, Sam." Charlie sprawled on a couch in her room and watched her pore over a sheet of notes on a clipboard. She looked up with a grin and threw a crumpled ball of paper that hit his left ear.

"You must be kidding. Me? Why would I look tired? I'm just dragging around the country with a bunch of eccentrics and a French poodle. Why should I be tired, Charlie?"

"I'm not tired." He looked virtuous and she made a face.

"No wonder. You never work."

"That's not my fault. I'm only the art director, here to

make sure that the film is artistically beautiful. It's not my
fault you're an ambitious bitch and you want to be C.D."
He had only been kidding, but suddenly Sam looked
serious as she sat down on the bed.

"Is that what you think, that I want to be C.D.?"

"No, my love." He smiled gently at her. "I don't really
think that's what you want. But I think it's what you'll get.
You're damn good at what you do. In fact, much as I hate
to admit it, sometimes you're brilliant. And Harvey
knows it, and the clients know it, and I know it, and everyone in the business knows it, and sooner or later you're
going to get yours. Either someone will hire you away at a
salary even you can't resist, or Harvey will retire, as he
keeps threatening to do, and you'll wind up the C.D."
Creative Director . . . it was an awesome thought.

"I don't think that's what I want. Not anymore."

"Then you better do something about it while you still
can, before it just comes at you and happens and it's too
late to stop it." And then, after he thought about it for a
moment, "What do you want, Sam?"

She looked at him for a long time and then sighed
softly, "Oh, Charlie, that's a long story."

"I had a feeling it would be." His eyes didn't waver
from hers. "There was someone in California, wasn't
there? On the ranch?" She nodded. "So what happened?"

"He left me."

"Oh, shit." And right after John too. No wonder she
had looked so rigid and unhappy when she had come
back. "For good?"

"I don't know. I'm still looking for him."

"Don't you know where he is?" She shook her head,

and he looked sad for her. "What are you going to do?"

"Keep looking." She said it with quiet determination and he nodded.

"Good girl. You're a strong lady, you know that, Sam?"

"I don't know, love." She smiled and sighed again. "Sometimes I have my doubts."

"Don't." He looked at her almost proudly. "I don't think there's anything you couldn't pull through. Remember that, kiddo, if the going ever gets too rough."

"Remind me."

"I will." They exchanged a warm smile and Sam was glad that he had come with her, he was the best friend she had, and it made the trip more fun to have him to joke with and laugh at and talk to, and behind all the clowning, there was a warm and intelligent man. It pleased her, too, to know that she had his respect and Harvey's. At first when she had come back from her months on the ranch, she had been aware that she was having to prove herself again, not only as assistant creative director, but as a person, as their friend. And now, in such a short time, she knew that she was back in the circle of their respect and affection. That meant a lot to her, and she stood up and went over to kiss Charlie on the cheek.

"You haven't told me anything about my namesake lately."

"She's great. Brushing her teeth, tap dancing, doing the laundry."

"Oh, shut up, you jerk. I'm serious. How is she?"

"Cute as a button. Girls sure are different from boys."

"You're very observant, dear. By the way, are you hungry yet? I'm starving, and we have to shepherd all our

little darlings to dinner at the taco joint down the street
or they're going to bitch and moan."

"That's what you're giving them for dinner? Tacos?"
He looked shocked. "I'm not sure little Mr. Vuitton will
like that, not to mention the poodle."

"Don't be nasty. Besides, in this town I doubt if there's
anything else to eat."

"Wonderful."

But as it turned out, they all had a marvelous time,
eating tacos, drinking beer, and telling jokes that got
increasingly raunchy as they got more and more relaxed
and more tired, and eventually the whole group went
back to the hotel and went to bed. Charlie waved a last
good night to Sam as he disappeared into his room, and
she spent another half hour going over her notes to
herself for the next day, and then, yawning, she turned off
the light.

24

It was six o'clock the next morning when they got together for breakfast. And seven thirty when they finally made it to the ranch. They had decided not to shoot a sunrise on the first day, but to settle for full day shots, and eventually try for a sunset. But it was almost noon by the time everything was set up to the film crew's satisfaction and they were fully rolling with Henry Johns-Adams riding a good-looking black mare, which made Samantha long for Caroline's Thoroughbred stallion. This was no Black Beauty Henry was riding, but she was a pretty horse and would look good on film. She had a pleasing gait as they cantered again and again over the same hills, filming take after take, but the horse was as even tempered as her rider, and by the end of the day everyone was tired, but there were no frayed tempers. They were a good group to work with, and Samantha was pleased with the way it was going. She went over to talk to the ranch foreman and thanked him for letting them film on the ranch. She had already sent flowers to the ranch owner's wife and a case of bourbon to her husband, in addition to what they were paying per day in order to film there. But now she handed the foreman several bottles too, and he looked pleased with the gift and chatted with her. He was even more impressed when he learned that she had spent most of the year working on a ranch in California, and for a little while they discussed ranch business and horseflesh and cattle, and Sam felt almost as though she had come home. After a while she happened to mention Tate Jordan, wondered if he'd met him, and said that there was a commercial she wanted to use him in, if he ever crossed the foreman's path. She described him as a fine man and someone she respected a great deal. Out of respect for Tate's sentiments about ranch people knowing about his relationship with her, she didn't let on about that. The foreman took her card and assured her that he'd be happy to let her know if he came across Tate, and after that she went back to the others and drove one of the bulging station wagons back to the hotel.

She struck out equally in her search for Tate at each stop of their trip in the next three weeks, although the filming of the commercials was going brilliantly. The production crew knew that they had gotten the most beautiful footage they'd ever had, and so far the entire shoot had gone off without a hitch. As a result spirits were soaring, friendships were cemented, humors were good, and everyone was willing to work endless hours in the hot sun and seldom complained. They had even managed to get two perfect sunrises on film and several sunsets. Only Sam seemed to be dragging by the time they got to their last stop. They were filming at a ranch in Steamboat Springs, Colorado, and Sam had just interviewed the last of the foremen and hung out for almost an hour with some of the ranch hands who had come by to watch them film. She knew now that if she found Tate it wouldn't be this time, and they were going home the next day, so once again her hopes had been dashed. She would go back to New York, and wait, and try again someday when she was near a ranch. And maybe, maybe, one day she would find him. Maybe. If.

As she stood looking at the mountains for a moment, she heard one of the men tell another that she had worked on the Lord Ranch in California. They knew of it, and the second cowboy looked her over with an appraising glance.

"Yeah?" She nodded. "I figured you knew horses, but I didn't know how. I saw you riding this morning. You got a good seat, good hands."

"Thank you." She smiled at him, but her sorrow had somehow crept into her eyes now. She looked tired and deflated and the man looked her over, wondering why she looked so down at the mouth.

"You see our new stallion?" he asked her, chewing on a

wad of tobacco. "Got him last week. He's out in the far barn."

"Could I see him?" Sam asked him the question more to be pleasant than because she had any real desire to see the stallion. She wanted to get back to the tiny motel where they were staying, wrap it all up, and get ready to go home the next day. For her, there was nothing left to stick around for. They had done the shoot, and she hadn't found Tate. But trying to look interested, she trudged after the old cowboy, and when she reached the barn beside him, she wasn't sorry she had come. What she saw in front of her was one of the biggest stallions she had ever seen, gray with a black mane and a black tail and a long white star on his forehead that seemed to make his eyes look even wilder as he pawed the ground. "My God, he's a beauty."

"Ain't he?" The ranch hand looked pleased. "He's a little devil to ride though. Gave everyone a toss or two yesterday." He grinned. "Even me."

Sam smiled. "I've spent plenty of time down on the ground too. But this boy is worth it." She ran a hand down his neck and he whinnied, as though he liked the feel of her hand on his flesh and he wanted more. He was so big and splendid an animal that just seeing him was almost a sensual experience. She told the ranch hand then about Black Beauty, about how she had ridden him and what a great ride he had been.

"Thoroughbred, eh?" She nodded. "Gray Devil here looks as fine to me. He runs like a racehorse, but he's a little too frisky for ranch work. I don't know but what Mr. Atkins may sell him after all. Damn shame too. He's a fine horse." And then, as though bestowing the ultimate gift on Samantha, he turned to her. "You want to ride him, miss? I warn you, you may land on your butt in the dirt, but I think you can handle him from what I seen you do today." She had ridden just off camera from Henry, urging him on at sunrise, almost angering him to make him seem less complacent and ride as hard as she wanted him to. In the process she had driven the horse she was riding as hard as he could be pushed, and Sam herself had accomplished the whole performance with obvious ease. She was a spectacular rider, and her precision and ability hadn't been wasted on the men who had watched her. They had talked about her over lunch, one of them had said that she looked like a little palomino filly, and it was a pleasure now to offer her Gray Devil, as he stood in his stall, waiting, as though he had been meant for her.

"Do you mean it?" She was awed by the offer, knowing that it was both a compliment and a gift. "May I ride him?" It was going to be her last ride for a long time. She was flying back to New York the next day, and there were no ranches in her immediate future. Only hard work at her desk in New York. "I'd love to."

"Go on. I'll get his saddle." He did so, and a moment later he had him saddled for Samantha, although he had to do it carefully so as not to get kicked. He had twice the devil in him that she had seen in Black Beauty, and he seemed to be almost bursting from his skin, aching to be allowed to run free. "He's a little fresh. Go easy with him in the beginning . . . Miss . . ." He hunted for her name.

"Sam." She smiled easily, suddenly anxious to get on the huge gray horse. He was even bigger than Black

Beauty, and suddenly it was as though she could sense Tate beside her, shouting at her as he had about Caro's black stallion, trying to force her to ride horses like Lady and Rusty. She grinned to herself. Hell, he had left her. She could ride anything she wanted to now. And as she thought of it the full pain of having lost him ripped through her once again; she took the leg up the old ranch hand gave her, pulled the reins taut, and let the huge gray stallion dance her around. She didn't let him get out of hand, and his two efforts to toss her were fruitless, much to the old man's delight.

Slowly she walked past the big barn, toward the old corral. By then several of the men had seen her, at first they watched with interest, and then they began to cheer as they saw how she controlled the prancing gray beast. As though everyone nearby suddenly sensed an intriguing performance, they turned to watch Samantha as she rode Gray Devil through the ranch's main compound, past her crew, and Charlie, and Henry and his friend and the poodle; and then sensing her own passion for horses and the countryside surge within her, she forgot them all and began cantering out into the fields beyond. She cantered for only a few moments and then she gave him what he wanted, letting him free to gallop at his own speed, racing until it felt as if he were flying, his hooves beating hard on the ground. As Sam rode Gray Devil she was smiling, with the wind on her face and her heart pounding as they rode along. Riding this horse was like waging a special kind of battle, against the horse's strength and his mind, with only her capabilities and her skill on her side. But she was an even match for Gray

Devil, and although several times he tried to throw her, he didn't succeed, and she felt all the tension and anguish and disappointment of not finding Tate well up within her, and she began to press Gray Devil forward, urging him to go even faster than he had before. She would beat him at his own game, if she could.

It was then that the crowd watching grew silent. Until then she had been a beautiful sight to see, her golden hair stretched out behind her, in sharp contrast to the black mane and tail of Gray Devil, as they flew across the fields. She moved as one with the giant stallion, her every muscle in tune with his. But now one of the ranch hands jumped off the fence to stop her, several others caught their breath, and the foreman shouted, as though she could hear him. But it was already too late. There was a hidden narrow stream out in the field she had just sailed into. It was narrow enough to jump with ease if she saw it, but it was also very deep, and if the horse stumbled, she would be thrown into a rocky ravine. The foreman was running now, waving wildly, and Charlie saw him and began to run too. It was as though both men knew what was coming, but at precisely that moment they saw her. The stallion stopped dead as he reached the stream he had seen before Sam did, and Samantha, unprepared, flew through the air with a wild, fearful grace, hair fanned out, arms extended, until she silently disappeared.

As Charlie saw it happen he ran for the station wagon, turned the key in the ignition, shoved it into gear, and surged forward—he didn't give a damn who he ran down. It was too far to run. He signaled wildly to the foreman, who hopped in, and they drove off with the tires screeching on the gravel and then bumping terribly as they crossed the fields. Charlie made horrible guttural sounds as he muttered to himself, praying all the way. "What's over there?" he asked the foreman, without taking his eyes off the field. He was going almost sixty, and Gray Devil had flashed past him only moments earlier, hell-bent on the barn.

"A ravine." The foreman looked tense as he answered, straining to see what was ahead. They could still see nothing and a moment later he shouted "Stop!" which Charlie did, and the foreman led the way through the grass, down a little incline to where Gray Devil had balked at the stream. At first they saw absolutely nothing, and then Charlie saw her, her white shirt almost torn from her body, her chest and her face and her hands lacerated almost beyond recognition, her hair fanned out around her, as she lay there broken, bleeding, and terribly, terribly still.

"Oh, my God . . . oh, my God . . ." Charlie began crying as he rushed toward her, but the foreman was already kneeling beside her, with two fingers pressed gently to the side of her neck.

"She's still alive. Get in the car, go back to the house, call for the sheriff, tell him to bring the helicopter out here right away. And if he can get one, bring a paramedic, or a doctor, or a nurse." The town of Steamboat Springs was not heavily endowed with medical personnel suited to the occasion. It was obvious from the position in which she lay, Sam had probably broken several bones, and possibly even her neck or her back. "Go on, man, get going!" he shouted at Charlie, who wiped his face on his sleeve and ran back to the car, shot back a little distance, turned around, and pounded on the accelerator, wondering frantically if Samantha would live. "Fucking horse," he was shouting to himself as he drove back to where the others waited tensely. And then he jumped out of the car and gave orders.

He went back to Sam then and knelt beside her, trying to hold her and stanch the flow of blood from the cuts on her face with a towel he'd found in the car. And when he got into the helicopter beside her twenty minutes later, his face was grim. The two assistants were left to wrap up with the others. They were all to meet him in the hospital in Denver later that night.

It seemed to take forever for the helicopter to reach Denver, and by the time it did, it was obvious that Samantha's life was in grave danger. A paramedic had traveled with them, and for the last ten minutes of the trip he had given her artificial respiration as Charlie had sat anxiously by. He was aching to ask the paramedic if he thought she would make it, but he was afraid, so he said nothing and just watched them and continued to pray. They set her down as gently as they could on the lawn of St. Mary's Hospital, having alerted all air traffic that they were coming through and coming down with a code blue. Charlie desperately searched his mind for what that meant, and thought he remembered that it meant someone was literally almost dead.

A doctor and three nurses were waiting on the lawn with a gurney, and she was rushed inside as soon as they landed, with Charlie left to follow as quickly as he could. He never thought to thank the young paramedic or the pilot, all he could think of was Samantha, so broken and so still. The only thing still recognizable about the long narrow form he saw draped in sheets a few minutes later was the tangled mass of golden palomino hair. It was then that he finally made himself say it, as two nurses stood by monitoring her vital signs while they prepared to take her to X ray and possibly surgery. They had already decided that the lacerations on her face were only superficial and could wait.

"Will she make it?" His voice was barely a croak in the brilliantly lit white hall.

"Excuse me?" His voice had been barely audible, and the nurse spoke to him without taking her eyes off of Sam.

"Will she make it?"

"I don't know." She spoke softly. "Are you the next of kin? Her husband?"

Charlie shook his head dumbly. "No, I'm—" And then he realized that maybe he should be. That if they thought he was family they'd tell him something more. "I'm her brother. She's my sister." He barely made sense as he stood there, feeling suddenly dizzy and sick as he realized that Sam might not live. She already looked as though she might be dead. But she was still breathing faintly, the nurse told him, and before she could say more, two residents, the doctor, and a whole flock of nurses in what looked like blue pajamas came to whisk Sam away. "Where is she going? Where is she . . . ?" No one listened and he just stood there, once again with tears coursing silently down his face. There was nothing they could tell him, they just didn't know.

It was an hour and a half later when they came back to find Charlie sitting frozen like a lost child in a waiting-room chair. He hadn't moved, he hadn't smoked, he hadn't even had a cup of coffee. He had just sat there, waiting, barely daring to breathe himself.

"Mr. Peterson?" Someone had taken his name when they had asked him to sign the admission forms. He had continued to claim that he was her brother, and he didn't give a damn if he lied, if it helped her, not that he was sure what difference it made.

"Yes?" He sprang to his feet. "How is she? Is she all right?" Suddenly he couldn't stop talking, but the doctor nodded very slowly and looked Charlie full in the face.

"She's alive. Barely."

"What is it? What happened?"

"To put it to you simply, Mr. Peterson, her back is broken. Her spine is fractured in two places. Bones are shattered. There's a hairline fracture in her neck, but we can work around that. The problem right now is her spine. There are so many small broken bones, we have to operate in order to take off some of the pressure. If we don't, there could be permanent damage to her brain."

"And if you do?" Charlie had instantly sensed that the sword had two edges.

"If we do, she may not live." The doctor sat down and indicated to Charlie to do the same. "The problem is that if we don't, I can almost guarantee you that she'll be a vegetable for the rest of her life, and probably a quadriplegic."

"What's that?"

"Entirely paralyzed. That means she'd have no control

of her arms and legs, but could possibly move her head."

"And if you do operate, that won't be the case?" Charlie
suddenly felt a desperate urge to throw up, but he fought
it. What in God's name were they discussing here, like
buying carrots and onions and apples, move her head or
her arms or her legs or . . . Jesus Christ!

The doctor was careful with his explanation. "She'll
certainly never walk again, Mr. Peterson, but if we do
operate, we might salvage the rest of her. At best she'll
wind up a paraplegic, with no use of the lower half of her
body. But if we're lucky, we can save her mind. She might
not be a vegetable if we go in now." He hesitated for an
interminable moment. "The risk is much greater though.
She's in bad shape, and we could lose her. I can't make you
any promises."

"All or nothing, isn't it?"

"More or less. In all fairness I should tell you even if we
do nothing for her, or if we do everything we can, she
might not live through the night. She's in very critical
condition." Charlie nodded slowly, suddenly understanding that it was his decision and feeling desperately
sorry that it was. He knew Sam had family still alive, but
he had gone this far, and besides, she was closer to him
than anybody. . . . Oh, poor sweet Sam.

"You want an answer from me, Doctor?"

The man in the white coat nodded. "I do."

"When?"

"Right now."

But how do I know you're any good, Charlie wanted to
ask him. What choice do you have? another voice asked.

Not to operate meant that Sam would die in effect, there would be nothing left but a lot of blond hair and a broken body, no mind, no heart, no soul—he choked at the thought. To operate meant they might kill her . . . but . . . if she lived, she'd still be Sam. In a wheelchair, but still Sam.

"Go ahead."

"Mr. Peterson?"

"Operate. Operate, dammit . . . operate!" Charlie was shouting and as the doctor hurried away, Charlie turned and began to pound the wall. It was when he stopped that he went to buy himself cigarettes and coffee and that he huddled in a corner, like a frightened animal, watching the clock. One hour . . . two hours . . . three . . . four . . . five . . . six . . . seven. . . . At two o'clock in the morning the doctor returned to find him wide-eyed and terrified and almost green with anguish as he waited, convinced that by now Sam must have died. She had died and no one had told him. And he had never been so frightened in his life. He had killed her with his lousy goddamn decision. He should have told the man not to operate, should have called her ex-husband, God, her mother. . . . He didn't even begin to think of the consequences of his decision. The doctor had wanted an answer. . . .

"Mr. Peterson?"

"Hmm?" He looked at the man as though he were in a trance.

"Mr. Peterson, your sister is all right." He gently touched his arm, and Charlie nodded. He nodded again, and then the tears came, and then suddenly he was clasping the doctor tightly in his arms.

"My God . . . my God . . ." was all he could whimper. "I thought she was dead. . . ."

"She's all right, Mr. Peterson. Now you should go home and get some rest." And then he remembered that they were all New Yorkers. "Do you have a place to stay?" Charlie shook his head and the doctor jotted the name of a hotel on a piece of paper. "Try that."

"What about Sam?"

"I can't tell you much. You know the stakes we were playing for. We reconnected as much as we could. Her neck will be fine. Her spine . . . well, you knew . . . she will be a paraplegic. I'm almost sure there was no brain damage, neither from the fall, nor from the pressure before we operated. But we just have to wait now. It was a very long operation." One could see that much on his face. "We'll just have to wait."

"How long?"

"We'll know a little more every day. If she makes it until tomorrow, we'll have much better odds."

Charlie looked at him then, realizing something. "If she . . . if she lives, how long will she be here? Before we can take her back to New York?"

"Ohh . . ." The doctor exhaled slowly, staring at the ground as he thought, and then looked back into Charlie's face. "That really is hard to say. I would say though that if she does exceptionally well we could move her in an air ambulance sometime in the next three or four months."

Three or four months? "And then?" He dared to say the words.

"It really is too soon to even think about all this," the doctor chided, "but you're looking at at least a year in the hospital, Mr. Peterson. If not more. She's going to have to make a lot of readjustments." Charlie shook his head slowly, only beginning to comprehend what lay in store for Sam. "But first, let's just get her through tonight." He left Charlie then, sitting alone in a corner of the waiting room, waiting for the others to arrive from Steamboat Springs.

They got there at three thirty in the morning, found Charlie asleep, hunched over with his head on his chest and snoring softly, and they woke him to hear the news. He told them what he knew, and there was sober silence among the others, and then quietly they left together to find a hotel. When they got there, Charlie sat staring in agony out the window at Denver, and it was only when Henry and his friend came to sit with him, that at last he let it all go, all the pain and the terror and the worry and the guilt and the confusion and the sorrow, and he sobbed for over an hour as Henry held him in his arms. And from that moment on, as they sat with him through the night and brought him solace, they were his friends. It was the darkest night that Charlie could ever remember, but when they called the hospital in the morning, it was Henry who dropped his face in his hands and cried. Samantha was still alive.

25

The day after Sam's accident the entire crew disbanded, but after several long phone conversations with Harvey, Charlie opted to stay. He didn't know how long he'd have to be there, and he couldn't leave Mellie alone with four kids forever, but right now he knew he wasn't leaving. She was alone in a strange city, and she was almost half dead. Harvey had been stunned when he had heard the news. It had been easy for Charlie to convince him to let him stay. But Harvey had also suggested that Charlie at least try to contact Sam's mother in Atlanta. She was, after all, Sam's only living relative, and she had a right to know that her only child was in intensive care in Denver with a broken back. But when Charlie called her, he discovered that she and her husband were on vacation for a month in Europe, so there was nothing more he could do. He knew anyway that Sam wasn't overly fond of her mother, thought her stepfather was a horse's ass, and her father had been dead for years. There was no one else to call. By then of course, though, he had called Mellie, and she had cried like a baby at the news. "Oh, poor Sam . . . oh, Charlie . . . how will she do it . . . in a wheelchair . . . and all alone . . . ?" They had cried for a few moments together, and then Charlie had gotten off the phone. He wanted to put another call in to Harvey, because he had wanted him to check on the doctor who did the operation, even though by now it was more than a little late. But he was relieved when he got back to Harvey. Harvey had called every bone man he knew in Boston, New York, and Chicago, he had even called a friend who was the chief orthopedic surgeon for the Mets.

"Thank God for your social connections, Harvey. Anyway, what did he say?"

"He says the guy's tops." Charlie let out a long sigh and a few minutes later he put down the phone. Now all he could do was go back to his waiting game. They let him see her for five minutes every hour. But there wasn't much he could do really. She hadn't regained consciousness yet, and she didn't all that day.

It was the next day around six o'clock in the evening, when he looked in on her for the eighth time that day. He expected only to stand there for a few minutes, as he had every hour on the hour since that morning, to watch her still, now bandaged face, and then, at the signal from the nurse, to close the door and walk away. But this time as he watched her he thought that something was different. The position of her arms had shifted slightly and her color looked better. As he stood there he began gently to run a hand down the long sun-streaked blond hair and softly say her name. He talked to her as though she could hear him, telling her that he was right there with her, that they all loved her, and that she'd be okay. And this time, before the nurse came to beckon him from her, Sam opened her eyes, saw Charlie, and whispered "Hi."

"What?" He looked astonished as he stood there, and his own word had sounded like an explosion in the highly monitored room. "What did you say?"

"I said hi." It was barely more than a whisper, and as she said it he wanted to give a war whoop of glee. Instead he bent low so that she could hear him and he whispered too.

"Hey, kiddo, you're doing great."

"Am I? . . . What . . . happened . . . ?" Her voice was fading and he didn't want to answer, but her eyes wouldn't let go of his.

"You kicked the hell out of some horse."

"Black Beauty?" She looked vague and groggy and he wondered if she was fading out again, but then the eyelids fluttered open. "No . . . now I remember . . . the gray stallion . . . there was a ditch . . . a river . . . something . . ." Something, all right. A something that had changed her whole life.

"Yeah. Anyway, it doesn't matter. That's all over."

"Why am I here?"

"So I can recover." They were still whispering, and he smiled at her and ever so gently took her hand. He had never been so happy to see her as he was right now.

"Can I go home?" She sounded sleepy and childlike as she closed her eyes again.

"Not just yet."

"When? Tomorrow?"

"We'll see." Tomorrow . . . it would be several hundred tomorrows, but Charlie couldn't bring himself to feel sorry. He was just so damn glad that she had made it. She was alive, and she was conscious—that had to be a good sign.

"You didn't call my mother, did you?" She eyed him suspiciously and he quickly shook his head.

"Of course not." He lied.

"Good. Her husband is an ass."

Charlie grinned at her, thrilled with the soft patter of conversation, and then the nurse appeared at the window and gave him the sign.

"I have to go now, Sam. But I'll come back tomorrow. Okay, babe?"

"Okay." She smiled sweetly at him, closed her eyes, and went back to sleep. And when Charlie went back to the hotel, he called Mellie and told her that Sam had regained consciousness at last.

"What does that mean?" She still sounded desperately worried, but he was buoyant with the news.

"I don't know, love. But right now it sure feels good. I thought . . . I thought maybe we had lost her."

Mellie nodded at her end. "So did I."

* * *

He stayed in Denver with her for another two weeks, and then both Mellie and Harvey started making noises about his coming home. He knew he had to, and he missed Mellie and the kids terribly, but he just hated to leave Sam. Still he knew he couldn't stay in Denver for another three months. But that night, as he tried to force himself to make a plane reservation for that weekend, he had an idea. And the next morning he waited for the doctor outside his office and nervously put forward his plan.

"What do you think, Doctor?"

"That it's very risky. Is it worth it? Why is it so important to take her back to New York?"

"Because she has her friends there. She has absolutely no one here."

"What about your parents? Couldn't they come out?" Charlie looked at the doctor blankly for a moment and then remembered that he was still masquerading as Sam's brother, and then shook his head.

"No. They're traveling in Europe, and I don't think that I'll be able to reach them for another month." By now he knew that if he had to reach her family Sam's stepfather's office could find him, but she had been adamant about it. She didn't want her mother called. "I just don't want to leave her alone out here, and I really should get back."

"I can understand that." The doctor looked pensive. "You know she would be in good hands."

"I know that." Charlie looked at him warmly. "But . . . right now . . . once she figures out what she's up against, Doctor, she's going to need everyone she's got."

He nodded slowly. "I can't argue with that. Right now she's really not in any danger, as long as we keep everything pretty constant for her and make sure she doesn't get pneumonia." That was still the greatest danger, and suspended on a great machine as she was in the giant plaster body cast—her "barbecue spit," as she called it—they turned her over, like a roast chicken, several times a day. But she still hadn't figured out the implications of what had happened, and the doctor didn't want to tell her until she was stronger. He felt that for the moment there was no need. "You do have a point, Peterson. Once she knows, and that day will come fairly soon, she's going to need all of you. I can't keep it from her forever. It's only been two weeks. But she's less groggy now, she's more alert, eventually she'll put two and two together, and when she figures out that she'll never walk again, it's going to be very traumatic for her. I'd like to have you here."

"Or her there. What do you think?"

"Can your firm charter a plane? Would they do it?"

"Yes." He had called Harvey that morning and Harvey had told him to spare no expense. "A nurse, a doctor, any kind of machinery you want. You run the show, we'll pay the bills."

"All right," the doctor said thoughtfully, "all right, if her condition stays stable for the next few days, I'll make the arrangements for you and we'll fly her to New York this weekend."

"You'll come too?" Charlie crossed his fingers and the

doctor nodded. "Hallelujah! Thank you, Doctor!" The doctor grinned, and Charlie hurried to tell Sam.

"You're going home, kid."

"I am? I can leave?" She looked both startled and thrilled. "But what about my barbecue? Won't they charge us a lot for excess baggage?" Although she was joking, he saw that she looked nervous at the prospect of leaving. She was beginning to understand just how much danger she had been in and that she wasn't totally out of the woods yet. The only thing she really didn't understand was about her legs. But she would. Charlie still cringed at the thought. As long as she was still in the cast, she wouldn't figure it out.

"No sweat—you should pardon the pun," he said, grinning. "We're taking the barbecue with us. Harvey says we can charter our own plane."

"But, Charlie, that's crazy. Can't they just set me up with crutches or something, or if worse comes to worst, stick me in a wheelchair with my stupid body cast and let me fly home on the plane?"

"Only if you want to give me heart failure. Look, Sam, the truth is you kicked the shit out of yourself, so now why take chances? Why not go home in style? I mean, if you're going to do it, baby, *do it!*"

"A chartered plane?" She looked hesitant but he nodded with a grin.

"Of course we'll have to see how you do in the next couple of days."

"I'll do fine. I want to get out of here." She smiled wanly at him. "I just want to go home to my own bed." He realized then with a jolt that by "home," she had understood her apartment, when all he had meant was New York. He mentioned it later to the doctor, who reassured him.

"I'm afraid you're going to see a lot of that, Mr. Peterson. The human mind is a wonderful thing. It only accepts what it can handle. The rest it just kind of puts away somewhere, until it can deal with it. Somewhere, deep in her psyche, she knows that she is still too sick to go home, but she's not ready yet to accept that. When she is, she will, you don't have to say anything. Not yet at least. We can discuss that little matter at the New York airport if we have to. But she'll deal with it when she's ready to, just like she'll deal with the fact that she can't walk anymore. One day all the information she already has will fall into place and she'll know."

Charlie exhaled softly. "How can you be so sure she'll understand?"

There was a moment's pause before the doctor answered. "She doesn't have any choice."

Charlie nodded slowly. "Do you think we'll be able to take her back there?"

"Sooner or later." The doctor answered calmly.

"I mean this weekend."

"We'll just have to see, won't we?" He smiled then and disappeared to make his rounds.

The next few days seemed to take forever, and Sam was suddenly impatient and nervous and jumpy too. She wanted to go home, but she was having problems. The body cast was chafing, she was coughing slightly, she had a rash on her arms from some of the medication, and her face itched terribly now that all the scabs were healing and dropping off.

"Christ, Charlie, I look like a goddamn monster!" She sounded irritated for the first time since she'd been there, and when he came into the room, he thought her eyes looked red.

"I don't think so. I think you look gorgeous. So what else is new?"

"Nothing." But she sounded sullen, and he watched her carefully as he toured casually around the room. She was no longer in intensive care, but had a small room, almost entirely swallowed up by the bed, and in the corner was a table covered with flowers, from Henry and his lover, Jack, the rest of the crew, another bunch from Harvey, and still more from Mellie and him.

"Want to hear some of the office dirt?"

"No." She lay in her cast and closed her eyes, and he watched her, praying that she wasn't getting sick. It seemed a long time before she opened them again. And when she did, she looked angry, and he saw that there were tears in her eyes again.

"What's up, babe? Come on, tell Papa." He sat down in a chair next to the bed and took her hand.

"The night nurse . . . the one with the funny red wig . . . " The tears slowly spilled over. "She said that when I go home . . . " Sam gulped down a sob and squeezed his hand, and as she did it Charlie was grateful that she could. "She said I'm not going home . . . that I'm just going to another hospital . . . in New York . . . oh, Charlie," she wailed like a small child, "is that true?" He looked at her, wanting to hug her, like one of his children, but there was no way to put one's arms around the huge plaster cast or her surrounding machine, all he could do was hold her hand and gently touch her face. He knew he had to tell her the truth.

"Yeah, babe, that's true."

"Oh, Charlie, I want to go home." She sobbed in anguish and then winced at the pain.

"Don't do that, silly, you'll hurt yourself, but it's all right to cry. Just keep it down." He tried to tease her, but inside he was sad at what was happening. For Sam, it was the beginning of a long, difficult road she had only just begun to travel. Her old life had ended in the flash of an instant, at the feet of a gray horse. "Come on, Sam, just getting back to New York would be a step in the right direction, wouldn't it?"

"I guess so."

"Sure it would."

"Yeah, but I want to go home. I don't want to go to a hospital."

"Well"—he grinned at her lopsidedly—"at least we know you're not crazy. But okay, so you have to go to a hospital for a while, so what? I'll be able to visit you, and Mellie and Harvey and whomever else you want. . . ."

"Not my mother!" Sam rolled her eyes and laughed through her tears. "Oh, shit, Charlie, why did this have to happen to me?" The smile faded, and the tears began in earnest again. For a long time he just sat there and held her hand, and then he said the only thing he knew to tell her.

"I love you, Sam. We all do. And we're right here with you."

"You're such a good friend, and I love you too." It made her cry more, but the nurse arrived then with her lunch.

"I hear you're leaving us, Miss Taylor. Is that true?"

"I'm trying to." She smiled at Charlie. "But I'll be back. Under my own steam next time, just to visit!"

"I sure hope so." The nurse smiled and left the room, as inwardly Charlie breathed a sigh of relief. For a moment he had been terrified that the nurse would give something away when Sam said "under my own steam."

"So," she looked at Charlie, sipping at some soup, "when are we going home?"

"Does Saturday suit you, or do you have other plans?" He grinned at her, immensely pleased. She was trying. Oh, God, she was trying.

"No, Saturday sounds okay to me." She was smiling as she looked at him, and he couldn't help thinking that the doctor had been right. When she was ready to know something, she would. He just wondered when she would be ready to face the rest. "Yeah, Saturday sounds just fine. What hospital am I going to, Charlie?"

"I don't know. Do you care?"

"Do I have a choice?"

"I'll find out."

"Try for Lenox Hill. It's in a nice neighborhood, and it's near the subway. That way everyone I want to see will be able to come visit." She smiled softly. "Maybe even Mellie." And then, "Do you think she could bring the baby?"

There were tears in Charlie's eyes when he nodded. "I'll sneak her in under my coat and tell them she's yours."

"She kind of is, you know. . . ." She looked embarrassed. "Kind of . . . after all, she's got my name." He bent over and kissed her forehead then, there was nothing more he could have said in answer without bursting into tears.

26

Charlie held his breath when the plane left the Denver airport on Saturday morning. They had Sam's orthopedic surgeon with them, as well as a young resident, two nurses, a life-support unit, and enough oxygen to blow them all the way to South America, but Samantha was slightly sedated, seemed very relaxed, and was excited to be going home. The doctor seemed pleased with her condition and had made all the necessary arrangements both at Lenox Hill Hospital and with an ambulance unit that would be waiting for them at the airport when they arrived. In addition they were getting special clearance all along their route and were making themselves known to air-traffic control from sector to sector. If Sam had suddenly needed help they couldn't provide in the air, they could have come down almost anywhere along the way at a moment's notice. Everything that could have been thought of had been, and all that remained now was to fly safely back to New York.

It was a brilliantly sunny day in August, and Sam did nothing but talk about going home. She was also slightly punchy from the sedative she'd been given, and she giggled a lot and made a number of jokes in poor taste, which everyone laughed at, except Charlie, who was a nervous wreck. Once again he felt the responsibility upon his shoulders, and he felt that if something went wrong now it would be his fault. He shouldn't have pushed, he had rushed them, he should have left her in Denver. The doctor found him halfway through the flight, staring out a rear window, and he gently touched his shoulder and spoke softly so Sam wouldn't hear in case she woke up. She had just gone to sleep.

"It's all right, Peterson. It's almost over. And she's doing fine. Just fine."

He turned to smile at the doctor. "She may make it, but what about me? I think I've aged twenty years in the last two weeks."

"It's a very trying experience, for the family as well." The craziest part was that he wasn't even family, but he was her friend. He would have done it for anyone, for his brother-in-law, for Harvey, for . . . Sam . . . he would have sat at Sam's bedside for another month if he had to.

PALOMINO

He felt so damn sorry for her. What in hell was her life going to be like now? And she had no one, no husband, no boyfriend, that damn cowboy she'd mentioned had run out on her and she didn't even know where he was. Who did she have to take care of her? No one. For the first time in a long time he found himself hating John Taylor again. If the bastard had stuck around, like a decent husband, she wouldn't be alone now. But she was. The bitch of it was that she was all alone. The doctor was watching him as he thought it out, and his hand pressed gently on Charlie's shoulder. "Don't overprotect her, Peterson. It would be a terrible mistake. When the time comes, she'll have to stand on her own, so to speak. She's not married, is she?"

Charlie shook his head. "No, not anymore. And that's what I was just thinking. It's going to be very rough."

"It will be for a while. But she'll get used to it. Others do. She can lead a full life. She can help herself, help others, she can go back to her job in time. Unless she's a tap dancer by profession, it shouldn't make that much difference, except psychologically. That's where the problems arise. But they won't let her leave Lenox Hill until she's ready, psychologically as well as physically. They'll teach her how to take care of herself, be independent. You'll see. She's a beautiful young woman, a strong one with a fine mind, there's no reason why she shouldn't adjust perfectly." And then after a moment he gave Charlie's shoulder one last squeeze and smiled. "You made the right decision . . . both times. It would have been a crime not to operate, to lose that spirit and that mind, and she should be in New York, surrounded by

305

friendly faces." Charlie turned to look at him then, with gratitude in his eyes.

"Thank you for saying that." The doctor said nothing. He only patted Charlie's shoulder and went back to take a look at Sam.

Two hours later they landed at Kennedy Airport. The transfer to the large ambulance unit went perfectly smoothly, and a life-support unit with three paramedics traveled alongside. Their lights were flashing but there were no sirens as they made their way along the highway at full speed. And half an hour later they reached Lenox Hill without a problem.

Sam was smiling up at Charlie as they made the last leg of the trip. "It's quicker this way, you know that, no baggage claim to hassle with and no cabs."

"Look, next time," Charlie said, grinning at her, "do me a favor. Hassle me a little with the baggage and let's take a cab."

She grinned up at him, but once they arrived at Lenox Hill, she was busy. It took them more than two hours to process her into the hospital and settle her comfortably in her own room. The doctor assisted with all the arrangements, then she met the new doctor who had been awaiting her arrival, thanks to Harvey once again. When it was all over she and Charlie and the doctor from Denver were all exhausted. The rest of the group had been dispensed with. They had all been paid before the trip and they would all be returning to Denver on the ambulance plane later that evening. The doctor was going to spend a few days in New York observing at Lenox Hill and would return to Denver by commercial jet.

"Think you'll be okay now, Sam?" Charlie looked at her with a tired smile as she accepted a shot and began almost instantly to drift off to sleep.

"Yeah, babe . . . sure . . . I'll be fine . . . give Mellie my love . . . and thank you. . . ." Five minutes later he was in the elevator with the doctor, and then he was in a cab, and ten minutes later he was on East Eighty-first Street with his arms tightly around his wife.

"Oh, baby . . . oh, baby . . ." He felt as though he had come back from a war zone, and suddenly he realized how desperately he had missed her and how exhausted he was. Sam's tragedy and Charlie's total responsibility for her had been an awesome weight to carry, and he hadn't let himself feel it until now, when suddenly all he wanted to do was make love to his wife. She had had the foresight to have hired a baby-sitter to be with the children, and after they all duly attacked their father, teased and played and ran him ragged, she shooed them off with the baby-sitter, closed the bedroom door, ran a bath for him, gave him a massage, and made love to him, before he smiled at her sleepily and fell asleep in their bed. She woke him up again two hours later, with dinner, champagne, and a little cake she had made for him that said I love you. Welcome home.

"Oh, Mellie, I love you so much."

"I love you too." And then, as they ate the cake, "Do you think we should call Sam?" But Charlie shook his head, he had given her all he had to give for a while. Just this once, just tonight, he wanted to be with Mellie. He didn't want to think of the horrible accident, of the gray horse that had haunted him in his sleep for three weeks, of Sam in her plaster cast or her "barbecue" or the fact that she would never walk again. He just wanted to be with his wife, and to make love to her, until he fell into her arms and passed out, which he did shortly after midnight, with a last sleepy yawn and a broad smile.

"Welcome home," she whispered to him softly as she kissed his neck and turned off the light.

27

"Mother, I'm fine really . . . don't be silly . . . there's no reason for you to come up . . . oh, for chrissake . . . yes, of course I'm still in a cast, but I'm fine here. No, I don't want to be moved to Atlanta. I just was moved here from Denver three weeks ago, that's enough . . . because this is my home, Mother. I don't know anyone in Atlanta. Yes, of course, I have you and George . . . Mother . . . now, Mother . . . please! I don't resent him. . . ." She rolled her eyes at Melinda as she walked into Sam's hospital room, and made a horrible face at the receiver, mouthing "My mother" to Melinda, who grinned. "Honestly, Mother, the doctor is wonderful, I like him . . . I know he's competent because he told me so and his mother loves him. Come on, Ma. Give me a break. I'm fine, I'll call you. You can call me. When I feel up to it, I'll come to Atlanta . . . I don't know when I can go home . . . but I'll tell you. I promise . . . no, Mother, I have to go now . . . the nurse is waiting . . . no, you can't talk to her . . . good-bye, Mother." She hung up then and groaned. "Hi, Mellie. Christ, what did I ever do to get saddled with my mother?"

"She's just worried about you, Sam."

"I know. But she drives me nuts. She wants to come up here to visit. With George, who wants to consult with my doctor, and turn the whole hospital upside down. Tell me what an ear, nose, and throat man from Georgia can possibly have to contribute to my broken back?" Mellie grinned at the thought. "How's life by you?"

"Okay. How are you?"

"Bored. I want to go home."

"What do they say?"

"Something inane about patience. How's my namesake?" She beamed at the mention of little Sam.

"Wonderful." Mellie smiled too. "She does more at two months than any of the boys did at four."

"It's the name," Sam assured her with a grin. "Just make sure she doesn't get into trouble with horses." Mellie didn't answer and Sam sighed. "I wish I knew how long I'll be stuck here." But Mellie suspected that she didn't really want to know. Charlie had told her that Sam would probably be in the hospital for a year.

She got visits from everyone including Harvey, who

sat nervously on the edge of his chair, fingering his hat, toying with his pipe, and staring nervously at Sam in her body cast lying helplessly on the bed.

"Don't look so uptight, for chrissake, Harvey. I won't bite you."

"Will you sign a document to that effect?"

"I'd be glad to." He smiled his rueful smile and she asked him when he was going to get smart and fire her.

"I can't, Sam. I'm saving you for my old age. Besides, I just saw the answer print of the first commercial from your great adventure out west. Sam"—he sounded almost breathless with admiration—"if you never do anything in your whole lifetime except lie there and eat chocolates, you can be proud of this."

"That good?" She sounded stunned. He was generally not lavish with praise. But she had heard from Charlie that morning that the stuff was damn good.

"It's better than that. It's superb. And they say the others will be better still. My dear, I'm in awe."

She looked at him for a long moment and then grinned at him. "I think I must be dying, for you to be talking like this."

"Hardly. We'll get it all put on tape for you eventually and bring it up here with a video machine for you to see it before we ever put it on the air. But I'm afraid after all this, Miss Samantha, I really am going to retire and make you C.D."

"Don't threaten me, Harvey." She glared at him. "I don't want your damn job, so you stay where you are, or I'll stay here."

"God forbid."

He came to see her once or twice a week, Charlie came to visit often at lunchtime, Henry Johns-Adams had already come to see her twice, bringing her a box of divine Godiva chocolates, and his friend had sent her a beautiful bed jacket from Bergdorf's, which she could hardly wait to wear when she got rid of her cumbersome cast. And Georgie, the French poodle, had sent her a get-well card and a book.

But a week later Sam got the visit to end all visits. Despite her protestations that she didn't want a visit from her mother, she arrived from Atlanta with her husband and did her best to turn the whole hospital upside down. She spent several hours trying to convince Samantha to sue her office, that if it weren't for them and their ridiculous commercials, she wouldn't have been on that trip, that it was obviously a dangerous assignment, that they didn't give a damn about her, and that her boss was undoubtedly some kind of a lunatic who didn't care two pins that she was now flat on her back. Her whole tack so enraged Samantha that she asked her to leave and then had to relent when her mother cried and insisted that Sam was a sadistic ingrate determined to break her mother's heart. On the whole it was an exhausting meeting, which left Samantha shaking and pale, but not nearly as upset as she was when her mother and George returned to see her the next day. They entered Sam's room with identical funereal expressions and it was clear that her mother had been crying, and once she sat down, she started again.

"Good God, Mother, what's the matter?" It made Sam nervous just to see them, and she was already upset. She had called Caroline Lord that morning to see how Bill was, and learned that he had had another heart attack, this one more serious than the first one. And chained to her bed in her body cast at Lenox Hill Hospital, she could do nothing to help Caro, and she suddenly felt useless and hemmed in. But Caro had been much more upset about the accident. She bit back the information about her own misfortune, thinking Caro had enough in her heart to carry around, but Charlie had obviously already told her. Caro was frantic with worry. Like all horsepeople, she knew the dangers involved but she nevertheless was in a state of shock over Sam. She made Sam promise that she would call again. And if not, she would call Sam herself when she had a free moment from Bill.

But now all thought of Aunt Caro was pushed from her mind as she faced her mother, who was, as always, elegantly dressed, in a blue linen suit and a white silk blouse. She wore neat little spectator pumps and three strands of pearls and pearl earrings, and although she was a little plump woman of sixty, she still had the same extravagantly beautiful hair as Sam. Hers was snow-white now, but once it had been as gold as Sam's. Her husband was tall and handsome and looked more like a naval captain than a doctor. He was barrel chested and florid, with a great shock of snowy white hair.

"Oh, Samantha . . ." her mother lamented as George held her hand and she sat back, almost inert, in the chair.

"For chrissake, what's wrong?" Samantha suddenly had an odd, creeping feeling, as though something terrible were about to happen to her, or maybe it already had.

"Oh, Samantha . . ."

"Jesus." If she could have, she'd have screamed, or maybe just tapped her feet. But her feet had only tingled and hung like dead meat since her body had been surrounded by what felt like cement. The nurses all told her that it was normal to feel that way in a body cast, and Sam had found that comforting. For a while there she had been worried that her legs were shot. "So what's up, guys?" She eyed them with irritation and hostility. She couldn't wait for them to go home. "Don't keep me in suspense." But her mother only cried more. It was her stepfather who eventually took the first step.

"Samantha, we have spoken at some length to your doctor this morning."

"Which one? I have four."

She felt like an irritable, sassy teen-ager as she watched them with suspicion. But she just wanted them to go away and leave her alone.

But her stepfather was a man of precision. "In fact we spoke to two of them. Dr. Wong and Dr. Josephs. They were both very informative and very kind." He looked at her with obvious pity, and his wife cast woeful eyes in his direction before she sobbed again and he went on.

"Did they say anything to bring all this hysteria on? Anything I should know?" She glanced at her mother in annoyance and then back at George.

"Yes, there is. And much as it pains us, we think it's time you knew. The doctors have simply been waiting until—until the right time. But now that we're here . . . " It sounded like the perfect beginning for a eulogy as he said it, and Samantha wanted to look around to see who was in the casket. He looked like an undertaker, not a sea captain, she decided and tried to fix her face politely as he went on. "Now that we're here, we feel it's time you knew."

"Knew what?"

"The truth." Suddenly, as he said it, a little alarm went off somewhere near Sam's heart. It was as if she knew. As if she had known all along, without knowing, as though she sensed exactly what they were going to say.

"Oh?" was all she said.

"Yes."

"The accident . . . well, Sam, it was a very grave injury you sustained when you fell. Your spinal column was severely fractured in two places. It was quite a miracle that you didn't die from the shock and those ruptures, and also that there was no brain damage, which of course they're sure now there wasn't."

"Gee, thanks. That's nice. But the rest?" Her heart pounded but her face gave nothing away.

"As you know, as for the rest, you weren't as lucky, or you wouldn't be here in that unfortunate cast." He sighed briefly but continued. "What you don't know, however, and we feel you should, as do your doctors, I might add—it really is time. What you don't know, Samantha, is that"—he hesitated for only a fraction of a second before lowering the boom—"you are now a paraplegic."

There was a moment's silence and she stared at him. "What exactly does that mean, George?"

"That you'll never walk again. You will retain the full use of your upper torso, your arms, shoulders, et cetera, but the real damage was done just at your waistline. One can see it perfectly on the X rays," he explained informatively with a professional air. "From that point on there's nothing. You may have some sensation, as I suppose you already do now, but that's all. You'll have no muscle control certainly, no ability to use your legs. You will of course have to use a wheelchair." And then he delivered the final shock. "But of course your mother and I decided this morning that you will come to live with us."

"No, I won't!" It was a shriek of panic, and both her mother and stepfather looked stunned.

"Of course you will, darling." Her mother stretched out a hand and Sam shrunk from it like a wounded animal, wanting desperately to run away. Her eyes were wild as she looked at them. They had no right to tell her this. It wasn't true . . . it couldn't be . . . no one else had told her . . . but she knew almost before she heard it that it was in fact the truth—and what she had been hiding from almost since the moment she'd gained consciousness in Denver. It was the one thing no one ever said. Except these two people. They had come here to tell her this, as though it were their mission, and she didn't want to hear anything that they had just said.

"I don't want to, Mother." She spoke through clenched teeth, but they refused to understand.

"But you can't take care of yourself anymore. You'll be as helpless as a baby." Her mother painted a picture that made Sam want to die.

"I won't! I won't, dammit . . . I'll kill myself first!" She was shrieking.

"Samantha! How dare you say such a thing!"

"I will if I want to, dammit. I will not be confined to

this life, to the life of a cripple. And I don't want to be as helpless as a baby, living in Atlanta with my parents at the age of thirty-one. How could this have happened to me, dammit . . . it can't have happened, I won't let it happen."

Her mother stood helplessly by as George put on his most professional bedside manner and attempted to soothe her but she just screamed louder, and her mother's eyes looked at her husband and implored him that they should go.

"Maybe we should come back and talk about this later. . . ." They edged slowly toward the door. "You need some time to yourself, Samantha, to adjust . . . we have plenty of time to discuss it, we're not leaving until tomorrow, and the doctors don't think you'll be leaving here anyway until May or June."

"What?" It was a final wail of pain.

"Samantha . . ." For an instant her mother looked as though she would approach her, and Sam could only snarl from the bed.

"Get out of here, for God's sake . . . please. . . ." She began to sob uncontrollably. "Just go. . . ." They did as she bid them, and suddenly she was alone in the empty room with the echo of their words. A nurse found her there half an hour later, sawing hopelessly at her wrists with the barely sharp edges of a plastic cup.

The damage she did was repaired with a few stitches, but the damage her mother and stepfather did took several months to heal.

28

"How's it going, kid?" Charlie shook the snow from his collar, took off his coat, and threw it on a chair. There was even snow in his beard and in his hair. "So?" He looked at her expectantly, and she shrugged.

"What do you expect? For me to sit in my chair wearing a pink tutu and do an arabesque for you when you walk in?"

"Ooohhhhh-eeee, charming today, aren't we?"

"Get fucked."

He looked at his watch with a pensive expression. "I'd like to, but Mellie has a PTA meeting, and actually I don't have time. I have a client meeting at two."

"Very amusing."

"That's more than I can say for you."

"Well, I'm not funny anymore. That's life. I'm thirty-one years old and I'm a cripple in a wheelchair. That is neither funny, nor amusing, nor cute."

"No, but it's not necessarily as pitiful as you'd like to make it either." He had seen her this way for three and a half months. Ever since her idiot stepfather had broken the news. She was out of the body cast now and wearing a brace and moving around in a wheelchair. But now came the hard part, the grueling months of physical therapy when she learned to live with her handicap, or not. "It doesn't have to be as lousy as this, Sam. You don't have to be a 'helpless cripple,' as your mother puts it."

"No? Why not? You going to make a miracle again and give me back the power over my legs?" She pounded on them as if they were old rubber.

"No, I can't do that, Sam." He spoke gently but firmly. "But you've got the power of your mind and your arms and your hands and"—he grinned for an instant—"the power of your mouth. You could do a lot with all of that, if you wanted to."

"Really? Like what?" Today he had come prepared.

"As it so happens, Miss Smartass, I brought you a present from Harvey today."

"One more box of chocolates from anyone and I'll scream." She sounded like a petulant child and not the Sam he knew. But there was still hope that she would adjust. The doctors said that in time she would very probably come around. It was a hell of a tough adjustment, for anyone, especially a beautiful, active young woman like Sam.

"He didn't send you chocolates, kiddo. He sent you work." For an instant he saw surprise in Sam's eyes.

"What do you mean, he sent me work?"

"Just that. We talked to your doctors yesterday and they said there's no reason why you can't do some of your work here. I brought you a dictating machine, some pens and paper, three files Harvey wants you to look over . . ." He was about to go on when Sam spun her chair away and almost snarled.

"Why the hell should I?"

But he decided that she had played the game for long enough. "Because you've been sitting here on your ass for long enough. Because you have a fine mind, and you could have died and you didn't, Sam, so don't waste what you got." He sounded angry and Sam was quieter when she spoke again.

"Why should I do anything for Harvey?"

"Why should he do anything for you? Why should he give you a five-month vacation because your husband left you, and then spare no expense to bring you home when you have an accident—I might remind you that you could still be sitting alone in Denver, if it weren't for Harvey— and then why should he give you unlimited sick leave and wait for you to come back?"

"Because I'm good at what I do, that's why!"

"Bitch!" It was the first time in months he had gotten angry at her and it felt good. "He needs your help, dammit. He's snowed under and so am I. Are you willing to pick yourself up again and stop feeling sorry for yourself, or aren't you?"

She was very quiet for a long moment, her back turned in her chair, her head bowed. "I haven't decided yet." She said it very softly and he smiled.

"I love you, Sam." And then she turned slowly to face him, and when she did, he saw that there were tears running slowly down her face.

"What the hell am I going to do, Charlie? Where am I going to live? And how? . . . Oh, Christ, I'm so afraid I'll end up with my mother in Atlanta. They call me every day to tell me what a helpless cripple I am now, and that's what I keep thinking . . . that I am. . . ."

"You're not. There's nothing helpless about you. You may have to make some changes in your life, but nothing as radical as Atlanta. Christ, you'd go nuts there." She nodded sadly, and he took her chin in his hand. "Mellie and I won't let that happen, even if you have to come and live with us."

"But I don't want to be helpless, Charlie. I want to take care of myself."

"So do it. Isn't that what they're teaching you here?"

She nodded slowly. "Yeah. But it takes forever."

"How long is forever? Six months? A year?"

"Something like that."

"Isn't it worth it, not to have to live in Atlanta?"

"Yes." She wiped her tears away with her fancy bed jacket. "For that, it would be worth five years."

"Then do it, learn what you've got to, and then come on back out in the world and do your thing, Sam. And meanwhile"—he smiled at her and glanced at his watch—"do me a favor and read those files and memos. For Harvey."

"Never mind 'for Harvey.' You're both full of shit. I know what you're doing, but I'll try it. Send him my love."

"He sent you his. He said he'd be up here tomorrow."

"Tell him not to forget my Mickey Spillanes."

She and Harvey were addicted to the detective books and Harvey kept shipping her copies of them to amuse herself with.

"Oh, Christ . . . you two." Charlie struggled back into his heavy overcoat, put on his galoshes, pulled up his collar, and waved at her from the door.

"So long, Santa Claus. Give my love to Mellie."

"Yes, ma'am." He saluted and disappeared, and for a long time she sat in her chair, staring at the files. It was almost Christmas again and she had been thinking of Tate all morning. Only a year before she had been on the Lord Ranch, and Tate had played Santa to the kids. It had been then that she had started to get to know him, then that it had all begun. It had been Christmas Day when he had taken her to the hidden cabin. Thinking about him made it all come alive again and she felt the familiar ache as she wondered again where he had gone.

She had talked to Caroline only that morning. Bill had had a small stroke after Thanksgiving, and in the past few months he had done nothing but go downhill. In the midst of the gloomy reports she hated to bother Caro with inquiries about Tate Jordan, but eventually she had anyway, and as always she had no news. Caroline herself was terribly depressed about the state of Bill's health. She had just hired a new foreman, a young man with a wife and three kids, and he seemed to be doing a good job. And as always she had encouraged Sam to push on. The physical therapy that Sam was enduring was the hardest work of her life and she wondered if it was worth it; strengthening her arms so that she could almost swing like a monkey, get herself in and out of her chair, in and out of bed, on and off the pot, anything she would need to do to live alone. If she would cooperate, the staff would train her to manage totally independently. She had resisted, balking at the help offered her—in her heart she felt it didn't really matter anyway—but now, now suddenly it seemed important to push on. Charlie was right. She had lived—that was reason enough to push on.

Christmas Day itself was a difficult holiday for her. Harvey Maxwell came by, and Charlie and Mellie and the kids. The nurse let them all in and she got to hold the baby, who was almost five months old now and prettier than ever. When they all left, she felt desperately alone. By the end of the afternoon she thought that she simply couldn't bear it, and out of sheer desperation she left her room and wheeled herself slowly down the hall. And then at the very end of the floor she found a little boy in a wheelchair like hers, sitting sadly by the window, staring out at the snow.

"Hi, my name's Sam." Her heart ached for him, and then he turned toward her. He couldn't have been more than six, and his eyes were filled with tears.

"I can't play in the snow anymore."

"Neither can I. What's your name?"

"Alex."

"What did you get for Christmas?"

"A cowboy hat and a holster. But I can't ride horses either."

She nodded slowly, and then suddenly she wondered. "Why not?"

He looked at her as though she were very stupid. "Because I'm in this wheelchair, dummy. I got hit by a car, riding my bike, and now I have to be in this thing forever." And then he looked at her curiously. "What about you?"

"I fell off a horse in Colorado."

"Yeah?" He looked at her with interest and she grinned.

"Yeah. And you know something, I bet I could still ride, and I'll bet you could too. I saw this article once in a magazine that showed people like us riding horses. I think they had special saddles, but they did it."

"Did they have special horses?" He looked enchanted at the idea and Sam smiled and shook her head.

"I don't think so. Just nice ones."

"Did a nice horse make you fall off?" He stared at her legs and then her face.

"No. He wasn't a nice horse. But I was pretty silly to ride him. He was a real mean horse, and I did a lot of stupid things when I was riding him."

"Like what?"

"Gallop all over the place and take a lot of chances." It was the first time she had been that honest with herself. It was also the first time she had talked about the accident, and she was surprised by how little it hurt. "Do you like horses, Alex?"

"I sure do. I went to the rodeo once."

"Did you? I used to work on a ranch."

"No, you didn't." He looked disgusted. "Girls don't work on ranches."

"Yes, they do. I did."

"Did you like it?" He still looked doubtful.

"I loved it."

"Then why did you stop?"

"Because I came back to New York."

"How come?"

"I missed my friends."

"Oh. You got kids?"

"Nope." She felt a small twinge as she said it, thinking longingly of little baby Sam. "Do you have kids, Alex?" She grinned at him and he guffawed.

"Of course not. You're silly. Is your name really Sam?"

"Yup. It's really Samantha. My friends call me Sam."

"Mine is Alexander. But only my mom calls me that."

"Want to go for a ride?" She was feeling restless and he was as good a companion as any.

"Now?"

"Sure. Why not? You expecting a visitor?"

"No." He looked momentarily sad again. "They just went home. I was watching them leave from the window."

"Okay, then why don't you and I take a little tour?" She grinned mischievously at him, gave him a push to start him, and told the nurse at the desk that she was taking Alex for a ride, and the entire nurses' station waved good-bye as they headed for the elevators and from there to the gift shop on the main floor. Sam bought him a lollipop and two candy bars, and some magazines for herself. Then they decided to buy some bubble gum too and they came back to their floor, blowing bubbles and playing guessing games.

"Wanna come see my room?"

"Sure." He had a tiny Christmas tree covered with little Snoopy decorations, and the walls were pasted with pictures and cards from his friends at school.

"I'm gonna go back too. My doctor says I don't have to go to a special school. If I do my therapy, I can be just like everyone else, almost."

"That's what my doctor says too."

"Do you go to school?" He looked intrigued, and she laughed.

"No. I work."

"What do you do?"

"I work at an advertising agency, we make commercials."

"You mean like to sell kids junk on TV? My mom says that the people who write them are ireessperonss . . . susperonsible, or something like that."

"Irresponsible. Actually I write commercials to sell junk to grown-ups mostly, like cars, or pianos, or lipstick, or stuff to make you smell good."

"Yuck."

"Yeah, well . . . maybe one day I'll go back to working on a ranch." He nodded wisely. It sounded sensible to him.

"You married, Sam?"

"Nope."

"How come?"

"No one wants me, I guess." She was teasing but he nodded seriously. "You married, Alex?"

"No." He grinned. "But I've got two girl friends."

"Two . . . ?" And the conversation went on for hours. They shared dinner that night and Sam came back to kiss him good night and tell him a story, and when she went back to her room, she smiled peacefully to herself and attacked a stack of work.

29

Alex left the hospital in April. He went home with his mom and dad, and then back to school. He sent Sam a letter every week, telling her that he was just like the other kids again, he even went to a special baseball game every Sunday with his dad, and a bunch of other kids in wheelchairs. He dictated the letters to his mother and Sam saved them all in a special file. She sent him letters too, and bubble gum, and pictures of horses, and anything she found in the gift shop that looked like something he'd like. Their connection somehow made Sam feel stronger. More like pushing on. But the testing time for Sam came at the end of the month, when her doctor brought up the question of going home.

"Well, what do you think? Think you're ready?" She panicked at the thought and shook her head.

"Not yet."

"Why not?"

"I don't know . . . I'm not sure I can manage. . . . I'm not . . . my arms aren't strong enough. . . ." Suddenly she had a thousand excuses, but that the doctor knew was normal. She felt safe in her cocoon, and she no longer wanted to leave. Doctor Nolan knew that when the time came they would have to push her gently, and she would resist them every inch of the way.

Indeed she had a comfortable routine all worked out for herself. Three hours of P.T. every morning, three hours of paperwork from her office every afternoon. The ads, which had won her seven new awards, and among them the much coveted Clio, had long since aired, and she was adding to the campaign with new concepts. Henry Johns-Adams and his friend and Charlie were about to head west to shoot two more ads.

One night Sam called Caroline to try one more time to use the ranch—thinking it would take Caroline's mind off Bill—but she was in for a terrible shock. Caroline picked up the phone, and when she heard Sam's voice, she broke down and sobbed deep racking sobs from the depths of her soul. "Oh, Sam . . . my God . . . he's gone . . . he's gone." Sam didn't know what to say—indeed what could she say—she simply kept in touch and tried to cheer her up. Now, a few months later, Caroline was still absolutely lost without him, and it killed Sam to hear her so bereft and so broken, her spirit spent, her soul torn, without the man she had loved for so long. It was Sam now who gave her the strength to continue, who encouraged her.

"But I have no one left, Sam. I have no reason to go on. All of my family is gone . . . and now Bill. . . ."

"You still have the ranch, and me, and there are so many people who care about you."

"I don't know, Sam." She sounded so tired. "I feel like my life is over. I don't even want to ride with the men anymore. I just let the new foreman handle everything for me. It doesn't mean anything without Bill, and"— Sam could hear the tears in her voice—"it all makes me so sad." She had had him buried on the ranch, and there had been a memorial service. He had had his way to the end. He had died as the foreman of the Lord Ranch, and not her husband, though it really didn't matter anymore. Whether people had guessed or not, they had respected both of them, and his loss was felt by many who sympathized with Caro for losing a good friend, even if they didn't know he'd been her man.

There was of course still no news of Tate Jordan. Sam didn't even ask anymore. She knew that Caro would have told her. All of those people she had contacted, all of those ranches she had driven to, and all of the ranch hands and ranchers she had talked to on her trips, and none of them had seen him, no one knew him. She wondered where he had gone, and if he was happy, if he remembered as she did. Now there was really no point in finding him. She had nothing left to give him. Now she wouldn't have let him stay with her. It would have been

Sam who would have run away. But she didn't have to. He had already been gone for a year.

It was spring when they finally pushed her gently from the nest, despite her mother's protests. Her doctor released her from the hospital on the first of May, on a splendid warm sunny day, and she went to see her apartment for the first time. She had had to rely once more on Charlie and Mellie, she had had to call movers and have everything packed up in her old place. With the stairs in her old apartment, she knew that there was no way she could manage entirely alone, and miraculously an apartment had turned up in Melinda and Charlie's building. It was a ground-floor apartment with a small sunny garden, and it was going to be perfect for Samantha because it had no stairs, an easy access, and a doorman. It was just exactly what the doctor ordered, and Samantha had instructed the movers to put the furniture as per the diagram she had drawn up for them and just to leave the crates of her belongings for her to unpack herself. It was going to be her first challenge after she left the hospital, and it was a big one.

She huffed and she puffed and she attacked the boxes and she sweated, and once she even fell out of her chair trying to hang a small painting on the wall. But she got up, she hung it up, she unpacked the crates, she made her bed, she washed her hair, she did all the things they had taught her. She felt so victorious by Monday morning that when she showed up at the office in a black skirt and a black turtleneck sweater, with fashionable black suede boots and a red bow in her hair, she looked younger and healthier than she had all that terrible year. When her mother called at noon to lament her daughter's fate, Sam was busy in a meeting. After that she went to lunch at Lutèce with Charlie and Harvey to celebrate her return, and by the end of the week she had seen her first client, and she had handled it with grace as well as ease. It intrigued her to see that men still looked at her like she was attractive, and even her terror that it was pity that motivated the looks couldn't dim the pleasure of knowing that even if she wasn't a functioning woman her femininity still existed. The question of dating was one she had refused to discuss with the psychiatrist at the hospital. She considered that a closed door, and for the time being they had left it alone and worked on the rest. She had made such progress in every other area that they figured sooner or later she would come around. She was after all only thirty-one, and incredibly pretty. It was unlikely that a woman like Sam Taylor would spend the rest of her life alone, no matter what she said now.

"Well." Harvey, wearing one of his rare smiles, lifted a glass of champagne. "I propose a toast to Samantha. May you live another hundred years, without taking a single day off from CHL. Thank you." He bowed and the three of them chuckled, and then Sam toasted them. By the end of the lunch they were half drunk and Sam was making bad jokes about not being able to drive her chair. She ran into two pedestrians on the way back to the office, and Charlie took over and pushed her, plowing her cheerfully into a policeman, who was almost brought to his knees.

"Charlie, for chrissake! Watch where you're going!"

"I was . . . I think he's drunk. Disgusting too, an officer on duty!"

The three of them laughed like kids, and had trouble sobering up when they got back to the office. Eventually they all gave up and left early. It had been a very big day.

That Saturday Sam took her little friend Alex to lunch, the two of them sunning in their chairs. They had hot dogs and French fries and she took him to a movie. They sat side by side in the aisle at Radio City, and his eyes were huge as he watched the show. When she took him home at the end of the day, she felt a little tug at her heart to give him back to his mother, and she took refuge at Mellie's apartment on the way home, where she played with the baby. Suddenly, as Sam rolled her wheelchair carefully and slowly across the room, little Sam stood up, and on tiptoe, with arms flailing, little Sam followed her, as "Big Sam," as they called her in the baby's presence, sat in her wheelchair and gaped. And then, as the child fell cooing to the rug, Sam shouted for Mellie, who arrived just in time to see the baby do the same stunt again, and she was only ten months old.

"She's walking!" Mellie shouted to no one in particular, "She's walking . . . Charlie! Sam's walking. . . ." He arrived in the doorway with an expression of shock, not having understood that it was the baby, and then Sam looked at him in astonishment with tears rolling down her face, and then she smiled and held out her arms to the laughing baby.

"Oh, yes, she is!"

30

Crane, Harper, and Laub won a Clio again that year for another of Sam's commercials, and by year's end, she had brought in two more major accounts. Her mother's premonitions of doom had not come to pass. Instead she was working harder than ever, managing her apartment with ease, seeing a few friends, and having occasional Saturday-afternoon movie dates with now seven-year-old Alex. On the whole Sam was happy with her life. She was glad she had lived—glad she had survived. Still, she wasn't entirely sure where it was all going. Harvey was still the creative director and still threatening to retire, but Sam never believed him until the first of November, when he called her into his office and pointed absentmindedly to a chair.

"Sit down, Sam."

"Thank you, Harvey, I am." She grinned at him with amusement and he looked momentarily flustered and then laughed.

"Don't make me nervous, dammit, Sam, I have something to tell you . . . no, ask you. . . ."

"You want to propose after all these years?" It was a standing joke between them. He had been happily married for the last thirty-two years.

"No, dammit, I'm not kidding around today. Sam"—he stared at her almost fiercely—"I'm going to do it. I'm going to retire on the first of the year."

"When did that hit you, Harvey? This morning?" She was still smiling. She never took his retirement threats seriously anymore, and she was perfectly happy with her job the way it was. Her salary had escalated satisfactorily over the years, and CHL had given her so much in terms of kindness and understanding during her various problems and illness that she felt an unseverable loyalty to them anyway. She didn't need Harvey's job. "Why don't you just relax and take a nice vacation with Maggie this Christmas, someplace warm, like the Caribbean. And then come back like a big kid, roll up your sleeves, and get back to work."

"I don't want to." He suddenly sounded like a belligerent child. "You know what, Sam? I'm fifty-nine years old, and all of a sudden I wonder what I'm doing. Who gives a damn about commercials? Who remembers anything we do by next year? And I'm missing the last of my best years with Maggie, sitting at this desk, working my ass off. I don't want to do that anymore. I want to go home, Sam, before it's too late. Before I miss my chance, before she gets sick, or I do, or one of us dies. I never thought that way before, but I'll be sixty years old next Tuesday and I just figured, screw it. I'm going to retire now, and you can't talk me out of it, because I won't let you. So what I called you in here to ask you was, do you want my job, Sam, because if you do, you can have it. In fact my asking you is only a formality, because whether you want it or not, it's yours."

She sat there, awed, for a moment, not sure what she should say. "Harvey, that was quite a speech."

"I meant every bit of it."

"Well, in a funny way I think you're right." She had spent months thinking about Bill King and Aunt Caro, and she wondered if they had enjoyed every moment they could, right until the end. They had been so busy hiding what they were doing for so many years that they had missed a lot of times together that they might otherwise have shared. To Sam, it seemed like a hell of a waste of energy they could have better spent together, but it was all in the past now. What concerned her more was Caro, who had been in such awful shape in the eight months since he had died. She had been in what Sam considered a deep depression for several months, and she wanted to go out and see her, but the one thing she hadn't tackled yet was traveling. She was comfortable on home turf now and knew she could manage, but leaving home to go any great distance still scared her. She hadn't been to Atlanta either, and knew she probably never would. But a visit to Aunt Caro would have been different. She just hadn't taken matters in hand and gotten organized to go. She was thinking vaguely about Christmas, but that wasn't sure. She had funny feelings about going back there at Christmastime and facing all her memories of Tate.

"Well, Sam, do you want to be C.D.?" It was a direct question that required a direct answer, and Sam looked at him with a small hesitant smile.

"You know, the funny thing is that I don't know. I like working for you, Harvey, and I used to think that being creative director was the end of the rainbow. But the truth is, in the last year or two my life has changed so much, so have my values, and I'm not sure I want everything that goes with it: the sleepless nights, the headaches, the ulcers, especially now. The other thing I'm concerned with is that the C.D. should really travel, and I'm just not comfortable doing that yet. I don't feel safe about it, that's why I haven't flown out to see my friend in California. I don't know, Harvey, maybe I'm not the right person anymore for the job. What about Charlie?"

"He's the art director, Sam. You know yourself how unusual it is for an art director to become C.D. It's a separate issue."

"Maybe. But he could do it and he'd be good."

"So would you. Will you think about it?"

"Of course I will. You're really serious though this time, aren't you?" She was as surprised by his decision as by her own hesitation to accept. But she wasn't sure anymore if that was what she wanted, and however well she was managing life from her wheelchair, she just wasn't sure if she had enough mobility for the job. "How soon do you want to know?"

"In a couple of weeks." She nodded and they chatted for a few moments before she left his office, and when she did, she had every intention of giving Harvey an answer at the end of two weeks time. But ten days later, life threw her a curveball, and she felt as though the sky had fallen in on her. She had felt like that fairly often in the last two years.

She sat in her office with the letter she had just gotten from Caroline's lawyer, and with tears running slowly down her face, she wheeled across the hall to Charlie's office and stopped in the doorway with a look of shock on her face.

"Something wrong?" He stopped what he was doing and came instantly toward her. It was a stupid question. She was white-faced and she nodded and continued into the room, holding out the letter, which he took and read, and then he stared at her with the same look of amazement on his face. "Did you know?"

She was crying softly now as she shook her head and then answered. "I never even thought of it . . . but I guess there's no one else." And then suddenly she flung out her arms to him, and he held her. "Oh, Charlie, she's gone. What am I going to do?"

"It's all right, Sam. It's all right." But he was as stunned as Samantha. Caroline Lord had died the previous weekend. For an instant Sam was hurt that no one had called her—where was Josh, why hadn't he let her know?

But the moment passed. They were drifters, it wouldn't have occurred to them to call her in New York.

In accordance with Caroline's will, the ranch had been left to Sam. She had died in her sleep, without pain or problem. And Charlie suspected, as Sam did, that she just willed it to happen. She hadn't wanted to live without Bill King.

Samantha wheeled slowly away from Charlie then and went to stare out the window. "Why would she leave me the ranch, Charlie? What the hell am I going to do with it? I can't do anything with it now." Her voice trailed off as she thought of the happy times she had spent there, with her friend Barbara, with Caroline and Bill, and with Tate. She thought of the secret cabin, of Black Beauty, of Josh, and the tears only flowed more swiftly down her face.

"What do you mean you can't do anything with it?" Charlie's voice questioned her, as did his eyes when she turned to face him again.

"Because however much I may not like to admit it, however much I may try to pretend I'm normal with my job and my friends and my living alone and my taking cabs, the fact is, Charlie, as my dear mother says, I'm a cripple. What the hell would I do with a ranch? Watch them ride the horses? A ranch is for healthy people, Charlie."

"You're as healthy as you allow yourself to be. The horse has four legs, Sam. You don't need any. Let him do the walking. It has a lot more style than your chair."

"You're not funny." She sounded angry as she said it, and she spun around and left the room.

But five minutes later he had followed her to her office, and he wanted to discuss it, no matter how angry she got, how loud she screamed.

"Leave me alone, dammit! A woman I loved a great deal just died and you want to bug me about how I should go out there and ride horses. Leave me alone!" She screamed the words at him but it didn't convince him.

"No, as a matter of fact I won't. Because I think the truth is that although it's damn sad that she died, she just gave you the gift of a lifetime, not because of what the place must be worth, but because that is a dream you could live with for the rest of your life, Sam. I've watched you here since you came back, and you're as good at it as you always were, but the truth of it is, I don't think you care anymore. I don't think you want to be here. I think that ever since you fell in love with that cowboy and worked on the ranch, all you want is that, Sam. You don't want to be here. And now your friend has given it to you, all of it, lock, stock, and barrel, and suddenly you want to play cripple. Well, guess what, I think you're a coward, and I don't think you should be allowed to play that game."

"And how do you plan to stop me from 'playing cripple,' as you put it?"

"Kick some sense into you, if I have to. Take you out there, rub your nose in it, remind you how much you love it all. Personally I think you're crazy and anything west of Poughkeepsie might as well be East Africa to me, but you, you're nuts about all that stuff. Christ, on that shoot last year, your eyes sparkled like light bulbs every time you saw a horse or a cow or talked to a foreman. It drove me nuts and you loved it, and now you're going to give all that away? What about doing something with it? What about bringing to life one of your dreams? You've talked so often to little Alex about that special riding class you'd read about once. The last time he came up here to pick you up for lunch, he told me you had said he could go riding one day, and maybe you'd take him—what about turning her ranch into a place for people like you and Alex, what about doing something like that?" Sam stared at her friend in amazement as the tears stopped rolling down her cheeks.

"But I couldn't do that, Charlie . . . how would I start it, how could I? I don't know anything about all that."

"You could learn. You know about horses. You know something about being in a wheelchair. You'll have plenty of people to help you run the ranch, all you have to do is coordinate it, like a giant commercial, and hell, you're good at that."

"Charlie, you're crazy."

"Maybe." He looked at her with a grin. "But tell the truth, Sam, wouldn't you enjoy being a little crazy too?"

"Maybe," she answered honestly. She was still staring at him with a look of amazement. "What do I do now?"

"Why don't you go out there and look around again, Sam. Hell, you own it."

"Now?"

"Whenever you have time."

"By myself?"

"If you want."

"I don't know." She turned away again and sat staring into space, thinking of the ranch and Aunt Caro. It would be so painful to see it again without her this time. It would be filled with memories of people she had cared about who were no longer there. "I don't want to go out there alone, Charlie. I don't think I could handle it."

"Then take someone with you." He sounded matter-of-fact.

"Who do you suggest?" She looked at him skeptically. "My mother?"

"God forbid. Hell, I don't know, Sam, take Mellie."

"What about the kids?"

"Take all of us, then. Or never mind 'taking us,' we'll take ourselves. The kids would love it, so would we, and I'll tell you what I think once we get there."

"Are you serious, Charlie?"

"Totally. I think this will be the most important decision you've ever made, and I'd hate to see you screw it up."

"So would I." She looked at him somberly and suddenly thought about something. "What about Thanksgiving?"

"What about it?"

"It's in three weeks, what if we all go out then?"

He thought for a minute and then grinned at her. "You've got a deal. I'll call Mellie."

"Think she'll want to go?"

"Hell yes. And if she doesn't"—he grinned—"I'll go alone." But Mellie offered no objection when he called her, and neither did the boys when they told them, and they didn't tell anyone else. They just quietly made reservations for a four-day trip over Thanksgiving. Samantha didn't even tell Harvey. She was afraid to upset him, and she still hadn't given him an answer about the job.

31

Samantha grew strangely quiet as they drove the last miles through the rolling hills on the familiar strip of highway. But the others didn't notice. The boys were so excited, that they were jumping up and down in the rented car. Mellie had left the baby with her mother, and the trip had gone smoothly so far. It was obviously an unorthodox Thanksgiving, the grown-ups at least thought it would be worth it. They had eaten a dry little slice of turkey and some dressing on the airline, and Mellie had promised to put together a real turkey dinner the next day on the ranch.

Samantha had spoken to Josh again only that morning. The boys were going to sleep in sleeping bags in one of the two guestrooms, and Charlie and Melinda were going to sleep in Aunt Caro's room. Sam would sleep in the room she had last had. The house was large enough to accommodate all of them, and Josh had assured her that there were groceries and that if she liked he would pick them all up at the plane in L.A. But Sam had insisted that she didn't want to spoil his Thanksgiving, she would see him when they got to the ranch. He had told her then, in his pained, halting way, how glad he was that she owned the ranch now and that he would do whatever he could to help her. He just hoped she wouldn't do something foolish like sell it, because he thought she could turn out to be one of the best damn ranchers around. She had smiled wistfully as he said it, wished him a happy Thanksgiving, and hurried to meet Mellie and Charlie and the boys in the lobby. They had had to take two cabs to the airport, and now they were crowded into a huge station wagon and the boys were singing songs.

But all Samantha could think of as they approached the ranch was how it had been the last time she had seen it, with Caroline and Bill King strong and healthy. Then she thought back once again to her days there with Tate. It all seemed like a dream now, it was so distant, the moments of joy she had shared with him, the hours at the cabin, the rides that they took on his pinto and Caro's handsome Thoroughbred stallion. She had been able to walk then. She felt a black cloud descend on her slowly as they turned the last bend in the road and she realized once again how much everything had changed.

"There it is." She said it softly from the backseat, pointing a shaking finger. They passed through the main gate, drove up the winding road, and then she saw it: Aunt Caro's house. But there were no lights on, and although it was only five o'clock in the afternoon, it looked bleak and lonely and sad in the failing light. "Josh said he'd leave the door open. If you want to go inside, Charlie, the living room lights are all on a panel on the right just behind the door." Sam just sat there with her eyes riveted to the house. She kept expecting to see the lights come on, to see the familiar white hair, to see Aunt Caro's smiling face and a wave of the hand. But as Charlie went in to turn the lights on and then walked quickly back to the car, there was no one beside him, and even the boys grew quiet as they looked around the ranch.

"Where are the horses, Sam?"

"In the barn, love. I'll show you tomorrow."

"Can't we see them now?"

She smiled at Charlie over their heads and then nodded. "Okay, let's get our stuff inside, and then I'll take you all over." But now that she was here, she didn't want to. She didn't want to go into the house, or the barn, she didn't want to see Black Beauty standing in his stall, or Navajo, or the other familiar horses. All she wanted was to see Caroline and Bill King and Tate Jordan, and live a life that she never would live again. There was a lump in her throat the size of an apple as she got herself into her wheelchair and let Charlie back her up the stairs. She rolled herself slowly into the house then and looked around. Then, ever so slowly, she began to roll toward her own room down the hall. A minute later the boys scampered past her, and she forced a smile as she showed them their room, and then she returned to the living room to find Charlie and Melinda. She pointed in the opposite direction, to their room, but she didn't want to see it. She didn't want to see the empty bedroom that had been Caro and Bill's.

"You all right?" Melinda looked at her gently and she nodded.

"I'm okay. Honest."

"You look tired."

She wasn't though, she was just desperately unhappy. "I'm fine." She was remembering once again with all too painful precision just how she had felt when she had left the ranch, not knowing where Tate was, or if she would ever find him, but still hopeful. And now she knew for certain that she would never see him again. Not only that but she had lost Caro. . . . The thought of it weighed on her like wet cement. And then as she sat gazing out the window at the dim hills in the twilight, she saw a bandy-legged little figure coming toward her, like an elf or a little wood sprite, and suddenly with damp eyes she was beaming. It was Josh. He had seen the lights in the house and he had hurried to see her. With a broad smile she pushed her way out the door and waited for him in her wheelchair on the porch. But as she did she saw him stop dead where he was standing, and she could see the look of shock on his face and hear the words. "Oh, my God. . . ." And then suddenly, without knowing when she had started, she was crying, and so was he, and he was halfway up the stairs and she was reaching down, and he bent over her and held her, as together they cried, for Bill and for

Caro and for Tate, and for Sam as well. For what seemed like hours there was only the muffled sound of their crying, and then after a time the wizened old cowboy sniffed loudly and stood up.

"Why didn't nobody never tell me, Sam?"

"I thought Miss Caro . . ." He shook his head with a look of despair.

"How did it happen?"

She closed her eyes for a moment and then opened them. It was as though she too had shared in his shock. As though suddenly she saw herself as he saw her, crippled, in a wheelchair, no more the proud young palomino who had run all over the ranch. It was as though her life were over, as though she had suddenly grown old. And at that moment she knew that she couldn't keep the ranch now. There was no way she could run it. All the men would react the same way to her as Josh had. She was a cripple now—no matter what they had told her at the hospital in New York.

"Sam . . ."

"It's okay, Josh." She smiled gently at him and took a deep breath. "It happened in Colorado, about fifteen months ago. It was something stupid I did with a horse." The memory was blurred now, but she would always remember the gray stallion . . . Gray Devil . . . and the endless moment when she had flown through the air. "I took a chance with a wild stallion. He was a real bitch to ride and he threw me into a ravine."

"Why—why did you do it?" His eyes filled again as he watched her. He knew instinctively that she had pushed the horse too hard, and she didn't deny it.

"I don't know." She sighed again. "I was crazy, I guess. I think Black Beauty made me think I could handle any stallion I ever came up against and I was upset about something." She had been depressed about Tate, but she didn't tell him that. "So, that's what happened."

"Will you . . . can they . . . ?" He didn't know how to finish, but she easily understood him and shook her head.

"No. This is it. I thought you knew though. I figured Caroline would have told you."

"She never did."

"Maybe she was too wrapped up with Bill. He had just had his first heart attack around that time. I wanted to come out but I was too busy with work, and then—" She faltered but went on. "I was stuck in the hospital for ten months." She looked around her at the familiar buildings. "I should have come back though afterwards, but I don't know . . . I think I was afraid to. Afraid to face what I couldn't do anymore, so I never saw her again, Josh"— her lip trembled—"and she was so damn sad after Bill died, and I never helped her." She closed her eyes and held out her arms and she clung to the old cowboy again.

"She was all right, Sam. And she went like she wanted to. She didn't want to hang around without him." Did he know, then? Had they all known? Had the pretense been a farce for all those years? Sam looked into his face and saw that it was no secret. "They was as good as married, Sam."

She nodded. "I know. They should have gotten married."

He only shrugged. "You can't change old ways." And then he looked down at her again, his eyes filled with

350

questions. "What about you?" He understood suddenly how unlikely it was that she'd keep the ranch now. "You going to sell this place now?"

"I don't know." She looked troubled as they lingered on the porch. "I don't see how I could run it. I think maybe I belong in New York."

"You live with your folks now?" He seemed interested in how she managed but she shook her head with a small smile.

"Hell no. I live alone. I live in the same building as the friends who brought me out here. I had to get a new apartment, one without steps. But I can take care of myself."

"That's terrific, Sam." There was only a faint hint that he was talking to a cripple, but she knew he'd still have to make the adjustment. In some ways she still did too, so she didn't hold it against him. And then what he said next shocked her. "Why couldn't you do that out here? Hell, we'd all help you. And shit, there's no reason why you can't ride. As long as you ride careful now." He almost glared at her as he said it, and then he smiled.

"I don't know, Josh. I've been thinking about it, but it's all pretty scary. That was why I came out here. I didn't want to make the decision to sell till I came out here again to see for myself."

"I'm glad you did. And you know"—he narrowed his eyes and stroked his chin, staring at the darkening horizon—"I think we got an old saddle in there I can fix up for you just fine. And I'll tell you one thing." He turned back to glare at her. "You ain't riding Black Beauty, if I have to kick your ass to keep you off him!"

"Try and stop me!" She was laughing now, it was almost like the old days, but he wasn't kidding around.

"It'll be my pleasure. I'd like to know who was the fool who let you ride that other stallion."

"Someone who saw me ride."

"Damn show-off." It was the kind of thing Tate would have said and her eyes grew serious again as she looked at Josh.

"Josh?"

"Yeah?"

"Did you ever hear any more about Tate Jordan?" It had been more than a year and a half since he left, but Josh just shook his head.

"Nope. Just another cowboy. Drifted off God knows where. He would have made you a good foreman though, Sam." Not to mention a good husband, but Sam didn't say what was in her heart.

"How's the new man?"

"All right. But he's leaving. He's already had an offer. He told the lawyer that yesterday morning. He don't want to take no chances that you might sell the ranch and he might lose his job, so he's movin' on while he can. He's got a bunch of kids," Josh said by way of explanation and Sam watched him thoughtfully.

"What about you, Josh? You staying?"

"Hell yes. This has been my home for too many years for me to go anywhere. You're going to have to sell me with the ranch."

"Tell you what, if I don't, how would you like to be foreman?"

"You kidding, Sam?" His eyes lit up with interest. "I'd

352

sure as hell like that, and my wife would be so full of herself she'd make us all sick. But I could live with that." They grinned at each other and he stuck out a rough hand, which she shook.

"Sam?" Charlie peeked out the screen door then, he had heard her talking and wondered who it was. She wheeled quickly in her wheelchair, made the introductions, and they talked for a few minutes about the ranch.

And then finally Josh looked down at her again. He had forgotten her for a minute in the conversation that went on above her head. "How long you staying, Sam?"

"Just till Sunday. We have to get back. Charlie and I work together in New York. He's an artist."

"I am not, I'm a genius." They all grinned.

"Can you ride?" He shook his head and Josh smiled broadly. "We'll teach you. And Sam says you brought your kids."

"Three of them. My sons."

"How many you got in all?" Josh raised an eyebrow.

"Four. We left a baby girl at home."

"Shit," he guffawed, "that ain't nothin'. I got six."

"God save me!" Charlie looked faint and they all laughed.

Josh came in then to meet Mellie and the boys, and then they all trooped out to the barn to look at the horses, and the boys were so excited that they were jumping up and down in the straw and squealing while the others laughed. Plans were made for the next day to give them lessons, and then Sam stopped for a few moments to look at Black Beauty, sedate and splendid as ever in his stall.

"He's a fine-looking horse, Sam, ain't he?" Even Josh looked him over with pride, and then he glanced at Sam as though he had just remembered something. "He's yours now, Sam."

"No." She shook her head slowly, looking at Josh. "He'll always be Caro's. But I'll ride him." This time she smiled, but he didn't.

"No, you won't."

"We can fight about that in the morning." He looked doubtful but they wandered back to the big house, and he left them on the porch, with a last tender look at Sam. It was then that she realized that it had been a homecoming. That even if the others were gone now, she still had Josh. And she had the beautiful ranch that Caroline had left her, and the memories of what her old friend had shared with Bill, and her own memories of Tate in their cabin—none of that would ever leave her, especially if she stayed right here.

32

"Okay now, Sam . . . we got you. . . ." Two cowboys
made a seat for her and held her while two more held the
horse firmly. It wasn't Black Beauty they held between
them, and not even Navajo, but a new horse named
Pretty Girl. But this time the name didn't annoy her. She
was surprised herself at how squeamish she felt and the
horse was supposed to be very docile. Suddenly she was
glad. They hoisted her into the saddle quickly, and Josh
tied a bunch of straps around her, and then she sat
there, perched in her saddle, staring down at them in
amazement.

"By God, we did it. Look at that, I'm riding!" She looked like an ecstatic kid.

"No, you ain't." Josh grinned at her with obvious pleasure. "You're just sittin'. Get her movin' a little, Sam, and see how it feels."

She looked down at him and whispered. "Would you believe it, I'm scared." She just sat there with a frightened expression alternating with a nervous smile, and after a moment Josh gently took the bridle and began to walk her on the quiet horse.

"You're okay, Sam. Come on, I'll walk you around the corral."

"Josh, I feel like a baby."

He looked over his shoulder with a tender smile. "You are. Got to learn to walk, you know, before you can trot." But a moment later he let go of the bridle and she began to trot slowly, and suddenly Sam's face broke out in a huge grin.

"Hey, guys, I'm running," she was shouting, "I'm running . . . look!" She was so excited, she could hardly stand it. For the first time in over a year, she wasn't moving along in a wheelchair, she was actually running again, and even if it wasn't under her own steam, the exhilaration of trotting along with the wind in her hair was the best feeling she'd known in years. It took Josh an hour to convince her that she'd had enough. And when they helped her down, she was so high, she was almost flying, her eyes were dancing, and her delicate face was framed by wisps of her golden hair.

"You sure looked good on that horse, Sam." He smiled gently at her as they set her down in her chair.

She grinned a grin of confession. "You know, at first I was scared to death."

"Stands to reason. You'd have to be crazy not to be after what happened." And then he looked at her thoughtfully. "How did it feel?"

"So good, Josh." She just closed her eyes and grinned. "Like I was a normal person again." The grin faded as she looked into his wise old eyes. "It's been a long time."

"Yeah." He scratched his chin. "But I keep thinkin', it don't have to be a long time anymore. Sam, you could come back here, and you could get back into ranchin'. . . ." He had thought about it all night, but now she looked at him pensively, her head cocked to one side.

"You want to know what I've been thinking?" He nodded. "Charlie and I talked about it in New York, and maybe it's totally crazy. But I wonder if, maybe, I could turn this into a special ranch, for"—she hesitated, not sure how to say it—"people like me. Kids mostly, but some grown-ups. Teach them to ride, help them get back to a normal life. Josh, I can't even begin to tell you what it just felt like. Here, in the chair, I'm different and I always will be. But up on that horse, I'm no different than I used to be. Oh, maybe a little, but I won't be once I get used to riding again. Imagine showing people that, giving them horses to ride, teaching them. . . ." She didn't notice but there were tears in his eyes and her own as she spoke. He was nodding slowly, glancing around at the buildings.

"We'd have to make some changes, but we could do it. . . ."

"Would you help me?"

He nodded slowly. "I don't know much about . . .

357

about . . ." He tried to be tactful, he had been about to say cripples. "About people like that, but hell, I know horses, and I could teach a blind man to ride if I had to. Had my own kids ridin' by the time they was three." She knew it was true too, and he had just been as patient and as loving as any therapist she had worked with. "You know, Sam, we could do it. Hell, I'd sure like to try it."

"So would I. But I have to think it over. It would take some money, and I'd have to have therapists and nurses and doctors, people would have to be willing to trust me with their children, and why should they?" But she was talking more to herself than to Josh, and a moment later Charlie and Mellie interrupted them to ask Josh more questions about the ranch.

Sunday morning came too quickly, and they all looked regretful as they said good-bye. Josh was almost heartbroken as he took Sam's hand before they left for the airport and squeezed it with a thousand questions written on his face. "Well? You goin' to keep it?" If not, he knew that he might never see her again. And he couldn't let that happen. He wanted to help her to find herself, and to build the ranch for special kids. He had sensed in the past few days how lonely and hurt she was.

"I don't know yet, Josh." She answered him honestly. "I have to do some research, and to think it over. I promise I'll let you know as soon as I make up my mind."

"How soon do you think that will be?"

"Has another job come up for you?" She looked worried.

"If I said yes," he said, grinning softly, "would that make you jealous enough to keep it?"

She laughed in answer. "You're a sly one."

His face sobered. "I just don't want to see you give up this ranch."

"I don't want to either, Josh. But I just don't know enough about ranching to make it worth it. The only thing that makes sense is if we do what we said."

"Well, why don't we?"

"Give me a chance to think it over."

"You do that." And then he leaned down and gave her a bear hug and turned to say good-bye to Charlie and Melinda and the three boys.

They waved good-bye to him for as long as they could see him, and in comparison to the trip out, it was a very quiet trip back. The boys were exhausted and disappointed that they were going back to New York. Charlie and Mellie alternated sleeping on part of the trip, and Sam was pensive all the way to New York. She had a lot to think about, about whether she herself could make it, about whether selling the livestock on the ranch would give her enough money to make the improvements, about whether or not it was what she wanted. Was she really ready to leave the safety of her life in New York? She had been so engrossed in the makings of her decision that all the way home she had barely thought of Tate.

She left Charlie and Mellie in the lobby of their building and disappeared into her apartment to make some notes, and she still looked preoccupied the next morning at the office when Charlie knocked on her door.

"Well, cowgirl, made up your mind yet?"

"Shhh!" She put a finger to her lips and beckoned him in. No one else knew in the office and she particularly didn't want Harvey to know yet. Not until she was sure.

"What are you going to do, Sam?" He threw himself down on the couch and grinned at her. "Want to know what I would do if I were you?"

"No." She tried to look forbidding, but he always made her laugh. "I want to make up my own mind."

"That's smart. Just don't make any mistakes and tell your mother what you're considering. She'd probably have you locked up in the nut house."

"Maybe she'd be right."

"Hardly. Or at least not for those reasons." He smiled at Sam and sat up just as Harvey's secretary appeared in the doorway.

"Miss Taylor?"

"Yes?" Sam turned to face her.

"Mr. Maxwell would like to see you."

"God himself?" Charlie looked impressed and went back to his office as Sam followed Harvey's secretary down the hall.

And when she reached his office, she found him looking tired and pensive. There was a mountain of papers on his desk and he only glanced at Samantha as he finished some notes. "Hi, Sam."

"Hi, Harvey, what's up?" It was another minute before he turned his attention to her, and he went over the amenities before getting down to the reason she had been called.

"How was Thanksgiving?"

"Very nice. Yours?"

"Fine. How did you spend it?" It was a loaded question and Sam felt suddenly nervous.

"With the Petersons."

"That's nice. At their place or yours?"

"Mine." But it was truthful, she reassured herself. The ranch was hers now after all.

"That's terrific, Sam." He smiled at her. "You're really doing amazingly well."

"Thank you." It was a compliment that meant a lot to her, and for a moment they exchanged a smile.

"Which brings me to why I called you into the office this morning. You haven't given me your answer." He looked expectant and Samantha sighed and slumped back in her chair.

"I know I haven't, Harvey . . . I feel awful about that, but I just needed time to think."

"Is it really a choice?" He looked surprised. What choice did she have after all? "If you're still worried about the travel, all you really have to do is hire a competent assistant"—he grinned at her—"like I did, and you'll be all set. The rest you can certainly handle. Hell, Sam, you've been doing my job and your own for years now!" He was teasing but she wagged a finger at him.

"Now you admit it! I should ask you to sign a statement to that effect."

"Not on your life. Come on, Sam, get me off the hook. Give me an answer." He sat back and smiled at her. "I want to go home."

"The bitch of it is, Harvey," she said, looking at him sadly, "so do I."

But it was obvious that he didn't understand her. "But this is your home, Sam."

She shook her head slowly. "No, Harvey, I just realized something this weekend. It's not."

"You're unhappy at CHL?" He looked shocked. That possibility hadn't even occurred to him. Did she mean that she wanted to quit?

But she quickly shook her head. "No, I'm not unhappy. Not here . . . but . . . well . . . I don't know if I can explain it, but it has to do with New York."

"Sam." He held up a hand to stop her. "I'm warning you, if you've come in here to tell me that you're moving to Atlanta with your mother, I will go into shock. Call my doctor now if that's what you're going to tell me." She could only laugh in answer and shake her head again.

"No, it is most certainly not that."

"Then what is it?"

"I've been holding out on you, Harvey." She looked guiltily at her boss of ten years. "My friend Caroline left me her ranch."

"Left it to you?" He looked startled. "Are you going to sell it?"

Samantha shook her head slowly. "I don't think so. That's just it."

"You're not going to keep it, Sam, are you? What could you possibly do with it?"

"A lot of things." And then, as she looked at him, she knew her answer. "It's just something I have to do. Maybe I won't be able to do it, maybe it'll be too much for me, maybe it'll be a terrible fiasco, but I just want to give it a try. I want to set it up as a place to teach handicapped kids to ride, teach them how to be independent, to cover ground in something other than a wheelchair—on a horse." Harvey was looking thoughtfully at her. "You think I'm crazy, don't you?"

He smiled sadly. "No, I was wishing that you were my daughter. Because I would wish you luck, and give you all the money I have and tell you to do it. I wish I could tell you that I think you're crazy, Sam, but I don't. It's a long way from being a creative director on Madison Avenue though. Are you sure that's what you want?"

"The funny thing is that I wasn't sure. Until right now when I told you, but now I know. I am sure." And then with a small sigh, "What are you going to do about the job? Give it to Charlie?" He thought for a minute and nodded.

"I guess so. He'll do a good job."

"Are you sure you want to retire, Harvey?" But she had to admit that he looked ready and that she would do the same thing in his place.

He nodded, looking at her. "Yes, Sam, I'm sure. As sure as you are about your ranch, which is to say that I want to retire and it's always a little scary to deal with the unknown. You never know for sure that you're doing the right thing."

"I guess not."

"Think Charlie will want the job?"

"He'll be thrilled."

"Then it's his. Because it has to be like that. You have to want to work fifteen hours a day, take it home on the weekends, louse up your vacations, eat, sleep, and drink commercials. I just don't want that anymore."

"Neither do I. But Charlie does."

"Then go tell him he has a new job, or should I?"

"Would you let me do it?" It was the last thing she would do at CHL that would mean something to her.

"Why not? You're his closest friend." And then he looked at Sam sadly. "How soon are you leaving us?"

"What would be reasonable?"

"Why don't I leave that up to you."

"First of the year?" It was in five weeks. That was a reasonable notice, and Harvey seemed to think so too.

"We'll retire together then. Maggie and I may even come to visit you on the ranch. My advanced age should be a sufficient handicap for us to qualify as guests."

"Bull." She moved her wheelchair around his desk and came over to kiss his cheek. "You'll never be that old, Harvey, not until you're a hundred and three."

"That happens to be next week." He put an arm around her shoulders and kissed her. "I'm proud of you, Sam. You're quite a girl." And then he coughed in embarrassment, fumbled on his desk, and waved her out. "Now go tell Charlie he has a new job."

Without saying anything further, she left his office and rolled her way down the hall, wearing a broad smile. She stopped in the doorway of Charlie's office, which was in its usual state of chaos, and she barged in on him as he attempted to find his tennis racket under the couch. He had a date to play at lunchtime, and all he could find were the balls.

"What are you looking for, slobbo? I don't know how you find anything in this mess."

"Huh?" He emerged, but only briefly. "Oh, it's you. I

364

don't. You don't happen to have a spare tennis racket, do you?" Only from Charlie could she take jokes like that.

"Sure. I play twice a week. Ice skating too. And cha-cha lessons."

"Oh, shut up. You're disgusting. What's the matter? Don't you have any decency, any taste?" He eyed her with mock outrage and she started laughing.

"Speaking of which, you'd better buy some of both, you're going to need them."

"What?" He looked blank.

"Taste."

"Why? I've never needed taste before."

"You were never creative director of a large ad agency before." He stared at her, not comprehending.

"What are you saying?" His heart pounded for a moment. But it couldn't be. Harvey was offering the job to Samantha . . . unless . . . "Sam?"

"You heard me, Mr. Creative Director." She beamed at him.

"Sam . . . ? Sam!" He jumped to his feet. "Did he—am I—?"

"He did. And you are."

"But what about you?" He looked shocked. Had they passed her over for the job? If that was the case, he wouldn't take it. They would both quit, they could open up shop together, they could . . .

She could see his mind racing and held up a hand. "Relax. The job is yours. Me, I'm going to California, Charlie, to run a ranch for handicapped children. And if you're real nice to me, maybe I'll let you and the kids come and visit me in the summers and—" He didn't let her finish. Instead he ran to her and hugged her tight. "Oh, Sam, you did it! You did it! When did you decide?" He was as thrilled for her as he was for himself. He was almost jumping up and down like a kid.

"I don't know." She was laughing as he held her. "I think just now in Harvey's office . . . or last night on the plane . . . or yesterday morning when I talked to Josh . . . I don't know when it happened, Charlie. But I did it."

"When are you going out?"

"When you get your new job. On January first."

"My God, Sam, does he really mean- it? Creative director? Me? But I'm only thirty-seven."

"It's all right," she reassured him. "You look fifty."

"Gee, thanks." He was still beaming as he reached for the phone to call his wife.

33

"So? How's it going? When do you open?" Charlie called her every week, to cry on her shoulder about all the work on his desk and find out about the progress at the ranch.

"We open in two weeks, Charlie."

"What is that? Like a bank? You give out toasters and balloons and party hats?"

She smiled into the phone. For the past five months, he had done nothing but encourage, and it had been a long haul. In the course of a lifetime five months was nothing, but her working sixteen and eighteen hours a day made it seem like ten years. They had torn down small buildings, put up new sheds, altered cottages, put in ramps, built a swimming pool, sold the livestock for the most part, except for a handful of cows to give them milk and to amuse the kids. There had been therapists to hire, nurses to see, doctors to contact, and then inevitably there had been the traveling. Sam had flown to Denver to see the doctor who had first operated on her back, to Phoenix, to Los Angeles, and to San Francisco, and then finally to Dallas and Houston, and in each city she had seen the top orthopedic men. She had hired a secretary to travel with her, which made it easier for her and made it look more businesslike. She wanted to explain her program to the doctors, so that they would refer patients to her, children who would spend four to six weeks on the ranch, learning to enjoy life again, to ride horses, to be with other children with similar disabilities, and to be independent of their parents and able to take care of themselves.

In her presentation she showed photographs of the ranch as it had been and architectural renderings of what it was going to be. She detailed the facilities and the plans for physical therapy, gave résumés of the staff and detailed references for herself. And everywhere she went, she got a warm reception, and the doctors were impressed. All of them referred her to other doctors, most of them invited her to their homes to meet their wives and families. And in Houston she could even have had a date, but she declined graciously, and still won the doctor over. By the time she had finished her travels, she was certain that at least forty-seven doctors in six cities were going to refer patients to her ranch.

She still called it the Lord Ranch and she had kept on a handful of the old cowboys. Josh was, as promised, made the foreman, and she had even given him a bronze plaque to put on his front door, and he had been thrilled. But what she needed was a new breed of ranch hands, and she and Josh had picked them all carefully, for their attitudes about children, about handicaps, about horses. She didn't want anyone too old, or impatient, or ornery, or willing to take risks with the children or the horses. Just hiring the men had taken them almost two months. But she had a dozen ranch hands now, two of them from the old days, and the other ten all new. Her favorite among them was a broad-shouldered, handsome, redheaded, green-eyed "young'un," as Josh called him, named Jeff. He was shy and closed up about his own life, but he was always willing to talk for hours about what they were going to do with the ranch. His references told her that at twenty-four he had been working on ranches since he was sixteen, and in eight years he had been on five ranches in three states. When she asked him why, he said only that he used to travel a lot with his father, but now he was on his own, and when she called the last two ranches he had worked at, they told her to do anything she had to to hang on to him, and if he didn't stay with her, send him back to them. So Jeff Pickett became assistant foreman, and Josh was pleased with his new team.

The only problem Sam had had for a while had been the money she needed, but it was amazing what could happen if you really wanted something badly enough, and she did. Caroline had left her a small sum of money, which had been absorbed by the alterations on the ranch within the first few weeks. After that the sale of the cattle had been a big help, and then Josh had come up with an idea to help her. They weren't going to need a lot of the fancier pieces of ranch equipment anymore, tools and tractors and trucks to transport the cattle, so she sold those and that paid for six new cottages and the swimming pool. After that she began to look into grants and discovered a wealth of untapped resources she hadn't considered, and once she'd gotten three of those, she applied for a loan at the bank.

Only a month before, Harvey had called her from Palm Springs, where he and Maggie were on vacation while he played golf in a tournament with some old friends, and he had asked if they could come to see her, and when they had, he had insisted that he wanted to invest fifty thousand dollars in her ranch. It was just over the final amount that she needed, and it was a godsend for her, as she told him when he wrote the check. And now she was going to be all right until they opened, and hopefully after that, within a year or two they'd be in the black and totally self-supporting. She didn't want to get rich on what she was doing. She just wanted to make enough money to be comfortable and support the ranch.

The opening date, as she now told Charlie, was June 7, and in a few days the rest of the physical therapists would be arriving, along with some new horses. The Jacuzzis were all installed, the pool looked terrific, the cabins were cozy, and she already had reservations for thirty-six kids over the next two months.

"When can I come?"

"I don't know, love, anytime you want. Or maybe, just

give me a chance to catch my breath after we get started. I think I'm going to have my hands full for a while."

As it turned out, that was the understatement of the century. She hadn't counted on being nearly as busy as she was. She was snowed under every morning, after they opened, with mountains of paperwork, letters from doctors, requests from parents, and she spent the entire afternoon teaching children, with Josh. One of the grants had gone toward having special saddles made for the children. They had fifty now, and had already applied for another grant for another fifty saddles, which Sam suspected they would soon need. Her patience with the children proved to be endless, as she taught them in groups of two or three. And invariably each time, after the initial terror as they sat there clutching the pommel, the horse would begin to walk as Josh led them, and the feeling of freedom and movement and actually walking would so completely overwhelm the children that they would squeal with glee. Sam never got over her own feeling of excitement and jubilation as she watched them, and time and again she watched Josh and the other cowboys stealthily brush away a tear.

All the children seemed to love her and, as the old ranch hands had more than two years before, they began calling her Palomino because of her sun-bleached fair hair. Suddenly everywhere on the ranch were shouts of "Palomino! . . . Palomino!" as she wheeled herself about, checking on children in therapy, at the pool, making their beds, or sweeping their rooms in the pretty little cottages. Sam kept an eye on them everywhere, and at night, in the main hall where everyone ate now, including Samantha, there were endless discussions about who would sit at her table, who would sit at her right or her left, and at the campfire, who would get to hold her hand. The oldest child there was a boy of sixteen, who had arrived surly and hostile from twelve operations over nineteen months, after injuring his spinal cord in a motorcycle accident in which his older brother had been killed. But after four weeks on the ranch he was like a new person. Redheaded Jeff had become his mentor, and the boy and he had become fast friends. The youngest was a little girl of seven, with enormous blue eyes, easy tears, and a lisp. Her name was Betty and she had been born with stumps instead of legs and she was still a little afraid of horses, but she was having a great time with the other kids.

Sometimes when she looked around herself in amazement, as the summer wore on and the numbers of children grew, Sam marveled at the fact that the handicaps didn't upset her. There had been a time in her life when only perfection seemed normal and when she wouldn't have known how to handle any of the problems that were now part of an ordinary day: children who wouldn't cooperate, artificial limbs that didn't fit, diapers for boys of fourteen, wheelchairs that got stuck, braces that broke. The mechanics of it all sometimes struck her as extraordinary, but most extraordinary of all was that it had become a way of life. And for a woman who had once longed for children, her prayers had been answered: by the end of August she had fifty-three. And now a new aspect had been added. They had bought a specially equipped van, with yet another grant, and made arrangements with the local school, so that after Labor

Day the children who came to her, or stayed on, would go to school. For many of them it would be a reintroduction to schooling with normal children, and it was a good place for them to make the adjustment before they went back to their hometowns. There was almost nothing that Sam hadn't thought of, and when Charlie and Mellie came out in late August, they were absolutely stunned by what they saw.

"Has anyone done an article about you yet, Sam?" Charlie was enthralled as he watched a group of advanced senior riders cantering back from an afternoon on the hills. The children, for the most part, loved the horses, and even the horses had been specially picked by Sam and Josh for their docility and the steadiness that they showed.

But now, in answer to Charlie's question, she shook her head. "I don't want any publicity, Charlie."

"Why not?" Living in the vortex of visibility in New York, he was surprised.

"I don't know. I like it this way, I guess. Nice and quiet. I don't want to show off. I just want to help the kids."

"I'd say you're doing that." He beamed at her as Mellie chased baby Sam down the road. "I've never seen kids look so happy. They love it, don't they?"

"I hope so."

They did, as did the parents, the doctors, and the people who worked there. What Sam had done had been a dream come true. It gave the children all the independence Sam had hoped to give them, gave the parents new hope for their children, gave the doctors a kind of gift to give to brokenhearted parents and children, and it gave the people who worked there a new meaning to their lives that they'd never had before. And most of the time they got children who made it all worth it. Now and then they got one whom even the most devoted therapists and counselors, and even Sam's loving efforts, couldn't help. There were those who just weren't ready or who didn't want help yet, or maybe never would. It was difficult to accept that they couldn't help a child, but they did their best nonetheless as long as the child stayed.

Amazingly enough, despite the magnitude of the handicaps with which they were dealing, it was always a happy place filled with laughter and smiling faces and squeals of delight. Sam herself had never been as happy and relaxed in her entire lifetime, and now when she met ranchers, or ran into ranch hands, or interviewed new personnel, she asked no questions except about the business at hand. Her endless, hopeless, fruitless search for Tate had finally been put to rest. And she accepted, with an equanimity that still upset Charlie, the fact that she would be alone for the rest of her life, running the ranch, and being with "her kids." It seemed to be all she wanted, and now and then Josh thought it was a damn shame. At thirty-two she was an extravagantly beautiful woman, and it pained him to think that she was alone. But none of the men who crossed her path seemed to intrigue her and she was always careful not to offer encouragement or innuendos when she met single fathers of new campers, or therapists or doctors. One sensed with Sam that her love life no longer existed, that for her it was a closed door. Yet it was difficult to feel sorry for her, surrounded as she was by children who adored her and whom she seemed to genuinely love.

It was in October that she was called to her office on an unusually warm day to see a new child coming in who was something of an exception. He had just been referred to the Lord Ranch by a judge in L.A. who had heard of what Sam was doing, and the child's "tuition" was to be paid by the courts. Sam knew that he was expected that morning, and she knew also that there were special circumstances regarding him, but the social worker had told her on the phone that he would explain it all to her when they arrived. She was intrigued by the nature of the new referral, but she had had some work to do with Josh that morning and she didn't want to wait in her office. She had a lot to do before the kids came back from school. There were currently sixty-one staying at the ranch. In her own mind she had already decided that eventually a hundred and ten would be their limit, but in the meantime they still had room to grow.

But when Jeff came to find her out near the Jacuzzis, talking to Josh, he wore an odd expression, and when she got back to her office, she saw why. In a small broken wheelchair sat a shrunken blond child with huge blue eyes, his arms were covered with bruises, and he was clutching a ragged teddy bear. As Sam saw him she almost stopped, because he looked so different from the others. For the past five months she had seen nothing but handicapped children, they had cried, they had wailed, they had argued, they had sulked, they had pouted on arrival. They didn't want to go to school, they were afraid of horses, they didn't see why they had to make their own beds now, but no matter how much they grouched and eventually adjusted, what they all had in common was that they were all children who had ben lavishly taken care of, almost pampered, by parents who loved them and were heartbroken at what had been dealt to them by the Fates. Never before had there been a child on the ranch who was so clearly unloved, so obviously bruised in spirit as well as in body, as this one, and as Sam wheeled her chair up closer to talk to him and held out her hands, he cowered from her and began to wail. She glanced quickly at the social worker, and then back at the child clutching his teddy bear, and spoke softly.

"It's okay, Timmie. No one's going to hurt you. My name's Sam. And this is Jeff." She waved at the young redhead, but Timmie squeezed his eyes shut and cried more. "Are you scared?" It was the merest whisper in her softest voice, and after a minute he nodded and opened one eye. "I was scared when I first came here too. Before I got hurt, I used to ride all the time, but I was afraid of the horses at first when I got here. Is that what you're scared of?" He shook his head vigorously. "You're not?" He shook his head again. "Then what are you scared of?" He opened the other eye and regarded her with terror. "Come on, you can tell me."

It was a tiny broken whisper as he stared at her. "You."

Sam was shocked, and with her eyes she signaled Jeff and the social worker and her secretary to back off. They wandered slowly across the room. "Why are you afraid of me, Timmie? I won't hurt you. I'm in a wheelchair just like you."

He looked at her for a while and then nodded. "How come?"

"I got hurt in an accident." She no longer told them that she was thrown by a horse. It didn't serve her purposes, trying to introduce them to riding. "But I'm okay now. I can do lots of things."

"Me too. I can cook my own dinner." Did he have to? she suddenly wondered. Who was this child and why was he so battered and bruised?

"What do you like to cook for dinner?"

"Spaghetti. It comes in a can."

"We have spaghetti here too."

He nodded sadly. "I know. They always have spaghetti in jail."

Sam's heart reached out to him and she gently reached out and took his hand. This time he let her, though the other one still clung tightly to his bedraggled bear. "Did you think this was like jail?" He nodded. "It's not. It's kind of like camp. Did you ever go to camp?" He shook his head, and she noticed that he looked more like four than six, which she knew he was. She also knew that he'd had polio when he was a year old. It had totally crippled both legs and hips.

"My mom is in jail." He volunteeered the information.

"I'm sorry to hear that."

He nodded again. "She got ninety days."

"Is that why you're here?" Where was his father . . . his grandma . . . anyone, someone who loved this child? It was the first admission she'd ever had that upset her. She wanted to shake someone for what they'd done to the boy. "Will you stay with us the whole time she's gone?"

"Maybe."

"Would you like to learn to ride a horse?"

"Maybe."

"I could teach you. I love horses, and we've got some real pretty ones. You could pick out one that you like." Right now there were still a dozen left unassigned. Each child always rode the same horse for his entire stay at the ranch. "How about that, Timmie?"

"Uh-huh . . . yeah. . . ." But he was glancing nervously at Jeff. "Who's that?"

"That's Jeff."

"Is he a cop?"

"No." She decided to speak his language. "We don't have any cops here. He just helps with the horses and the kids."

"Does he beat kids?"

"No." She looked shocked, and then she reached out and touched his face. "No one here will ever hurt you, Timmie. Never. I promise." He nodded, but it was obvious that he thought it was a lie. "As a matter of fact, how about if you and I stick together for a while, huh? You could watch me teach riding, and we could swim in the pool."

"You got a pool?" The eyes began to light up.

"We sure do." But the first pool she wanted to get him in was the bathtub. He was filthy from head to foot. He looked like he hadn't had a bath in weeks. "Would you like to see your room?"

He shrugged, but she could see that interest was dawning, and with a small smile she handed him a coloring book and some crayons and told him to wait there. "Where are you going?" He looked at her with suspicion and fresh fear.

"I think the man who brought you here wants me to sign some papers. I'll do that and then I'll take you to your room and show you the pool. Okay?"

"Okay." He began to pull out the crayons and she crossed the room in her wheelchair and signaled to the social worker to join her in her secretary's office. In a whisper she asked Jeff to stay.

The social worker was a tired man in his late forties. He had seen it all by now, and this kid was no worse than the rest. But a child in Timmie's condition was new to Sam.

"Good Lord, who's been taking care of him?"

"No one. His mother went to jail two weeks ago, and the neighbors thought he had been sent somewhere else. The mother never even told the cops about him when they picked her up. He's just been sitting around in the apartment, watching TV and eating out of cans. We talked to his mother though." He sighed and lit a cigarette. "She's a heroin addict. She's been in and out of jail for years, in and out of treatment centers and hospitals and God knows what. The kid was a trick baby, and she never got him any of his shots. Hence the polio." The social worker looked annoyed and Sam looked confused.

"I'm sorry. What is a 'trick baby'?" He didn't look like any trick to her, that child was real. But the social worker smiled.

"I forget that there are any decent people left who don't know expressions like that. A trick baby is a child conceived by a prostitute. She doesn't know the father.

He was a 'trick,' a 'john,' whatever. Charming, isn't it?"

"Why is she allowed to retain custody? Why don't the courts take him away from her?"

"They might. I think the judge is considering it this time. In fact she's thinking of giving him up. She considers herself one of the early Christian martyrs, being stuck with a crippled kid, having taken care of him for six years, she's had it." He hesitated for a moment and then looked Sam in the eye. "I might as well tell you, there's also a question of child abuse here. The bruises on his arms—she beat him with an umbrella. Almost broke the kid's back."

"Oh, my God, and they'd even consider giving him back to her?"

"She's been rehabilitated now." He said it with all the cynicism that went with his job. Sam had never been exposed to anything like it before.

"Has he had any psychiatric help?"

The social worker shook his head. "Our assessment of him is that he's normal, except for his legs of course. But mentally, he's all right. As all right as any of them are." Sam wanted to scream at him, how all right could he be if his mother had been beating him with an umbrella? The child was terrified. She had already seen that much. "Anyway, she's been in for two weeks, and with time off for good behavior and credit for time served, she'll be out in two months. You got him for sixty days." Like an animal, like a car, like a rental. Rent-a-Kid. Rent-a-Cripple. It made Sam feel sick.

"And after that?"

"She gets him back unless the court decides otherwise or she doesn't want him. I don't know, maybe you could keep him as a foster child, if you want to."

"Can't he be adopted by decent people?"

"Not unless she gives up custody, and you can't force her to do that. Besides"—the social worker shrugged—"who's going to adopt a kid in a wheelchair? Any way you look at it, he's going to wind up in an institution." "Jail," as Timmie had already said himself. What a grim life for a six-year-old child.

Sam looked sorrowful as the social worker walked to the door. "We're happy to have him. And I'll keep him longer if necessary. Whether the court pays or not." The social worker nodded.

"Let us know if you have any problems. We can always keep him in juvenile hall till she gets out."

"Isn't that like jail?" Sam looked horrified and he shrugged again.

"More or less. What else do you think we can do with them while their parents are in jail? Send them to camp?" But the beauty of it was that they just had.

Sam turned the chair around and went back into her own office, where Timmie had torn a page out of the coloring book and scribbled across it relentlessly in brown.

"Okay, Timmie, all set?"

"Where's the cop?" He sounded like a little gangster and Sam laughed.

"He's gone. And he's not a cop, he's a social worker."

"Same thing."

"Well, anyway, let's get you to your room." She

attempted to get his chair going for him but it locked every few feet and one of the sides had fallen down. "How do you get anywhere in this thing, Timmie?"

He looked at her strangely. "I never go out."

"Never?" She looked shocked again. "Not even with your mother?"

"She never takes me out. She sleeps a lot. She's very tired." I'll bet, Sam thought. If she was a heroin addict, she must have slept a hell of a lot.

"I see. Well, it seems to me that the first thing you're going to need is a new chair." That was one commodity they didn't have. They didn't have any spare chairs, but she kept a narrow extra one in the back of her station wagon, in case anything ever happened to her own. "I've got one you can use for now. It'll be a little big, but we'll get you a new one by tomorrow. Jeff"—she smiled at the young redhead—"can you get me my spare chair? It's in the back of my car."

"Sure." He was back five minutes later and Timmie was ensconced in the big gray chair, as Sam wheeled along beside him, helping him with the wheels.

As they wheeled past the other buildings, she explained to him what everything was, and they stopped at the corral for a few minutes so he could look at the horses, and as he did he stared at one of the horses and then at Sam's hair. "That one looks like you."

"I know. Some of the other kids call me Palomino. That kind of horse is a palomino."

"Is that what you are?" For a minute he looked amused.

"Sometimes I like to pretend that I am. Do you ever pretend stuff like that?" Sadly he shook his head and they drove on to his room. Now she was especially grateful that she had reserved him this particular room. It was big and sunny and all done in blue and yellow. There was a big cheerful bedspread and there were drawings of horses in frames on the walls.

"Whose is this?" He looked frightened again as she wheeled him into the room.

"Yours. While you're here."

"Mine?" The eyes were as big as saucers. "You mean it?"

"I mean it." There was a desk, without a chair, a chest of drawers, and a little table where he could play games. He had his own bathroom, and there was a special speaker in case he got in trouble and needed help from one of the counselors nearby. "Do you like it?"

All he could say was "Wow!"

She showed him the chest of drawers and then told him that that was where he could put his things.

"What things?" He looked blank. "I don't have any things."

"Didn't you bring a suitcase with some clothes?" She suddenly realized that she hadn't seen one.

"Nope." He looked down at the spotted T-shirt that had once been blue. "This is all I've got. And Teddy." He squeezed the bear tight.

"Tell you what." Sam glanced at Jeff and then back at Timmie. "Right now we'll borrow you some stuff, and then I'll go into town later and get you some jeans and stuff. Okay?"

"Sure." He didn't seem to care one way or the other, he was happy with his room.

"Now, about a bath." She wheeled herself into the sunny bathroom and turned on the tap after flicking a special switch at a comfortable level that would close the drain. Everything had been specially installed. And the john had hand bars on each side. "And if you want to use the toilet, all you have to do is push this button and someone will come and help."

He stared at her, not comprehending. "Why do I have to take a bath?"

"Because it's a nice thing to do."

"You gonna do it?"

"I could have Jeff do it if you like." She wasn't sure if at six he'd be modest, but he wasn't and now he vehemently shook his head.

"Uh-uh. You."

"Okay." For her this was a new adventure. It had only taken her ten months to learn how to bathe herself, but to bathe a child from a wheelchair, that was going to be something new.

She sent Jeff off to find clothes that would fit Timmie, rolled up her sleeves, and told him how to get himself in, but when he slipped and she tried to grab him, they both almost wound up on the floor. In the end she managed to get him into the bathtub, wound up soaked herself, and as she helped haul him out, she got him into the chair she had lent him just in time to lose her balance and fall out of her own. And for some reason she found herself on the floor, looking up at him and laughing as he laughed down at her too.

"Pretty silly, huh?"

"I thought you were supposed to teach me how to do it."

"Well, there are other people here who do that." She hoisted herself carefully off the wet floor and back into her chair.

"What do you do?"

"Teach riding."

He nodded and she found herself wondering what he was thinking, but mostly she was grateful that he no longer seemed to be afraid of her, and when Jeff brought them the clothes he had borrowed from various cabins, Timmie almost looked like a new child. But she was soaking wet from his bath and she had to go back to her room to change. "Want to come see my house?" Hesitantly he nodded, and after she helped him dress, she led the way. There was an easily accessible ramp into the big house now, and he followed her into the living room and down the hall to her bedroom, while she pulled some fresh jeans and a shirt out of the closet, which had been entirely rebuilt for her. She kept Caroline's old room as her best guest room, but she almost never used it, and visited it as seldom as she had to. It still pained her to feel its emptiness without her old friend.

"You got a nice house." Timmie was looking around with interest. The teddy bear had come with him too. "Who sleeps in the other rooms?"

"No one."

"Don't you have kids?" He looked amazed.

"No. Except all the kids who live here on the ranch with me."

"You got a husband?" It was a question a lot of the

children asked her and she always smiled and said no, and it ended there.

"Nope."

"Why not? You're pretty."

"Thank you. I just don't."

"Do you wanna get married?"

She sighed softly as she looked at the beautiful blond child. He was actually very pretty now that he was clean. "I don't think I do want to get married, Timmie. I lead kind of a special life."

"So does my mom." He nodded his understanding, and Sam was at first shocked and then laughed but she couldn't say "Not like that."

She tried to explain her views to him. "I just think I wouldn't have enough time for a husband with the ranch and you kids here and stuff."

But he was looking at her intently, and then waved at her chair. "Is it because of that?" What he had just asked her hit her like a punch in the stomach, because it was the truth, but she couldn't admit it, not to anyone, and barely to herself.

"No, it's not because of that." But she wondered if he knew she was lying, and then, without giving him time to ask her more questions, she ushered him back outside. They visited the stables and the main hall, looked at two cows in a pen, and went to the swimming pool, where she took him for a quick swim before lunch. There were only a few younger children on the ranch at that hour of the day in October. The others were all in school, having been dropped off by the huge adjusted school bus that Sam had bought to get the kids there. But the children who were around greeted Timmie with warmth and interest, and when the others got back at three thirty, he was hardly even shy. He watched them have their riding lessons, swoop down on the pool in their wheelchairs, and chase each other down the wide well-paved walks. He met Josh and solemnly shook his hand, and watched Samantha during all her lessons, and when she was finished, he was still standing by.

"You still here, Timmie? I thought you'd have gone back to your room." He only shook his head, holding on to his teddy bear with big eyes. "Want to come back to my house before dinner?" He nodded and reached out for her hand, and hand in hand, they wheeled back to the big house where she read him stories until the big old school bell sounded, and it was time to go eat.

"Can I sit with you, Sam?" Once again he looked worried, and she reassured him. But she suspected that by now he was tired after his long first day at the ranch. He sat beside her at dinner, yawning loudly, and before dessert had arrived, she turned to see that his little chin had dropped onto his chest and he was slumped in a corner of the big gray wheelchair. The teddy bear was still clutched in his arms, and she smiled gently and took off her heavy sweater, settled it around him like a blanket, and left the table to take him home. In his room she gently lifted him from the chair to the bed with one powerful smooth gesture, her own arms had gained much strength from the constant use they got. She took off his clothes as he stirred gently, undid his braces, changed his diapers, turned off the light, and ran a gentle hand over the soft blond hair. For a brief moment she was suddenly reminded of Charlie's children, of the sweet faces and the big blue eyes, and she suddenly remembered that fierce longing she had felt when she had first held their last baby, little Samantha, and how she had known then that it was a void that, in her life, would never be filled. And now, as she looked at Timmie, she felt her heart reach out and embrace him as though he had been her child. He stirred gently as she kissed his forehead, and whispered, "Good night, Mommy . . . I love you. . . ." Sam felt tears spring to her eyes. They were words she would suddenly have given her life for, and then, with head bowed, she wheeled out of the cabin and closed the door.

34

By the end of the first month Timmie was riding the pretty little palomino. Her name was Daisy and he loved her the way any little boy would have loved his first horse. But far more than the palomino, he loved Samantha, with a passion that startled everyone with its vehemence and strength. He appeared at the big house every morning, knocked on the door, and waited for her to come and answer it. Sometimes it took her longer than others, because sometimes she was already making coffee and sometimes she was still in bed. But the moment he saw her, his face lit up like a sunburst, and as he wheeled in the chair that she had bought him, he always looked around him, like a puppy who's been kept outdoors all night. They had a comfortable early morning patter. Sometimes he told her what he'd dreamed about, or what one of the kids had done at breakfast, or what the palomino had been doing when Timmie sped past the corral in his chair to bid the gentle horse good morning. And Samantha told him what she would be doing that morning, they'd talk about his riding lesson, and once or twice she inquired if he had changed his mind about school, but he remained adamant on that subject. He wanted to stay on the ranch, not go to school with the others, and Samantha figured that for the first month at least she would let him settle in.

The bruises that his mother had inflicted upon him had long since faded, and the social worker called once a week to see how Timmie was, and when at the end of the month he came out to see them, he looked from Timmie to Samantha and then back again, and he was clearly stunned.

"What in God's name did you do to him?" he asked her when they were finally alone. Prying Timmie from Sam's side wasn't easy, but she had sent him to check on Daisy and tell Josh that they would be riding in a few minutes to show the social worker how well he had done. "He looks like a different child."

"He is a different child," Sam said proudly. "He's a child who's been loved and it shows."

But the social worker only looked at her sadly. "You know how hard you've made it for him?" She thought he

390

was joking and she started to smile but she saw then that
he meant it and knit her brows.

"What do you mean?"

"Do you know what it'll be like for him to go back to an
apartment in a tenement with a drug-addict mother who
feeds him stale crackers and beer?"

Sam took a deep breath and stared out the window. She
wanted to say something to him. But she didn't know if it
was the right time. "I wanted to talk to you about that,
Mr. Pfizer." She turned to face him again. "What about
the possibilities of not sending him back?"

"And keep him here?" She nodded, but he started to
shake his head. "I don't think the judge would buy that.
The courts are paying for it right now, but it was just kind
of a trial thing, you know. . . ."

"I don't mean like that." She took another deep breath
and decided to ask him. What could she lose? Nothing.
And she might win everything . . . everything. . . . For
the third time in her life, Sam had fallen in love. And this
time not with a man, but a six-year-old boy. She loved
him as she had never loved another human being, with a
kind of depth and feeling she had never even suspected
that she had, as though some sort of well had reached
right past her heart into her spirit and now she was able
to give him all she had to give. And there was a lot of
loving left over from the men who had left her, a lot that
she had left to give. And now it was Timmie's, with all of
her heart. "What if I adopt him?"

"I see." The social worker sat down heavily in a chair
and looked at Samantha. He didn't like what he was
seeing. He could see that she loved the child. "I don't

know, Miss Taylor. I would hate to get your hopes up. His mother may still want him."

A strange light came into Sam's eyes. "By what right, I might ask, Mr. Pfizer? As I recall, she beat him, not to mention her drug habits—"

"All right, all right . . . I know." Oh, Jesus. This he didn't need, not today—not any day, in fact. People only got hurt thinking the way she did. The truth was that his mother could most likely keep him, whether Sam liked that idea or not. "The fact is that she's the boy's natural mother. The courts lean over backward to respect that."

"How far do they lean?" Her voice was both frightened and cold. It was frightening to have let herself love the child as much as she did now, and to have to face the possibility that he might leave.

The social worker looked at her sadly. "To tell you the truth, they lean pretty far."

"Couldn't I do something?"

"You could." He sighed. "You could hire a lawyer and fight her, if she still wants him. But you might lose . . . you probably will." And then he thought to ask her about the child. "What about the boy? Have you asked him? That could weigh with the court, even though he's still very young. A natural mother would have a strong case here, no matter how rotten she is. You know, the worst of it is that with the state rehabilitating her, we really can't afford to say now that she's not okay. If we do, then we're admitting that our whole rehabilitation system doesn't work, which it does not. But it's kind of a Catch-22 situation. See what I mean?" Sam nodded vaguely. "What about the boy, have you asked him?" She shook her head. "Why don't you?"

"I will."

"All right. Then give me a call after that. If he wants to go back to his mother, you should let it go. But if he wants to stay here"—he paused, thinking it over—"I'll go talk to the mother myself. Maybe she won't give you any problem." And then he bestowed a wintry smile. "I hope for your sake that she makes it easy, the boy would sure be better off here with you."

It was an understatement but Sam let it pass. The fact was that Timmie would be better off anywhere than with her, and Sam was determined to protect the child with all her will.

They went out to see Timmie ride then, and as happened with parents who saw their children ride for the first time, Martin Pfizer, the hardened, tired, old social worker, had to wipe away a stray tear. It was incredible to see what had happened to Timmie. He was beautiful and blond and clean and happy, he laughed all the time now, looked at Sam with an air of pure adoration, and he was even funny, and the oddest thing of all was that he even looked quite a lot like her.

When Martin Pfizer left at the end of the day, he said something again to Sam in a whisper as he squeezed her arm. "Ask him and call me." And then, tousling Timmie's hair, he shook Sam's hand and waved a last good-bye as he drove off.

It wasn't until after dinner that night when she took Timmie back to his room that she asked him, while he buttoned his pajamas and she put his braces away.

"Timmie?"

"Yeah?"

She turned to look at him, feeling something tremble inside her. What if he didn't want her? If he wanted to go back to his mother? She wasn't sure if she could stand the rejection, but she had to ask him. And that would only be the beginning. "You know, I was thinking about something today." With a look of interest he waited. "I was wondering what you would think about sticking around here. . . ." It was ghastly, she hadn't realized that it would be so hard to ask him. "You know, kind of like forever . . . I mean—"

"You mean stay here with you?" His eyes grew huge in the little tanned face.

"Yeah, that's what I mean."

"Oh, wow!" But she knew as he said it that he hadn't understood her. He thought she just meant an extended visit, and she knew that she had to tell him it would mean giving up his mom.

"Timmie . . ." He had his arms around her now and she pulled him away so she could see his face. "I don't mean just like the other kids here." He seemed puzzled. "I mean . . . I mean . . ." It was like a proposal of marriage. "I want to adopt you, if they'd let me. But you have to want that too. I would never do anything you didn't want." She was having to fight back tears and he stared at her in amazement.

"You mean you want me?" He seemed astounded.

"Of course I want you, silly." She hugged him tight again, the tears spilling from her eyes. "You're the best little kid in the whole world."

"What about my mom?"

"I don't know, Timmie. That would be the hard part."

"Would she come to see me?"

"I don't know. Maybe we could arrange that, but I think it would be harder for everyone that way." She was being honest with him, she knew she had to. It was a big step for him to take.

But he looked frightened when she looked down into his face again and she could feel him tremble. "Would she come and beat me?"

"Oh, no." It was a cry of anguish. "I wouldn't let her do that."

And then suddenly he started to cry and he told her things that he had never told her, about his mother and what she had done to him. When it was over, he lay in Sam's arms, spent, but he was no longer frightened, and after she pulled the sheets up to his chin, she sat next to him in the dark for over an hour, just watching him sleep and letting her tears flow. The last thing he had said to her as his eyes closed was "I want to be yours, Sam." And it was all she had wanted to hear.

35

The next morning Sam called Martin Pfizer and told him what Timmie had said. She also told him some of the other things he had told her, about the beatings and the neglect, things he had kept inside for a long, sad time. Pfizer shook his head.

"I hate to say it, but it doesn't surprise me. All right, I'll see what I can do."

But by the next day he knew that he could do nothing. He had spent two hours with the woman, tried to reason with her, had talked to her counselor at the facility where she had been incarcerated, but he knew that it was useless to say more. With a heavy heart he called Sam that evening and found her alone in the big house.

"She won't do it, Miss Taylor. I tried everything, reason, threats, everything. She wants him."

"Why? She doesn't love him."

"She thinks she does. She spent hours telling me about her father and mother, how her father beat her, her mother whipped her. It's the only thing she knows."

"But she'll kill him."

"Maybe. Maybe not. But there isn't a damn thing we can do now until she tries."

"But can I sue for custody?" Sam's hand trembled as she waited.

"Yes. That doesn't mean that you have a chance. She's the natural mother, Miss Taylor. You're a single woman, and a—a handicapped person." He caught himself quickly. "That won't look well in court."

"But look what I've done for him already. Look at the life he could have here."

"I know. That makes sense to you and me, but there's an element of precedent involved, and you'll have to convince the judge. Get yourself a lawyer, Miss Taylor, and give it a try. But you have to be realistic. Treat it as a test case, an experiment. If you lose, you lose, if you win, you get the boy." Was he crazy? Didn't he understand that she loved Timmie and he loved her?

"Thank you." Her voice was chilly when she hung up, and she spun around the room half a dozen times, mumbling to herself and thinking, and it drove her nuts that she had to wait until morning before she could call.

But when Timmie turned up the next morning, she gave him several errands to do for her, so that she could call Caroline's old lawyer and see if he could refer her to someone who might take the case.

"A child-custody suit, Samantha?" He sounded surprised. "I didn't know you had children."

"I don't." She smiled grimly into the phone. "Yet."

"I see." But of course he didn't. But he gave her two names of lawyers he had heard of in L.A. He knew neither of them personally, but assured her that their reputations were first-rate.

"Thanks." When she called them, the first lawyer was on vacation in Hawaii, and the other was due back from the East the next day. She left a message for him to call her and spent the next twenty-four hours on pins and needles, waiting for him to call. But he did, as his secretary had promised, at exactly five o'clock in the afternoon.

"Miss Taylor?" The voice was deep and mellifluous, and she couldn't tell if he was young or old. In as little time as she could, she explained the problem, told him what she wanted to do, what Timmie wanted, what the social worker had said, and where Timmie's mother was. "My, my, you do have a problem, don't you?" But he sounded intrigued by what she had told him. "If you don't mind, I'd really like to come out and see the boy." She had told him that both she and Timmie were bound to wheelchairs, but she had explained to him about the ranch and how well Timmie had done. "I think an important part of your case would hinge on the surroundings, and I should see them if I'm to make any sense. That is, of course, if you decide that you'd like me to represent you." But so far she had liked what he had said.

"How do you feel about the case, Mr. Warren?"

"Well, why don't we talk about it at greater length tomorrow? On the surface I'm not overly optimistic, but this could be one of those highly emotional situations that get resolved in a most unorthodox way."

"In other words, I don't have a chance. Is that what you're saying?" Her heart sank.

"Not exactly. But it won't be easy. I think you know that already."

She nodded. "I suspected that much from what the social worker said. It doesn't make any sense to me though, dammit. If that woman is a junkie and a child abuser, why is she even considered a possibility as Timmie's custodial parent?"

"Because she's his natural mother."

"Is that really enough?"

"No. But if he were your son, wouldn't you want every chance to keep him, no matter how screwed up you were?"

Samantha sighed into the phone. "What about the good of the child?"

"That's going to be our best argument, Miss Taylor. Now tell me where you are and I'll come and see you tomorrow. Route Twelve, you said? Let's see, how far is that from . . ."

She gave him the appropriate directions and he appeared the next day at noon. He was driving a dark green Mercedes, wore a pair of dark brown slacks and a beige cashmere jacket, an expensive silk tie, and a very good-looking cream-colored shirt. He was a man clearly in his mid-forties. His watch was Piaget, his hair was iron-gray, and his eyes were steel-blue. His full name was Norman Warren. And Samantha couldn't resist a smile when she saw him. She had worked for too many years among people who looked so much like him. She held out a hand from her wheelchair with a grin.

"Forgive me, but are you from New York?" She had to know. But he laughed right out loud.

"Hell yes. How did you know?"

"So am I. Not that you can tell anymore." Nonetheless she had worn a soft lilac sweater with her jeans today instead of her usual flannel shirt, and her dark blue cowboy boots were brand-new.

They shook hands and exchanged pleasantries, and she led him to the big house, where she had prepared sandwiches and hot coffee, and there was a hot apple pie she had "stolen" from the main hall when she took Timmie to lunch there a few minutes before. He had been very annoyed when she had left him but she had explained that she was expecting a grown-up for lunch at the house.

"Why can't I meet him too?" He had pouted ferociously as she left him with Josh and the handful of kids who weren't in school. They all accepted Timmie as their mascot, he was the youngest in the place and he looked so much like Samantha that somehow they regarded him almost as though he were her son, and of course she did too.

"You'll meet him but I want to talk to him first."

"What about?"

"Business." She grinned at him in answer to the question he didn't quite dare ask. "And no, he is not a cop." Timmie laughed his bright little laugh.

"How did you know that was what I thought?"

"Because I know you, silly, now go eat." He had gone off with the others, complaining because they were eating leftover stew. She had promised to come and get him when they were finished talking business.

And as she sat over her own lunch with Norman Warren, she told him everything she could about the child. "May I see him?" he finally asked. When they went to find him at the main hall, Warren looked around himself with interest and eyed the dazzlingly beautiful woman in the lilac sweater, perfectly at ease in her chair. Just being there was an experience for Norman Warren, he could see from the way the place was kept, and from the happy people he saw around them, that what Samantha had done was a success. But nothing had prepared him for what he saw when he met Timmie, or when the boy mounted a palomino with Josh's help, or when he saw Sam ride beside him on Pretty Girl, or when the others came home from school and took their lessons. Norman Warren didn't leave until after dinner, and when he did, he did so with regret.

"I want to stay forever."

"I'm sorry, I can't adopt you too." Samantha laughed with him. "And fortunately you don't qualify to come here as a student. But anytime you'd like to just come and visit and ride with us, we'd love it."

He looked sheepish and almost whispered, "I'm scared shitless of horses."

She whispered back, "We could cure you."

Another sotto voce, "No, you couldn't. I won't let you." And then they both laughed and he drove off. They had come to terms on the agreement—she would pay him a fee of ten thousand dollars to represent her in her suit. She liked him very much, and he seemed to like Timmie, and there was every reason to hope that she at least had a chance to win him, and if she didn't, she could appeal it. He stressed once again that it wouldn't be easy, but it wasn't impossible either, and there were a lot of sympathetic factors in her favor, not least among them the way she and Timmie loved each other, and he hoped the fact that they were both in wheelchairs would add drama and sympathy to her side rather than work against them. But that remained to be seen. She had signed papers that afternoon. He would file the complaint in Los Angeles the next morning, and they would get a hearing date as soon as they could.

"Think he can help us, Sam?" Timmie looked up at her sadly as she accompanied him back to his room. She had explained to him who Norman Warren was and what he was going to do.

"I hope so, love. We'll see."

"What if he can't do it?"

"Then I'll kidnap you and we'll hide in the hills." She was teasing but his eyes sparkled as she pushed open the door to his room and turned on the lights for him.

"Okay."

Only when she left the room did she begin to wonder

the same thing . . . what if he couldn't . . . but he had to . . . he had to win the case for her. She couldn't bear losing Timmie. And by the time she got back to her own room, she convinced herself that she never would.

36

They shared Christmas in peace, and for the first time in Timmie's life he had the kind of Christmas of which children dream. There were presents stacked high in boxes, things to wear, and games, and puzzles, a bright fire engine with a hat for him to wear, and a sweater for his teddy bear, and even some things Sam had made for him. And in the main hall was a huge tree surrounded by presents. There were toys for all the children currently staying at the ranch. And one of the counselors, at her request, had dressed up as Santa, and it reminded Sam and Josh of the year when Tate Jordan had been Santa.

The memory of the man she still so loved placing the angel on the Christmas tree came back to her like a knife stab to her heart. Suddenly she was reminded of so many things about Tate and about John, whom she so seldom thought of now. They had had another baby, she knew, and Liz had finally been fired by the network, because she was so tiresome on the air. John Taylor's career was still booming but once in a great while when Sam watched him she found him plastic and empty and too pretty and terribly boring, and she wondered why she had ever cared. It seemed amazing now to watch eleven years of one's life fly out the window and not even care, but she just didn't. It was different when she thought of Tate.

"Sam . . . can I ask you a crazy question?" Josh asked her as they stood apart in a corner, watching the kids open their gifts.

"Sure. What?" But she already knew.

"Were you in love with Tate Jordan?" She looked into Josh's eyes and nodded her head slowly.

"Yes, I was."

"Was that why he left?"

"I suppose. He decided not to work things out, I guess. And I had told him I didn't want to play the same game as Caro and Bill. But he didn't think a lady should love a ranch hand. At least not openly." She looked sad as she spoke. "So he left."

"I figured it was something like that."

"And he had some kind of fit when he found out who my ex-husband was . . . thought he wasn't good enough for me, or something equally dumb. . . ."

"Shit." Josh looked instantly angry. "He was worth ten of that jerk. Oh—" His face flushed bright red. "I'm sorry, Sam. . . ."

She chuckled. "Don't be. I was just thinking the same thing."

"And he never wrote you or nothing?"

"No. I think I must have looked for him on every ranch in this country, but I never found him."

Josh looked sorry again as he glanced at Sam. "It's a damn shame, Sam. He was a good man, and I always thought that he loved you. Maybe he'll turn up someday, just to say hi to Bill or me or Caro, and find you here instead."

Sam shook her head with a taut expression on her face. "I hope not. He'd be in for one hell of a shock." She meant her legs, but this time Josh shook his head.

"You think he'd care?"

"It doesn't matter, Josh. I would. That's all over now. I've got the kids instead."

"At your age, Sam? Don't be crazy. What are you, twenty-eight, twenty-nine?"

She grinned at the old man. "Josh, I love you. I'm thirty-three."

"All sounds the same to me. Try fifty-nine and see how you like the feel of that."

"On you it looks good."

"Sweet-talker, but I love it." He grinned at her, and then his face grew serious again. "You're talking bullshit though, you know, about Tate. And it don't matter if it's Tate or someone else, you're too damn young to treat yourself like an old maid." And then he narrowed his eyes and lowered his voice. "The truth is, Sam, you're a damn liar. You spend all your time teaching these kids that they don't have to live or think or act like cripples, and then in your heart you think of yourself as one." He had hit a nerve but she said nothing and kept her eyes on the kids. "It's true, Sam . . . dammit, it's true. I saw that lawyer from Los Angeles talking to you the other day. He likes you, like a woman, dammit, and do you pay him any mind? No, hell no, you just act like a happy little old lady and give him iced tea."

"There's nothing wrong with iced tea." She grinned at him this time.

"No, but there's a lot wrong with pretending you're not a woman anymore at thirty-three."

"Watch out, Josh," she said, trying to glare at him, "I may attack you the next time we're alone." And with that, she blew a kiss in his direction and wheeled herself into the midst of the kids. It was her way of telling him that she didn't want to hear any more. He had come a little too close to home.

It took them all two days to recover from the excitement of Christmas. There weren't even any riding lessons, just some casual groups that rode out over the hills, but neither Timmie nor Sam were among them. They were both spending a lot of time alone, as though they each had a deep need to be together. The hearing was set for December 28.

"You scared?" The night before the hearing, she had put Timmie in her smallest guest room, next door to her own room, and she was just tucking him into bed.

"About tomorrow?" Her face was close to his, and she

touched it with one long graceful hand. "A little. Are you?"

"Yeah." She saw now that the big blue eyes were filled with terror. "A lot. What if she hits me?"

"I won't let her."

"What if she takes me?"

"She won't." But what if they let her take him? That was the ghost that haunted Samantha, and she couldn't promise him that that wouldn't happen. She didn't want to lie. She had already told him that if they lost it she would appeal it, if that was what he wanted, and she had also told him that if what he wanted was to be with his mommy then that was okay too. It tore at her heart to give him that option, but she knew she had to. She didn't want to steal him from his own mother. She wanted him to come to her with an open heart. "It'll be all right, sweetheart. You'll see."

But she didn't look nearly as certain the next day as Josh pushed both their wheelchairs up the ramp at the Los Angeles County Courthouse. She and Timmie were ferociously holding hands, and when they pressed into the elevator in their wheelchairs, they both felt awkward and conspicuous until Josh helped pull them out. Norman Warren was waiting for them just outside the courtroom, in a dark blue suit. He looked eminently respectable, as did Sam. She had worn a pretty pale blue wool dress, which was a remnant of her New York wardrobe, a matching light blue mohair coat, and plain black leather Gucci shoes. She had bought Timmie new clothes especially for the occasion, little navy blue slacks with a matching jacket and a pale blue turtleneck sweater,

409

which accidentally matched Sam's dress. They looked very much like mother and son as they sat there waiting, and Norman once again noticed the striking resemblance of his towhead, her blond hair, and the same enormous blue eyes.

The hearing took place in a small courtroom, and the judge entered, wearing glasses and a quiet smile. He did his best not to intimidate Timmie when he looked at him, and he sat at a desk on a slightly raised platform, which was less impressive than some of the desks he had sat at in other courts. He was a man in his early sixties, and he had been doing child-custody hearings for a great many years. He was admired in Los Angeles for his fairness and his kindness to children—a number of times had saved children from unfortunate adoptions. He had a profound respect for children and natural mothers, and often encouraged the mothers to think over their decisions before they gave away their babies, their faces drenched in tears. Many women had come back to thank him, and it was something he would always carry with him when he retired. And now he looked at Timmie with interest, and at Samantha and her attorney, and a few minutes later at the tiny, fragile-looking young woman who slipped into the courtroom with her attorney. She was wearing a gray skirt and a white blouse and she looked more like a schoolgirl than an addict or a hooker. And Sam learned then for the first time that she was only twenty-two. She had a kind of fragile beauty and looked like the sort of girl who couldn't possibly take care of herself. One wanted instantly to love, cherish, and protect her. It was part of why Timmie had always felt sorry for her after she beat him. Because she looked so hurt and so distraught herself. It always made him forgive her and made him want to help her, instead of expecting her to help him.

The court was called to order, the files were handed to the judge, but unnecessarily, as he had already read all the existing documents the day before. He said at the outset that it was an interesting case because of the aspects introduced by Samantha, a handicapped child, a handicapped adopting mother, but they had to keep in mind, all of them there, that what was being looked for by the court, and should remain everyone's goal, was the ultimate good of the child. The judge offered the option to have the child removed, but Sam and Timmie had already discussed it. He said he wanted to be there, he didn't want to be "taken away by the cops." She assured him that he could wait outside with Josh, but he insisted that he wanted to be with her. She noticed then that he never let his eyes roam toward his mother, as though he were frightened to acknowledge her presence, or even see her, and he kept his hand in Sam's and his eyes toward the judge.

The opposing attorney called Timmie's mother as his first witness, and as Sam sat staring her full in the face, she realized full well what she was up against. A sweet face, a soft voice, a sob story from beginning to end, and the assurance that this time she had learned a lesson and had done nothing but read psychology books to learn more about herself and how she might help her precious son. Timmie's eyes fell into his lap the whole time her testimony was being heard and he didn't raise them again until she'd left the stand. Sam's attorney put on record that he would cross-examine her later, and the next witnesses were called, a psychiatrist who had examined Timmie's mother for the county, declaring her to be a warm, feeling young woman who had had an unfortunate youth. They felt that she had no intention of hurting her child, but had been under enormous pressure financially, but that now that she was about to go to work in a big hotel downtown everything was looking up. Norman Warren made the psychiatrist look foolish, and the implication was made that she would have ample opportunity in the hotel to start picking up johns. The comment was stricken from the record, Norman was admonished, and the witness was excused from the stand. There were additionally two counselors called, and then a doctor attesting to the mother's health and to the fact that she was in no way addicted to drugs anymore. And last of all, there was a priest who had known her since she was eleven, in fact he had baptized Timmie. He said that he felt absolutely certain that the child belonged with the mother who loved him, and as he said it Sam felt her stomach flip over in her gut. She held tightly to Timmie's hand through the entire proceeding, and when the priest left the stand, they adjourned for lunch. Norman had cross-examined them all except the mother herself and the priest. He was going to call Timmie's mother to the stand after the lunch break, but he explained to Sam that he had no intention of tackling the Catholic Church on the stand.

"Why not?"

"The judge is Catholic, my dear. Besides, what am I going to do to impeach what the man is saying? We're better off not touching that one." Nonetheless he had made all the others look slightly shady, and he interrogated them almost with an air of amusement and derision, as though their testimony itself was tainted due to association with the woman herself. But none of what he had done to them even came close to what he did to Timmie's mother, and at a sign from Sam, Josh had firmly wheeled Timmie out of the room, protesting in a hoarse whisper, but he wasn't given any choice by Samantha, who blew him a kiss and turned back to watch what was happening on the stand. The girl was shaking in her seat, and almost before she started talking, she started crying. And it was admittedly difficult to envision this frail child as the villain in the piece. But despite what she looked like it was nevertheless made clear that she had discovered drugs at twelve, heroin at thirteen, had been arrested for prostitution at fifteen, gotten pregnant with Timmie at sixteen, had had five abortions to date, had been in seven drug programs, had been arrested nine times as a juvenile, and three as an adult.

"But," her attorney insisted as he objected, "the court must keep in mind that this woman is no longer addicted, that she has just been through a very arduous state-run drug program, and if we are to say that this woman is not rehabilitated, then we are in fact saying that our entire system of rehabilitation does not work." The objection was duly noted and sustained. Her arrest record was stricken from the record as per California law, the rest stayed.

Her testimony took well over an hour, she sobbed throughout and talked remorsefully about "my baby"

413

whenever she had the chance, but every time Sam looked at her, she thought of the shots she hadn't gotten for him, which was why he had contracted polio, she thought of the beatings he had had at her hands, the torment, the loneliness, the terror, and all Sam wanted was to rise out of her wheelchair and scream.

For their side, Norman Warren called the social worker, Martin Pfizer, who was unemotional, matter-of-fact, and not particularly exciting as a witness; there was Sam's own physician; Josh; and there had been a packet of letters from important people, like judges and doctors, about the marvelous work she was doing on the ranch. And then at last there was Sam herself. The fact that she was divorced was brought out, that she was not remarried and had no "prospects," as the opposing attorney put it, at the present time, the fact that she was indeed irreversibly handicapped. The whole sad, long list was emphasized over and over until Sam almost started to feel sorry for herself. Norman objected and got that line of questioning stopped. In the end she wound up sounding like a kindly, interested do-gooder who wanted to help Timmie, but unlike his half-hysterical mother she did not shout "my baby" and have to be led from the room.

The final witness was the hardest. It was Timmie himself, and his mother was asked if she could possibly quell her tears, or if she would like a recess during which she might compose herself once again. She chose to subdue herself then and there, still sniffing loudly as she listened while Sam watched the look of terror in the child's face. Everything that had previously been brought out was now tested. What his life was like with his mother, what his life was like with Sam, how his mother provided for him, what Sam bought him and gave him, how he felt about the two women, and then suddenly, "Are you afraid of your mother, Timmie?" But the question itself obviously frightened him so much that he shrank back in his wheelchair, holding his teddy, shaking his head violently.

"No . . . no!"

"Does she ever beat you or hit you?"

There was no answer and then he shook his head and was finally asked to speak up. All they got was a hoarse "No." Sam closed her eyes in despair. She understood what he was doing. There was no way he could tell the truth with his mother there. It went on for another half hour and then they were all sent home. The judge kindly asked them all to return the following morning. He said that he had all of their phone numbers, and that if, for some reason, he felt that he would not be able to reach a verdict that quickly, he would let them know. But if they did not hear from him that evening, they were to return to the same court the next morning, bringing Timmie— this was a glance at Sam—and the verdict would be returned. He felt that in the interest of the child, and to avoid any additional pain to all parties, it was best to have the verdict returned right away. With that, the judge rose and the bailiff announced that court was adjourned.

On the drive back to the ranch Sam felt her whole body ache with exhaustion and Timmie fell asleep in her arms almost as soon as they left the curb. He had trembled with terror as his mother had begun to approach him, clutched at Sam's hand, and Norman had whisked him from the courtroom as Josh helped Samantha, and they got away as quickly as they could. She realized later as she held him what a brave thing Timmie had done by being willing to try to go through the custody hearings. If his mother won him back, she might do anything to get even, and he had known that better than anyone. But Sam understood it now too as she held him close. How on earth was she going to give him to that woman if she had to? How could she bear it? As she lay in bed that night she knew she couldn't, that it would kill her. For hours she lay there and thought of taking him and running away somewhere. But where and how, and what was the point really? Two people in wheelchairs wouldn't get very far, and then she thought of the secret cabin, which she hadn't visited since she got back to the ranch. But she knew that even there they would find her. It was hopeless. All they could do was believe in justice and hope for the best.

37

Sam was awake long before sunrise the next morning. In fact, she realized as she looked at the clock, she had only slept for an hour and a half. But when she wheeled her way into Timmie's room, beside hers, she found that he was awake too.

"Hi, sweetheart. . . ." She kissed him on the tip of the nose and reached for his braces. "Good morning."

"I won't go with her."

"Why don't we worry about that after breakfast?" Sam tried to sound lighthearted, but he burst into tears and clung to her. Thus had begun the day. They had eaten breakfast alone again that morning. The rest of the children had no idea what was going on, and only a few of the therapists and counselors had been told by Samantha. They were all trying to keep it as low-key as they could. But it was obvious when she left again with Josh and Timmie that something major was going on. As though they sensed something wrong around them, the children were unusually quiet as they boarded the bus to go to school.

In Los Angeles Samantha and Josh and Timmie met Norman outside the courtroom, and they all looked grim.

"Take it easy, Sam." Norm gently touched her arm. She was wearing gray slacks and a gray cashmere sweater, and Timmie was wearing the same suit as the day before, this time with a red and white plaid shirt.

The judge began the proceedings by asking to have Timmie in the room, and then addressed himself to the boy, explaining that he had listened to all the evidence and had tried to make a good decision that would make Timmie happy for a very long time. He smiled at him like a benevolent grandfather and then asked him if he could wheel himself to the front of the room, explaining that it was only a formality, because he was the most important person there, after all, and all of this was about him. Timmie looked questioningly at Sam then and she smiled and nodded, and he rolled himself front and center as the judge had asked.

With that, the judge turned his attention to Sam, explaining that he understood that what she was doing was not only admirable, but saintly, that he had talked to several people about the ranch, and that he was impressed beyond anything he could describe to her. Once again he favored her with a warm smile. But then he went on to say that although there was no doubt that her intentions were excellent, and that she could certainly materially provide better for Timmie than could his mother, and although Timmie had certainly had a difficult life with this young woman who had tried so hard to find the right road for herself and her handicapped child, he did however feel certain now, particularly after talking to Father Renney, that Timmie's mother had found her feet at last. Therefore, he beamed down at Timmie, he had found that Timmie belonged with his rightful mother. "And now"—he gestured to the startled young girl in the pink blouse and with the tousled hair—"you may reclaim your son." And then with an official bang of his gavel that felt like Sam's heart hitting bottom as she stared, he announced in a booming voice, "The court finds in favor of the natural mother." He got up then and left the room as Sam tried desperately not to scream. Timmie's mother, however, did not restrain herself in a similar fashion, and ran to him, almost knocking him out of his chair. All Sam could see was Timmie flailing wildly, trying to move away from her, and his chair being firmly held by the lawyer as he was embraced by his mother shrieking loudly all the while, "My baby . . . my baby . . ."

"Sam . . . Sam!" It was a plaintive wail that almost tore her asunder and instinctively she turned toward him and tried to push her wheelchair past Josh and Norman to reach the child. But Josh grabbed the handles on the back of the wheelchair and Norm blocked her, the two men had instantly understood each other without a word. It would do no good now. The mother was all over her child.

"Stop . . ." Sam pushed at Norm. "I have to see him."

"You can't, Sam!" He spoke quietly but firmly, and Josh wouldn't let go of the chair as she pushed.

"I have to, dammit . . . Josh, let go!" She was beginning to sob now, but already Timmie's mother's lawyer was pushing his little wheelchair from the room as in anguish Timmie turned back toward Samantha, waving his little arms with a grief-stricken face.

"Sam . . . Sam!"

"I love you!" she called out. "I love you, Timmie! It's okay!" And then he was gone. And as though the last ounce of strength had left her, she dropped her face in her hands and began to sob. For a long moment neither man knew what to do, and then Norman knelt beside her.

"I'm so sorry, Sam . . . we can appeal it."

"No." She could barely speak as she reached for her handkerchief and shook her head at Norm. "No. I can't do that to him." He nodded and stood up and then signaled Josh. There was no reason to stay there. It was all over for Samantha and Timmie. The boy was gone.

38

For the rest of the week Sam stayed at the big house, never leaving the building, and for the first day not leaving her room. Norman had come to pick up Timmie's things to return them to the social worker for Timmie, but Sam had refused to see him. Josh was taking care of everything for her. Twice that morning Norman had knocked on the door. He had even tried to call her. But she didn't want to see anyone, except Timmie. She had just lost the last love of her life.

"Will she be all right?" Norm asked Josh with a look of

sorrow, and the old man shook his head with tears in his eyes.

"I don't know. She's tough, but she's lost a lot. And this . . . you don't know how she loved him."

Norman nodded sadly. "Yes, I do." For the first time in his career, as he left the courthouse the previous evening, he had stepped on the gas as hard as he could in his Mercedes, and as he drove home at eighty miles an hour he had cried too. "I'd like to see her when she's ready. And I want to talk to her about an appeal. I think it would be worth it. This is an unusual case, because what she has against her is the fact that she is both single and crippled. But it's absolutely incredible that the court should find for a prostitute and a drug addict because she's a natural mother against a woman like Sam. I want to take this one all the way to the Supreme Court."

"I'll tell her." Josh looked as though he approved. "When I see her."

And then suddenly Norman looked worried. "She wouldn't do anything crazy, would she?"

Josh thought for a while. "I don't think so." He didn't know she had tried that once before in the hospital in New York. But this time she wasn't suicidal. She just wished she were dead, but some faint, irrational hope that one day she might get Timmie back kept her from doing anything truly crazy. Instead, she just lay in bed, without moving, without eating, only dragging herself to the bathroom, for two whole days. She just cried and slept and then cried some more when she awoke, and at the end of the second day she awoke to hear someone pounding on her door. She lay silently in bed, fully intending not to answer, and then she heard glass breaking and knew that someone had just come through her front door.

"Who is it?" She sounded frightened. Maybe it was a burglar, she wondered. But as she sat up in bed with a look of confusion and terror, the lights in the hall suddenly went on, and she saw Jeff with his shock of red hair. His arm was bleeding as he stood there and then he looked suddenly embarrassed, and as always he flushed beet-red. "What are you doing here?"

"I came to see you. I couldn't take it anymore, Sam. I haven't seen a light on in here for two days, and you didn't answer the other times when I came to the door . . . I thought maybe . . . I was afraid . . . I wanted to know if you were all right." She nodded, smiling at him for caring, and then the tears came again and suddenly he was holding her tightly in his arms. The odd thing was that as he held her it was a familiar feeling, as though he had held her before, as though she knew his arms and his chest and his body, but she knew that it was a crazy thought and she pulled away from him and blew her nose.

"Thanks, Jeff."

He sat down on the edge of the bed and looked at her. Even after two days of just lying there, she looked lovely. And for just an instant he had a wild urge to kiss her, and as he thought of it he flushed bright red again. But as he did she was suddenly laughing through her tears and he looked at her in confusion. "What are you laughing at?"

"When you get embarrassed, you look just like a radish."

"Thanks a lot." He grinned. "I've been called carrot-top, but never radish-face." And then with a gentle smile, "You okay, Sam?"

"No. But I will be, I guess." And then another trickle of tears coursed down her face. "I just hope Timmie'll be okay."

"Josh says your lawyer wants to appeal it, all the way to the Supreme Court."

"Yeah?" She looked cynical and angry. "He's full of shit. He doesn't have a chance of winning. The fact is that I'm a cripple and I'm single. They probably don't even care if I'm single, but I'm a cripple. That's enough. Prostitutes and drug addicts make better mothers than cripples, or didn't you know?"

"The hell they do." He almost snarled it.

"Well, that's what the judge decided."

"The judge sucks." She suddenly laughed at the outrageous comment and then realized that she smelled beer on his breath. She frowned as she looked at the young redhead.

"You drunk, Jeff?"

He looked embarrassed and blushed again but he shook his head. "I just drank two beers. It takes more than that."

"How come?"

"It just does. I usually don't get tight till five or six."

"No." She laughed at him. "I mean how come you drank the two?" She didn't like the men to drink around the kids and Jeff knew it, but she knew from the darkness outside that it was after hours.

"It's New Year's Eve, Sam."

"It is?" She looked surprised and then counted

424

backward . . . the hearing had been on the twenty-eighth, the verdict on the twenty-ninth, that had been two days ago. "Oh, shit. So it is. And you're going out partying?" She smiled gently at him.

"Yeah. I'm goin' over to the Bar Three. Did I ever tell you I used to work there?"

"No, but you seem to have worked on every damn ranch in the West."

"I forgot to tell you about that one."

"Are you taking a date?"

"Mary Jo." This time he turned fire-engine red.

"Josh's girl?" She looked amused and he grinned at her. "Yeah."

"What did Josh have to say to that?"

"That he'd kick my ass if I got her drunk. But hell, she's almost nineteen. She's legal."

"I'd watch out though, if I were you. If Josh said he'd kick your ass, he means it." And then her face grew sober again. "How is he?"

"Worried about you." Jeff's voice was gentle in the quiet room. "We all are, the ones who know. Your lawyer was here yesterday."

"I figured he would be. To pick up Timmie's things?" Jeff hesitated and then nodded. "Did he get all his Christmas stuff?" She began to cry again. "I want him to have all of it."

"He has it, Sam." And then, not knowing what else to do for her, he took her in his arms and held her, and she lay her head against him and cried. He wanted to tell her then that he loved her, but he was afraid to. He had loved her the first time he saw her, with that incredible pale gold hair. But she was nine years older than he was and she never acted like she was interested in any man. He wondered sometimes if she could still do it, but he didn't even care, he just wanted to hold her and tell her he loved her one day. They lay like that for a long time, and then the tears stopped.

"Thank you." She looked at him for a long, quiet time, stirred by his strength and his youthful beauty. "You'd better get out of here now or you'll end up spending New Year's Eve with me instead of Mary Jo."

"You know something?" His voice was deep and sexy. "I'd like that."

"You would, would you?" Her eyes were teasing but she could see that his were not. But she didn't think what she was suddenly feeling was what Jeff needed. He didn't need an older woman, and a cripple yet, on his hands. He was young. He had his whole life in front of him, filled with girls like Mary Jo. But she was suddenly so desperately lonely that she wanted to reach out to him, and before she did something foolish, she wanted him to go. "Okay, kiddo, go celebrate New Year's Eve in style." She sat up in her bed and tried a smile.

"And you, Sam?"

"I'm going to take a hot bath, make myself something to eat, and come back to bed. I guess maybe tomorrow I'm going to have to come out of my hole and face the world."

"I'm glad to hear it. For a while there you had me scared."

"I'm tough, I guess, Jeff. Time does that to you." Time, and heartbreaks, and loss.

"Does it? It sure makes you beautiful too."

"Go on, Jeff." She looked worried. "It's time for you to go."

"I don't want to leave you, Sam. I want to stay here."

But she shook her head as she looked at him, took his hand, held it to her cheek, and then kissed the fingertips gently as she let it go. "You can't stay, Jeff."

"Why not?"

"I won't let you."

"You don't believe in ranchers and ranch hands mixing?" He bridled like a young stallion and she smiled.

"No, nothing like that, love. It's just that my life is behind me now and yours isn't. You don't need something like this."

"You're crazy. Do you know how long I've wanted you?"

She put a finger to his lips. "I don't want you to tell me. It's New Year's Eve, people say things they shouldn't on nights like this. I want us to be friends for a long time, Jeff. Please don't spoil it." And then, with tears in her eyes again, "I need you right now. You and Josh, and the children, but especially you and Josh. Don't do anything to change that. I just . . . I couldn't take it . . . I need you too much." He held her once again then, kissed the top of her head, and then stood up and looked down at her.

"I'll stay if you want me to, Sam."

She looked up into the brilliant green eyes and shook her head. "No, babe, it's okay. You go." He nodded slowly then and stood looking at her for one last moment in the doorway, and then she heard his cowboy boots echo in the hallway and the front door close.

39

"Sam? . . . Sam?" It was six o'clock in the morning on New Year's Day and she was dressed and in her kitchen, making coffee for the first time in three days, when she heard Josh pounding on the door. She smiled to herself. One by one they would all break her door down if she didn't come out now. She still felt the terrible emptiness of Timmie's loss, but she knew that she couldn't let herself go. She owed more than that to the other kids. Slowly she wheeled her chair to the front door and opened it, looking out into the gray light before dawn as Josh stood in his heavy jacket on the front porch.

"Hi, Josh. Happy New Year."

He stood there, saying nothing, and she wondered what was wrong. He looked as though he had been crying. "You okay?" He shook his head and walked slowly into the room. "Come and sit down." She had thought that he had come to offer her solace and now she knew that he was in trouble. "What is it?" She eyed him, her own brow furrowed with worry, and he gazed at her as he fell heavily into a chair and then dropped his head into his hands.

"The kids. Jeff and Mary Jo. They went out to some party last night"—he stopped and swallowed hard—"and they got drunk as skunks, and then drove home." Sam felt her heart begin to race. She was afraid to ask the next question but he answered it for her. He looked up with an air of great pain and she saw two great big tears creep down his face. "They ran into a tree and bounced off into a ravine . . . Mary Jo broke both her arms and legs, and tore up her face pretty bad . . . Jeff's dead." Sam closed her eyes and reached for his hand, thinking of the boy who had held her only the night before and wondering if she had asked him to stay with her after all, that none of it would ever have happened. But it would have been wrong for her to seduce a boy of twenty-four, she told herself as she thought back over the night before. Wrong? she questioned herself. Wrong? Was it better for him to be dead?

"Oh, God . . . " She opened her eyes and looked at Josh, and then she reached out and held him. "Will Mary Jo be okay, Josh?" He nodded and then sobbed into Sam's arms.

"But I loved that boy too." He had only been with them

for a year but it felt like half a lifetime, and now she
understood the references he'd had from other ranchers,
still wanting him to come back.

"Does he have folks we should call?"

"I don't know." He blew his nose on a red handkerchief
from his pocket and then replaced it with a sigh. "I guess
we should go through his things. I know his mom was
dead, because he said something about it once or twice,
but I don't know if he has sisters or brothers or a dad. He
never talked about his life much, just about the kids here,
and you, and how happy he was around the kids and the
horses."

Sam closed her eyes again and took a deep breath.
"We'd better go through his stuff. Where is he now?"

Josh sighed and stood up. "I told them to keep him at
the hospital, and we'd call and tell them what to do. If his
folks are somewhere else, they may want him sent back."

"I just hope we find something in his things that tells
us who they are. What do we do if he doesn't have
anything like that, Josh?" This was a new problem for
her.

"Bury him with Bill and Miss Caro, I guess, or in town."

"We can bury him here." He was one of her people
now, and he had loved the ranch. It was mad to be talking
of burying that boy though, only a few hours before he
had been standing in her bedroom doorway, and sitting
on a corner of her bed, and holding her in his arms. She
forced the memories from her mind, reached for her own
jacket on a low peg near the front door, and turned her
wheelchair slowly out the door.

Josh looked at the broken window in surprise then and turned to Sam. "What happened?"

"Jeff. He wanted to be sure I was okay last night. He came to see me before they went out."

"I had a feeling he'd do that, Sam. He looked at this house for two days and I knew all he could think about was you." Sam nodded and said nothing more until they reached his cabin. For her it was bumpy going, because the paths to the men's cabins didn't need the smoothly paved walks that were everywhere else to allow for the wheelchairs. But Josh pushed her over the bumps and ruts and eased her wheelchair into the comfortable little cabin. She looked around at the unmade bed and moderate chaos that the boy had left, and felt that if they looked hard enough, they would find him. Maybe he would come staggering out of the bathroom with a grin, or poke his head out of the covers, or come wandering in singing a song. . . . He couldn't be dead . . . not Jeff . . . not that young boy. Josh looked at her with his own look of pain and sat down at the small maple desk and began to pull out papers. There were photographs and letters from friends, souvenirs from old jobs, pictures of girls, programs from rodeos, and everything except what they needed to find now.

Finally Josh came up with something that looked like a little leather billfold and in it he found a card with Jeff's social security number on it, some insurance papers, a couple of lottery tickets, and a slip of paper. On the paper it said, "In case I get hurt, please contact my father: Tate Jordan, Grady Ranch," and there was a post-office-box number in Montana.

As Josh looked at it his mouth dropped open and he stared, and then suddenly he remembered . . . the Bar Three . . . why hadn't he thought to ask? Sure, Tate had had a boy over there. He looked up at Sam in disbelief and she frowned at him.

"What is it?"

There was nothing he could say to her now. He only handed her the slip of paper and walked slowly outside for a breath of air.

40

Sam stared at the piece of paper for almost half an hour, trying to decide what to do and feeling her heart pound in her chest while she thought of it. She had almost made love to Tate's son the night before—what an insane quirk of fate. And now because she hadn't, he was dead, and she had to call his father. But she knew that even if they had made love, he might have gone out drinking and could have died then too. Whatever had happened, there was no changing fate. And now she had to face the problem of what to tell Tate Jordan and how. It was ironic that after all the searching she had done, and all the looking and asking and calling, there it was finally, his address, lying in the palm of her hand. She slipped the piece of paper into her jacket pocket and wheeled outside.

Josh was waiting for her there, leaning against a tree, as the sun rose slowly in the morning sky. "What are you going to do, Sam? You going to call him?" He knew the truth now, and he hoped to hell she would.

She nodded somberly. "We have to. It's only right."

"You gonna do it?"

"No, you are. You're the foreman."

"You scared?"

"No, if it were anyone else, I'd do it, Josh. But I don't want to talk to him. Not now." It had been almost exactly three years since he'd run off.

"Maybe you should."

"Maybe so." She looked at him sadly. "But I'm not going to."

"Okay." But when Josh called, they told him that Tate was in Wyoming for the week, at a cattle auction with some of the other hands. No one seemed to know where they were staying or how to reach them, and it meant that Jeff was going to have to be buried, either at the ranch or in town. They couldn't wait a week.

The funeral was simple and painful for all. But it was part of nature, part of life, Sam told the children, and Jeff had been their friend, so it was right that they should bury him together. The local minister said a little piece over the casket, and that day the men buried him next to Caro and Bill, and the children rode out over the hills, each of them carrying a bunch of flowers, which they left on the fresh grave. And afterward they all stood around and

sang their favorite songs. It seemed a fitting way to bury
someone who had been one of them and had been a friend
to many. And as they turned their horses back toward
the ranch and cantered over the hills, Samantha watched
them, with the sun setting to their right, and their
horses' hooves beating softly on the ground, and the
air cool around them, and she thought that she had
never seen anything as lovely in her life. For a moment
she felt as though Jeff were riding alongside them, and in
silent tribute to their lost friend, the ranch hands had led
out Jeff's horse riderless, with his colorful Western
saddle. For some reason it brought back her own
memories of Timmie, and once more she felt tears sting
her eyes.

And as she wrote to Tate that night from her desk at
the big house, it helped her to hold out a hand to him,
whatever had passed between them and whatever was no
more. She, too, had lost a child now, though he had been
hers differently than Jeff had been Tate's, but still she
knew the agony of that loss and she felt it again now even
more deeply as she wrote to the man she had sought in
vain for so long. She found herself wishing, too, that she
knew what Jeff had told him. The one thing she didn't
want him to know was what had happened to her. But she
decided to twist the truth a little and pray that Jeff had not
told at all.

"Three years doesn't seem like a very long time," she
wrote from her kitchen table after the initial paragraph
in which she told him the news as simply as she could.
"But what a great deal has changed here. Caroline and Bill
are both gone now, resting next to where we laid Jeff

today, in the hills, near their cabin. And the children who share the ranch with me rode out with flowers to leave on Jeff's grave as the men led his horse in the sunset. It was a difficult moment, a beautiful day, a sad loss for us all. The children sang the songs he loved best, and somehow, as we rode back, I had the feeling that he was near us. I hope, Tate, that you always feel him near you. He was a wonderful young man and a dear friend to us all, and the waste of such a young life is a source of disbelief and sorrow and immeasurable pain. I can't help but feel though that he accomplished more in his short lifetime than most of us with so many more years, which we spend so much less well.

"I don't know if you were aware, but Caroline had left the ranch, after her death, for a special purpose. She wished it to be made into a special facility for handicapped children, and Josh and I worked for months afterward to get it ready. It was just before we opened our doors to these special children that Jeff joined us, and he had a gift for this kind of work that truly touched the heart. He did things that would take hours to relate but that should make you proud of him, and I will see now if in the slew of photographs we took in the beginning there are any of Jeff, which I will send you. It will undoubtedly give you a clearer idea of what he did here. The ranch is very different from what you once knew.

"Certainly none of us had realized that this was Caroline's intention for the ranch, but it has served a worthy purpose, as has your son. I grieve for you in your loss, I wish you well, and we will be sending you all of his things to avoid the need of your making this painful journey. If there is anything that we can do here in this regard, please don't hesitate to contact us. Josh is always here and I'm sure would be happy to help you." She signed it "Cordially, Samantha Taylor."

There was no trace in her letter of what had passed between them, and the day after the funeral, Sam had Josh and some of his boys pack up Jeff's things and ship them air express to Tate. And that night she herself went through the ranch albums as promised and carefully took out each of the photographs of Jeff, searched for the corresponding negatives, and the next day went into town with the whole stack. When the pictures came back a week later, she carefully went over them again to make sure that there were none of her, and there weren't, and then she put them in an envelope, without anything else, and mailed them to Tate. For Sam, that ended the chapter of Tate Jordan. She had found him at last. She had had the choice of reaching out to him, of telling him she still loved him, of even asking him to come. But just as she had sent Jeff away that fateful night, because she knew it would be selfish of her to reach out and wrong for the boy, now she turned away again, for her own reasons, and she congratulated herself afterward for what she had done. She didn't belong in Tate's life anymore, not the way she was. And she wondered as she lay in bed that night if she hadn't been crippled if she would have reached out to Tate now. There was no way to know, of course, because if she hadn't been crippled, she wouldn't have had the ranch, wouldn't have known Jeff, wouldn't have . . . She drifted off to sleep and was only awakened the next morning by the phone.

"Sam?" It was Norman Warren and he sounded excited at the other end.

"Hi." She was still half asleep. "What's up?" And then she realized that he probably still wanted to discuss the appeal. With Jeff's funeral and the difficult letter to write to Tate, she hadn't gotten back to him after their last conversation, but she had definitely decided that she didn't want to put Timmie through the ordeal. She had spoken to the social worker twice, he had told her that Timmie was having a rough time readjusting and he wanted to come back to her, but that there was nothing anyone could do, and he had told Timmie as much the last time he'd stopped by at their home. She had asked him if his mother was being decent to him this time, but the social worker was vague and said that he assumed she was.

"Sam, I want you to come to L.A."

"I don't want to discuss it, Norman." She sat up in bed with an unhappy frown. "There's no point. I won't do it."

"I understand that. But there are some other matters we have to work out."

"Like what?" She sounded suspicious.

"There are some papers you didn't sign."

"Send them to me."

"I can't."

"Then bring them to me." She sounded annoyed. She was tired and it was early. And then she realized, as she blinked again, that it was Sunday. "What are you doing, calling me on a Sunday, Norm?"

"I just didn't have time to get to it last week. Look, I know this is an imposition, Sam, and you're busy too, but couldn't you please do me a favor? Could you come in today?"

"On Sunday? Why?"

"Please. Just do it for me. I'd be very grateful."

And then suddenly she panicked. "Is something wrong with Timmie? Is he hurt? Did she beat him again?" Sam felt her heart race but he was quick to reassure her.

"No, no, nothing like that. I'm sure he's fine. I'd just appreciate winding it all up today once and for all."

"Norman," she sighed and looked at the clock. It was seven in the morning. "Personally I think you're demented. But you were a big help, and you tried, so I'll do you a favor, just this once. Do you realize what a long drive that is for us?"

"Will you bring Josh?"

"Probably. Where shall we meet you? At your office? And what exactly am I going to sign?"

"Just some papers that say you don't want to appeal."

What could he be up to? "Why the hell can't you mail them?"

"I'm too cheap to buy a stamp."

She laughed at him. "You're crazy."

"I know. What time will you be here?"

"I don't know." She yawned. "How about after lunch?"

"Why not get it over with early?"

"You want me to come in my nightgown, Norman?"

"That would be nice. Shall we say eleven o'clock?"

"Oh, shit," she sighed. "All right. But it better not take too long. I have a lot of things to do here."

"Fine."

She called up Josh then and told him and he sounded as

annoyed as she had. "Why the hell can't he mail you the stuff?"

"I don't know. But if we have to do it, we might as well go in on a Sunday. I don't have time all week. I'm going to be too busy with the kids." She was expecting eleven of them from different states.

"All right. Want to leave in half an hour?"

"Make it an hour."

He did, and she swung herself into the car, wearing jeans and a red sweater, there was a red ribbon in her hair, and she was wearing her favorite red cowboy boots.

"You look like a valentine, Sam."

"I feel more like Halloween. I don't know why the hell we have to go to L.A. on a Sunday morning." And when they reached Norman's house, he seemed terribly hyper and revved up and insisted they had to go to the courthouse, because he didn't have all the papers he needed there after all.

"On Sunday? Norman, have you been drinking?" She really was not amused.

"Just trust me, for God's sake."

"If I didn't, I wouldn't be here." Josh looked at him suspiciously and drove the car to the courthouse on the other side of town from where Norman lived. But when they got there, Norman suddenly looked as though he knew what he was doing. He flashed a pass at the guard downstairs, the guard nodded and let them in. "Seventh floor," he told the lone elevator man on duty, and when they got out of the elevator on the seventh floor, they turned left and then right and then left again and then suddenly they were in a brightly lit room with a uniformed matron at a desk and a policeman chatting to her, and suddenly Sam gave a gasp and a shriek and she raced toward him. It was Timmie, sitting in his wheelchair, with his teddy, looking filthy dirty again, but wearing his good suit and a grin.

He held her tight for a long time and she felt him tremble in her arms, and he said nothing and all she said was "I love you, Timmie . . . I love you, darling . . . it's all right . . ." She didn't know how long she would be able to see him, if it would be a minute or an hour or a day, but she didn't care, she would give him everything she had for as long as she could, for as long as they would let her. "It's all right . . ."

"My mom's dead." He stared at Sam and said the words as though he didn't understand what they meant. And then Sam saw that there were deep circles under his eyes and another bruise on his neck.

"What happened?" She looked horrified, as much by what she saw as by what he had just said. "What do you mean?" But Norman came toward them then and took Sam's arm gently.

"She OD'ed, Sam, two days ago. The police found Timmie alone at the house last night."

"Was she there?" Her eyes were wide as she held Timmie's hand.

"No, she was somewhere else. Timmie was alone at the apartment." And then he took a deep breath and smiled at the woman who had become his friend. "They called the judge last night about Timmie, because they weren't sure if they should put him in juvie—juvenile hall," he translated for her, "—and he called me. He said he'd meet us here this morning with Timmie's file. Sam, it's going to be all over." There were tears in Norman's eyes.

"Right now?" Norman nodded. "Can he do that?"

"Yes, he can reverse his decision based on what has just occurred. Timmie won't have to go through all the business of becoming a ward of the court on an interim basis. He's yours, Sam!" He turned and looked at the small child in the wheelchair, holding Samantha's hand. "You've got your son." It had been two weeks since Samantha had seen him wheeled, screaming, from the courtroom, and now he was hers. She reached out and pulled him onto her knees and held him, sobbing openly now and laughing and kissing him and stroking his hair, and slowly he began to understand and he held her and kissed her and then in a quiet moment he touched her face with his small grimy hand and said, "I love you, Mom." They were words Samantha had ached to hear all her life.

The judge arrived half an hour later with the file he had collected from his office on the way, signed several papers, had Sam sign them, the matron witness them; Josh cried, Norm cried, she cried, the judge grinned, and Timmie waved his teddy bear at the judge with a broad grin as they wheeled into the elevator. "So long!" he shouted, and when the doors closed, the judge was laughing and crying too.

41

"And then I'm going to ride Daisy . . . and play with my train and my fire engine and—"

"Take a bath," Sam filled in for him with a grin on the drive back. My God, what a gift they had just given her. She was laughing and giggling almost hysterically, she was so happy, and for the first time since the accident that had killed Jeff and broken Mary Jo's arms and legs, Sam saw Josh laugh. They had already told Timmie about Jeff when he had asked for him, and he had cried for a minute and then nodded.

"Just like Mom. . . ." But he said nothing else about

her, and Sam didn't want to press him. She knew from the little that Norm had told her that it had been rough. But now that part of Timmie's life was over, and whatever he remembered in years to come would be counterbalanced by the love she would lavish on him in the time ahead.

She told him about the new children coming in and the garden they were going to plant in the spring, and then she looked at him with a big grin. "And guess what you're going to do in a few weeks."

"What?" He looked excited, despite the dark circles under his eyes.

"You're going to school."

"Why?" He looked less than pleased at the thought.

"I just decided."

"But I didn't before." It was a whine just like that of any child and she and Josh exchanged a smile.

"That's because before you were special, now you're regular."

"Can't I be special again?" He looked at her hopefully and she laughed and tucked him under her arm. They were sitting three abreast in the front seat of the big station wagon, with Timmie in the middle.

"You'll always be special, sweetheart. But now we can just live a regular old life. We don't have to worry about you going away, or being taken away, or anything. You can just go to school like the rest of the kids."

"But I want to stay home with you."

"You can for a while, but then you've got to go to school. Don't you want to get smart like me and Josh?" She was giggling again, and suddenly Timmie was laughing too, and he groaned at what she had just said.

"You're not smart . . . you're just my mom now!"

"Thanks a lot!" But it was obvious that the love affair between them was far from over. That afternoon they baked cookies and visited the rest of the kids, and she read him a story before he went to sleep in the room next to hers, and before she had finished it, he was snoring softly. She stayed like that for a long time, just watching him sleep, and touching his hair, and thanking God for bringing him back to her.

It was two weeks later, when he had finally started school and the new arrivals had been admitted and had started to settle down, before Sam got to spend almost a full day in her office. She had worked her way through three stacks of mail, much of it from doctors, and some of it from the East, which was new for her. So far they had only had referrals from western cities.

It was then, as she was putting down the last letter, that she saw him. She happened to glance out her window, and there he was, as he always had been, as tall and as lovely, with his raven-black hair and his broad shoulders and his sharply etched face, and his cowboy hat and his boots . . . only now she saw that there was a little more salt mixed in with the pepper at his temples, but if anything, it improved his looks, and she caught her breath as she watched him stop and talk to some of the kids. As she watched him she remembered how well he had played Santa. But suddenly she shrank from her office window, pulled down the shade, and called her secretary to her. Her face was flushed and she looked terribly nervous, and she glanced around the room as though she might hide. "Find Josh!" was all she told her. And five minutes later he was in the room. By then, outwardly, she had regained her composure. "Josh, I just saw Tate Jordan."

"Where?" He looked startled. "Are you sure?" Hell, it had been three years, he must have changed, maybe she had dreamed it.

"I'm sure. He was out in the big yard, talking to some of the kids. I want you to go find him, find out what he wants, and get rid of him. If he wants to see me, tell him I'm not here."

"Do you think that's fair?" Josh looked at her reproachfully. "His boy just died on the ranch, Sam. It ain't been five weeks, and he's buried out there." He waved toward the hills. "Don't we at least owe him some time here?"

Sam closed her eyes for an instant and then opened them to look at her old friend. "All right, you're right. Show him Jeff's grave and then please, Josh, get him out of here. There's nothing to see. We sent him all of Jeff's things. There's no reason for him to be here."

"Maybe he wants to see you, Sam."

"I don't want to see him." And then as she saw the look in his eyes she grew fierce and turned her wheelchair to face him. "And don't tell me about fair, dammit. It wasn't fair to walk out on me three years ago. That wasn't fair. Now I don't owe him a damn thing."

Josh stopped in the doorway for a moment with a look of regret on his face. "The one you owe, Sam, is yourself."

She wanted to tell him to go to hell, but she didn't. She sat in her office and waited, she didn't even know for what, but she just sat there, thinking. She wanted him to leave the ranch, to go away again, to leave her alone. It was her life now, he had no right to come back and haunt her. Except that she knew that there was some truth in what Josh had just said. He had a right to see where his son was buried.

Josh came back half an hour later. "I let him ride Sundance to go out and see the boy."

"Good. Has he left the barn?" Josh nodded. "Then I'll go home. When you see Timmie, tell him I'm there." But when he got back, he had a riding lesson with some of his friends, and she sat in her house alone, wondering if Tate had left yet. It was so strange knowing that he was so nearby, that if she had wanted to she could have gone out and touched him, or seen him, or talked to him, and she wasn't even sure of what she was afraid of. Her own feelings? What he might say? Maybe she wouldn't feel anything at all if she had a chance to spend some time with him, maybe what had left the wound open for so long was the fact that he had left her without any real explanation and no chance to fight back. It had been like sudden death, with no reprisal, and now, three years later, he was back and there was nothing left to say. Or at least nothing that seemed worth saying, nothing that she would let herself say.

It was almost dark when Josh knocked on her front door and she cautiously opened it. "He's gone, Sam."

"Thanks." They looked at each other for a long moment and he nodded.

"He's a nice man, Sam. We talked for a long time. He's real torn up about the boy. He said he'd stop by and see Mary Jo tonight at the hospital and tell her he's sorry. Sam . . ." His eyes questioned her and she shook her head. She knew what he was going to say, but instinctively she held up a hand.

"No." And then, softly, "Does he know . . . about me? Did he say anything?" Josh shook his head.

"I don't think so. He didn't say anything. He asked where you were, and I said you were gone for the day. I think he understood, Sam. You don't walk out on a woman and then come back three years later. He just said to thank you. He was real touched by where we buried Jeff. He said he wanted to leave it just like that. You know," he sighed softly and looked out at the hills, "we talked about a lot of things . . . about life, about people . . . Caroline and Bill King. . . . Life sure does change in a few years, don't it?" Josh looked sad tonight, it had done something to him to see his old friend. Sam didn't ask but he volunteered the rest of what he knew. "When he left here, he went up to Montana. Worked on a ranch. Saved his money, and then took out a loan and bought a small spread and turned rancher. I teased him about it. He said he was doing it to have something to leave the boy. He did real good, and now Jeff is gone. He says he just sold his place last week."

"What's he going to do now?" Sam looked suddenly nervous. What if he stayed around there, or got a job at the Bar Three?

"He's going back up there tomorrow." Josh had seen the fear in her eyes. And then, "I'll see him

450

tonight, Sam, if you should change your mind."

"I won't."

Timmie came home then and she thanked Josh again and went in to make dinner. For some reason she didn't want to eat in the main hall, and Timmie had been with the other kids all day. But she was nervous and jumpy all evening, and that night as she lay in the dark all she could think of was Tate. Was she wrong? Should she see him? What did it matter? It was too late now and she knew it, but suddenly, for the first time since she'd been back to the ranch, she wanted to go back to their old places, just to see them . . . the cabin he had lived in behind the orchards, the hills they had ridden, and the secret cabin. In all the time she'd been back on the ranch, over a year now, she had never gone back to the cabin or the little lake, until they buried Jeff nearby. But you couldn't see the cabin from the graves. She had promised herself for months that one day she would go out there, just to retrieve Caroline's things. She really ought to take the place apart, but she didn't have the heart to, or even to see it. All she would think of there would be Tate . . . Tate . . . Tate . . . his name rang in her ears all night long.

In the morning she was exhausted and shaken, and Timmie asked her if she felt sick when they went to breakfast in the main hall. She was relieved when he went off to school with the others and she had time to herself. She wheeled slowly over to see Black Beauty. Occasionally she took the stallion out for a ride, but she hadn't ridden him in a long time, and she kept him now more out of sentiment than anything else. He was too high-strung for most of the others to ride, the ranch hands didn't really like him, he wasn't Josh's kind of horse, and when she taught or led the children, she really needed a quieter horse like Pretty Girl. But now and then, when she was alone, she still rode him. He was a sensitive animal and now he seemed to gear himself down to accommodate her. Even after Gray Devil in Colorado, she wasn't afraid of him.

And now, as she looked at him, she knew what she had to do. She asked one of the men to saddle him up, and a few minutes later he lifted her up into the saddle. Sam walked the huge horse slowly out into the yard and turned toward the hills with a pensive expression. Maybe now was the time when she finally had to face it, when she had to go back and see it and know that it could no longer touch her, because none of it belonged to her anymore. Tate Jordan had loved a woman she hadn't been for years now, and never would be again. And as she began to canter slowly over the hills she knew that, and she looked at the sky and wondered if she would ever love a man again. Maybe if she faced it once and for all and let his memory go, she could let herself care for someone, maybe someone on the ranch, or a doctor she met through the children, or a lawyer like Norman, or . . . But how pale they all looked next to Tate. As she thought of him in the yard only the day before, she smiled softly, and then piece by piece she remembered the time they had shared, the times they had run over these hills, the days they had worked side by side, the respect they'd had for each other, the nights she had spent in his arms . . . And then, as the full impact of what she had felt for him began to hit her, she came over the last hill, rounded the trees, and there she saw it, the little lake and the cabin where she had come with him. She didn't want to go any closer. It was as though, for her, it were haunted. It belonged to another lifetime, to different people, but she saw it and saluted it, and then slowly she wheeled the powerful black stallion and cantered over the little knoll where they had laid Jeff to rest. She stood there for a long moment and smiled at the people they had left there, a man and a woman and a boy, all of them people she had cared about a great deal. But suddenly, as she stood there, with tears running slowly down her face, she felt Black Beauty sidestep and buck gently, he whinnied and she looked around and saw him, sitting tall and proud in the saddle as always, Tate Jordan, astride a new Appaloosa she had just bought. He had come to say a last good-bye to his son. For a long moment he said nothing to her, and there were tears on his cheeks too, but his eyes bored into hers and she felt her breath catch as she watched him, not sure whether to say something or simply ride away. Black Beauty was dancing gracefully around, and as she reined him in she nodded at Tate.

"Hello, Tate."

"I wanted to see you yesterday, to thank you." There was something infinitely gentle in his face. Gentle and yet so powerful. He would have been frightening, had he not looked so kind. But his frame was so large, his shoulders so broad, his eyes so deep set. He looked as though he could have picked up Samantha and her stallion and set them down gently somewhere else.

"You don't have to thank me. We loved him." Her eyes were like blue velvet as she looked into his.

"He was a good boy." He shook his head slowly then. "He did a real foolish thing. I saw Mary Jo last night." And then he smiled. "My, she's gotten big."

Sam laughed softly. "It's been three years."

He nodded, and then he looked at her, with a question in her eyes, and slowly he let the Appaloosa approach. "Sam?" It was the first time he had said her name and she tried to feel nothing as he did. "Will you ride with me for a few minutes?" She knew that he wanted to see the cabin, but she couldn't bear the thought of returning there with him. She had to fight with everything she had to keep her distance, not to reach out to this gentle giant who suddenly stood facing her across a chasm of three years. But each time she wanted to say something to him, to say his name, to reach out while she had the chance, she looked down at her legs, tightly strapped to the saddle, and knew what she had to do. Besides, he had left her three years ago, for his own reasons. It was better left as it had been.

"I should get back, Tate. I have a lot to do." She also didn't want to give him time to figure out why there was a strap around her legs. But he hadn't seemed to notice. He was much too intent on her face.

"It's quite a place you put together. What made you do it?"

"I told you in my letter, it was in Caroline's will."

"But why you?" Then he didn't know. She felt a sweep of relief.

"Why not?"

"You never went back to New York?" That seemed to shock him. "I thought you would." *Did you? Was that why you left, Tate? So I would go back to where you thought I belonged?*

"I did. For a while." She sighed softly in the early morning. "I came back after she died." She looked out at the hills as she spoke. "I still miss her."

His voice was soft beside her. "So do I." And then, "Can we ride? Just a few minutes. I won't be back here for a long time." He looked at her, almost pleading, and then feeling her heart pull inside her, she nodded and let him lead the way. When they rounded the knoll, they stopped as they came to the little lake. "Do you want to get down for a minute, Sam?"

"No." She shook her head firmly.

"I don't mean go into the cabin. I wouldn't do that." And then he looked at her with a question. "Are their things still there?"

"I haven't touched them."

He nodded. "I'd like to talk to you for a minute, Sam." But this time she shook her head. "There's a lot I never said." His eyes pleaded but hers were gentle.

"You don't have to say it, Tate. It's a long time ago. It doesn't matter anymore."

"Maybe not to you, Sam. But it does to me. I won't bore you with a long speech about it. I just want you to know one thing. I was wrong." She looked at him, suddenly startled.

"What do you mean?"

"To leave you." He sighed softly. "The funny thing is that I even had a falling-out with Jeff about it. Well, not about you, about running from the ranch. He said that all my life I ran away from the important things, from the things that mattered. He said I could have been a foreman, or owned a ranch if I wanted to. He and I drifted for about six months, and then we gave each other hell. I went up to Montana then and bought that little ranch." He smiled then. "I made a damn good investment, too, and all with a loan. I did it to show Jeff he was wrong, and now"—he shrugged—"it really doesn't matter anymore. Except for what I learned from it. I learned that it doesn't mean a damn if you're a rancher or a ranch hand or a man or a woman, if you live right and you love well and you do good, that's all that matters. Those two"—he nodded toward the cabin—"look at them, in the end they're buried together side by side, because they loved each other, and no one cares whether or not they were married or whether Bill King kept it a secret all his life that he loved her. What a damn waste of time!" He looked annoyed at himself, and she smiled at him and held out her hand.

"It's all right, Tate." Her eyes were damp but she was still smiling, and he took her hand and raised it to his lips. "Thank you for what you just said."

"It must have been hard as hell on you when I left, Sam, and I'm sorry. Did you stay long after?"

"I looked for you everywhere for about two months and then Caro pretty much threw me out."

"She was right. I wasn't worth the effort." And then he grinned. "Then."

She laughed at the correction. "And I suppose you are now?"

"Maybe not. But I'm a rancher now too." This time they both laughed, and how comfortable it felt to be talking to him. It was almost, but not quite, like old times, when she first knew him, after they had begun to become friends. "Remember the first time we came here?" She nodded, knowing that they were getting onto delicate ground and they had already come far enough.

"Yes, but that's a long time ago, Tate."

"And now you're an old woman."

She looked at him oddly. "Yes, I am."

He returned her gaze. "I thought you'd remarry."

Her eyes turned hard for a moment. "You were wrong."

"Why? Did I hurt you that much?" He looked sad for her, but she only shook her head and didn't answer, and he held his hand out to her again. "Let's go for a walk, Sam."

"I'm sorry, Tate, I can't now." She grew sad and insistent. "I have to get back."

"Why?"

"Because I have to."

"Why won't you let me tell you what I'm feeling?" His eyes looked very green and very deep.

"Because it's too late." She spoke softly, and as she said it he happened to glance down at her saddle with a look of despair. As he did he frowned and was about to ask her a question, but she seized the opportunity to begin to ride away.

"Sam . . . wait. . . ." And then, as he watched her ride along, suddenly he knew the answer, the piece that had been missing from the puzzle for the past two days, why she had done it, why she had come back and not remarried, why it was too late. . . . "Sam!" But she wouldn't listen. It was as though she sensed something different in his tone now, and smacking the reins against Black Beauty's neck, she urged him to go faster, and as he watched her again for a long moment he was sure. The heels that had been so tight in the stirrups, that had pressed the stallion's flanks three years before, hung lifeless, toes pointed down. Never would she have allowed that to happen if she'd had any control. Now he understood the strange aspect of her saddle. He'd been so busy watching her that he hadn't seen the most important thing of all. But now he had to spur on the Appaloosa to catch her, and finally, just before the last hill before they got back to the main complex, he urged on the Appaloosa like a racehorse and reached out to the stallion's bridle and reined it in. "Stop, dammit! I have something to ask you!" His green eyes bored into hers, but when she turned, her blue eyes blazed.

"Let go, dammit!"

"No, now I want to know something and I want the truth or I'll knock you off that damn horse I've always hated and we'll see what happens!"

"Try it, you bastard!" Her eyes dared him and she fought him for the reins.

"And then what would happen?"

"I'd get up and walk home." She prayed that he would believe her.

"Would you? Would you, Sam? Well then maybe we ought to try it. . . ." He made to push her gently from her seat and she forced the stallion sideways.

"Stop, damn you."

"Why won't you tell me? Why?" His eyes were the greenest she had ever seen and on his face there was almost immeasurable pain. "I love you, dammit, woman, don't you know that? I've loved you every minute since I left here three years ago. But I left for your sake, not for mine, so you could go back to where you belonged with the people you belonged with and forget about me. But I never, ever, forgot you, Sam, I've dreamed of you every lousy night for the last three years, and now suddenly here you are again, ten times more beautiful, and I want you just as much and you won't let me near you. Why? Is there someone else? Tell me, I'll go away and you'll never hear from me again. But it's something else, isn't it? You're like the others, aren't you? Like the children? And you're as big a fool as I was then. I thought being a ranch hand made a difference, now you think not being able to walk does, don't you, because you can't walk, can you, Sam? Can you? Dammit, answer me!" It was an anguished roar as the tears poured slowly down his cheeks and she looked at him, torn between despair and anger, and nodded slowly, and then, with her own tears pouring freely, she pulled the stallion's reins from him and began to walk the horse away.

But first she looked back over her shoulder. "That's right. You're right, Tate. But the funny thing is that you were right. Oh, not then, but now. Some things do make a difference. And believe me, this does." She wheeled the horse slowly. "Now do me a favor. You've said good-bye to your son and you told me what you had to tell me, now go. For both our sakes, go."

"I won't." He was adamant, more powerful than the

stallion that she rode. "I'm not going, Sam. Not this time. If you don't want me, you tell me, and we'll see, but not because of your damn legs. I don't care if you can't walk or crawl or move. I love you. I love your head and your heart and your mind and your soul. I love what you gave me and what you gave my son, and what you've given to those children. He told me, you know, Jeff did. He wrote to me about the extraordinary woman who ran the ranch. The stupid thing is that I never understood what he was doing. I never knew that it was you. He had a lady boss here, that's all I knew. I figured some saintly crazy had started something new on Caro's ranch. But I didn't know it was you, Sam . . . and now I'm not leaving."

"Yes, you are." Her face was hard. "I don't want pity. I don't want help. I don't want anything anymore, except what I have—the children and my son." It was the first he had heard of Timmie, and he still remembered what she had said in the past about not being able to have kids.

"You can explain that one later. Now what do you want to do? Race me for the hills? The barn? The highway? I'm not leaving you, Sam." She glared at him for a moment, and then in utter fury she urged the stallion on again, back over the hills at an insane pace the Appaloosa was barely able to keep up with, but everywhere she went, Tate was right behind. At last, with even Black Beauty winded, Sam knew she had to stop. They were at the far boundaries of the ranch now, and Sam looked at him almost in despair as she slowed to a walk.

"Why are you doing this, Tate?"

"Because I love you. Sam, what happened?" She

460

stopped at last and told him, and he shielded his eyes from the sun for a moment. She had told him about looking for him everywhere, about her trips and the commercials, about Gray Devil and the fateful ride. "Sam, why?"

"Because I was desperate to find you . . ." And then she whispered softly, "Because I loved you so damn much . . . I didn't think I could live without you."

"Neither did I." He said it with the sorrow of three years of lonely days and nights. "I worked so hard day and night, and all I did was think of you, Sam. Every night I'd lie there and all I could think about was you."

"So did I."

"How long were you in the hospital?"

"About ten months." And then she shrugged. "The funny thing is, I don't mind that anymore. It happened. I can live with it. I just can't force it on someone else."

"Is there anyone?" He hesitated and she smiled and shook her head.

"No, there isn't, and there won't be."

"Yes." He brought the Appaloosa right up next to her. "There will." And then, without further warning, he kissed her, pulling her body close to him and tangling his fingers in the precious golden hair. "Palomino . . . oh, my Palomino . . ." And when she heard the words that she had longed for for so long, she smiled. "I won't ever leave you again, Sam. Never." His eyes held her tight, and then she threw all caution to the winds and told him.

"I love you. I always loved you." Her voice was filled with awe as her eyes drank him in. Tate Jordan had finally come back. And when he kissed her this time, she murmured, "Welcome home." He took her hand then, and slowly, riding their horses as close together as they could, they walked them over the hills and went home.

Josh was waiting in the big yard when they rode slowly toward it, but he turned and walked into the barn, pretending not to have seen them. And when they reached the barn door, Sam reined in the handsome stallion and looked at Tate. Slowly, solemnly, he dismounted and stood looking into her face. His eyes asked her a thousand questions, and his heart poured into hers. She hesitated for only a moment, and then she smiled as he said the familiar words.

"I love you, Palomino." And then in a voice that only she could hear, "I want you to remember that every day, every hour, every morning, every night, for the rest of your life. From now on I'm going to be here with you, Sam."

Her eyes never left his, and then slowly, ever so slowly, she began to unstrap her legs from the saddle. She sat there for a minute, watching him, wondering if she could trust him after the endless three years. Was he really back now? Or was it all an illusion, a dream? And would he run away again? Tate could sense the terror that she was feeling, and as he stood beside her he held out his arms. "Trust me, babe. . . ." And then after a long moment, "Please." His arms never wavered as she sat there, still and tall and proud in her saddle. There was nothing defeated about Sam. Nothing crippled. Nothing broken. This was no half-woman. This was a woman and a half. But Tate Jordan was more than just a man. "Sam?" As their eyes held and they watched each other, it was as though the years between them melted, and as Sam put her hands carefully on his shoulders, one could almost feel the bond between them begin to form again.

"Help me down." The words were quiet and simple, and he swept her from the saddle into his arms with ease, and then, having watched what was happening, Josh appeared suddenly with her chair. Tate hesitated for only a moment and then put her in it, fearing that when his eyes met hers again he would see sorrow and pain. But when he looked into her face now, she was smiling, and deftly she began to roll away. "Come on, Tate." She said it matter-of-factly, and suddenly he knew that things had changed. This was no frail broken woman for him to rescue, this was a woman of strength and beauty for him to love. There was a deep smile in the green eyes as he hurried to walk along beside her.

"Where are we going, Sam?" He strode along, and she looked up into his face with a look of peace mingled with unbridled joy.

She smiled at him and rolled on, whispering the word as she looked at him once more. "Home."

When they reached the big house, she sped up the ramp with Tate only a few steps behind her. She pulled open the door and watched him carefully for a long moment, his eyes tender with memory as they stood there remembering another time, another life. He wanted to carry her over the threshold, but he wasn't sure she would want that, so with a last look at Sam he quietly stepped inside, then she rolled in behind him and closed the door.

Thomas W Simpson
352-3694